BENEATH A DIFFERENT SKY

JESSICA GRAYSON

Purple Fall
Publishing

Copyright @ 2020 by Jessica Grayson

Beneath A Different Sky. All rights reserved under International and Pan American Copyright Conventions.

No part of this text may be reproduced, transmitted, downloaded, decompiled, reverse-engineered, or stored in or introduced into any information storage and retrieval system, in any form or by any means, whether electronic or mechanical, now known or hereafter invented, without the express written permission of Jessica Grayson except for the use of brief quotations in a book review.

This is a work of fiction. Names, characters, businesses, places, events and incidents are either the products of the author's imagination or used in a fictitious manner. Any resemblance to actual persons, living or dead, or actual events is purely coincidental.

Published in the United States by Purple Fall Publishing. Purple Fall Publishing and the Purple Fall Publishing Logos are trademarks and/or registered trademarks of Purple Fall Publishing LLC.- purplefallpublishing.com

Publisher's Cataloging-in-Publication Data

Names: Grayson, Jessica, author.

Title: Beneath a Different Sky / Jessica Grayson.

Series: V'loryn

Description: Purple Fall Publishing, 2020.

Identifiers:

ISBN: 978-1-64253-091-9 (paperback)

ISBN: 978-1-64253-116-9 (Ebook)

ISBN 978-1-64253-037-7 (Audiobook)

Subjects: Vampires--Fiction. | Dragons--Fiction. | Shapeshifting--Fiction. | Fairies--Fiction. | Human-alien encounters--Fiction. | Science fiction. | Romance. | Love stories. | Paranormal romance stories. | BISAC FICTION / Romance / Science Fiction | FICTION / Science Fiction / Space Opera

Classification: LCC PS3607 .R3978 B46 2020 | DDC 813.6--dc23

Edits by Tera Cuskaden

Cover Design by Maria Spada

PRINTED IN THE UNITED STATES OF AMERICA

Please Note

This story is a continuation of the characters in Lost in the Deep End and is for readers who wanted more of their favorite couple. Don't start here! Start with Lost in the Deep End. Available on Amazon as Kindle ebook, Audio book, or Paperback.

Dedication

To my husband: You aren't just my husband, you are my best friend. I'm so blessed that we found each other. I love you more than words can say.

CONTENTS

Prologue	1
Chapter 1	3
Chapter 2	8
Chapter 3	16
Chapter 4	23
Chapter 5	34
Chapter 6	39
Chapter 7	52
Chapter 8	70
Chapter 9	81
Chapter 10	93
Chapter 11	107
Chapter 12	110
Chapter 13	115
Chapter 14	123
Chapter 15	130
Chapter 16	141
Chapter 17	157
Chapter 18	168
Chapter 19	180
Chapter 20	184
Chapter 21	195
Chapter 22	204
Chapter 23	218
Chapter 24	226
Chapter 25	235
Chapter 26	239
Chapter 27	242
Chapter 28	252
Chapter 29	265
Chapter 30	272
Chapter 31	279

Chapter 32	282
Chapter 33	288
Chapter 34	293
Chapter 35	310
Chapter 36	313
Chapter 37	317
Chapter 38	324
About Jessica Grayson	331

PROLOGUE

Sometimes a minute can feel like an eternity. I know this from experience. A single moment begins a chain of events that spiral rapidly through the universe, leaving behind destruction in its wake.

If this is the moment…if this is the minute…that could end in his death, I've decided I will not live with any more nightmares or regrets. I've had enough of each to fill a lifetime.

I will save him, or I will die trying. He is mine, and I am his. Fate brought us together, and I won't allow anything to tear us apart.

CHAPTER 1

ELIZABETH

Awareness slowly trickles back into my mind as Marek's arm tightens around my waist. With his body curled protectively around mine, I snuggle back into the warmth of his chest.

He pulls on the comforter, tucking it over my shoulder. His masculine scent—like a mixture of cinnamon and earth—surrounds me and I release a soft sigh of contentment. I'm not sure how long he's been awake, but it has probably been hours. V'loryns don't need as much sleep as Terrans, but he stays in bed because he says he loves holding me. Opening my eyes, I blink several times, adjusting to the soft morning glow of sunlight filtering in through the curtains. I love waking up like this with him every day.

With a small yawn, I stretch my entire body and turn in his arms to face him. I give him a sleepy smile. "Good morning, my love."

He presses a soft kiss to my forehead. "Good morning, my Elizabeth."

His glowing green eyes stare deep into mine as I reach out and trace my fingers lightly over the sharp, pointed tip of his elvish ear.

My gaze drifts to the three slight cranial ridges that run from just between his prominent brows—one straight up the center to the top of his forehead and the other two forming a V that extends to his temples, disappearing into his short-cropped raven-black hair. Idly, I wonder if our children will inherit his alien features or if they'll look more Terran, like me.

When I cup my hand to his face and gently brush my thumb across his full, perfect lips, the soft purring sound of his tr'llen begins low in his chest.

His lips quirk up slightly in his V'loryn smile. "What are you thinking, my Si'an T'kara?"

I smile and take his hand in mine, entwining our fingers. "That I can hardly wait until our bonding ceremony."

Through the touch of our palms, he opens a small connection between us, sending a wave of love and warmth across the tenuous bridge. It's stronger now—this faint bond we share—the one his people call the fated bond: the si'an'inamora.

We will be married—bonded—in less than a month and I am so happy, I can't stop smiling. As his mind joins with mine, his happiness fills me with warmth. He loves me with the kind of love that only exists in myths and legends. We'll be the first V'loryn/Terran couple to marry. I sometimes feel like I should be a little nervous about it, especially with all the attention from his people and mine, but I've never been more certain of anything in my life as I am about bonding to Marek.

Leaning forward, I brush my lips to his. He responds by tightening his arms around me, pulling me closer until there is no space between our bodies. Intense desire flares brightly through our bond, and I inhale sharply as his consciousness sinks deep into my own. He traces his tongue along the seam of my lips, asking for entrance. His hands dip beneath the hem of my silken sleep gown and move across my already sensitive skin with an urgency that steals the breath from my lungs.

His mouth tastes of cinnamon and warmth as his tongue strokes against mine in a branding kiss. *"You are mine."*

I gasp as his words arc through me like fire. Something dark and primal unfurls from deep within him, reaching across the connection to claim me and wrapping thickly around my mind. Enveloping and all-consuming—these emotions are strong, possessive, and entirely V'loryn in their intensity. His love is as deep as the ocean and constant as the stars. A soft moan escapes my lips as the overwhelming sensation moves through me, suffusing my body with delicious warmth.

"Yours," I whisper back through the connection.

Desire surges through the bond and he rolls me beneath him in one fluid motion. He floods my mind with fervent longing to join our bodies as one.

I'm breathless and panting with want as his hips settle between my thighs. Wrapping my arms and legs around him tightly, I run my fingers through his hair and barely manage to whisper between kisses. "I love you, Marek. I'm yours, my love."

Like soft silk over hard steel, his muscles flex beneath my hands as I knead his back and shoulders. He growls low in arousal as he rolls his hips against mine, creating a delicious friction against the entrance to my core. I want him so much it's maddening.

He pulls back just enough to stare down at me; his gaze intense and possessive. His eyes swirl from glowing green to black and I watch, transfixed, as his fangs extend into sharpened points. Panting heavily, his gaze drifts down to the curve of my neck and shoulder, his body tense. With a slight clench of his jaw, he squeezes his eyes shut and softly shakes his head. Through the touch of our skin, I can sense the conflict within. His desire to claim me is so strong it almost overwhelms his fear that I will be hurt during the formation of the permanent mental bond—the S'acris.

When he opens his eyes again, they are the normal glowing green that is typical of all V'loryns. And despite the intense need that pulses through our faint connection, he stares down at me with a strange mixture of pain and devotion. I'm one of only a handful of Terrans who knows the truth about his people. Their ancestors came here long ago; their race is the inspiration for the ancient Terran vampire myths.

To form the permanent bond, he must claim me in the sacred blood ritual of the S'acris—biting my neck and drinking my blood to seal me to him. Because his ancestor, Kaden, nearly killed his Terran bondmate when he did this, Marek fears the same could happen to me.

But I'm not afraid. I trust him. Completely.

~

MAREK

My heart clenches as her ocean-blue eyes stare up at me with complete trust. I am both grateful and anxious that she does not fear me as she should. My desire for her is unlike anything I have ever known, and if I were certain that I could maintain my control during the formation of the permanent bond, I would have sealed her to me a long time ago.

Her long red hair fans around her head like a beautiful halo as she reaches up to cup my face. Her soft lips are slightly swollen from our kisses, and her skin is flushed in a beautiful rose-colored hue. As my gaze lingers on her, a pink bloom spreads across her cheeks and the bridge of her nose, accentuating the many spots that she calls freckles on her otherwise pale skin. I am captivated as she softly bites her lower lip in the way that drives me mad. "What's wrong, my love?"

Rolling us both so that we are laying on our sides facing one another, I press my forehead gently to hers. "I don't want to hurt you."

She runs the soft pad of her thumb across my cheek. "You won't hurt me, Marek."

Her words break me. She does not know how easily I could harm her, how hard it is to maintain my control of the dark and primal part of me just beneath the surface that demands I claim her as mine. Her people are so fragile compared to my own; we possess nearly two to three times the strength of Terrans. "We must wait, my Si'an T'kara. I have arranged for a Healer. L'Tana will remain nearby on the night of our bonding in case something—"

She presses a finger to my lips, silencing me abruptly. "We'll be fine." Her luminous eyes stare deep into mine. "Brienna survived her bonding with Kaden."

She reminds me of the recent discovery of the ancient V'loryn ship, the *N'emera*, and my Ancestor—the lost Prince Kaden of House D'enekai. His vessel crashed on Terra thousands of cycles ago and he took a Terran for his bondmate. Aside from myself, Kaden is the only other V'loryn to take a mate outside of our species. In his recordings he laments nearly killing her when they formed the S'acris. And I cannot bear the thought of harming my Elizabeth.

The small chime of my communicator on the side table rips me from my dark thoughts as it signals the start of our morning. Elizabeth rolls away just enough to reach out and shut it off.

As she sits up in bed, her long, crimson hair spills down her back and shoulders. My fingers ache to run through the silken strands and pull her back down to me. I settle for reaching up to smooth a hand across the petal-soft skin of her shoulder, down the length of her arm. She is more precious to me than anything, and I am addicted to touching her.

As we ready for work, the sharp chirp of her communicator draws her attention to the display. She studies it a moment before lifting her gaze to mine. "It's Anton. He's already at the lab. He says one of our scientists on Mars Colony is requesting our help analyzing some strange audio files they picked up from a deep-space scan. He's waiting for them to come in."

I still. "Did they give him any more detail than that?"

She shakes her head.

Dread trickles down my spine. The deep-space scanners are how my people first became alerted to theirs. We have long feared that the Terrans might attract other hostile races if they continue to blindly send signals out into the dark void of space. Until we listen to the files, I can only pray that day has not come.

CHAPTER 2

MAREK

As soon as we reach the V'loryn Embassy's Long-Range Communications System Array (LRCSA) lab, I'm surprised to find Anton and Maya already there. Our Terran colleagues and Elizabeth's best friends, they used to be the last ones to arrive for work every day, but I suppose their new quarters at the Embassy make it easier for them to get here on time.

Anton greets us with what Elizabeth refers to as his boyish grin. With his warm bronze skin, chestnut hair and hazel eyes, he is considered very attractive for a Terran. I remember how I used to worry that he had romantic intentions toward my Si'an T'kara. But he is her best friend and as close to her as a brother.

He looks to Elizabeth. "The audio files still haven't come in yet," he says, answering her unspoken question. "But I got breakfast for all of us while we wait." My gaze drifts to the several to-go bags of food on the table before him. A light jab to my side from his elbow startles me abruptly. I snap my head toward him, and he winks. "I even got some V'loryn items as well."

Suppressing a very un-V'loryn-like sigh of frustration, I dip my chin in a subtle nod of thanks. I like Anton and already consider him as I would a brother, but I often find it difficult to adjust to the increasing amount of touch contact the growing closeness of our relationship brings.

Terrans are a very tactile species—especially the more familiar they are with someone. A slight jab to my side, an unexpected hand on my shoulder, a sudden clap on my arm. Having spent most of my life actively avoiding touch, as is the norm for polite V'loryn society, it is still rather jarring to be handled so often.

My people are touch telepaths. It is forbidden to touch one to whom you are not bonded through marriage or family. With Elizabeth, I do not have to worry about keeping my mental transference shields in place to avoid the transfer of emotions through the bare contact of my skin. But with others, it is something I must be ever mindful of.

Taven enters the lab. His blond hair and pale skin stand out in sharp contrast to his dark tunic and pants. His eyes meet mine, and he quirks his brow. "Is there a particular reason Anton's quarters were placed directly beside my own?"

Prior to the announcement of our betrothal to her people, Kalvar —my uncle and the V'loryn Ambassador to Terra—arranged for Elizabeth, Anton, and Maya to move into the V'loryn Embassy under the guise of aiding in the transition of their postings from Terra to V'lora within the next few months. Kalvar suggested it would be helpful to fully immerse them in our culture.

In truth, I suspect he did this more for their safety than anything else, especially considering how violently the Terra United terrorist group has responded to the news of our upcoming bonding. The announcement that was supposed to have brought our people closer together seems to have also added fuel to their terrorist movement. There have been protests outside the Embassy every day for the past few weeks.

I had no hand in assigning quarters to any of the Terrans except for my Si'an T'kara. I made certain her apartments were next to mine.

Anton rolls his eyes at Taven. "Look, I said I was sorry for all the noise last night. How was I supposed to know you could hear me snoring through the walls?" He spreads his arms wide in exasperation. "I'm fine now, by the way," he adds, and I notice the hint of sarcasm laced in his tone. "I went to see Doc, and he gave me an injection for my allergies, so I shouldn't keep you up again."

Taven purses his lips. "We shall see."

Maya starts laughing beside him, while Ruvaen's mouth quirks up slightly in amusement. Her warm brown eyes dart briefly to his. "I slept okay." She grins. "Since my new apartment is next to Ruvaen's, we watched movies last night and both of us fell asleep on the couch."

Ruvaen's glowing green eyes widen slightly at her admission as a light-green bloom spreads across his cheeks and the tips of his ears. They are in the "dating" phase of the Terran courtship ritual. I have not asked, but I suspect they have a secret door between their apartments as Elizabeth and I do.

My people do not believe in any form of intimate contact prior to bonding. Kalvar was aghast at the idea of Elizabeth and me formally sharing quarters here at the Embassy despite my having spent so many nights at her previous apartment before now.

I am addicted to her touch and to falling asleep with her in my arms. So, in an act that could possibly be construed as defiance but was actually one of desperation because I could not bear to be apart from her, I had Ruvaen create a door to link our quarters. He is an engineer and my friend; I trust his discretion. And if Kalvar suspects anything, he has said nothing of it.

My thoughts turn back to the transmission we're awaiting from Mars Science Station, and I look to Anton. "Did they give you any details about the message they are sending?"

"No. But it must be something important for them to have contacted me in the middle of the night about it."

Ice fills my veins.

He continues. "I figured they would have sent it by now, but there was a strong solar flare shortly after they reached me. That's probably why the message has been delayed."

My gaze darts to Taven and Ruvaen. Their expressions are neutral, but their eyes betray their concern. Long have our people feared the Terrans would make contact with another space-faring race—one that may not be as hospitable as ours.

Elizabeth, Anton, and Maya were in the last year of their degree a little over four cycles ago when they developed the program that allowed Mars Science Station to both send and search for communication signals in deep space. It is how my people first became alerted to Terra's existence and also why the three of them were chosen by their government to work on the LRCSA project team here at the V'loryn Embassy in Seattle.

The LRCSA is one of the most important scientific achievements of both their race and mine. It allows V'lora and Terra to communicate directly without having to bounce transmissions off the ships in route between our two planets.

Our people hope to have another one in orbit around V'lora within a cycle to expand our communication capabilities to our deep-space ships. The Council was pleased to hear that our entire team would be transferring to the Terran Embassy on V'lora next month to begin work on this project.

Anton and Taven are the physicists in our group. Their job is to ensure that the LRCSA's signals reach their intended destination unimpeded. Maya and Ruvaen are the chief engineering team, and Elizabeth and I are in charge of the computer core and the translation program.

Elizabeth frowns at her workstation display. "I thought there was a glitch in the translator program, but it looks more like a spelling error."

I follow the line of her delicate finger as she points at the screen. My mouth drifts slightly open when I notice the mistake. I quickly snap it shut as my cheeks and the tips of my ears flush with warmth. "Yes, I see it. That extra letter"—I motion to the word—"should be removed because that particular spelling refers to an anatomical structure that is specific to the males of my species."

Tapping a few keys on the keyboard, Elizabeth deletes the character, correcting the issue. She turns to me, dropping her voice to a low whisper as a pink bloom spreads across her face. "That was the word for 'knot,' right?"

Slightly embarrassed, I give her a subtle nod. I remember how surprised Elizabeth was when the Healers explained this part of V'loryn anatomy to her. It seems that knotting is something specific to my species. The l'ok of Terran males does not expand at the base during mating as ours does. Just before release, we knot inside the female to ensure that the l'ok remains in place while the tip seals over the cervix. This forces the seed directly into the womb and stimulates the female to climax, increasing the chances of conception.

I am glad she caught this error before anyone else noticed it.

It is fortunate that Terra created Terran Common—a standard world language—within the past century. It allowed them to work together more effectively to stabilize their planet when it experienced great earth shifts and drastic climate changes. This also made it more efficient to create a translation database between our two languages.

Anton turns to me. "So, is this how it's going to be at the Terran Embassy on V'lora?"

I quirk my brow.

He continues. "You know. All of us living at the Embassy while we work on the V'loryn LRCSA."

"According to the plans Kalvar was given, it seems we will each have apartments at the Embassy if we choose to remain there." I look to Elizabeth. "But we will most likely stay at our home, just outside the city, and commute back and forth." I shift my gaze back to Anton. "You are all welcome to stay there as well if you wish. There is plenty of room for everyone."

Elizabeth gives me a dazzling smile. We'd anticipated this very question from our friends and colleagues and had already decided to invite them to stay with us on my family's Estate.

Taven dips his head in acknowledgment. "Thank you for the generous offer, but my home is near the Embassy and I will be staying there with my sister Tayla. Any of you are welcome in my residence as well."

Anton crosses his arms over his chest and gives him a pointed look. "Even if we snore?"

Taven rolls his eyes in mock frustration. "In that case, you will be given a small cot to sleep in the storage unit outside." A slight smirk twists his lips. "I cannot have you keeping Tayla awake all night with your snoring. She is in the last cycle of her studies."

Anton's jaw drops but he quickly snaps it shut. "Fine," he huffs. "And after all I'm doing to try to help you find a nice Terran girl to settle down with. I see how it is." He walks over to my Si'an T'kara and wraps an arm around her shoulders. "I'll just go live with Elizabeth and Marek then. At least *they* appreciate me."

Taven sighs heavily while Elizabeth and Maya laugh. I try but fail to suppress the smile that tugs at the corner of my mouth.

∼

ELIZABETH

I'm still laughing at the deep scowl on Taven's face in response to Anton's teasing when a blinking light at my station draws my attention.

Scanning the display, I realize it's an urgent message from Mars Science Station.

Dr. Elizabeth Langdon,

We picked this up with one of the deep-space transponders. It appears to be a communication of some sort, but we are unable to decipher it. Any help you can give us in this regard would be much appreciated.

Best,

Dr. Drew Reese

Tapping the controls, I activate the audio file. Loud static buzzes over the speakers a moment before a frantic clicking noise fills the room. Closing my eyes, I lean forward and concentrate on the strange and rhythmic cadence. I once heard a man make a similar noise by clicking two spoons together. This reminds me exactly of that.

A sudden rush of air startles me, and I open my eyes to find Marek and Taven on either side of my station staring intently at the screen.

Marek turns a worried gaze to me. "Where did this come from? What region of space?"

I open my mouth to answer, but another strange noise begins. The hairs rise on the back of my neck as soft words elongated by a subtle hissing sound conjure images of a snake in my mind. Whatever this is, my body instinctively reacts to it with fear.

Marek's nostrils flare, and he wraps a protective arm around me, tugging me into his side. The frantic clicking begins again, and my jaw drops when I realize this is language. Both of these strange sounds are two different languages.

Anton steps forward. "Are those two different species communicating with each other?"

Panic flares brightly across the faint bond between us, and when I look up at Marek, his expression is set in a mask of concern.

Despite his impassive face, Taven's eyes flash with worry as he replies. "It is a Zovian and an Anguis speaking to one another."

"Wow!" Maya chimes in behind us. "Two new species."

Something in Marek, Taven, and Ruvaen's expressions tells me this isn't something to be excited about. I place a hand on Marek's arm, drawing his attention away from the screen. "What's wrong?"

"Did they say where this came from?" he asks again. Something about his tone sends a chill down my spine.

"No, they just sent this to me to see if I could run it through my new translation algorithm. All they said was that they picked it up from one of the deep-space transponders."

Marek and Taven exchange a worried glance.

I don't like that look, and I certainly don't like being left out of the loop. I take his hand in mine, entwining our fingers to strengthen the connection between us. "Marek, why are you so worried?"

I'm surprised when I feel nothing and realize he has raised his mental transference shields to prevent the sharing of thought and emotion across the tenuous link. But when he turns his gaze to mine, there is no mistaking the panic behind his eyes. "We must contact

Mars Science Station and warn your people not to reach out to this signal."

Before I can ask any more questions, he taps his communicator.

Kalvar answers immediately, and the next words out of Marek's mouth fill my veins with ice. "Zovian and Anguis slavers are searching for the Terran home world."

CHAPTER 3

ELIZABETH

All the color drains from Kalvar's face, in the viewscreen, as Marek informs him of the transmission from Dr. Reese. He's usually so stoic. To see him this visibly upset is mildly terrifying, to say the least.

His glowing emerald-green eyes meet mine evenly. "Inform your colleagues on Mars Science Station that they should not, under any circumstances, reach out to this signal. I must speak with the Prime Minister at once." Before I can respond, he leans forward and shuts off the display.

Without hesitation, Anton activates the LRCSA to contact Mars. I only hope we're not too late. After what feels like an eternity but I'm almost certain was probably no more than five minutes, a middle-aged man with peppered gray hair and thick glasses appears in the viewscreen.

"Ah, Dr. Langdon." He grins. "I assume you have received my message." His gaze drifts past my shoulder to Marek and Taven. "Greetings," he adds in broken V'loryn.

Despite his terrible accent, the fact that he acknowledged them and made the effort to do so in their language tells me that he isn't among the many Terran scientists who harbor an inherent distrust of the V'loryns. Much of it is rooted in the fact that Marek's people refuse to share all the secrets of their technology with us.

"Greetings," Marek and Taven reply in unison.

He smiles brightly at them before turning his attention back to me. "So, what do you think? Is it something your algorithm can decipher?"

"There was no need to run it through the computer. Our colleagues"—I motion to Marek and Taven—"were able to translate the message."

His face is practically beaming with excitement. "Excellent. What did it say?"

Marek steps forward. "It was a communication between a Zovian and an Anguis. They are slavers searching for the Terran home world. Do not attempt to reach out to this signal. If you do, they will most certainly be able to trace it back to your system."

Dr. Reese pales and his eyes go wide. He nods shakily. "Of course. I will make sure no one tries to—"

He stops speaking abruptly as a man enters the room with a grave expression on his face. "Dr. Reese, a communication just came in from the Prime Minister. It's marked as 'urgent.'"

The man hands him a tablet, and Dr. Reese gives us an apologetic look. "Excuse me for a second." Sliding his glasses down his nose, his lips move slightly as he reads the display under his breath.

After a moment, he lifts his gaze to mine. "The V'loryns are sending two of their people to the Mars Station to translate any further signals we receive from the deep-space transponders. A V'loryn cruiser and two Terran defense ships are also en route and will be deployed in defensive positions in orbit above the planet."

"Good," I reply.

He nods. "Until they arrive, I will forward any other rogue signals we pick up in the meantime. I will keep you apprised of any further developments."

"We'll be here," Anton says behind me before we shut off the display.

Ever since our conversation with Dr. Reese this morning, the LRCSA has been in continuous use as Terran government officials coordinate with the V'loryns, and I'm so exhausted I can barely keep my eyes open. My algorithm seems to be working well, for the most part, but every now and then it messes up on some of the translations. It seems like just as Marek and I address one issue, another one pops up.

I enter a sequence of commands and the computer shuts off abruptly as the words "signal lost" appears across the screen.

"Dammit!" Anton curses at the display. His hands fly across his console as he tries to fix it.

"There is the problem." Taven points at the screen, and although his voice is neutral, his frustration is easily read in his features. All of us are tired.

With a heavy sigh, I brace my elbows on my workstation and rest my head in my hands, rubbing my temples as if that will somehow ease my throbbing headache.

Warm hands settle on my shoulders and begin to gently massage my tense muscles. "You should rest, my Si'an T'kara." Marek's breath is soft and warm against my ear.

With a tired sigh, I lean back against his chest, and he slips his arms around me, practically holding me up.

Anton's voice calls teasingly from his station. "It must be nice to have a work partner that cares so much about your well-being."

A hint of irritation shifts into Taven's gaze as he turns to my best friend. "If you are tired, all you must do is say so, and I will continue to work while you rest. Despite what you may think, I *do* care about you."

Anton's eyes widen in shock. "Wow, Taven. I think that's one of the nicest things you've ever said to me. What happened? Did you make a New Year's resolution to be nicer or something?" he teases.

Taven's lips form a tight thin line.

Anton laughs. "Don't give me that face. I was just joking. You know you're one of my best friends."

Taven quirks his brow. "Do I?"

Clapping a hand on his shoulder, Anton flashes his boyish grin. "Yeah, you do."

Marek's voice draws my attention back to him. "You need sleep."

Exhausted, I barely manage to nod.

Marek looks to Taven and Anton. "I am taking Elizabeth to rest, but I will return shortly to assist you."

Ruvaen and Maya walk in. "There is no need," Ruvaen says. "Maya and I will monitor the LRCSA if the rest of you need a break."

With a quick thanks, we leave the lab and head for my quarters. Several pairs of glowing green eyes watch us as we make our way through the Embassy to the staff apartments. Marek used to stay over at my place quite a bit, before I moved into the Embassy, to avoid this kind of unwanted attention. But now that I'm staying right next to him, I suppose intense scrutiny is just something we're going to have to get used to until we're officially bonded.

V'loryns do not cohabitate before bonding, and I realize what we're doing could be considered scandalous among his people. But no one has looked at me with an expression of disgust. Instead, I find only open fascination and curiosity when their eyes meet mine.

Despite my fatigue and all the curious stares, happiness blooms in my chest as I think on our bonding ceremony. When we enter the apartment I stretch up on my toes, wrap my arms around Marek's neck, and press a gentle kiss to his full, perfect lips. Pulling back slightly, I take his hand in mine and entwine our fingers. "I can hardly wait to get married, my love."

The moment I touch his skin, I'm surprised when I sense something strange from him through the connection. A hesitation that is about more than just his imposed rules of abstinence. I search his glowing green eyes in concern. "What's wrong?"

He drops his forehead gently to mine and gives me a hesitant look. "There is something I must tell you."

Something about his tone fills me with dread. "What is it?"

"The Emperor and the Great Houses of G'alta and M'theal tried to pass a vote before my people came to Terra."

"A vote for what?"

Reaching out, he cups the back of my neck and swallows thickly as his gaze holds mine. "They wanted to enslave your people if you were found to be breeding compatible with ours. Our males greatly outnumber our females, and they believed this was the answer to the repopulation of our race. And when we found Kaden and Brienna, their child was proof of our compatibility, and they tried to pass the vote again."

Ice floods my veins. "What stopped them?"

"House D'enekai, A'msir, and L'eanan," he replies soberly. "Together we have the majority vote on the Council. We would never allow such a measure to pass."

His words hit me like a physical blow, and I step back. Shocked not only by this information, but by the fact that he's kept this from me until now, I turn away from him to face the window. The bright lights of the city below are a sharp contrast to the dark skies overhead. Thunder rolls in the distance, echoing my mood as the first drops of fresh rain patter softly against the glass.

Tears of hurt and anger threaten to spill from my lashes, but I blink them back, brushing away the stray one that manages to escape and roll down my cheek.

"Elizabeth?" His voice is soft, an uncertain edge in his tone.

Steeling myself, I struggle to keep my voice even. "Exactly how long have you known?"

Holding my breath, I wait and pray for him to say that he knew nothing before today, but he doesn't. And deep down, I already knew that he couldn't.

Turning to face him, I stare at him accusingly. "Your people approve the building of a Terran Embassy on V'lora, and all the while you know that your Emperor desires to enslave us—to use us like breeding stock." Swallowing against the bile rising in my throat, I tilt my chin up and demand an answer to my question. "How long have you known, Marek?"

Guilt flashes behind his eyes, and he lowers his gaze to the floor.

"After you saved me." His voice is barely a whisper. "When I fell through the ice."

Clenching my jaw, I draw in several deep breaths, attempting to push down my anger.

"Please, Elizabeth." With a pleading look, he extends his open palm out to me. "May I have your thoughts?"

I shake my head. "Trust me. You don't want them right now."

He recoils his hand as if struck and, although he is V'loryn, it is easy to see the pain in his eyes.

"Why didn't you tell me *then*, Marek?" I snap. "And—why bother telling me now? After all this time?"

"At the time, it would have been treason against my government to do so. But more importantly, I didn't want to lose you." He reaches for me but then stops abruptly, curling his fingers into his palm as he lowers his hand again to his side. "I am sorry, Elizabeth. Please forgive me. I should have told you a long time ago. I am telling you now because you need to understand what kind of man the Emperor is. What kind of people rule the Great Houses of G'alta and M'theal. You will be K'Sai of the Great House D'enekai. You need to be aware of the danger you may face by coming with me to V'lora."

Although I'm still upset, his words give me pause. Taking a step toward him, I reach up to cup his cheek and stare deep into his eyes. "I'm not going to lie. Part of me is angry that you kept this from me, but another part of me understands why you did…and why you had to. But I want no more secrets between us." I lift my open palm to him, and he does the same. Gently pressing my hand to his, I entwine our fingers and allow my emotions to flow across the connection. "I love you, Marek. I choose you, my love. The truth, no matter how difficult, will never drive me away."

"You forgive me." He breathes these words like a sigh of relief as he drops his forehead to mine. Wrapping his other arm around my back, he pulls me close.

I lean forward and give him a tender kiss before whispering against his lips. "Take me to bed, my love. I want to sleep wrapped in your arms."

MAREK

It doesn't take long before Elizabeth's breathing becomes soft and even. Closing my eyes, I'm about to drift off as well when my communicator chirps loudly. Quickly pressing the display, I still when I notice the message from Kalvar asking us to meet with him.

It is marked as urgent. This cannot be good.

Despite my wanting to know what it is, my Si'an T'kara worked herself to the point of exhaustion today, and she needs her rest. I tap out a reply informing him that we will meet him as soon as she awakens.

CHAPTER 4

ELIZABETH

Soft light from the early morning sun filters in through the curtains. Sensing I'm awake, Marek softly brushes the hair back from my face, tucking it back behind my ear as he presses a soft kiss to my temple.

Slowly, I turn in his arms. He stares across at me intently. "How long was I asleep?"

"Only four and a half hours," he whispers softly. "Kalvar wishes to meet with us as soon as you are ready."

"Why? Has something happened?"

"I do not know. I informed him you were resting. If it had been an emergency, I believe he would have told me."

He's right. If it was important, Kalvar would have insisted we meet with him even if I was tired. But still, I can't help but worry that it's something to do with the message we received yesterday.

When we reach Kalvar's office, we find Vanek there as well. With short-cropped, deep-chestnut hair and expressive glowing green eyes, he looks so much like his sister L'Tana they could be twins. As second T'Hale of the Great House A'msir and one of Marek's closest friends, I realize that the fact he is the only other person here means that whatever Kalvar has summoned us for is something important.

Kalvar's face is set in a typical stoic V'loryn mask, but I don't miss the hint of worry that reflects behind his eyes, their deep-green coloring the only indication of his advanced years. V'loryns do not otherwise outwardly age after their fortieth cycle. His appearance is so similar to Marek's anyone would know they were family. But it's strange that to the untrained eye you would think Kalvar is not much older than my beloved. Although he is the V'loryn Ambassador to Terra, as Marek's uncle and only living relative, it is easy to see the concern etched in his features as his gaze travels over his nephew. And the fact that he appears so concerned is unsettling to say the least.

Having sensed the tension in the room, Marek wraps one arm around me, pulling me close to his side as we sit across from Kalvar and Vanek.

Kalvar's eyes meet mine evenly. "Before they contacted you, Mars Station had already attempted to respond to the rogue signal. We can only hope that it did not get through. That the damage hasn't already been done."

Panic tightens my chest.

Vanek leans forward in his seat. "If they received the attempted communication, it would not be hard for the Zovians or the Anguis to follow the signal back to the station and then eventually to Terra."

I shudder inwardly as my thoughts drift to the Terran transport—the *Intrepid*. Just last week it disappeared without a trace on its way to Mars. It's the second ship this year to unexpectedly vanish, and now I find myself wondering if their disappearance was more than just an accident. I look to Marek's friend. "What if they are behind the disappearance of the *Intrepid* and the *Voyager*? That could explain their presence near our system. It wouldn't be hard for them to access the computer of either one to help them find our planet."

Vanek looks to me and something—an emotion—flashes behind his eyes, but it's gone too quickly for me to know what it was. "I have considered this as well, and I pray to the Goddess that we are both wrong." His gaze shifts to Kalvar. "Our ships are on heightened alert, scanning for any further evidence of Anguis or Zovian vessels near the Sol system."

"How do they even know of the Terrans?" Marek asks. "None have traveled beyond their planetary system yet. Elizabeth will be the first Terran to do so, the first to step foot on V'lora."

Kalvar's brow furrows deeply. "I do not know." He lowers his gaze. A long exhale escapes through his nostrils before he looks back up at me and Marek. "There is another pressing concern. The Emperor has invoked the Right of Sanction."

Vanek's head snaps up; a low growl rumbles deep in his chest. "He cannot do that."

Kalvar sighs heavily. "He is the Emperor. It is law."

Vanek scoffs. "A law that has not been invoked in at least two thousand cycles."

I place my hand on Marek's forearm, drawing his attention back to me. "What is the Right of Sanction?"

The slight tic of the muscles along his jaw already tell me that whatever this is, I'm not going to like it. "It is an ancient law that states that any heir to one of the Great or Lower Houses must receive the blessing and approval from the Emperor or Empress prior to bonding."

My stomach twists as I stare up at him in shock. "He'll never give us his blessing."

Vanek turns to me. "I believe that is his purpose in invoking this ancient law. He has not given up on the idea of bonding Marek to his daughter so he can absorb House D'enekai and all its holdings under his."

Marek's eyes burn with anger as he looks to his Uncle. "Elizabeth is *my* choice. I do not care what the Emperor says, and I do not need his blessing to choose my bondmate."

Kalvar meets his gaze evenly. "If you bond now without the

Emperor's sanction, you'll forfeit your status and title. Your children would be Outcast, and your act of defiance could be construed as treason."

Disbelief ripples through me. "Treason? This is ridiculous!"

Vanek curls his hands into fists at his sides as he grits through his teeth. "The Emperor has gone too far. He has no right to judge something that has already been blessed by the Goddess herself." His eyes turn black with anger as his fangs extend into sharpened points. In his rage, he is every bit the vampire of Ancient Terran lore as he turns to Marek. "The reign of House K'voch must end. Say the word and my House will join with yours to remove him from his throne. I swear it to the stars. My vow."

Kalvar slams his fist down on the table before him so hard, the indentation stays in the metal after he's lifted it away. "We are not going to war! Not unless we have no other choice. There is another way."

Many of my people mistakenly believe the V'loryns are incapable of feeling emotions. Marek explained that they suppress them because their ancestors were savage, bloodthirsty warriors. As I stare at Kalvar, Vanek and Marek—all of them bristling with barely contained rage—a glimpse of their heritage reflects behind their eyes and I understand now why they do this.

Marek clenches his jaw. "What is it?"

"There are many on V'lora who already view your refusal to bond with V'Meia as an act of defiance. There are whispers of revolution to overthrow his tyrannical reign." He pauses. "And now he and his supporters are questioning the validity of the si'an'inamora between you and Elizabeth."

Marek's arm tightens around me. "I refuse to bond to the Princess. Our people have seen the vidcam footage from when I used the Balance to restore Elizabeth's life, proving that she is my Si'an T'kara."

Kalvar shakes his head. "I know this, and so does the Emperor. But he would spread doubt to gain support, trying to garner sympathy for his daughter being cast aside for an off-worlder."

Frustration burns through me as I meet Kalvar's gaze evenly.

"Before Empress K'Lura used the Balance to restore the life of her Si'an T'karan, there were others who also shared the fated bond. I read about it when I studied the history of your people. And according to the ancient texts, the High Omari—the religious leader of V'lora—can verify the presence of the si'an'inamora."

Marek gently cups my cheek, drawing my attention back to him as he stares deep into my eyes. "*We* do not have to prove anything, my Elizabeth. I fell in love with you because of who you are, not because of the bond." He turns to Kalvar. "Let the people believe what they want. All that matters to me is that I am Elizabeth's, and she is mine. We will be bonded in less than a month here at the Embassy as we have already planned."

Kalvar gives him a pained look. "I wish it were that simple, but you know that it is not. Our Great House—House D'enekai—has always had the most support on the council and among the people. The Emperor has called for the Right of Sanction in a desperate attempt to force you into bonding with his daughter so he can absorb that power for himself. Elizabeth is right. If you go before the High Omari and she verifies the si'an'inamora, he will have no choice but to sanction your bonding."

Marek's nostrils flare. "We will not postpone our ceremony. The Emperor *will not* keep me from bonding to my mate."

Kalvar sighs heavily. "If you do not do this, you risk allowing the Emperor to spread further dissent among the Great Houses and among our people. You could lose everything. And if he accuses you of treason, you would be exiled."

Vanek narrows his eyes. "What if *that* is his plan?"

Marek cocks his head to the side to regard him. "What do you mean?"

"The Emperor is a very clever male. That is what makes him so dangerous. I do not doubt that he would have anticipated the very move that we are contemplating now." He turns to me with a piercing gaze. "When Marek chose *you* over the Princess, you became the one thing that stands between him and the control of House D'enekai. All of the Embassy guards are those loyal to my House—House A'msir—

and House D'enekai. The Emperor knows he cannot touch you here. I would not put it past him to make an attempt on your life when you go to V'lora. And if he can assassinate you before your bonding is complete, Marek would not suffer L'talla and would be free to bond with Princess V'Meia."

Vanek is right. The Emperor knows that once Marek and I are bonded, if I were to die, he would suffer L'talla—broken bond sickness. Most V'loryns do not survive the loss of their mate; my death would be Marek's as well. That's why he'll do everything he can to prevent us from bonding. He needs Marek to marry his daughter so he can absorb House D'enekai's influence and power.

Marek tenses and tucks me even closer to his side. His fear for my safety is so palpable and thick it floods the link between us, and I feel as though I'm drowning in it.

Attempting to quell his panic I take his hand in mine, sending a wave of reassurance through the tenuous bridge. "Despite the risk, we have to go before the High Omari, my love. It is the only way."

He opens his mouth to protest, but Kalvar interrupts. "She is right."

Before Marek can say anything else, I level a determined gaze to his Uncle. "How soon can we leave?"

"As soon as I can arrange for Captain Ryven and several of our guards to come to Terra. They will escort you both back to V'lora."

"My ship will travel with yours as well," Vanek adds. "To ensure your safety."

Marek gently cups my face. His eyes stare deep into mine with a strange mixture of panic and devotion. "We are not going. I will not place you in danger, my Elizabeth."

"From the moment you refused the Emperor's daughter, you have both been in danger," Kalvar's booming voice cuts in. "The only way to keep the two of you safe is to rally support for your bonding. And the surest way to secure it, is to have the High Omari verify the blessing of the si'an'inamora between you."

Marek stills. His despair and resignation flow across the faint bond between us. We have no choice. If we want to be together, this is the only way.

Vanek places a hand on his shoulder. "Whatever happens, my friend, you will always have the support of House A'msir."

∼

When we leave Kalvar's apartment, Marek walks beside me in silence.

Gently probing the link between us, I can sense nothing. He is purposely shielding himself from me, and perhaps that's for the best. I don't want him to feel my disappointment that we'll have to postpone our wedding.

When we enter the lab, Anton and Taven are in the middle of an argument about something on the display. Although I cannot see what it is, I'm sure they'll figure it out. This is nothing out of the ordinary for them; they always seem to have a different opinion about what works best for the LRCSA. These professional disagreements are actually what make them a better team, to be honest. It forces them to consider every angle of a problem. To come up with a better solution.

Marek sits down at his workstation. From the tense set of his shoulders, even without the bond, it is easy to see that he's still upset over our conversation with Kalvar and Vanek.

He's so quiet throughout the morning it's unnerving. And whenever I ask him a question, his answers consist mostly of one word, "yes" or "no." It's as if we're having an argument like Anton and Taven…except instead of constant bickering, ours consists of silent V'loryn brooding.

Having noticed the tension between us, Anton sends me a message asking what's wrong on my communicator.

When I type out a lengthy reply about what happened this morning, he starts to come over to me, but I subtly shake my head. I don't feel like talking about it right now. Not until I've had a chance to discuss it with Marek.

It's almost lunchtime, I'm hungry, and I've had just enough of his moodiness. Stalking over to his desk, I place my hands on my hips and stare down at him. "What's wrong? What are you thinking about so hard over here?"

He lifts his gaze to mine, quirking his brow. "*Now* you would ask for my thoughts?"

His question and the slight biting edge to his tone catch me off guard. "What are you talking about?"

"You dismissed my concerns for your safety as if they were nothing when we were speaking with Kalvar," he says darkly. "The Emperor wants you dead. *You* may be prepared to risk your life by going to V'lora, but *I* am not."

Exasperated, I huff. "Marek, we can't show him fear. We have to—"

He shoots up from his chair and grips my shoulders, staring down at me with a tortured look. "You *died* in my arms, Elizabeth. I watched the light leave your eyes. I *know* what it is to lose the one thing most precious to me in the entire world. The Emperor is a dangerous man, and he would see you dead for standing in his way. For ruining his plans of bonding his daughter to my House—of acquiring our holdings and our lands to secure his power." He shakes his head. "I will not place you in danger just to hold onto a title. You mean more to me than that."

The pain is easily read in his features and my frustration melts away. How can I be upset with him when he says something like this? The memory of my death still haunts him. It is burned in his mind. I've experienced it when we've linked our minds in the al'nara. Losing me is his greatest fear.

"Marek," I sigh, "I don't want to argue about this."

He gives me a slight condescending quirk of his brow. "Then it logically follows that if you will only do as I ask, Elizabeth," he says pointedly, "we will not need to argue about this anymore."

His words reignite my anger. Crossing my arms over my chest, I practically glare up at him.

Anton laughs. "You know you're about to die, right?"

I turn to find him and Taven watching us intently. I had no idea they were listening to us argue.

Narrowing his eyes at my best friend, Marek purses his lips and draws in a deep breath through his nostrils, clearly not amused by the teasing.

"Don't ever say I wouldn't take a bullet for you." Anton gives him a conspiratorial wink before turning back to me. "Look, Elizabeth, he's just trying to keep you safe. The Emperor's still upset about the broken betrothal to his daughter and—"

Angry, not just at Marek, but also at my best friend and Taven for listening in on what should have been a private argument, I snap. "I don't care. I'm not going to change my mind." Tilting my chin up defiantly, my gaze sweeps back to my stubborn V'loryn fiancé. "I'm *going* to V'lora. We'll go before the High Omari together and have her verify our bond. Then, we'll be married, just like we planned."

"Elizabeth, please listen to reason, my Si'an T'kara. I cannot bear the thought of losing you."

My anger dissolves almost instantly. I understand his pain. He looks so vulnerable in this moment, I want only to reassure him. Reaching out, I cup his face and run the soft pad of my thumb across his cheek. He tilts his head into my palm as if relishing the touch of my skin upon his own. This is why we complement one another. I am fire, and he is water. When I am quick to anger, he is just as quick to calm. "You won't lose me, my love. You are mine, and I am yours. I chose *you*, Marek. And if we want our future together, this is the risk we'll have to take."

A look of resignation flashes briefly across his expression and I know I've won this argument. With a heavy sigh, he slips his arms around me and pulls me to his chest. "I cannot change your mind?"

I melt into his embrace. "No."

With a slight clench of his jaw, he nods. "Fine. We will do as you wish, my Si'an T'kara."

"Marek, I do not think it is wise—" Taven starts to protest but stops abruptly when I give him the Terran death stare.

"Elizabeth, please do not be angry with me," he pleads. "I worry for you as well. You are my friend," he says, but his eyes betray his true feelings.

Taven is a good person. But my heart has always been Marek's.

"I appreciate your concern, but everything will be fine. Besides, you'll all be there shortly anyway, right?"

Anton steps forward. "I'll admit it. It's funny to see you get mad at Marek." He grins for a moment before his face becomes serious. "But I've got to be honest. I don't like the idea of you going either. Especially now that we know these guys are"—he darts a glance over his shoulder at Taven before lowering his voice to barely a whisper—"vampires."

Taven quirks his brow. "I *can* still hear you, you know."

Anton whips around to face Taven, placing his hands on his hips. "Okay, you know what, Taven? *Maybe* I'm just trying to be quiet so that the Terrans who *don't* know your little secret won't hear me and flip the hell out, okay?"

Taven rolls his eyes in mock frustration, and I laugh, because Anton's completely rubbing off on him. It's hilarious.

"All right, look," I tell Anton. "You, Taven, Ruvaen, and Maya will be coming soon to start working on the new V'loryn LRCSA project. By then, everything should be settled, and we'll have our bonding ceremony. And you"—I point at my best friend—" get to be my maid of honor."

Taven quirks his brow. "There is no maid of honor in a V'loryn bonding ceremony."

Anton's jaw drops. "What? At least tell me there's a reception and dancing."

Taven cocks his head to the side in confusion.

My best friend gives me an incredulous look. "You're not going to have a reception or *dancing*?"

Casting an annoyed glance at Taven, I open my mouth to reply, but Anton cuts me off.

His eyes dart to Marek. "Oh, *that's* right. As soon as the ceremony's over, you have to whisk her away to your secret lair and bite her, right? To complete your bond? Meanwhile, I'm stuck with Mr. Personality over here." He motions to Taven. "And there's not even a reception to look forward to?" He says, completely exasperated. "What the hell, you guys?"

I place my hand on his shoulder. "We can still do what we'd originally planned. A private V'loryn bonding ceremony and then a Terran traditional wedding complete with a reception a few days later. The only thing that's changed is the venue. Now it will be on V'lora instead of Terra."

"Oh, thank God." He hugs me tightly. "I'm going to be the best maid of honor ever, Elizabeth. I promise." He pulls back and then winks at Marek as a wide smile splits his face. "Don't worry, I won't go wild planning the bachelorette party."

Marek tilts his head slightly forward in attention, raising both eyebrows in a questioning look. "Bachelorette party?"

I glare at Anton. I've already told him "no" at least a dozen times about the bachelorette party.

"I'll...explain it to you later, buddy." He flashes his boyish grin at my clueless fiancé before turning back to Taven, clapping a hand to his shoulder. "Let's go finish up those calculations so we can go eat. I'm starving."

Marek tracks Anton and Taven as they walk back to their workstations. I hear the word "bachelorette" and realize Anton must be explaining the party to Taven. And even though I can't make out the rest of the conversation, I can tell by the look of concentration on Marek's face that he certainly can...and he's listening very intently.

Across the room, Taven's jaw drops at the same time Marek's brows shoot up toward his hairline. Blinking several times, he gives me a stunned look. I can only imagine what he overheard Anton telling Taven.

A smile tugs at my lips as I take his hand in mine. "Whatever you heard Anton talking about, it's not going to happen. I already told him I don't want a wild bachelorette party."

A sigh of relief escapes him.

My communicator chirps loudly, drawing my attention. I glance down at the display, and my eyes widen in shock.

Marek gives me a curious look. "What is it?"

"It's the Terran Prime Minister. She wants to speak with me."

"When?"

"Tomorrow."

CHAPTER 5

ELIZABETH

When we reach the Embassy gardens, Terran Prime Minister Martinez is already there. She greets me formally. "Dr. Langdon, it has been too long."

Although I've spoken with her several times, we're not on a first-name basis with each other. "It is good to see you too, Prime Minister."

Marek stands beside me, his hand in mine. She studies him with a piercing gaze before a polite smile curves her mouth. "It is agreeable to see you again, Marek—nephew of Ambassador Kalvar," she says in flawless V'loryn.

He dips his chin in a subtle nod. "And you as well."

Her eyes shift to me. "I'd like to speak with you. Alone."

Despite her words, the way she says this makes it sound less like a request and more like a demand. Marek must feel the same as well because he bristles slightly beside me.

Giving his hand a reassuring squeeze, I look up at him. "Can you give us a moment?"

Reluctantly, he nods and then leaves.

As soon as the door closes behind him, I meet the Prime Minister's gaze expectantly. "What is this about?"

"The rogue signal from Mars Station. Did the program translate it? Or did the V'loryns?"

"The V'loryns," I reply, wondering why she's asking this. "The computer can only translate V'loryn, Terran, and a small amount of Mosauran that I've begun to program into it as I've been learning the language."

Her gaze sweeps over the garden as if checking to make sure we're alone before she steps forward. "I came here to warn you."

Her statement catches me off guard. "Warn me about what?"

She meets my eyes evenly. "There are many in our government who do not trust the V'loryns. They question why a superior species would come to our planet and forge an alliance without asking for anything in return."

I say nothing as I wait for her to continue. What can I say? If I tell her about the Emperor and the Council holding a vote to decide whether to enslave us, it will only heighten their suspicions and mistrust of Marek's people. And I know for a fact that not all V'loryns are bad; their entire race shouldn't be judged against only a few. I give her a wary look. "Why are you telling me this?"

"A little over one hundred years ago, President Adana had to decide in under five minutes whether to authorize the use of weapons of mass destruction against his government's enemy. If he had, it would not only have devastated the enemy population, it would have resulted in a retaliation that would have likely meant the death of our world."

My mind drifts back to the most famous historical "near miss" in Terran history. When Adana's Pan American allied forces were almost tricked into firing first on their perceived enemy—Eurasia—based on the faulty intelligence planted by a rogue and violent group of radicals. This group had conspired to wipe out both of their enemies in one fell swoop by forcing them into open conflict with one another. Fortunately, it didn't work out like they'd planned.

She continues. "In the end, it all came down to a game of chess."

I frown in confusion. *This* part of the story, I've never heard. "Chess?"

She dips her chin in a subtle nod. "President Adana's Foreign Secretary, Carlos Martinez, and his counterpart, President Thrace's Foreign Secretary, Michael Cho, each secretly feared the use of the devastating weapons at the disposal of their governments. It's uncertain who approached who first. But the result is what saved our planet from almost certain destruction." A sly grin curves her lips. "They were chess players, you see. Having discovered their mutual interest in this ancient game of strategy, they decided to set up a backchannel of communication under the guise of playing a harmless game on their communicators."

She leans forward. "Neither of their governments realized that they were playing each other because the names on the program were randomly assigned and untraceable back to the actual player."

My mouth drifts open slightly as I listen to the unedited version of a history I thought I knew so well.

"When the information came through that President Thrace had already launched weapons in a first strike, President Adana was pressured to retaliate instantly. The rogue group who'd instigated this action had planted the information so perfectly, it appeared as though the intelligence was solid. Martinez immediately sent an emergency message to his counterpart, Cho, via the chess game. Cho assured him that his government had not launched a first strike." She pauses. "Martinez presented this information to President Adana, who then decided to stand down weapons before they launched, thus saving our world from catastrophic devastation."

Blinking several times in shock as I process her story, I ask, "How do you know all of this? I've never heard any of this before."

A faint smile tugs at the corner of her mouth. "I'm the great-granddaughter of Foreign Secretary Martinez. As such, I understand, better than most, the importance of maintaining several levels of communication both official and non in the ever-changing landscape of politics." She tilts her head to the side. "Our records indicate you are an exceptional chess player, am I correct?"

From her story and her question, I understand now exactly what she's asking. Although I rarely play chess anymore, I have become a fair strategist at the V'loryn game of v'oltir—similar to Terran chess, but much more complex. "My preferred game now is v'oltir," I inform her. "It's on my communicator."

"Yes." She grins. "I'd heard that you played. It is on mine as well." Raising her arm, she brings her communicator close to mine. It chirps three times, indicating that our v'oltir profiles have linked so we may now play one another.

My eyes snap up to meet hers. "You understand that what you've told me today, I will share with my fiancé and Ambassador Kalvar." I say this as a statement, but it is also a question. I'm informing her in no uncertain terms that I will not keep secrets from my family.

"That is why I chose you and why we met here"—she gestures to the gardens that surround us—"at the Embassy." With a thoughtful look, she lifts her gaze to the sky, tracking a V'loryn transport as it ascends into the upper atmosphere. "Our people have never ventured beyond our planetary system, nor made contact with any other species. The universe is vast and full of many different races—some of them intent upon conquering lesser worlds." Her eyes meet mine evenly. "I do not possess the hubris of many of my colleagues and am not so naïve as to believe that there will not come a day where we will need the help of our friends—the V'loryns. I believe in the Terran/V'loryn Alliance, and I will do everything I can to ensure it is not broken." She studies me with a sharp gaze, gauging my reaction to her words.

"I feel the same," I reply.

After a moment, she dips her chin in a subtle nod. "I am glad we understand one another. It was nice speaking with you, Dr. Langdon."

"You as well."

Without another word, she turns to leave, disappearing back into the Embassy.

As soon as she's gone, Marek returns.

He listens carefully as I tell him everything about our conversation. "She was wise to come to you."

"I don't understand why she didn't just approach Kalvar. He wants to maintain the alliance as much as she does."

"You are Terran, and you will be K'Sai of House D'enekai. One of the most powerful of the Great Houses of V'lora. The logical choice to represent both worlds."

"But you and Kalvar are the leaders of your House."

He takes my hand and gently brushes his thumb across my knuckles. "You will have just as much power and authority as he and I once we are bonded. You will have the right to address and vote on the Council. It is V'loryn tradition and law."

His words shock me. I hadn't realized this before now. I thought my title would be in name only. "I'm not a politician, Marek. I don't know how to lead a House."

With a subtle quirk of his brow, the edges of his lips quirk up slightly. "You have a brilliant mind, Elizabeth. You are one of the most intelligent people I have ever known. Just as Kalvar taught me how to lead, we will teach you as well. You will learn, and I do not have any doubt that you will be able to govern our House wisely." He pauses. "And now…we must speak with Kalvar and inform him of your meeting with the Prime Minister."

CHAPTER 6

MAREK

Kalvar listens with an impassive expression as Elizabeth informs him of her meeting with the Prime Minister. When she is finished, he looks down, his brows knitting together in deep contemplation as he steeples his hands before him.

After a moment, he lifts his gaze back to her. "Your discussion with Prime Minister Martinez confirms much of what I've suspected. We've heard rumors that there are many in the Terran government who are secret supporters of Terra United. And despite the risk posed by the presence of Anguis and Zovian slavers so close to the Sol system, your government is balking at the idea of our sending V'loryn cruisers to orbit Mars and Terra to enhance your defenses."

"Why?"

"They say that because this is Terran space, we must ask for their approval before sending for any more of our ships to patrol your system." He shakes his head in frustration. "Do they not realize it would only require a mere handful of our cruisers to take down your defenses? If our intent was to conquer, it would have been done so long ago."

My eyes widen slightly at his candid admission in front of my Si'an T'kara, but I'd told him she asked for nothing to be withheld from her concerning our people. That he actually voices this to her proves that not only does he trust her, but he's already accepted her as family and a future leader to our Great House.

Elizabeth is silent for so long after his statement, I begin to worry. But when I search the faint bond between us, I sense only a slight ripple of disbelief. Even she is surprised that he's given her what would be considered a damning truth if the wrong people in her government heard it. After a moment, she leans forward and meets his eyes evenly. "Perhaps you could order your cruisers to patrol just outside the borders of our system instead—offering protection without violating the sovereignty of Terran space."

Pride fills me. She is brilliant. This is an excellent strategy that will ensure the safety of her people and dissuade her government from the notion that we have intent to overthrow their rule.

Kalvar's sharp gaze studies her a moment and something akin to admiration flashes briefly behind his eyes. He dips his chin in a subtle nod. "You already think like a leader. Our Great House will do well with you as K'Sai. I will send word for our people to patrol the borders of the Sol system."

∽

When we leave Kalvar's apartment, we head straight to the Embassy Med Center. Our Healers must give Elizabeth a serum to help her body adjust more easily to the higher gravity on my home world. Almost all spacefaring species receive this treatment, but I was reluctant to have it given to my Si'an T'kara before Doc and several other Terran Healers studied it thoroughly and gave their approval.

As soon as we enter the Med Center, Doc greets us with a wide grin. "I've been expecting you two."

His face quickly falls when Elizabeth does not appear as enthusiastic to see him. He frowns and runs a hand through his dark-brown hair. The soft hints of peppered gray that surround his temples make him appear a bit older than his age of twenty-eight cycles. He claims they are the result of work-related stress. With all that we have recently learned, I suspect my Si'an T'kara's hair will soon begin to take on this coloring as well. "I guess you're not too happy to be here?" he teases.

"Don't take it personally, Doc." Elizabeth gives him a nervous laugh. "You know how I am about these things."

My Si'an T'kara hates injections. Her anxiety pulses through the faint bond between us, and I take her hand in mine, sending a wave of peace and calm.

"You don't have to worry," Doc says as he leads us to an exam room. "I already injected myself three days ago, and aside from being a bit more tired than usual the first couple of days, I haven't had any problems."

The tense set of her shoulders relaxes a bit, and I give Doc a subtle nod of thanks because I'm certain that he did this to help ease her fears. He is not only a competent Healer, he is also a very good friend.

As soon as she's seated on the table, he produces the injection and asks her to hold out her arm.

All the color drains from her face. The acrid scent of her fear is so thick it calls forth my protective instinct to defend my mate. I know Doc will not hurt her, but rational thought be damned at this moment. Attempting to quell my primal reaction, I grip the chair arms so tightly the wood begins to creak and splinter beneath my hands.

Doc's eyes dart briefly to mine, and he gives me a nervous look before turning his attention back to my Si'an T'kara.

She does her best to give me a reassuring smile as she shakily extends her arm for the injection. "It's all right, Marek."

Clenching my jaw, I jerk my chin down in a reluctant nod.

"So." Doc smiles at her. "Anton says V'loryn bonding ceremonies don't include a reception afterward. Is that true?"

"Yes," her voice quavers slightly. "We're going to have a Terran ceremony a few days after, with a reception too."

Doc launches into a series of questions about the V'loryn ceremony, and Elizabeth becomes so caught up in conversation that the scent of her fear begins to dissipate. She doesn't even flinch when he places the injector to her arm. My gaze darts to his, and when our eyes meet, I dip my head in a subtle acknowledgment of thanks. He is very skilled in the art of distraction. A smile tugs at the corner of his mouth before he looks back to my Si'an T'kara.

"Okay, deep breath," he says, and her eyes drop to her arm, widening slightly. "One. Two. Three." She inhales sharply at the sudden click of the injector. As soon as he removes it, she places her hand over the site, rubbing it gently as if to ease the slight sting.

Standing, I slip my arms around her back and pull her close. I run my fingers lightly through the long silken strands of her soft, crimson hair and place a kiss to the top of her head.

She lifts her gaze to mine. "I'm okay, Marek. Really. I promise."

Despite her words, small echoes of her fear still linger in the bond, calling forth my primitive instinct to protect my mate. I hold her against my chest, smoothing a hand up and down her back soothingly as I give her my truth. "I cannot stand to see you in discomfort, my Si'an T'kara. And when you are afraid, the scent of your fear is..." I pause just before the word "unbearable" leaves my mouth and instead say, "Most distressing."

I shudder inwardly, and my mind drifts to thoughts of my mating cycle. I dread its approach. It usually begins sometime between the ages of twenty-eight to thirty-three cycles, and I will reach this age soon. It is marked by three days of intense and compulsive mating. Males are known to become aggressive—feral even—during their time. Females often fight the males if they become too insistent. This is why I fear for Elizabeth when it happens. Her species is physically much weaker than mine.

We've had several discussions with L'Tana about the best way to prepare, but the truth is, we're the first V'loryn/Terran pairing aside from Kaden and Brienna. Kaden's recordings detailed exactly what happened between him and his Si'an T'kara during his mating cycle.

Panic and guilt gripped me in an iron vise as I listened to his logs. Kaden broke down while recounting the multiple injuries Brienna sustained. Pulling Elizabeth tighter in my arms, I clench my jaw in frustration as my eyes turn to Doc's. I have to protect my Si'an T'kara. "Doc, I...I have something I must ask of you."

He gives me a puzzled look. "What is it?"

Elizabeth's eyes flick up to meet mine. I'm certain she's already guessed what I will ask him. We've discussed it many times, and she always tries to talk me out of it because she doesn't want me to be embarrassed. I do not want that either, but *she* is more important than my pride.

She slips her hand in mine, entwining our fingers and giving my hand a gentle and reassuring squeeze as I force the words past my lips. "I would ask that you please provide Elizabeth with several sedative injections and ensure that she is taught the best way to use them, should she need to administer them to me."

Doc's head jerks back in surprise. "Sedatives? What do you need that for?"

Drawing in a deep breath, I begin. As I explain the details of the V'loryn mating cycle to him, his eyes widen slightly despite his obvious attempt to appear unfazed as befits his profession.

When I'm done explaining, he does exactly as I've asked without any further questions. But when his gaze meets mine briefly while instructing Elizabeth, it is easy to read the worry behind his eyes.

～

We leave the Med Center to meet with Lorne in the work lab. If not for him, I might have lost Elizabeth forever. I am immeasurably grateful that he contacted me before our ship could leave the Sol system to inform me that, my ancestor, Kaden had not been responsible for the death of his Terran mate, Brienna.

Staring intently at his display, he runs a hand through his short, dark-blond hair and sighs heavily. He and I have spent many hours trying to decipher Kaden's logs. With the help of Elizabeth's new algorithm we've managed to recover almost the entirety of the recordings.

Despite the faint upward quirk of his lips as he greets us, his fatigue is easily visible in his features.

Elizabeth moves to the station beside him, studying the read-out before her intently as they scan the *N'emera*'s information.

The wrecked ship of my ancestor who crashed on this planet over two thousand cycles ago is fascinating to my people because of its history. But to Elizabeth, she is drawn to the technology as well. Her people have only begun venturing into space less than two hundred cycles. "I can't believe your people were so advanced two thousand years ago," she says, more to herself than to us.

"Advanced but savage," I remind her. This is why her people have been kept in the dark about our discovery of the ancient ship, and of Kaden and Brienna.

She turns to face me, standing up on her tiptoes and twining her arms around my neck. "So were my ancestors." She smiles against my lips. "But you're not that way now…and neither are we."

Despite his attempts to appear otherwise disinterested, Lorne watches us from the corner of his eye. It is no secret that he desperately desires a mate of his own. He is near the Age of Joining, and if he does not find someone before his first mating cycle, he will likely be paired with a veritable stranger.

He moves to the far side of the room and opens the door to make one last check of Kaden and Brienna's stasis pod to ensure it is ready for transport. We will be taking their bodies to V'lora to inter them on my family's Estate.

Elizabeth inhales sharply. "Is that Kaden and Brienna?"

I nod solemnly.

Cautiously, she walks toward the pod as if afraid of what she will find inside. When she reaches it, she stops. Tears gather in the corners of her eyes as she gently rests her hand atop the glass casing.

Lorne turns to me with an apologetic look written in his expression as I move toward Elizabeth, slipping my arms around her from behind. My nostrils flare at the distinct saline scent of her tears as her growing sadness fills the bond between us.

"They look like they're asleep," she whispers. Reaching up to wipe the tears from her cheek, she shakes her head softly. "I can't even imagine how awful that must have been for her, and for him to have found her like he did. How desperate he must have been to save her…"

As I stare at my ancestor and his Terran mate, heavy with their child, I shudder inwardly. Ever since I listened to his logs, recounting the details of her death, I have had many nightmares of finding Elizabeth like Kaden found Brienna—struggling in the deadly embrace of an A'kai as it drains her of her lifeblood.

My people share so many physical traits with the A'kai that it is believed we share a common ancestor. They have the same pointed elvish ears, glowing green eyes, three slight cranial ridges, fangs, claws, and the same ability of touch telepathy. The only difference between us is their green-tinged skin and silver hair—thought to have evolved as an evolutionary side effect of adapting to the constant darkness on their home world: A'kaina. They are still blood drinkers that prey upon other races, while my people abandoned this practice long ago.

Elizabeth's voice rips me from my dark thoughts. "If they had lived…do you think your people would have accepted Brienna? Accepted their daughter?"

Clenching my jaw, I swallow thickly. I have often wondered this myself. I do not know, but I understand why she asks this question. She wonders if my people will accept her, if they will accept a child that results from our bonding. I want nothing more than to assuage her worry. But the truth is, she may face much judgment from my people when we reach V'lora. While many have accepted her here, there are those that believe her people inferior.

I gently turn her in my arms to face me. Staring deep into her ocean-blue eyes, I give her my truth. "I do not know if they would have been accepted or not. I only know that Kaden never regretted his decision to take Brienna as his bondmate. The proof is not only in his logs, but in his actions. He chose to disable the distress beacon of his ship for fear that they would be discovered by a hostile race. In making that decision, he chose to remain stranded on this planet because of his love for his bondmate and child." I cup her chin and skim the tip of my nose alongside hers before pressing a soft kiss to her lips. "In this, I am of the same mind as my ancestor. I would give up everything for you. It matters not to me where we make our home. I only wish for your happiness. And if my people do not accept you and you wish to stay on Terra, we will make our life here. My home is wherever you are. That is all that matters to me."

She wraps her arms tighter around me, and as I hold her close, my gaze drifts over her shoulder to Brienna and Kaden. I squeeze my eyes shut as if that will remove the terrible memory of Elizabeth's death that is burned in my mind. If I had been unable to use the Balance to restore her life, she would have died in my arms that terrible day in the Embassy gardens.

I can only imagine the pain Kaden must have felt when he was unable to save his Si'an T'kara. He used the Balance to heal her wounds, but it was not enough to save her. She had already lost too much blood when the A'kai fed from her.

Wanting to distance myself from the painful image before me, I lead Elizabeth from the room.

Lorne turns to face us, crossing his arm over his chest and bowing deeply before turning his eyes up to Elizabeth. "Any who would judge you based solely upon your race are not worthy of your attention."

She smiles warmly at him. "Thank you, Lorne."

He dips his chin in a subtle nod and then turns his attention to me. "I've discovered something in the logs."

"What is it?"

His gaze darts briefly to Elizabeth, and something akin to guilt flashes briefly behind his eyes, but it is gone so quickly I wonder if I only imagined it. He leans forward and hands me a data crystal. "In one of the recordings I transcribed just this morning, Kaden mentions that Terra was considered a pleasure planet."

My muscles tense and I swallow thickly. I had suspected as much given the heavy similarities of the ancient Terran myths to many of the other races, but I'd hoped I was wrong.

"What does that mean?" Elizabeth asks.

Lorne hesitates a moment before answering. "Our ancestors, the Mosaurans, the A'kai…they all knew of this place. They hunted here."

She stills. "Hunted?" her voice is barely a whisper as the horrific meaning of his words sink in. "You mean they hunted my people… Terrans, right?"

Unable to hold her gaze, he lowers his head and nods grimly.

"But why did they leave?" She turns to me, but I cannot meet her eyes either. The shame of what my ancestors did to hers is too great. "If they knew about our planet and they all hunted here, why didn't they stay? Conquer our world?"

Lorne motions to the data crystal. "Our people and several other races used to travel back and forth from this world and many others by use of something called the Passage."

"What was the Passage?" she asks.

"From what we know from the ancient texts, it must have been some kind of wormhole or subspace conduit that allowed for fast travel over great distances," he explains. "When Kaden brokered peace between the three warring Empires—ours, the A'kai and the Mosaurans—he wanted to ensure that it would last. To do so, he destroyed the Passage. He thought it would prevent further expansion of their Empires and subsequent fighting over territory. And in doing so, he trapped not only himself, but several other enemy ships here as well."

The confusion is easily read in my Si'an T'kara's expression as she stares across at Lorne, so I interject. "This was before FTL travel. That is why the Passage was so important. Even if Kaden had been able to repair his ship, it would have taken him at least ten cycles to return to V'lorys. And the trip would have been much longer for the A'kai and the Mosaurans."

Lorne turns back to his workstation display, bringing up the stellar map to show Elizabeth exactly how far Terra is from each Empire's home world. He looks back at us. "According to Kaden's logs, he was out hunting when a group of A'kai discovered his ship. They came down to salvage it for parts. And when they found Brienna…"

Elizabeth's voice quavers softly as she finishes his sentence. "They attacked her and drank her blood." Her gaze drifts back to the stasis pod and a tear slips down her cheek. "She was pregnant. How could they do that?"

Lorne shakes his head softly. "They did not consider your people to be sentient beings. To them, Terrans were little more than animals to be culled during their great hunts."

This, I believe, would still be truth if the A'kai were to rediscover Terra. Ice fills my veins at the thought of them ever coming to this planet. It is one of my greatest fears and the reason our government has so desperately tried to convince the Terrans from setting out in deep-space ships to explore beyond their system. Elizabeth's people are not ready for the horrors that await them in the dark void of space.

～

When we leave the lab, Elizabeth leads me out into the Embassy gardens, looping her arm through mine. My eyes drift over all the newly replanted vegetation. According to Kalvar, it only took my people a day to restore the garden to its original state after I burned through all of it when I restored her life.

I shudder inwardly when we pass the spot. The very location where I held Elizabeth as she drew her last breath. My fingers flex at my side with the memory of her crimson blood on my hand as I held it against her wound. I placed the other on the ground and channeled the life force of every living thing rooted in the earth within a five-acrum radius to pull her back from the Goddess of Death.

Elizabeth stops abruptly. Her soft presence fills my mind, and when she turns to me, she cups my face, having sensed my dark thoughts. Her eyes search mine as she lightly brushes the pad of her thumb across my cheek. "We have so many beautiful memories here in this garden, Marek. Don't let what happened erase all of those."

Reluctantly, I nod. *She* wasn't the one who had to watch their cherished one die in their arms. She doesn't know how deeply this affected me. The echoes of remembered devastation and pain still linger in my thoughts and replays often in my nightmares.

We walk a bit farther to the back wall. She refers to this as "our spot." It is lined with rosebushes. All of them are bare and dormant, except for one.

"This one is special," she says, running her fingers gently across one of the scarlet blooms. "Its flowers never fade."

Turning my attention to the rosebush, I realize it is the one I picked her rose from. The one that I made bloom. Cupping my hand, I gently cradle one of the roses and close my eyes as I feel of its lifeforce. The beating pulse of energy travels from the tips of my fingers and down my arm to spread through my body like a strong current. My eyes snap open, and I find Elizabeth staring at me in confusion.

"I came here one night when I was thinking of you," I explain. "The plant was only covered with immature buds, but I wanted to know what color they'd be. So I transferred some of my energy to this bush, and that's where your rose came from. It seems that much of my energy still lingers here, allowing it to stay vibrant despite the changing of seasons."

She gives me a puzzled look. "I don't understand."

"My people are able to sense and connect to the lifeforce of the earth around us. Using the Balance, we're able to both give or take energy from nature. It is why V'lorys—our original home world—was so vibrant and green before its destruction."

"And V'lora?" she asks, referring to our current home world. The planet where we've been rebuilding our society ever since the destruction of V'lorys.

"Most of the land is bare, devoid of any life. There is not enough lifeforce to encourage much growth. It is why we must rely upon terraforming." It will be at least three more generations until V'lora is completely terraformed and the red-orange planet resembles anything even remotely close to the lush green color that defined V'lorys that was.

As her eyes search mine, I decide to try something. Holding out my hand, a smile tugs at the corner of my lips. "May I?"

Without hesitation, she gives me her hand, threading her fingers through mine. Reaching again for the rosebush, I close my eyes and concentrate, allowing Elizabeth to feel the pulsing energy that runs through me from the vibrant, flowering plant.

Her joy and wonder flood the link between us, suffusing my entire body with warmth. It is addicting to experience her emotions in this way. The soft brush of her mind to mine is intoxicating. An intimacy I both cherish and crave. When I pull back from the connection, I find her staring up at me with a dazzling smile. "That was incredible," she whispers.

Despite her joy, her fatigue is easily read in her features. It is an effect of the treatment Doc gave her earlier, and I know she should rest.

When I suggest this, her smile tips into a frown. "I'm not tired, Marek. Besides, I still have so much to do before we leave."

She is right. There is much I still must do as well in preparation for our departure to V'lora. Although I am excited at the idea of showing her my world, I worry not only about the Emperor, but also about how she will be received by our people.

The first test will be with my guards tomorrow when they arrive with the transport. Ryven is the captain among our guard and has been my friend for many cycles. He served with me and Vanek in the V'loryn Defense Force during our mandatory five-cycle service. At its completion, he asked to pledge himself as a guard of House D'enekai. Kalvar and I accepted him without hesitation.

It is an honor to become a guard to one of the seven Great Houses of V'lorys. Many males aspire to this after their service on the Defense Force. My House—the Great House D'enekai—is one of the oldest of the seven Great Houses and also the one with the most power. More than two-thirds of the Lower Houses have pledged themselves to ours.

House A'msir—Vanek and L'Tana's House—is the second most powerful among the Great Houses, and House L'eanan—K'Sai Milena's House—is not far behind.

Kalvar told me later that he feared we'd lose House L'eanan's support when K'Sai Milena expressed disapproval of my attachment to Elizabeth. But after she witnessed my using the Balance to save Elizabeth's life, thus proving the si'an'inamora between us, she has never once wavered in her commitment to the solidarity among our three Great Houses.

The remaining Great Houses of M'theal, G'alta, and S'tiran are smaller. G'alta and M'theal have close blood ties to the Emperor's Great House of K'voch. While S'tiran only ever takes a side if they believe it will somehow be to the benefit of their House.

Elizabeth's voice rips me from my thoughts. "It will be nice to finally meet Ryven. Especially after all you've told me about him."

It did not take him long to rise to the rank of captain—head of the House D'enekai guards. He is a trusted friend, and I am eager to introduce him to Elizabeth. I am certain he will not be speciest toward her, but I am uncertain about the rest of my guard. If there are any that disrespect her, they will be dismissed from their service immediately. "Ryven is a most agreeable person. He has already been assigned to remain at your side as your constant guard."

She blinks several times in shock. "Like a bodyguard?"

I nod.

From her expression and the emotions that bleed across our bond, it is easy to see that she was not expecting this. But instead of arguing against it, as I'd expected she might, she says nothing. She realizes how much of a threat the Emperor poses.

I suspect that tonight will be the last night I sleep well for a long time. Because I know once we leave for V'lora, we will be closer to the Emperor. In the back of my mind, Vanek's words of caution replay in my memory, and I pray to the Goddess we are not walking into a trap.

CHAPTER 7

ELIZABETH

Anton hugs me tightly as we stand on the transport platform. When he finally pulls away, his eyes are bright with tears. He sniffs, looking between me and Marek. "It's not too late to change your mind. Both of you."

My best friend is usually so lighthearted and quick with a smile. I hate seeing him so concerned and I try to offer some comforting words. "We have to go. Besides, you'll all be joining us soon anyway."

He gives me a pained look. "I'm just worried about you, you know."

"We'll be fine, Anton."

It is only now, staring into my best friend's eyes and hearing his pleading words that I'm actually feeling nervous about this. Maybe he's right. Maybe we shouldn't go. The Emperor is a dangerous man. Once we're on V'lora…

I turn to Marek and open my mouth to speak, but as I look at him, I realize that I cannot ask him to give up everything for me. The Emperor has summoned him for the Right of Sanction. If he doesn't go, he could be exiled from his planet…from his people.

Anton shakes his head softly. He gives Marek a half-smile that doesn't quite touch his eyes. "Why'd you have to be a real Elf Prince? Why couldn't you just have been a regular V'loryn instead of royalty?"

Marek quirks his brow as he opens his mouth to protest that he is a T'Hale and not a Prince, but before he can even finish his sentence, Anton steps forward and gives him a hug. "Love you like a brother, Marek."

No doubt surprised by the unexpected contact, Marek's eyes widen noticeably for a moment before he looks down at Anton and slowly raises his arms to return the embrace. Although he looks awkward returning the hug, I can tell by the softened expression on his face that he appreciates Anton's words and gesture.

∽

Nervous anticipation runs through me as the metal doors slowly open to reveal at least a dozen D'enekai guards. Each of them dressed in some sort of fitted obsidian armor that, instead of being bulky, seems to mold to their bodies and is emblazoned with the same dragon, or v'rach as the V'loryns call them, that I'd seen on the tapestry in Kalvar's office not long ago.

The first one on the right steps forward to greet us. His armor has an extra insignia on his shoulder, differentiating him from the rest of the guards. With dark, close-cropped chestnut hair and rich, olive-toned skin, his piercing, glowing green eyes meet mine. I see the surprise and shock that flash briefly behind them before he crosses his arm over his chest and bows deeply. "T'Hale. K'Sai," he greets us.

Marek places a hand on his shoulder and the guard straightens. "This is Ryven. Captain of my Guard. And my good friend."

The fact that he already addresses me as K'Sai even though Marek and I are not officially bonded is unexpected. But he is Marek's friend, and I suppose this must be his way of showing acceptance of me despite the fact that I'm not V'loryn. I smile. "It is an honor to meet you, Ryven."

He inclines his head politely, but I notice the tense set of his shoulders. "The honor is mine, K'Sai." His gaze sweeps briefly over the rest of the guards before returning to me. "All are eager to meet you."

As we move down the line of guards, Ryven introduces each one. They stare at me with the same curious fascination as the V'loryn scientists who visited the LRCSA lab a few months ago. I am the first Terran they have seen up close, and I realize it must be as strange an experience for them as it was for me when I first met one of their people.

After the last introduction, Ryven turns to Marek, concern flashing behind his glowing green eyes. "We should leave as soon as possible. We have not detected any Zovian or Anguis ships, but we are ready if we encounter them during our travel."

Worry pulses through the faint bond between us. I look up to Marek, whose expression betrays nothing. It's unnerving that both he and Ryven are so concerned about the Anguis and the Zovians. I am glad Vanek's ship will be accompanying us.

When Marek leads me to the bridge, I'm surprised by how large and spacious it is. The transports don't look that big on the outside, but clearly, it's some kind of optical illusion. Everything is polished metal and glass, shining with sparkling clarity. It's a sharp contrast to the worn and battered outer hull.

As if sensing my thoughts, Marek's eyes meet mine. A subtle smile quirks his lips. "The outer appearance of our transports is intentional. A precaution of our race when dealing with other species. We prefer not to draw attention to our technology."

I've worked enough with V'loryn computers that I suppose they're right to be cautious. Technology as advanced as theirs could be dangerous in the wrong hands. And unfortunately, I'm not even certain if my own people would be responsible enough to hold that kind of power and not abuse it somehow.

As the transport lifts off, I stare out the viewscreen. The beach and the Embassy below us grow smaller before disappearing completely from view as we rise above the clouds.

When we break through the atmosphere and head toward the orbital station above Terra, my eyes scan the impressive structure as we approach. I'm surprised at how large it is. On one side, dozens of transports are docked while at least that many larger V'loryn and Terran ships are on the opposite side. Constructed of L'omhara—a platinum colored metal—the V'loryn vessels appear both sleek and powerful. Beautifully designed, they easily dwarf the Terran ones stationed beside them.

My gaze is drawn to the energy field of a massive V'loryn cruiser. It surrounds the ship like an iridescent shield of pulsating waves, alternating between silver and gold as the engines spin up in preparation for FTL travel. Side by side, it is easy to see the superiority of their ships compared to ours. We are lucky their people reached out to us in peace, because I know Kalvar's words are true. We would be no match for them if they had voted otherwise.

With my eyes glued to the viewscreen, I watch in wonder as the entire ship disappears in a brilliant flash of light. The brief display of color leaves behind only the darkness of space, punctuated by millions of distant and glowing stars.

Terran ships utilize FTL travel, but not as efficiently as V'loryn ones. Though, with the help of their scientists, we are making great progress converting our engines for optimum performance.

As if reading my thoughts, Marek wraps his arms around me from behind. "It is the L'sair crystals that power our ships that allow them to travel so quickly. It is why our space-faring vessels are unmatched by any in the known universe for both speed and defense.

I turn to him. "But don't other species trade with you for L'sair to power their ships and weapons as well?"

He nods. "Yes, but we only sell lesser-quality crystals to off-worlders and keep the purer ones for ourselves."

"Can't they just refine it anyway?" I ask, thinking of fossil fuels that used to be utilized on Terra.

"Many have tried, including our scientists. But L'sair cannot be refined without damaging its composition."

"And it's only found in the V'loryn planetary system?"

He nods. "Other races used various fuels for space travel before they encountered my people. But once they discovered L'sair, even in its less than pure state, there is nothing in the known universe that is superior for powering ships, weapons, even entire cities and civilizations. Almost every race trades with us for our crystals."

I never realized before now what a powerful position that puts V'lora in. The only thing holding them back from being an even more formidable race is their lack of people after the destruction of their home world—V'lorys. Something that will soon be corrected if more Terrans decide to bond with V'loryns. I shudder inwardly at the thought that the only thing that stopped them from enslaving my people—forcing us to become breeders—was a vote.

My dark thoughts are interrupted as the dull sound of the transport docking with the station echoes loudly throughout the metal hull. From the various images I remember my grandfather showing me, it used to be much smaller, used only for transports to and from Mars. And yet, it was impressive that my people had even been able to build such a structure, signaling our commitment to explore our system and our advancements in science.

After all I'd heard of this place from my grandparents and my Aunt Liana, when I was a child, I'm excited to finally see it up close. With his hand in mine, Marek and I step off the transport. His guards follow in tight formation closely behind us as we walk through the sparse, utilitarian interior. Bright lights cast a harsh glow on the seamless metal walls that seem to have withstood the wear of time without visible damage or aging.

Several Terran crews stare silently as we pass, many of them smiling in greeting. This is a historic event. I will be the first Terran to travel beyond our system and the first to step foot on V'lora.

Space travel is part of my family's legacy. My grandparents were among the early travelers to Mars Colony. My Aunt Liana was the first baby conceived on the red planet. My grandfather always insisted that's where she got her love of the stars. As a child of Mars, he'd said it was in her blood.

Although I've never been here before, I've heard the station described often enough it feels almost familiar to me. A wistful smile crests my lips as my thoughts turn to Aunt Liana and my grandparents. How many times did they come through here? Staring down at the polished metal floor beneath us, I wonder even now if I'm walking where they once did.

I turn to Marek, about to ask if he knows if this is the new part of the station or the original but stop abruptly when I notice the plaque along the far wall. My mouth drifts open. I recognize this marker from my grandfather's stories.

Gently pulling on Marek's arm, I guide him toward it.

He cocks his head to the side in a curious look but follows me without question.

His guards remain close behind us, all of them watching silently as I stop in front of the decorative metal plating. Running my hands over the commemorative marker, my fingers trace reverently across the engraving. This is where it all started. If my grandmother hadn't decided to accept a posting on Mars Colony, she never would have met my grandfather here.

My gaze sweeps up to the pictures above the plaque, along the wall. During the first two years of travel between Terra and Mars, there weren't many ships going to the red planet. The trip took at least three months each way, and that was before the stasis sleep pod technology was developed. Each crew and their passengers had their pictures taken before disembarking on the long journey. Although the wall is covered with at least a dozen photos, my eyes instinctively find my grandparents.

I turn back to Marek and smile as I thread my fingers through his. "My grandparents met here in this exact spot. There." I point to one of the images. "That's my grandfather, Antonio Garza. And there"—I motion to the smiling woman beside him—"is my grandmother, Grace Taylor."

With his gaze locked on the picture, Marek moves forward, studying it closely.

I continue. "My grandfather was a pilot, and my grandmother was a botanist on her way to Mars Colony. They met right here in front of this plaque before they disembarked, and when they reached Mars my grandfather proposed, and they got married. My Aunt Liana was the first baby conceived on the red planet."

Standing in the exact same spot where my grandparents first met, I'm overcome with emotion. In my study of physics, I have always believed that time is not something that flows impassively around us. No. I ascribe to the theory that the past, present, and future coexist all at once, but it is our inability to perceive this that causes us to believe it is linear—an ever-constant and flowing river that drags us always forward.

Closing my eyes, I imagine my grandparents and my Aunt Liana, standing here in this exact space. Separated only by time, it is as if echoes of their presence still linger here. They are my past. Marek is my present and my future—the man I'm going to marry. Holding his hand, I place the other reverently on the sacred plaque connecting me to the memory of my family, and for the first time, after so many years of grieving, my heart feels inexplicably whole.

In this moment, I understand now, the complete and utter devastation of all that Marek's people have lost. In losing V'lorys—their original home world—they lost everything that connects them to their past. There are no markers or commemorative plaques, old structures or buildings that carry the memory of their ancestors. All those things were taken from them when their planet was destroyed. There is no physical connection between the people they are now and the ones they were before. Perhaps that is why the finding of the *N'emera* and Kaden is so important to them. It is something that survived—a tangible piece of their history—from the time before.

I turn my attention back to Marek. His head is bowed slightly, and his eyes are closed. When he opens them again, his gaze meets mine.

"What were you doing, my love?"

He cups my face, brushing the soft pad of his thumb across my cheek. "Sending a silent prayer of thanks to the Goddess S'Mira, the Goddess of Fate, for bringing your grandparents together, here in this place. If they had never met, you would not exist now."

His words melt my heart, and I stretch up on my toes to press a gentle kiss to his lips. In the back of my mind, I realize that what should be a private moment between us is being watched very carefully by all of his guards and several Terrans walking past. V'loryns rarely touch one another, and according to Marek, they certainly don't kiss. Under the intense scrutiny of their gazes, for the first time, I wonder if I should restrain my natural inclination to touch him like this.

Here on the station, poised at the edge of all I've ever known, I'm almost hesitant to step onto the V'loryn cruiser that awaits us. As we walk up the ramp, I'm acutely aware that I'm entering Marek's world. I thought working for so long at the Embassy would have prepared me for this, but as the glowing green eyes of his guards stare at me from behind stoic expressions, I feel a bit uncertain of myself. Suddenly, all of the differences between us are brought into razor-sharp focus.

I never realized, in all the time I worked at the Embassy, that the familiarity of so many expressive Terran faces around me seemed to balance the impassive masks of the V'loryns. Marek's eyes meet mine, and I can see the concern that flashes briefly behind them. He must sense my apprehension. I do my best to give him a reassuring smile, but I can tell by his expression that it falls short. He knows me too well.

Despite my trepidation, I embrace my future. I will learn to navigate my way in his world as he has learned to do in mine. With my arm looped through his, I push down my worry and turn my attention to studying the ship.

Much larger than it appeared from outside, just like the transport, I stare gaping at all the smooth, polished silver metal and glass. All rounded corners and soft edges, it is nothing like I imagined a V'loryn ship would be. I'd pictured hard angles and a completely utilitarian space, but it's beautiful in here. A soft white glow emits throughout, lending an organic warmth to the space.

Marek takes my hand in his, opening a small connection between us. His consciousness carefully reaches across the tenuous bridge as he searches for the source of the mild anxiety I'm trying to shield from him. Gently, I push back as he's taught me to do, keeping my

JESSICA GRAYSON

troubled thoughts to myself. It's normal to be slightly nervous in a new situation. But he's so protective, he might mistake my nerves for fear and do something drastic like insist we return to Terra.

Having sensed my wish to keep my thoughts to myself, he gives me a subtle nod to acknowledge that he understands. A moment later, he raises his mental shield, erecting a barrier between our minds and respecting the privacy that I've silently requested.

He leads me down a long hallway, while Ryven and the guards go in the opposite direction. The ship seems so large, it feels like forever before we turn a softly rounded corner and Marek stops before a blank wall. Lifting my hand, he carefully presses my palm to a slight indentation in the smooth metal. Warmth travels through my palm and down my arm, and my mouth drifts open as a bright white light zips through the smooth surface in the shape of a door. After a moment, the glowing outline shimmers and recedes into the wall, opening into a large room.

I stare in wonder at the open doorway before turning my attention back to Marek. "I coded my quarters to recognize you," he explains.

In the V'loryn Embassy, our quarters were accessed similarly, but the doors weren't hidden in the wall like this one was. In awe of this strange and impressive technology, it takes me a moment to realize he said, "my quarters." Does that mean I'll be sleeping somewhere else? I'm about to ask, but another V'loryn appears beside us.

"Elizabeth, this is Tolav."

He bows deeply. With dark-blond hair and flawless light-brown skin, only the deep emerald color of his eyes speaks to his age. Although his face remains a perfect stoic mask, when Tolav's gaze meets mine I recognize the shock that flitters briefly behind it as he addresses me. "Your quarters have been made ready, K'Sai."

"Thank you," Marek and I reply in unison. I guess this means I'll be sleeping elsewhere then. Disappointment washes through me. We rarely sleep apart, and the times that we do are only when he is locked away in the lab with Lorne, working late on the translation of Kaden's logs.

Marek told me that even bonded V'loryns rarely ever share a bed, but he knows my people are not that way. I suppose it would be scandalous for us to share quarters here, and I have to remind myself that this is his world now, his customs. I should respect them as he respected mine. We're not on Terra anymore.

My eyes widen as we step farther into his quarters. Large is an understatement. This room is palatial to say the least. An enormous bed on the opposite wall of the floor-to-ceiling viewscreen draws my attention. It's unlike anything I've ever seen before. A massive, white, rounded canopy curves overhead, reminding me of a large but open cocoon. The bedding is covered with a shimmering silver material, embroidered in white thread with a thick pattern of curling vines full of heart-shaped leaves.

It looks so inviting and romantic that heat blooms across my cheeks at the mere thought of lying there wrapped up in Marek's arms. A desk in the far corner and a table with two chairs appear to be made from ornately carved L'kir, lending an almost fairytale-like appearance to the space. Everything about this ship is a strange mixture of technology and intricately sculpted elegance. I'm a Terran that has literally stepped into an outer space version of the Elven Kingdom I used to read about when I was a child.

Marek draws my attention to the viewscreen. Standing behind me, he slips his arms around my front and pulls me back against the solid wall of his chest as he points to another ship. "There is Vanek's vessel." A massive cruiser, the same design as this one, drifts closer to us and comes to a stop. A deep, rumbling sound reverberates throughout the metal walls, and I watch in wonder as a shimmering light envelops Vanek's ship and then expands to cover ours as well.

I tip my head back to look up at Marek. "What is that?"

"An energy lock. Our ships are capable of traveling in tandem, sharing an energy shield. We are able to travel faster this way, and also more securely."

"Wow." I cannot hide the awe in my voice as my mind begins to spin with all the possibilities of what exactly V'loryn technology is capable of. "How does that work?"

"The two engines together create a feedback loop of energy

between them, accelerating our FTL travel. And sharing the energy field does the same for our shields. It strengthens them into an impenetrable barrier."

"Impenetrable?"

"There is no race that has the ability to damage our ships with their weapons when we travel this way. That is why I was glad of Vanek's offer to accompany us back to V'lora."

The tension leaves my shoulders, and I sag against him in relief. My anxiety drains away at the knowledge that we'll be traveling in something so secure that it can withstand an attack from any Zovian or Anguis slave ships.

One hand reaches up to cup my cheek, turning me back toward him. His eyes search mine intently. "You were afraid?"

I'm reluctant to admit my fear, but I don't want to lie to him either. "Yes, but now I'm not."

He gives me a pained look. "And yet, you still chose to come with me. To be by my side."

His voice is soft, and I realize he's saying this more to himself than to me.

"Always," I whisper in reply.

He turns me to face him and drops his forehead to mine, pulling me close. Although he tries to hide it, his worry pulses through the faint bond between us.

I brush my lips to his in a soft kiss and then whisper against them. "It's going to be all right, my love."

The ship's countdown begins, and the engines spin up for FTL travel.

Marek's lips quirk up slightly, in response to my words, but there's a sadness behind his V'loryn smile.

Taking my hand, he opens his mind to me. His thoughts those of complete and utter devotion as he stares at me like I'm a rare and precious thing. "We do not have to do this. We can return to Terra and live out the rest of our lives there. V'lora is not my home...*you* are, my Si'an T'kara."

My heart clenches. His words touch something deep inside me. In his eyes, I see the truth. He *would* give up everything for me.

"V'lora is your home, and the V'loryns are your people. I will not allow you to give up everything you've ever known just for me."

Tortured emotions play across his face. "Do you not realize that I would give up everything to keep you safe?" Gently, he brushes the hair back from my face, tucking a stray tendril behind my ear. "I cannot lose you, my Elizabeth."

"You won't lose me, my love." I wrap my arms around him and meet his gaze evenly. "Where you go, I will go. Where you stay, I will stay. Your people will be my people, and your home will be my home. I will love you for the remainder of my days. I am yours, and you are mine." Pressing my lips gently to his, I seal my vow.

He opens his mouth, deepening our kiss. When we finally pull away, I'm breathless and panting as his glowing green eyes meet mine intensely, full of desire and longing. "Stay here, with me, in my quarters."

"What about your people? I thought it was improper for me to stay with you until after we've formed the permanent bond."

"I do not care what they think. You are Terran. Our life together will always be a blending of two cultures. Falling asleep with you in my arms is the greatest intimacy I've ever known, and I will not give it up just to conform to the traditions of my people. We are the first of many mixed V'loryn/Terran bondings to come. Even now, my guards watch us with discreet curiosity. Our relationship will set the precedent for what comes after. My people will have to learn to adapt to new ways if they are going to create a future with yours." Gently pressing his forehead to mine, he whispers. "It is two days until we reach V'lora, and I do not wish to be apart from you…even while you sleep. You are mine and I am yours."

My heart flutters at his possessive statement. "I don't want to be parted from you either. I was worried that things were going to be different between us now that we're not on Terra any longer."

He cocks his head slightly to the side. "That was the source of your apprehension I felt earlier?"

"Yes."

He pulls me into his arms, pressing a soft kiss to my forehead. "I will never ask you to change. I fell in love with *you*, my Elizabeth"—he pulls back just enough to stare deep into my eyes—"and I will never ask you to be anyone other than who you are."

I smile up at him, softly biting my lower lip.

A low growl rumbles deep in his chest. "Please do not do that, my Si'an T'kara."

I jerk my head back slightly in confusion. "Do what?"

"When you bite your lower lip like that, it drives me half-mad."

At first, I think he's joking, but the intense hunger in his expression suggests otherwise. Heat flushes my skin as his eyes drift down to my mouth. "Okay. I'll try to remember not to do that until *after* we've formed the permanent bond."

His gaze is fiery, possessive and all-consuming. My heart quickens its pace.

He lifts me into his arms as if I weigh nothing and captures my mouth in a branding kiss. I love the way his tongue moves expertly against mine as if he cannot get enough of my taste. I wrap my legs around him. A soft moan escapes my lips as he presses my back against the wall, pinning me in place. I run my fingers through his hair and then down his shoulders and back. I want him so much. He groans as he rolls his hips against mine, and I know he wants me too.

"Elizabeth," he whispers between kisses in a low warning growl that tells me he's having a hard time resisting temptation. "We must stop."

But even as he says this, he grips me even tighter as one hand moves beneath my shirt to cup my breast. I gasp and he swallows my breath with a kiss, filling my mind with all the ways he longs to touch me and make me his.

Panting heavily with want, desire pulses through me so intense that I wonder for a moment if it's mine or if it's his. I don't want to stop, and I don't want to wait any longer. I stare deep into his glowing green eyes. "I'm not as fragile as you think I am. You're not going to hurt me, Marek."

With a slight clench of his jaw, he softly shakes his head. "I have three times your strength. I will not risk accidentally hurting you. We must wait until we have formed the permanent bond. When it is in place, I will be as aware of your body as I am of my own. Only then will I be more certain that I will not harm you during our joining."

Sighing heavily in frustration, I drop my forehead to his and give him a reluctant nod. He wants to wait…so, we'll wait.

This is going to be torture.

∼

MAREK

Watching the soft and steady rise and fall of her chest, I marvel at her beauty as she sleeps. I wrap my arms even tighter around her and am pleased when she nestles instinctively into my embrace, molding her perfect form against mine. She is everything to me, and I am so afraid to lose her.

She hopes the Emperor is a reasonable man. That he will be appeased once the High Omari confirms that she is, in fact, my Si'an T'kara. While I want to believe this will satisfy him, I'm not certain that it will. Neither is Kalvar. Once the High Omari confirms the presence of the si'an'inamora, the Elders will follow as well. Then, the Emperor will have no choice but to sanction our bonding.

According to Vanek, there is not a single V'loryn who has not seen the vidcam footage of my using the Balance to restore Elizabeth's life —proof of the fated bond between us. Only those blessed with the si'an'inamora can heal their mates in this way. Without the bond, I would have died in the attempt to save her.

Long tendrils of fear take root deep within me. I know what I risk by taking her to V'lora. I risk her life and a war on my House, but I can see no way around this. The Emperor will not stop until we remove every shred of doubt he has placed in the minds of our people regarding the validity of our fated bond.

Pulling back from my dark thoughts, I carefully run my hand

through Elizabeth's soft red hair, brushing it back from her face. Fierce possessiveness, primal and dark, unfurls from deep within me. It grows stronger with each day, and I worry that my mating cycle approaches. I long to possess her in every way—body, mind, and soul. "Mine," I whisper. I gently nuzzle her temple, drawing her delicious scent deep into my lungs. "Eh'leh-na, my Si'an T'kara."

A smile ghosts her lips, and she nestles even closer into me. In the back of my mind, the gentle hum of her contentment flows through the faint connection between us. It is stronger now than it was before. Kalvar could not hide the fear in his eyes when I told him I could feel it strengthening. He is worried, afraid he will outlive me.

Because the Terran lifespan is so short compared to my people, I will forfeit over half of my life by bonding with Elizabeth.

Her hand moves over my chest and up to my jaw as she cups the side of my face. She looks up at me through a half-lidded gaze. "Are you all right?" she whispers softly.

"I am fine. Rest, my Si'an T'kara. I am here."

She smiles sleepily and moves her hand back down to my chest, resting her palm over my heart as her body relaxes into sleep once more. I listen as her breathing becomes soft and even before closing my eyes and allowing myself to drift off as well.

∽

Stumbling through my nightmare, I'm unable to awaken as my mind replays the logs of the *N'emera*. Kaden's voice is full of sadness as he recounts Brienna's death.

"I will never forgive myself for what happened to my Si'an T'kara. I was out hunting when I felt her distress through the S'acris. Overwhelming fear battered at my mind through our connection as I tore through the forest. When I finally reached the ship, I found her trapped in the arms of an A'kai hunter. Her eyes were wide with terror and her mouth open in a silent scream.

"Rage roared through me as I attacked, ripping him away from my mate before plunging my dagger deep into his chest, ending his life. I turned back

to her, but another appeared. As I fought him, her life force began to wane, slipping away as the link between us grew fainter and fainter. After finally killing the other, I rushed to her side. Her face was pale with the loss of her lifeblood. Tears flowed freely down her face as her pain and anguish flooded our bond.

"Lifting her into my arms, I used the Balance to heal her. But I could not replace the lifeblood that she'd lost. Placing my hand over her abdomen, I could no longer detect the lifespark of our child. I carried her back to the ship and to the med bay, trying everything in vain." His voice quavers softly. "As I felt her lifeforce fading, I begged her to stay. Pleaded with her to not leave me. She used her last breath to tell me how much she loved me.

"I cannot bear to place the bodies of my bondmate and child in the cold, damp earth. No. I will place them in one of the stasis pods. Already, the effects of L'talla move through me. I cast my thoughts out to the void, seeking my beloved. The silence that echoes in reply is deafening, and I can bear it no longer. My Si'an T'kara and our daughter await me in the next world. I go to them now."

My eyes snap open and instinctively search for Elizabeth. She is still asleep in my arms. Drawing in a shaking breath, I wrap my arms tighter around her, breathing in her scent and reminding myself that she is alive.

I will kill the Emperor and any who dare try to harm her or take her from me. I swear it to the stars. My vow.

She murmurs something against my chest, and I gently brush the hair back from her face.

"Elizabeth?" I whisper, but she does not reply. She is still asleep; perhaps she is dreaming.

Resting my fingers lightly on her temple, I dive into her subconscious, careful not to delve too deeply. Her mind is still unused to such intimate mental contact.

She is dreaming, but this feels different from her dreams that I've observed before. Gently tracing along the edge of her consciousness, I observe her staring into a darkened sky. Intense fear floods the connection between us as she whispers. "They're coming."

JESSICA GRAYSON

Taking her hand in mine, I try to bring her attention back to me. "Who, Elizabeth?"

Her eyes remain transfixed on the dark sky overhead.

Black clouds roll and swirl above us in a tangled mass against the darkness. Lightning arcs across the sky, illuminating a large shadow hidden behind the clouds. It feels...ominous somehow, and Elizabeth's heart rate and breathing quicken as she stares transfixed.

Whatever this is, it terrifies her.

Wrapping my arm around her form, I cup my other hand under her chin, forcing her gaze away from the clouds and to my face. "Elizabeth, you are dreaming; this is not real."

Her eyes are open yet unseeing as I stare down at her. Now, *I* am afraid—unable to break her from this strange spell she is under. Gently brushing the hair back from her face, I try to push down my panic as her ocean-blue eyes seem to stare right through me.

Rolling thunder breaks the silence as a large shadow parts the clouds. A bolt of lightning streaks across the sky, illuminating the darkness to reveal the outline of a massive ship. The metallic hull is pitch-black metal that absorbs all light as it begins a slow descent.

Although I know it is only a dream, panic coils tight in my chest. "Elizabeth, who are they?"

Her gaze remains fixed on the strange vessel. "You called them," she whispers. "They are coming."

Breaking the connection, I cup my hand to her face, turning her toward me. "Elizabeth! Wake up!"

Her eyes snap open, and the fear quickly drains from her features.

"Elizabeth, you were having a nightmare, and I—"

"It wasn't a nightmare, Marek." Her voice is calm, but her eyes betray her worry. "I think it was a warning."

"I do not understand."

"I—I don't know how to explain it to you. It wasn't just a nightmare. This was...different."

I stare down at her in concern.

"I know you don't believe me..." Her voice trails off as she looks away.

Placing my fingers under her chin, I tip her face up to mine. "Elizabeth, I will always believe you. My vow."

"Before the accident. I dreamed that my mother died. I thought it was just a nightmare, but it was a warning." Her voice is thick with emotion as a tear rolls gently down her cheek. "It happened only a week later. My dream was a warning, Marek. Something bad is coming. I can feel it."

I run my hand gently through her long, red hair, the soft strands spilling through my fingers. I cannot deny that her words have unnerved me. *Could Elizabeth be a seer like my mother?*

When I was born, my mother insisted that Kalvar be named my guardian in case anything happened to her and my father. There were many on both sides of my family that questioned her decision in this. It was well-known Kalvar's mind had suffered greatly from the loss of his wife, K'Lena, and their children. But my mother stood firm in her decision, and my father supported her, as he did in all things.

Kalvar told me that he often wondered if my mother somehow knew that he would end up raising me. He had always suspected that she had the gift of foresight.

I turn my focus back to Elizabeth, tugging her closer. Gently pressing my forehead to hers, I stare deep into her impossibly blue eyes. "Whatever it is, we will face it together. My vow."

As soon as she falls once more into sleep, I turn and tap a quick message on my communicator to Ryven, requesting that he double the number of guards that will greet our ship at the V'loryn orbital station. We will be prepared if anyone dares threaten us.

CHAPTER 8

ELIZABETH

"Elizabeth." Marek's deep, rich voice awakens me. Wrapped in the warmth of his arms, I inhale deeply of his distinct cinnamon earthy scent and sigh in contentment. I turn to face him. His glowing green eyes sparkle with barely contained joy. "I want to show you something."

"What is it?"

He slowly stands from the bed and reaches his hand out to take mine.

His shields are down just enough that I can feel his happiness and anticipation through the connection as he leads me to the viewscreen.

My mouth drifts open. A massive red-orange planet at least twice the size of Terra fills the screen. "Is that V'lora?"

"Yes."

Studying Marek's home world, I stare in awe as we approach. Missing the familiar blue and white that defines Terra, V'lora is dominated by various shades of red and orange. As we move closer, dark patches of black and green punctuate the surface, but they are so minimal they are easily lost in the warmer colors.

Dozens of softly blinking lights catch my eye, drawing my attention away from the planet and to a mammoth structure off in the distance. Constructed entirely of L'omhara, the platinum color stands out like a glowing beacon against a vast multitude of stars in the black void of space. "Is that the V'loryn orbital station?"

"Yes, that is A'tena Station."

My jaw drops. A'tena is massive compared to the Terran orbital station. But I suppose it has to be. Marek says that almost all trade is conducted there. It is rare for any off-worlders to be allowed down to the planet's surface. This is an added protection to guard the safety of their people ever since the destruction of their original home world—V'lorys.

Marek pulls me back against his chest, and I melt into his embrace. Soon we'll be on his planet, and I'm excited to see his home. He presses a tender kiss to my temple and then speaks softly in my ear. "We will board a transport for the surface from there."

As we move closer, I notice the dozens of ships of varying shapes, colors, and sizes docked along the outer ring. More than three quarters of them are larger than any Terran spacefaring vessel I've ever seen. I tip my head back to look up at Marek. "Are those all V'loryn ships?"

"Most. But many different species come here to trade for our L'sair crystals." His muscles tense, and he growls low in his throat. "A few appear to be Mosauran and Anguis."

"They trade with your people as well?"

He nods. "As you are aware, the Mosaurans are mostly a warrior race. While not formally allies, they are not enemies either. We have a pact of nonaggression between us and trade many goods with their Empire. The *Anguis*"—I can feel a ripple of disgust flow through the bond at the mention of their name—"are a reptilian race. Similar in appearance to the cobras of Terra but possessing a humanoid form of two arms and legs in addition to their tale and wide-hooded face. Many of them are mercenaries and slavers."

A cold chill runs down my spine. "Slavers?"

"I doubt any would dare practice that despicable trade here. All races know that the penalty for trafficking slaves anywhere in V'loryn space is death. We will be safe, my Elizabeth. I have requested more guards to meet us once we dock, to escort us to V'lora."

We already have over a dozen guards with us now, and that doesn't even include the ones that travel with Vanek. "Why?"

He gently cups my cheek, lifting my gaze to his. "I did not wish to take any chances with your safety, and Ryven agreed. More of my guard have come from the surface to escort us from the docking station to V'lora and then on to the Estate."

Long tendrils of fear uncoil and wrap around my spine. It's not just Marek and Kalvar who worry that the Emperor might try to harm me. Apparently, the captain of Marek's guard does as well. I force myself to push down the rising panic in my chest.

Taking a deep and steadying breath, I steel myself. This is Marek's world, and these are his people. *My love for him is stronger than my fear.* I repeat these words in my mind like a mantra as we drift closer to the station.

"Elizabeth?"

His soft voice calls my attention back from the viewscreen. He stares at me intently. I'm thankful that we do not yet have the permanent bond between us. If he knew how terrified I am in this moment, he'd turn the ship around and never return to V'lora. He would allow himself to become an exile from everything he's ever known, just to make me feel safe.

His glowing light-green eyes search mine in his intense V'loryn gaze.

"I'm just a little nervous, my love. That's all," Attempting to hide my fear, I give him a small smile of reassurance. "I've never been off-world before."

~

A dull sound reverberates along the outer hull as the docking clamps attach to the ship. Marek's hand on the back of my elbow steadies me as the slow yet abrupt stop makes me rock back on my heels.

I look across at him, so regally dressed in the colors of his House—dark gray and black with the silver D'enekai dragon sigil across his chest. My own outfit was tailored to reflect them as well. Kalvar made certain I had V'loryn clothing that identifies me as part of their House, despite the fact that Marek and I are not bonded yet. My gray pants hug my legs and blend seamlessly into my boots. My stark-white dress-like tunic is soft as silk against my skin. It looks almost ethereal as it floats softly behind me as I walk. The House D'enekai dragon sigil is intricately woven in glowing silver thread across the chest. It's beautiful. Like something straight out of the Elf Prince book I'd read as a child. For the first time, I feel like a true princess.

My heart pounds as the metal doors slowly open to reveal at least a dozen V'loryn males—more of Marek's guards.

The first one on the right steps up to greet us.

His eyes widen slightly when I meet his gaze before it's quickly replaced by a typical stoic V'loryn mask. I suppose I should be used to it. The color blue does not exist in the V'loryn planetary system. Crossing his arm over his chest, he bows deeply. "T'Hale. K'Sai." He greets us formally.

The guard straightens, and Marek gives him a subtle nod. "This is Daenor. My Second."

I give him a warm smile in greeting. "It is an honor to meet you, Daenor," I reply in V'loryn.

He blinks several times, a look of surprise flitting across his features before he inclines his head politely. "It is an honor to finally meet you as well, K'Sai. Your accent is flawless." His sharp gaze shifts to Marek and Ryven. "We should leave this station as soon as possible. There are Mosaurans and Anguis nearby."

The loud sounds of booted steps draw my attention off to the left to find Vanek, followed by at least a dozen of his guards. Their uniforms are similar in appearance to those of Marek's men except displaying the rich crimson color of Vanek's house. Emblazed across their chest in silver thread is their House sigil of the t'sar—an animal similar to a large Terran panther but with obsidian scales instead of fur.

He dips his chin in subtle greeting, but his eyes betray a hint of worry as he motions for us to follow him. "This way."

Marek loops his arm through mine. Ryven moves ahead of us, greeting Daenor briefly before ordering the men to make a closed formation around us both.

They form a tight barrier between us and everyone else. I'm surprised when Vanek positions himself next to two of the lead guards. Although their faces are perfect stoic masks, it is easy to read their tension as we make our way through the station. Are they worried about the Anguis and Mosaurans? Or is it the Emperor?

As if sensing my concern, Marek takes my hand and sends a wave of reassurance and calm through the connection.

I can barely see much of the station over the shoulders of his guards. His people are generally taller than mine, but because I'm not exactly a tall person myself, being surrounded by so many V'loryns, now, I feel so small.

Only able to glance at the upper levels that line the promenade, I'm surprised at not only how large it is, but how impeccably clean and elegantly designed. It reminds me so much of the V'loryn Embassy in Seattle. Soft light illuminates the entire station. If I didn't know better, I'd think we were walking beneath the Terran sun. There are no sharp angles here. Rope-like, deep crimson vines cascade over the edges of the upper levels, lending an organic yet modern feel to the entire space. A rich, fresh, and earthy scent fills the station so thick that if I closed my eyes I could easily imagine myself in the middle of a forest. Every surface is polished to a brilliant platinum hue so bright that even when I look down at the floor panels, my image is reflected back to me with sparkling clarity.

Marek explained that almost all of the trade and commerce with other races is done here on A'tena instead of on the planet's surface. The station reflects that. Each time the guards part just enough to allow me a small glimpse beyond their protective formation, I'm shocked at the myriad species that are here.

An alien with bright red feathers from head to toe and a strange-looking beak instead of a mouth stares warily at Marek's men as they approach. My jaw drops when his bright-red eyes meet mine and long red peacock-like feathers spread out behind his back in a brilliant display of color. Marek and Ryven growl low in their throats, and he folds them back together with an audible snap and then scurries away.

The guards group together even tighter, blocking my view, but I'm still able to make out some details of the station. As we walk farther, the space opens up to reveal several more levels in concentric loops. The large area in the middle looks like a park. Covered in deep red, green, and purple vegetation, a small bubbling stream winds along one of the many inviting, tree-lined paths. The warm scent of V'loryn spice wafts through the air, rich and enticing. It's probably coming from the restaurant directly across from us on the next level up, full to overflowing with diners.

Several of the patrons turn in my direction, their eyes practically boring into mine with their curious stares. A man with large sweeping horns and glowing lavender eyes flares his nostrils as his gaze zeros in on me. His skin flashes from stone gray to green and back again as his wings expand from his sides briefly before he tucks them against his back again. Leaning over the railing as if to look more closely at me, he grips the metal handrail, revealing long, lethal, black claws where a Terran's nails would be. He reminds me of a gargoyle like you'd see perched atop one of Terra's ancient structures—both strong and menacing. Despite my determination to appear unfazed, a small tremor of fear moves through me.

We halt abruptly, and Marek's body tenses, mirroring the rest of the guards. Ryven's voice is loud as he commands someone to step aside.

Wrapping his arm protectively around me, Marek pulls me close against him.

One of the guards shifts slightly, and two reflective silver eyes zero in on mine with burning intensity.

As tall as the V'loryns, his face is Terran-appearing, but his brows, nose, and cheekbones are accentuated by strangely sharp ridges. His entire body is a grayish-silver that shimmers with an iridescent glow beneath the light. Instead of skin, smooth scales line his heavily muscled form. His cheeks, forehead, and neck have a subtle orange-red hue. Large cranial ridges start at the top of his forehead and spread out like a V across his skull, disappearing into his short, raven-black hairline. From the way this man carries himself, it is easy to see that he is a warrior.

He shifts, and a dark-gray leathery wing is just barely visible, tucked tightly against his back. Instead of being terrified or scared of his strange, dragon-like features, I'm nothing short of fascinated. He must be Mosauran. Beside him is another with green eyes, obsidian scales and purple markings on his brow and cheeks.

For the past four months, I've been studying the Mosauran language modules that Marek gave me. Ryven glares at the Mosauran and says something that—if I'm right in my translation—is considered extremely rude as he orders him to move aside.

He replies in the harsh guttural tones of his language, "I demand to speak with the Terran."

Fear coils tight in my chest as his piercing silver reflective eyes find mine, and I realize he's referring to me.

Stepping forward in an aggressive stance, he continues. "I am Rowan of—"

Lightning fast, Ryven and Daenor push the Mosauran aside, and we move quickly. Intense panic bleeds through the faint bond. Marek's expression is frantic as he scans for any threats in the crowd as we rush through the station.

Another loud commotion stops us up ahead. The hair rises on the back of my neck as Marek's glowing green eyes swirl into obsidian black orbs. His lips part, and he bares his fangs. A deep growl rumbles in his chest as he glares up ahead at something I cannot see. The rest of the guard mimic this action. Without warning, he scoops me into his arms, tucking me tightly against his chest.

I squeak out in surprise at his strong grasp but quickly wrap my arms around his neck. Intense panic mixed with unbridled fury floods the connection between us. When his bare hands touch my skin, it expands exponentially. It's all-consuming in its intensity, and the air rushes from my lungs, my pulse pounding in my ears.

Peering between his guards, large raven-black eyes with yellow vertical-slit pupils stare hungrily at me. Two massive snake-like aliens with deep-crimson scales open their mouths to reveal two large fangs as they flick their bifurcated tongues, scenting the air and pointing at me as they look between each other.

Those must be Anguis. Cold fills me as their menacing gazes lock on mine.

Vanek rushes forward with inhuman speed. Wrapping his hand around the nearest Anguis's throat, he lifts him into the air as if he weighs nothing.

Marek was right. These guys do look like cobras with their hooded faces and long, deadly sharp fangs. His long whip-like tail lashes wildly as he writhes in Vanek's grasp, kicking frantically at the air. A gurgled choking sound emits from his mouth as he struggles to breathe.

I notice the other Anguis not only doesn't make any move to help his partner, he also does not try to run away either. V'loryns are able to move so fast, I suspect he realizes it would be futile of him to try anything.

Without releasing his grip on the Anguis, Vanek turns to Marek. "Get her safely to the surface. I will deal with this scum," he grits through his teeth. His eyes burn with rage as he looks back at the Anguis and orders his guards. "Search their ship. Leave nothing unturned."

From the unmistakable look of panic on the other Anguis's face, I'm almost certain they have something illegal on their vessel.

Wasting no time, Ryven roughly pushes the other Anguis aside, and we begin moving again. This time faster than before. All eyes seem to watch us as we move briskly through the station.

Marek holds onto me so tightly his grip is almost bruising; I can barely move.

When we finally reach the transport, the guards usher us inside. Marek quickly sets me down in one of the seats and begins fastening my belt. I move my hands to stop him, ready to protest that I can do this myself. But I stop when I realize I don't know the first thing about this strange harness. His tension is escalating through the bond, sending me into full-blown panic mode.

He wants to get out of here. Now.

If he's worried, it's for a good reason. Trusting his instincts, I sit back and allow him to adjust my restraints without any interference. I can learn how to do it later...for next time.

Slamming into the seat beside me, he instructs the captain to take off immediately.

I turn to him. "Why were—" I start but stop abruptly as the transport lurches forward, throwing me back in the seat and forcing the air from my lungs.

My stomach twists, and I breathe through pursed lips, swallowing against the bile rising in my throat as the transport roughly maneuvers away from the station. I squeeze my eyes shut, gripping the chair arms so tightly my hands begin to go numb.

"Elizabeth?" I hear Marek's panicked voice beside me.

I don't want to throw up. Especially not in front of Marek's guards. Swallowing thickly, I barely manage to reply, "It's okay...just a little nauseated."

The ship levels out, and I open my eyes to find him staring at me with open concern. Despite my best efforts to appear unaffected, my hand trembles slightly as I reach across to gently take his, forcing myself to smile weakly in an attempt to reassure him. "I'll be okay in a sec."

He unbuckles my harness and pulls me into his arms, brushing my hair to the side to lightly rest the tips of his fingers against the back of my neck. Warmth radiates from his touch, suffusing my body with comforting warmth. The nausea quickly dissipates. "Does this help, my Elizabeth?"

"Yes," I practically sigh the words in relief as I relax against him.

"We will be home soon."

Able to focus now that my nausea has passed, I look up at Marek. "I don't understand what just happened back there. Why were the Mosaurans and Anguis so interested in me?"

"I do not know. The Mosauran was demanding to speak with you."

He pauses and something—a strange mixture of rage and panic—seeps through our bond.

I reach up to cup his cheek. "What is it?"

"When the Anguis saw you, I overheard them mentioning you were worth thousands of credits."

I inhale sharply. "They wanted to buy me?"

He shakes his head. "No, they would never have approached us in that way. They understand that the penalty for operating in the slave trade is death. Despite the fact that we were on a V'loryn station, I feared they might try to take you by force." He pulls me closer, drawing in a deep breath as if struggling to contain his emotions. "I'm sorry. I panicked. When I was on the V'loryn Defense Force, we liberated many slaves from Anguis ships." A small shudder runs through him. "The thought of even one of them touching you…" With a slight clench of his jaw, he looks away as if the very idea is more than he can bear.

Placing both hands on either side of his face, I force his gaze back to mine. "What's wrong?"

"I know you can take care of yourself, but my people are very protective of their mates." He wraps his arms even tighter around me. "This compulsion of our biology becomes even more pronounced when we are nearing our mating cycle. The way I reacted…I am concerned that it may be approaching soon." He inhales deeply, allowing a long exhale to escape through his nostrils as guilt threads through our connection. "I should never have brought you here. We haven't even touched down on the planet's surface and already you are in danger. If anything were to happen to you, I—"

I press a quick kiss to his lips to silence him. "I'm fine, Marek. It's going to be okay."

He nods in agreement, but the sadness behind his eyes tells me he doesn't believe this.

"Two minutes to arrival," Ryven calls out over his shoulder.

The ship is steady enough that we are able to stand. When I reach the viewscreen, Marek slips his arms around me and pulls me back against the solid warmth of his chest. The red-orange sun is so bright,

I squint my eyes as we hover just above the surface. Tall white, buildings of exquisite and detailed architecture stretch out before us, reminding me a bit of ancient Terran European structures and yet more sleek and elegant in their design. Veins of gray and black streak through the marble-like stone, shimmering beneath the V'loryn sun. K'ylira—the capital city of the D'enekai province—is so breathtakingly beautiful it's like something straight out of a fairytale. Various sleek glass and metal transports zip back and forth both in the sky and on the ground.

Just beyond the city's edge, a large and spectacular castle looms in the distance. Gleaming white towers spiral up to the thin wisps of light-gray clouds as the vast sea-green ocean spreads out behind it.

Staring in awe, I raise my hand to the viewscreen as if to touch the beautiful structure—alabaster stone against a pale yellow-orange sky.

Marek reaches around me and points to the castle before curling his fingers around mine. He leans forward, his lips brushing against my ear as he whispers, "There is our home, my Elizabeth."

CHAPTER 9

ELIZABETH

The transport shakes turbulently beneath our feet before a dull thud echoes loudly as we touch down on the planet's surface. The engines spin down, and Marek moves to my side, taking my arm in his as we move to the outer doors.

Ryven and the guards move into formation around us as we wait for the transport to open.

A thought occurs to me and I turn to Marek. "Most of the people in this city...they've pledged themselves to your House, right?"

He nods.

"Then we should not exit the ship with your guards surrounding us, as if we expect them to do us any harm."

Ryven spins to face me. "You would be exposed. At risk, K'Sai, and—"

I lift my hand up in a silent request to allow me to speak. "Do you normally escort Marek and Kalvar like this?"

"No. Usually only me or Daenor guard them."

"Then, allow the people to welcome their T'Hale back openly. If we exit the ship surrounded by guards, we're sending a message that we don't trust the people and that we're afraid the Emperor."

Ryven protests. "The Emperor would see you come to harm, K'Sai. Of this, I am certain."

I meet his gaze evenly. "I am not afraid, and we will not show the Emperor any fear."

His eyes widen slightly before he darts a quick glance to Marek. Something unspoken passes between them because when he returns his gaze to mine, he steps aside and motions for his guards to do the same. This time, they form two lines on either side of us.

I suppose it's a good compromise. After what happened on the station, I'll admit that I am afraid, but I'm also the first Terran to ever come to V'lora, and I understand that's why so many of them have gathered here to see us off the transport. I push down my fear. If I am the first Terran they will see, I will make sure they know my people are strong.

If what Taven has told me is true, Marek and Kalvar are highly respected and revered in their society. Glancing down at the v'rach in threaded silver across my chest, I steel myself. I will not allow any to question the strength of Marek's House. I will allow none to see my fear; I'll walk proudly and unafraid beside my Si'an T'karan.

Glowing green eyes watch intently as we step to the front, waiting for the outer doors to open. Marek's gaze holds mine a moment before he offers me his arm. I twine mine around it as we stand side by side. He turns, straightening his back, and I do the same, tilting my chin up slightly in defiance of the small twinge of panic that ripples through me. I will not allow the Emperor or the people to see my fear. Marek is mine, and I am his. I *will not* be afraid.

With a deep and steeling breath, the words repeat in my mind: *My love for Marek is stronger than my fear.*

As the outer doors slide open along the metal track the outside air rushes in, bringing with it the scent of rich and exotic spice balanced by the crisp saline breeze of the ocean. I'd always thought because it was mostly a desert planet that it would be hot here, but it seems I am pleasantly wrong. I understand now why the V'loryns chose Seattle as the location of their Embassy on Terra.

Silence greets us as we step onto the platform. Hundreds of impassive faces watch us from below, their glowing green eyes staring up with a mixture of fascination and curiosity.

The wind catches my hair, lightly lifting my long scarlet strands as the hem of my dress floats softly around my legs. The wedge of my boots provides a few inches of height, and as I look over at Marek, I have a hard time suppressing the smile that curves my lips. With his face set in a stoic mask, he looks so handsome and regal in his dress tunic.

Having noticed my attention on him, he turns and gives me a subtle nod, his eyes holding mine intently before turning back to face the crowd. "People of K'ylira, I present to you my Si'an T'kara, Elizabeth Langdon of Terra, future K'Sai of House D'enekai. We go now to the Temple to formalize our betrothal as was done during the time of the Ancient Ones."

More silence follows his words, and a small measure of panic rushes through me. What if they dislike the idea of him taking a Terran bondmate? What if someone tries to attack us like Terra United did? He assured me this wouldn't be the case, but now, as I look out at the crowd of people staring in silence before us, I'm not so sure.

Together, we take the first step. My dress billows out behind me as the wind whispers through my hair. I gasp lightly as a sea of heads bow low, folding forward in a rippling wave of bodies as we make our way down the platform.

As we pass, they lift their gazes, their eyes widening slightly as they stare openly at me. To my great relief, I see nothing indicating hatred or disgust. Instead, I recognize their curiosity and fascination. The same expressions I saw on almost every V'loryn that first saw me after they arrived at the Embassy.

Ryven and the rest of the guards trail behind us, their bootsteps echoing along the stone walkway as we make our way from the transport hub to the Temple.

Row upon row of quaint shops and buildings, reminiscent of old-world European architecture but with a hint of modern design, and open-air market stands line the streets. Overflowing vegetation in varying shades of red, orange, green, and purple fill the space. Crimson vines with vibrant purple blooms climb several of the buildings. Large trees line the walkways with trunks and branches that twist at varying angles as they reach for the sun, thick with red heart-shaped leaves that remind me a bit of the Spanish oaks of Terra. Marek told me the cities were recreated to appear as they were on V'lorys, but this looks like a perfect oasis in the middle of a desert; nothing at all like I imagined it would be, given that we are on a mostly barren planet.

People stare transfixed as we pass and when I turn to face Marek, a hint of a smile tugs at his mouth. He leans down, and his soft lips graze my ear, sending a small shiver of anticipation straight through me as he whispers. "You are more beautiful than anything they have ever seen, my Elizabeth."

Happiness blooms in my chest, and I smile brightly at his words.

The corners of his lips quirk up slightly in his signature V'loryn smile. "The Temple is just up ahead. And when we leave here today, we will be formally betrothed, according to the traditions of my people."

A mixture of joy and anticipation flows across the faint bond between us, and I wish we were alone so I could wrap my arms around him. But that will have to wait until later.

Turning my attention to the Temple just up ahead, I stare in wonder at the impressive structure. Larger than any cathedral I've ever seen on Terra, the gleaming white stone with veins of black and gray stands proudly beneath the brilliance of the V'loryn sun. The futuristic architecture blending seamlessly with what could best be described as a hint of Terran European old-world style—much like the rest of the city's structures. Marek's people must have come to Terra many times to have influenced our culture to such a degree.

We climb the many steps to the entrance while the people wait below. As soon as we step inside the sacred space, a woman in light-gray robes greets us. From her dress, I realize she must be one of the Omari—a person pledged to serve the Temple. Her face is set in an impassive mask as her piercing emerald-green eyes drift over my form. "Follow me," she finally says.

Our footsteps echo through the large, domed interior. Beautifully carved beams and molding made of L'kir speak of something centuries old, but this planet was only settled in the past few decades.

As if sensing my question, Marek turns to me. "Almost everything from V'lorys that was has been recreated in exact detail here on V'lora."

Both shocked and impressed by this information, I scan the beautiful structure around me with even more appreciation than before. The level of technology it must have taken to do this is astounding. "That's amazing. How long did it take to build?"

Although I've asked the question of Marek, it is the Omari who answers. "Our architects and engineers were able to construct all of this within a year of our..." she pauses as if searching for the right word before she finally says, "*settling* on this planet."

As amazing as it all is, there is something deeply sad about the fact that they recreated their cities exactly as they were on V'lorys. While such a feat speaks to their strength and resilience as a people, it must have been difficult to be surrounded by something so familiar—a constant reminder of all that was lost. And yet, I suppose it was done purposefully as a tether from the old world to the new. An attempt to anchor the collective emotions and memories that were attached to these landmarks and structures—the things that shaped the history of their people.

∼

MAREK

Aside from Ryven, the rest of our guards remain outside, forming a protective grouping near the entrance to the inner sanctuary. The High Omari steps forward. Her sharp gaze scans Elizabeth, and she stares with a mixture of fascination and wonder at Elizabeth's ocean-blue eyes before she speaks.

She inclines her head in polite introduction. "I am High Omari L'Naya."

"I am—" Elizabeth starts, but L'Naya cuts her off.

"Elizabeth Langdon of Terra," she says solemnly, appraising Elizabeth again before she shifts her attention to me, "and Marek of House D'enekai. I have eagerly awaited you both. Now, please kneel." She motions to the floor. "Facing each other."

We do as she instructs. Elizabeth smiles across at me, but beneath her expression, I sense her growing anxiety as nervous energy flares brightly through our joined hands.

High Omari L'Naya turns her piercing gaze to mine. "Marek of House D'enekai, you are here today because you claim that the si'an'inamora exists between you and Elizabeth Langdon of Terra."

"Yes."

She dips her chin in acknowledgment and then turns her eyes to the other Omari gathered around us. "I will need two witnesses to join with my mind as I link with theirs. After the presence of the si'an'inamora has been verified, I will perform the ancient Betrothal Ceremony."

A shiver of panic runs through Elizabeth, bleeding across the faint bond.

I squeeze her hands gently in reassurance and whisper in a low voice, "Only High Omari L'Naya will touch our minds, my Si'an T'kara. The other two will be linked only to hers to experience what she sees. It is how they witness and validate their findings. No one else will enter your mind but myself and the High Omari. My vow."

L'Naya's brows furrow slightly as she cocks her head to the side. "Is something wrong?"

Elizabeth meets her eyes evenly. "Marek is the first and the *only* one that has ever touched my mind. I...do not like the idea of anyone else inside my head."

Fierce and primal possessiveness surges through me. I am pleased beyond measure that she dislikes the idea of another mind, beside my own, touching hers. Gently, I squeeze her hands again to reassure her. "We do not have to do this, my Elizabeth."

L'Naya's expression softens. "Your fidelity to your chosen one is admirable. Yours is the first Terran mind I will have ever linked with; I promise to take great care if you still wish to proceed."

Elizabeth nods. "I do." Turning her attention back to me she takes a deep and steadying breath before exhaling through pursed lips and then closing her eyes.

Pressing her open palms to mine, I entwine our fingers and strengthen the connection. *"I am here, Si'an T'kara,"* my mind projects to hers as I lower my shields and we form the al'nara. I slip into the familiar ocean of her consciousness as our minds become one. For a moment we are alone, basking in the combined warmth and strength of our love for one another.

"Like Icarus flying too closely to the sun." Her mind whispers to mine as together, we surrender to the intensity of the mental bond, allowing ourselves to sink deeper into the al'nara.

Another presence joins us, and I know it is L'Naya as she searches my thoughts. The memory of the first moment I looked into Elizabeth's luminous blue eyes flashes through my mind. *Si'an'i-namora. Like the solving of an infinitely complex mathematical equation or the gravitational pull of the stars as they align…my world shifts in an instant.*

Glowing eyes stare back at me. This is Elizabeth's memory. *His gaze searches mine, and I see warmth and something else…but I'm uncertain what it is. The same eyes look away, and the warmth is gone from them because it is only for me.*

An elderly woman with red hair streaked with white, and eyes as blue as the sea appears in my thoughts. I recognize Elizabeth's memory of her grandmother before she softly speaks. *"You'll know when you meet your soulmate, Elizabeth, just like I knew with your grandfather."*

The image fades to be replaced with another. *My own panic-filled eyes stare down at me—this is Elizabeth's memory of her death. "I love you, Marek," she whispers, and my heart clenches as devastation washes over me anew.* Her pain was immense, yet she used her last breath to speak words of truth before she passed from this world to the next.

As quickly as they appeared, the memories fade as we are pulled from the al'nara by a powerful mind.

My eyes snap open, and I gaze at Elizabeth a moment before a sharp inhalation draws my attention to the High Omari. A single tear runs down her cheek as she stares at us in shock.

The two witnesses appear equally affected.

Elizabeth's uncertainty flares through the connection.

My people do not cry.

The Omari's eyes are bright with tears as she stares down at us. "An effect of the mental transference," she whispers to explain her outward display of emotion.

She turns to Elizabeth, staring at her in open wonder. "I always doubted its existence; I believed it was only a legend. But I have seen it when your beloved restored your life by using the Balance and now…I have felt it for myself. The si'an'inamora is strong and does indeed exists between you, Marek of House D'enekai and Elizabeth Langdon of Terra." She pauses, a hesitant look on her face. "But there are things you must know."

Something about her tone sends a chill down my spine. "What is it?"

She turns her piercing gaze to Elizabeth. "Many believe you are one of the Great Uniters foretold in the Ancient Tomes of the Saraketh."

Elizabeth's brow furrow softly. "What does that mean?"

I still, as does Ryven beside me. I know of what she speaks. Kalvar warned me that there were whispers of this prophecy circulating among our people after I used the Balance to restore Elizabeth's life. If this prophecy is truth, it would mean the end of the Emperor's reign. He is already paranoid and, if this belief is spread any further, he may become even more dangerous to my Si'an T'kara than he already is. He is power hungry and will not tolerate any threat to his rule.

Ryven knows this as well as I do. I give the High Omari a warning look, but she continues. "It means that the Emperor considers you a threat. He will try to do anything he can to prevent your bonding."

Elizabeth stands straight, tilting her chin up slightly in defiance as she replies evenly. "He will not succeed."

Something akin to admiration flashes behind Ryven's eyes as he stares at my Si'an T'kara.

High Omari L'Naya bows her head slightly in agreement. "I believe you are correct. It has been foretold that he will fail." She motions for us to follow her outside. "Now come. We will perform the ancient Betrothal Ceremony."

Although Elizabeth's eyes are full of questions, she takes my hand in hers, and we follow the High Omari to the Temple entrance. Through the touch of our bare skin, I can sense her eagerness to understand L'Naya's words tempered by her desire to perform the ceremony as soon as possible because it means leaving for the safety of the Estate soon after it is done.

Our guards move to flank us, forming a protective wall on either side. My gaze drifts down to the sea of people below. I've never seen this many come to bear witness for an event at the Temple. But I suppose it is expected. Kalvar announced our arrival days before we landed.

I'll admit I was upset with him for drawing attention to us, but I now understand his reasoning. Elizabeth is not only the first Terran to come to V'lora, she is the first Si'an T'kara in over two thousand cycles and the first ever to be found outside of our race. I lift my gaze to the several dozen vidcams recording this historic event and realize the genius behind his plan. My uncle knew our people would support us, and he wanted to make certain the Emperor was aware of this as well.

All eyes are fixed upon my Si'an T'kara, standing proudly and dressed in the colors of House D'enekai. The silver v'rach sigil embroidered on her chest reflects brightly beneath the V'loryn sun. A fierce and powerful reminder that she will be K'Sai of our great and noble House.

The people stare in awe and wonder not just because she is so rare, but because she represents hope for our race—a sign that the Goddess has chosen to restore her blessings upon us by gifting the si'an'i-namora that she has withheld for over two thousand cycles.

The Betrothal Ceremony is an ancient one that has not been used in several hundred cycles. Its use fell out of favor as the Elders and the Council asserted more power over the matches between couples. I chose to honor this sacred ceremony to send a message to the Emperor and the people. Elizabeth is as much my choice as I am hers. We do not need the Elders, the Emperor, or the Council to sanction our intent to bond.

And now that the High Omari has verified the presence of the si'an'inamora between us, this ceremony signifies that regardless of whether they approve of our bonding, it matters not. I am hers, and she is mine. The Emperor would be a fool not to sanction our bond. It would be considered sacrilege to do so now after our betrothal has been blessed and sealed in the sacred Temple.

When the High Omari verifies her findings before the Council and the Elders, it will leave no room for doubt that Elizabeth and I have been blessed with the si'an'inamora. All will know that I did not break my betrothal with V'Meia to slight the Emperor. It was broken by love as much as by the fate determined in the stars long ago.

High Omari L'Naya motions for us to face each other.

I turn to my beloved, taking both her hands in my own. Her happiness bleeds through our connection. Several audible gasps rise up from the crowd below when she gives me a dazzling smile that rivals the brightness of the V'loryn sun. My Si'an T'kara is unrivaled in her beauty.

I stare deep into Elizabeth's ocean-blue eyes as the High Omari speaks the words of the ancient ceremony. That she would choose me when she could have had any other, humbles me beyond words.

L'Naya places three fingers lightly to each of our brows as her voice echoes down the steps of the Temple to the still crowd below. "What the Goddess S'Mira has brought together, let us bind in the ways of our ancestors."

Entwining our fingers, I gently rest my forehead to Elizabeth's as we close our eyes and recite the betrothal vows. Soon, we will speak the ancient words of the V'loryn bonding ceremony and then I will claim her. She will be mine completely, just as I am already hers. I long for the intimacy of the S'acris, when our minds are joined in the permanent mental bond, just as much as I desire the joining of our bodies as one. In her gaze I can already see our future, imagining the family we will someday create.

The bells of the Temple begin ringing as soon as we finish, and when I open my eyes, the entire crowd is kneeling before us. The High Omari bows as well. When she straightens, her gaze shifts briefly to Ryven, silently standing guard behind us. She meets my eyes evenly. "I will present my findings—the proof of the si'an'inamora—to the Elders and the Council when you go before the Emperor. Keep your guards close."

I appreciate her words of caution, but they are entirely unnecessary. It has always been my plan to ensure Elizabeth is protected at all times. "I will."

Having overheard our conversation, Ryven dips his head in a subtle nod to me before ordering the guards into formation to escort us to the transport. Many in the crowd stare openly at us with a look somewhere between awe and reverence. Elizabeth was right. Although I'm sure there are still some who consider her people inferior, it appears that those gathered here have come to show their support.

I suppose it is just as it is on Terra. There will always be those who are speciest, but there are many more who are not. And for the first time since we touched down on the planet, I breathe a deep sigh of relief. Perhaps she will not face as much prejudice here as I feared that she would.

As we make our way to the transport, the crowd parts just enough to let us through. Careful to maintain enough distance to allow us to walk, they position themselves as near as possible for a closer view of my Elizabeth.

With her arm looped through mine as she moves in step beside me, wearing the colors of my House and the v'rach sigil emblazoned proudly across her chest, happiness unlike anything I've ever known spirals through me. I have imagined this moment many times. Bringing her to my home world and presenting her proudly as K'Sai of House D'enekai—my chosen one and my bondmate.

Soon, she will carry my mark, and someday our child. I can hardly wait to show her the surprise I asked Tolav to prepare before our arrival. I believe it will please her greatly.

As we step onto the transport and head for the Estate, the future is stretched out before us and I am both happy and anxious to meet it. It is difficult to contain my elation at the thought of showing her our home. Of the seven Great Houses our castle is the known for its beauty as well as its strength. Perched atop a cliff at the edge of the ocean there is nothing on V'lora that rivals the majesty of its view. And now, there is no one on the entirety of V'lora more intelligent or beautiful than the K'Sai of House D'enekai.

The connection between us hums with excitement as we wait to lift off, and I am uncertain if it is hers or mine, but I suspect it is a combination of both. When I turn to her for confirmation, I find her already staring up at me with a breathtaking smile.

My lips quirk up slightly at the edges in answer. "You are happy, my Si'an T'kara?"

Already nestled against my side in the seat, she leans closer and presses a soft kiss to my lips. "More than words can say."

Gently squeezing my hand, she sends a wave of love and emotion so powerful it catches me off guard, and I inhale sharply. That she is able to project so strongly is both unexpected and wonderful since her race are not natural touch telepaths. Carefully, I raise my shields just enough so that she will be unable to sense the surprise I have awaiting her. In my study of Terran courtship rituals, I've learned that a gift of great value is most often appreciated more when it is presented as an unexpected token of affection.

She narrows her eyes and then gives me a teasing grin. "What are you hiding, my love?"

I quirk my brow. "It is a surprise."

CHAPTER 10

ELIZABETH

As our transport lifts off, I stare out the viewscreen to the bustling city below. The V'loryn architecture, ornately beautiful, stands proudly in defiance of the sparse desert that comprises most of the planet around it. Vibrant green fields define the outer edges of the city. The sharp lines of vegetation marking the advance of the V'loryn efforts at terraforming.

It is at once harsh yet beautiful. Different from anything I've ever seen, it perfectly captures the essence of Marek's people. They are survivors forging a new life in a barren land. With steeled determination and infinite patience, they carve their way into the desert, molding the earth and the sand into something familiar—the planet that they lost.

Marek says it will be at least three generations before the terraforming is complete. Even knowing they will never live to see the fruits of their labor, they press on for the generations that are to come —to remake this world into a beautiful paradise as close to their original home world—V'lorys—as possible.

I've seen V'lorys that was in Marek's mind, explored the planet of his youth in his memory as we've joined in the al'nara. Except for the red sands of V'lora, he's held back any other visions of this place, telling me that he wanted me to see it with my own eyes before viewing it through the lens of his own. Now, I long to explore and learn more about this planet that his people call home. I've imagined being here with him many times.

I turn to get his attention but smile when I realize I already have it. His glowing green gaze is studying me intently, a look of pure love reflected in his eyes. "I'd like to explore the city some more after we get settled."

His lips curl up slightly at the edges in his V'loryn smile. "Of course. There is so much I wish to show you." His gaze sweeps to the viewscreen before us. "Starting with our home."

My eyes follow his, and I'm speechless as the castle grows larger in the distance. I stare in wonder at the expanse of the sea-green ocean behind it. The red-orange sun dips low on the horizon scattering brilliant rays of light across the shimmering waves. It's nothing short of breathtaking.

I turn to smile again at Marek, but my eyes go wide as a large shadow passes overhead, blocking the light of the sun. A deafening roar shakes the transport, and my heart stops in my chest.

Marek takes my hand and transmits a wave of calm. "It's all right, Elizabeth. It is Errun coming to greet me."

When he points out the side window, I blink several times in shock at the large emerald-green dragon flying beside us. The sun glints off his scales, iridescent beneath its rays, as massive wings billow out like great sails as he dips and weaves effortlessly through the wind. "How does he know you are home?"

"V'rachs have a heightened sense of smell. They are able to scent things as far as fifty acrums away."

In all my wildest imaginings as a child, I never believed I'd ever see such a thing. Unable to tear my eyes away from Errun, I don't realize that we've finally reached the castle until we've already begun our descent. The transport halts its forward movement, and the floor vibrates slightly beneath us as we hover over the ground a moment before a low thud signals that we've landed. Marek unbuckles my harness and helps me out of the large chair. I never realized how small all the furniture on Terra must have been to the V'loryns, now that I see what their standard seats are here.

When he takes my hand in his, excitement thrums across the tenuous bridge between us. The cool saline breeze teases through my hair as we walk down the ramp, reminding me so much of Seattle. But that's where the similarity ends. We step out of the transport, into an open courtyard filled with beautiful trees like the ones I admired in the city. Thick dark-gray trunks and branches twist up toward the sky, covered in heart-shaped leaves of various shades of orange and red. The grass beneath us is varying shades of lush green—deeper and more beautiful than any of the verdant shades I've ever seen on Terra.

"This courtyard and the gardens inside the Estate are Kalvar's greatest indulgence." Marek says. "They remind him of V'lorys that was."

If I thought the vegetation was lush in the city, that was nothing compared to the courtyard here. It's filled and overflowing with deep-crimson vines that hang like thick curtains over the walls, dotted with small violet blossoms that span their entire length. They sway as the cool breeze travels through them, carrying a soft floral scent mixed with the crisp, salted air that surrounds us. Tall, thick bushes of varying shades of purple and green bloom with vibrant petals similar to red roses found on Terra. If I'd never seen the planet's surface from the ship or the transport, I'd never know that most of it was a desert.

"This is all so beautiful, Marek," I whisper.

"This is only the front courtyard." His lips quirk up slightly at the edges. "There are gardens in the back, much larger than this space."

If this is the small courtyard, I cannot imagine how grandiose the gardens must be. My gaze drifts to the surrounding walls. This place, while extremely beautiful, is obviously also a fortress. Muted white stone polished to a brilliant sheen like marble, lined with black-and-gray-streaked veins remind me of the city's structures. I rest my hand against the smooth surface and it's cool against my skin. It is striking and impressive against the contrasting various shades of red, orange, green, and purple all around us.

Marek leads me through a massive set of doors that shimmer a moment before they disappear to reveal an opening, just as the ones on the ship did. "I can't believe we're actually here...in your home," I whisper.

His brow creases slightly. "It is your home now as well. Does it not please you?"

"It's beautiful. It's just that I didn't realize that it was so...big."

He flashes his subtle V'loryn smile and tips his chin up slightly with pride. "Ours is one of the seven Great Houses of V'lora. House D'enekai was once the ruling House. This Estate is an exact replica of the Estate as it was on V'lorys."

I still have a hard time wrapping my mind around the knowledge that the V'loryns have such superior technology, they were able to recreate entire cities to appear as they had on their original home world.

Ryven steps forward. His glowing green eyes meet mine, and he dips his head in a subtle bow. "The rest of the household is eager to meet their new K'Sai."

We enter into a large room with patterned stone flooring that seems to echo each step as we move farther inside. Bright light floods the interior from the floor-to-ceiling windows that completely line the opposite wall that look out onto the gardens and the ocean beyond it. The view is only broken by two wide and elegant staircases that curve along the side, winding up to the second floor where I notice a large terrace on the other side of the glass.

This space is sparsely decorated aside from the alabaster carving in the center of a v'rach. It is so large the top almost reaches the second level. With its wings spread wide and two large sparkling green jewels for eyes, it appears both fierce and menacing.

A symbol of strength, it is in direct contrast to the intricately carved L'Kir that runs throughout the Estate. Images of vines and flowers are etched into the wood in such fine detail it appears as if they are growing along the baseboards and crown molding, lending an enchanting elegance to the interior. If not for these soft architectural touches, this place would feel intimidating simply because of its enormous size. Instead, despite the lack of furnishings it feels almost cozy and warm in a way that I never suspected a castle might be.

As Marek introduces me to each member of the household, I'm met with the same stares as I was with the guards. A strange mixture of fascination and disbelief. I manage to appear more composed than I feel as I greet each one, remembering that this must be how Marek's people felt when they first came to Terra.

After I've been introduced to everyone, Marek leads me up a curved staircase to another floor and down a long hallway as we make out way to a double set of doors.

When we reach them, he gestures for me to raise my hand and press the panel beside them. Cautiously, I do so, and they shimmer and fade away, revealing a large bedroom. As soon as we enter, they seal behind us and blend almost seamlessly into the solid wall. "These are our rooms," he says, motioning to this one and another set of doors at one end.

"Rooms?" I blink several times in shock. "As in...more than one?"

"Yes."

I've only begun to scan the space when a low, rumbling growl draws my attention to the far wall of floor to ceiling windows. I gasp as Errun's large glowing green eyes stare back at me through the glass.

Marek makes a tsking sound, and his lips turn up slightly at the edges as he extends his hand to take mine. "He is curious about you."

Threading my fingers through his, I take a deep breath and follow him out onto the expansive balcony overlooking the sea. The crisp salted air surrounds us in a gentle breeze, carrying the dull roar of the ocean and the crashing of the waves along the rocks and shoreline below.

Errun stares down at us, and I inhale sharply at his massive size. He's larger than any animal I've ever seen on Terra, and the balcony trembles beneath our feet as he settles down on his haunches, curling his long, thick tail around behind us, as if to draw us even closer to him. A trickle of panic runs through me at both the way his gaze seems locked on me and also at the thought that perhaps the balcony cannot handle so much weight.

My eyes dart to Marek. He doesn't seem concerned, so I push down my worry.

Errun lowers his head, and a small tremor of panic snakes down my spine when I notice the sharp fangs that peek out from beneath his lips as he opens his mouth to make strange low rumbling sounds that I can only assume are in greeting.

"It is good to see you too, old friend," Marek says, as he extends his free hand and gently pets Errun's snout.

Large cat-like irises lock onto mine, and it is easy to see the intelligence behind them. His nostrils flare, and he cocks his head to the side as he regards me curiously a moment before his gaze returns to Marek with an almost questioning look.

"She is my mate," Marek says, and his possessive words cause a shiver of excitement to run through me.

Errun dips his head a bit lower toward me, and I cautiously reach out and rest my palm along his jaw. His emerald-green scales are soft like silk as I trace my fingers lightly across his face and up to the hard, bony ridge of his cheek. With proud, sweeping horns that curve back and up from his head, he is more magnificent than any dragon I've ever imagined from my childhood stories. "You are beautiful," I whisper.

He tips his head slightly into my hand, nuzzling against my palm.

A wide smile curves my mouth as I stare at him in wonder.

"He likes you." My heart flutters as Marek's lips brush against the shell of my ear.

A thunderous roar sounds above us, and I gasp as another v'rach circles overhead. Covered in obsidian scales and slightly larger than Errun, it swoops down so low, I raise my hand to shield my eyes from the wind and dust stirred up by its wings.

Errun lifts his head, answering with a strong bellowing cry in return. He gives us an almost hesitant look before turning and lifting into the air. His wings flapping furiously in his eagerness as he lifts from the balcony and flies toward the other v'rach.

"Is that his mate?"

Marek stares in rapt fascination as Errun and the other v'rach circle one another. They spin and weave in an almost synchronous dance of sorts as they move across the sky. As one, they fold their wings tightly against their backs and dive over the cliff edge. I gasp as I watch them fall with dizzying speed, worried they're going to crash onto the shoreline below.ABRUPTLY, they snap open their wings, halting their descent abruptly before disappearing into the cliff face wall.

"They are sharing a cave," Marek says, a hint of his V'loryn smile on his face. "They are bonded at last."

Now that my attention is no longer on the v'rachs, I marvel at the structure of the Estate. We're standing on a large upper balcony that hangs slightly over the cliff's edge, providing a breathtaking view of the ocean. Another door farther along the wall of windows must lead to the adjoining room Marek pointed to earlier.

The grounds below seems to expand out from the line of our bedroom. The cliff edge curves out from this spot and connects to the gardens which takes up a much larger portion of the Estate than I realized. A protective railing follows along the cliff ledge, and as I think of our future children I'm glad that it's there.

The garden area is thick with vegetation. Dozens of trees with large twisting trunks are heavily laden with leaves of vibrant orange and red. A carpet of deep-green grass covers almost the entire space except for a few small streams the wind throughout. Several smaller bushes and shrubs of various shades of green with purple flowers dot the landscape, and if not for the many pathways that run throughout, I'm almost certain it'd be easy to get lost. Near the edge of the lower terrace is a large clear space covered by marbled white stones of alternating patterns along the ground. On the far side is a cleared grassy area and several smaller structures that look almost like rows of homes or some kind of elaborate storage buildings.

Following my gaze, Marek answers my unspoken question. "That is the training area. Many of the unbonded guards live there. Most of the bonded ones have homes in the city, but a few choose to remain with their families on the Estate."

I blink in shock at his words. "How much property does the Estate cover?"

He quirks his brow. "It is the largest Estate on V'lora. We will tour the grounds tomorrow if you wish."

"I'd like that," I tell him as I continue to scan the area below.

The entire space is surrounded by a massive marble stone wall, except for the see through railing along the cliff edge overlooking the sea, like something you'd see in old Terran castles for fortification. But Marek explains that what I can see here is only one smaller section of the Estate. That there are more walls beyond this one that encompass a much larger area.

The sun slowly sets over the water, taking the last of the day's warmth with it as a cold breeze whips up from the ocean below. Staring down at the beach, I gaze in wonder at the hundreds of glowing pearlescent stones along the onyx sands. "I thought the sand on V'lora was red."

Marek's gaze drifts over my hair before settling on my eyes. "The sands of the desert are red, while those along the beach are coarse obsidian grains." He looks down at the shoreline. "The glowing stones are similar to L'sair in that they are able to store energy. The light of the sun charges them during the day, giving them their soft glow at night."

Part of me still cannot believe I'm here. On an alien planet. One that will soon be my home. "Your world is so beautiful, Marek."

His slips his arms around my back and drops his forehead to mine before gently running his fingers through my hair. "I am pleased that you find it so."

The chirp of his communicator draws his attention. His entire body goes still, and his shoulders tense as he stares down at the display.

"What's wrong?"

"I must speak with Ryven. We need to ensure the grounds are safe." Although he replies in an even voice, his eyes betray a hint of worry.

Panic tightens my chest as my mind conjures images of the Mosauran and the Anguis. "Safe from what?"

His eyes meet mine, but instead of answering me he moves to the door. "I will return as soon as I can. Tolav will bring your things to the room and help you settle."

His tone is urgent, and I open my mouth to ask more questions, but he leaves the room with his inhuman V'loryn speed and I don't get the chance. Although I've already seen him move this fast before, I wonder if I'll ever get used to it.

Now that he's gone, my gaze travels over the room. The massive bed is made up of four posters, similar to a Terran bed, but carved from L'kir with intricate patterns of greenery and small animals. I imagine they must be images of V'lorys that was. It's covered by a plush silver comforter with embroidered white leaves that looks so inviting, I'm tempted to lay down.

The floor is soft beneath my feet and covered in several thickly woven rugs of black and dark gray. The walls are beautifully whitewashed stone with carved moldings and baseboards of L'kir, similar to the rest of the castle. Along the left wall is a large concave structure that reminds me a bit of a Terran fireplace but has no chimney, and instead of firewood, it is stacked with L'sair crystals. There are two massive gray sofas. One faces the fireplace and another facing the windows with a gorgeous view of the sea.

Large tapestries decorate the walls with various scenes of v'rachs and V'loryns dressed in what could best be described as something similar to the armor worn by ancient Terran knights.

A gentle knock on the door rips me from my thoughts.

"Enter," I call out.

Tolav comes in, bowing slightly before me in respect. "I have brought your belongings, K'Sai."

I smile. "Thank you, Tolav."

His eyes widen slightly before he looks toward the set of doors at the end of the bedroom.

"Shall I show you to your room?"

"My...room? I thought *this* was our room."

JESSICA GRAYSON

"*This* is the T'Hale's room," he corrects me. "*Your* room is through those doors."

His statement catches me off guard but I follow him anyway as he leads me into the adjoining space.

"Your resting chamber has been cleaned and prepared for you as per the T'Hale's instructions," he says with a hint of pride in his voice. "I saw to it myself."

This bedroom is just as large as the...T'Hale's bedroom, and the bed is an exact replica as well. I realize it's a mirror of the other room.

He said the T'Hale instructed him to ready this space. I thought we'd already discussed this. Why would Marek request I have a room separate from his? Maybe it's like back at the Embassy, where we had to maintain the appearance of sleeping in separate apartments because of Kalvar's insistence that we follow the rules of V'loryn propriety.

"Do you require anything, K'Sai?"

"If you could please tell me where the kitchen is so I can fix myself something to eat. That would be great."

He tips his head to the side. "Anything you wish, you need only to ask. I will have some food prepared and brought to you at once."

I start to insist that I can prepare my own meal but decide against it. This is Marek's home, and until I can talk to him about how all of this works, I'll just go with the flow...for now.

"Thanks, Tolav."

His eyes lock on mine a moment with a look of intense curiosity before he looks down at the floor. "Forgive me, K'Sai. Your eyes...I have never seen this color before, and your appearance is...unique."

"There is nothing to forgive, Tolav. You're just curious. I myself was the same way when I first saw V'loryns."

He lifts his gaze to mine. "I have heard that even on your world, your phenotype is rare. Is this truth?"

It's hard to suppress a laugh at the memory of the first time I met Marek and he commented on my "spots," but somehow, I manage to do it. "Yes, it is."

"It is no wonder the T'Hale is worried," he whispers under his breath.

"What do you mean?"

His shoulders visibly stiffen. "I will see to your meal." He bows.

"Wait, Tolav. What did you mean, 'the T'Hale is worried'?"

His face remains impassive, but his eyes betray his concern. "I overheard Ryven talking about how the Mosaurans and the Anguis tried to gain access to you on the station." He pauses, a hesitant look on his face before he continues. "You are a rarity...even among your own species. That would make you more valuable to slavers. Mosaurans have strong anti-slavery laws, so I do not understand what they wanted with you. But the Anguis? They will be very interested in your race, and that is concerning."

Recalling our encounters on the station, I shudder inwardly at the memory.

"I will return shortly." He bows again and then leaves the room.

Sitting down on the edge of the bed, I sigh heavily. I wish I knew where Marek went. I have so many questions to ask him. I thought we would have time once we got here, but he left so quickly. And now, I know it's because he's still worried even though he said we'd be safe on the Estate.

Glancing around the room, my thoughts turn to Terra and all that I left behind—everything I've ever known.

After all the time I've spent learning about his culture, I thought I was more than prepared to understand his world and his people. Now, I realize I have so many questions; I feel so lost. Is this how *he* felt on Terra?

At least on Terra, he was surrounded by other V'loryns. Here...I am alone. The only one of my kind. The Embassy is not finished yet, and Anton and everyone else won't be here for at least another month.

Crossing the room, I step out onto the balcony. The dull roar of the rolling waves as they crash against the shoreline below is familiar enough that if I close my eyes, I can imagine I'm back on Terra.

So strange to find myself beneath a different sky. I wonder if it will ever feel as familiar to me as the skies of my home world. Will I ever think of it as mine? The fresh saline breeze whips through my hair as I move to the edge of the balcony and peer down below at the white cliff wall. It shimmers as it reflects the last of the sun's rays as it makes its slow descent into the sea-green ocean.

Light reflects off something in the distance, and as I study it further, I realize it's a strange translucent glow in the sky around and above me. Iridescent in places, it reminds me of a soap bubble. It must be an energy defense shield like the one at the V'loryn Embassy on Terra. Although I never actually got to see it deployed, I recognize the technology from Marek's description.

I don't know when he's going to get back, but I'm already tired. I was so anxious about coming here that I didn't sleep much last night. Part of me wonders if most of my nervousness might have come from him, through our connection.

He's on edge, and whatever happened back on the station with the Mosaurans and the Anguis made it exponentially worse. Even now, his anxiety floods across our tenuous bond, and I don't know how to separate myself from it. My body is filled with nervous energy. I want to go for a run, but I don't know where I can even do that here, and I know that if I'm gone, Marek would be even more worried if he returned and couldn't find me.

I sigh. We're going to have to have a long and serious talk when he gets back. He can't just leave me like this while he goes off to take care of everything. We're a team, and if this is going to work between us, I have to be involved and not sheltered like some damsel in distress.

My gaze drifts to a meditation firepot in the far corner of the room. Looks like I'm going to have to try meditation. Marek's been walking me through it for the past few months, but we usually end up having a make-out session as a result. It's difficult to be so close to him and keep my hands to myself. He's so good at kissing, you'd think V'loryns had been doing this as long as my people have.

I light the firepot and then settle on the floor, crossing my legs in front of me. Drawing in a deep breath, I stare intently into the flames and do my best to relax my shoulders. Time to see if I actually learned anything from Marek.

Slowly, I descend into a meditative state, allowing my thoughts to drift untethered through my mind. A soft chime snaps me back into awareness.

"Enter," I call out as I stand to face the door.

Tolav enters with a tray full of a colorful variety of foods and places it on the nearby table. He tips his chin up with pride as he presents it to me. "I brought a sampling of various items to see which you prefer, K'Sai."

"That was very thoughtful of you, Tolav. Thank you."

"Of course." He bows low and then leaves.

Some of the foods he's brought me I recognize immediately as selections they served at the V'loryn Embassy. But there are several items I've never seen before, and I'm not sure what to try first. I should have asked Tolav about these before he left.

The first thing that catches my eye is a round, dark-orange fruit or vegetable; I cannot tell which. It has a soft, outer fleshy layer similar to a peach. I take a cautious bite and, a crisp, sweet taste, like a cross between raspberry and blueberry, explodes across my tongue. It's exquisite. I think I have a new favorite V'loryn food.

After sampling various other items, I make a note to ask Marek about their names later. Sitting on the couch, I stare out at the sea-green ocean. I can't believe I'm actually here, on an alien planet. How many times did I stare up at the stars as a child and dream of strange new worlds?

When we accepted our postings at the new Terran Embassy here, we talked about making this our permanent residence. If we decide to stay here indefinitely, someday this will be home to my children. Will Terra be home to them as well? Or will it feel as alien to them as V'lora feels to me now?

The last rays of the orange-red sun peek out above the water, and I wrap my arms around myself as the air grows cooler. Glancing at the walls, I don't see anything that resembles an environmental control unit. As Marek has pointed out multiple times, V'loryns are able to regulate their body temperatures much more effectively than Terrans, so I suppose this type of chill doesn't really bother them.

I take the blanket off the large bed and drag it to the sofa, wrapping it around me like a cocoon. Pulling my legs up to my chest, I prop myself against the arm of the couch and lay my head on one of the soft cushions.

The large sofa and plush upholstery practically swallow me, and I wonder if I'll ever get used to the size of the furniture here. Everything seems so much bigger than on Terra. Then again, Marek's people *are* taller than mine.

Nestling into the comforter, I watch the rolling waves as the tide comes in until my eyes refuse to stay open. I'll just rest a bit until Marek gets back. Hopefully, that won't be long.

CHAPTER 11

MAREK

Ryven's face is a mask of concern as he stares across at me. "The two Mosaurans we encountered on the station are requesting an audience with you, T'Hale. They are demanding to speak with the K'Sai."

Fierce protectiveness arcs through me. "No." Ryven's eyes widen slightly as the word escapes my mouth with more force than I'd intended. "The Mosaurans are aggressive and unpredictable. I do not want them anywhere near her."

"I agree, Marek," he replies, reverting to the familiar use of my given name. We trained and served together when we were younger in the V'loryn Defense Force, and while I've insisted that he address me this way, he only does so when we are alone.

I don't understand why they are so interested in her, and their interest makes me worry. The Mosauran Empire is vast, and they are a race of formidable warriors. We have a treaty of non-aggression with them, but it has always been tenuous at best. I shake my head in frustration. What could they possibly want with my Elizabeth? "They knew she was Terran, Ryven. How do their people even know about hers? She is the first to venture beyond their planetary system."

"I do not know."

A knot of worry forms in the pit of my stomach. "Alert the Terran government about what happened on the station. The first Terrans will be arriving within the month to begin staffing their Embassy. Until we know more about the intentions of the Mosaurans and the Anguis toward their people, it is best to be cautious."

"Agreed. I've made sure extra security measures are in place to protect the K'Sai."

"The shields surrounding the Estate?"

"All have been raised."

My thoughts drift back to this afternoon when we first arrived and the crowd there to greet us. "The people bowed to her, Ryven. Why would they do that?"

He tips his head to the side and gives me a look that borders on disbelief. "Do you not realize that we have all eagerly awaited the arrival of your K'Sai ever since the news came that you were bringing her here?"

His question stuns me. "I was not aware."

He continues. "Many have requested to be allowed to attend the interment ceremony for Prince Kaden and Princess Brienna."

"Why?"

"They are demonstrating their support for your House, for your choice of a Terran bondmate. It is as much out of approval for K'Sai Elizabeth that they wish to attend as it is for respect of House D'enekai. Kaden was a beloved Prince of legend. Now that word has spread of his tragic story, people wish to show honor and reverence to his Princess and child."

My mouth drifts open slightly at Ryven's words before I quickly snap it shut again. I nod. "Any who wish to attend the ceremony shall be allowed."

"There is one other thing."

"What is it?"

He gives me a grim look. "The Emperor will be in attendance as well."

Ice cold dread fills my veins. "Do you believe he will try anything?"

"I believe he has not given up on the idea of aligning you with his House, and that he will do anything he can to ensure that it happens."

The gravity of his words and suggestion settle in my stomach like a heavy stone. He is right. Elizabeth is a threat to the Emperor's plans, and he is not a male who accepts defeat lightly. Kalvar said he threatened war between our Great Houses when my mother refused his betrothal and bonded with my father instead.

Ryven opens his mouth as if to speak but then closes it again and says nothing. He gives me a hesitant look. One that I recognize as the expression he makes when he's about to tell me something I may not wish to hear.

"What is it, my friend? You know you can always speak freely to me."

His eyes meet mine evenly. "I admit, I was surprised that you brought her back with you. The Emperor is a dangerous man."

Looking down at my hands, I sigh heavily in frustration. "She is very…determined. I could not convince her otherwise."

Ryven nods. "My father was the same way. He could deny my mother nothing."

"Are not all males this way when they find their mate? It is what we were told when we were growing up. And now…" A smile tugs at my lips. "I find it is truth."

His eyes sparkle with barely contained amusement before his expression sobers and he is once more the soldier and guard who first earned my respect before we became such close friends. "She is the future of our House. You both are," he adds. "We will protect her. My vow."

"Thank you, my friend."

CHAPTER 12

MAREK

When I finally return to our chambers, I scan the room for Elizabeth. Alarm bursts through me when I do not find her. Crossing the bedroom with the speed possessed of my people, I rush into the adjoining apartment and sigh in relief when I notice the shock of red hair beneath a blanket on the sofa.

She is asleep. The comforter is wrapped around her like a cocoon. Even the tip of her small button nose is tucked beneath the fabric. My heart stops when I notice her visibly shivering. Angry at myself, I clench my jaw in frustration. I should have realized that the night air is much cooler than she is used to. My people are able to easily adapt to a wide range of temperatures, but Terrans are not.

I move to the warming pit along the wall and am glad to see that Tolav made sure there were plenty of L'sair crystals stacked inside. He did this for both apartments. It seems that at least *he* was prepared for my Si'an T'kara to stay here, even though I was not. With a quick tap of one crystal to another it activates their energy, emitting a soft warm glow that should heat the rooms rather quickly.

Returning to Elizabeth, I kneel beside her and gently run my fingers through her hair, brushing the long, soft, scarlet strands back from her face.

Her eyelids flutter open, and she gives me a sleepy smile. "You're back."

My heart clenches. "And you are cold, my Si'an T'kara," I whisper.

"Just a little," she replies, although the chattering of her teeth suggests otherwise.

Scooping her up into my arms—comforter and all—I walk her back to our room and lay her down in the large bed, covering her with yet another blanket. Removing my tunic and shoes, I settle in next to her and wrap my arms around her form, trying to give her warmth.

"That's better." She smiles, nestling against me as she molds her body to mine. The cold press of her small feet against my shins fills me with guilt. I have to take better care of my mate; I cannot forget that she is different from my people. "Is it always so cold here at night?"

I shake my head. "This is the coldest season of the cycle. Forgive me. I forgot that your body is unable to adjust as well as mine is to—"

She places her finger to my lips to silence me. "It's okay. We just got here. You've had a lot on your mind."

I gently nuzzle her hair as I pull her closer against me.

"Marek?"

"Yes?"

"Why did you instruct Tolav to put me in a different room from yours?"

It takes me a moment before I realize my error. In having him prepare the adjoining space, I did not explain to him why. "I believe he misunderstood my intent. As you know, most V'loryn bonded pairs sleep separate and do not share a room or a bed. I wanted the room ready so you could see it in the..." I pause a moment, searching for the correct Terran idiom, before finally continuing, "...best light."

Her brows knit together in confusion.

I trace my fingers lightly over her cheek and down to her jaw, tipping her chin up as I run my thumb across her soft, pink lips. She is the most beautiful thing I have ever beheld. "Although it will be a while before we start a family, I wanted to know your thoughts on making that room into a nursery in the future."

Her mouth drifts slightly open as I continue. "Most of the children born of the Great Houses are given to a Healer to care for in a separate part of the Estate shortly after birth. It is to encourage emotional independence from an early age. I have seen how involved Terran parents are with their young. Because you are Terran, our children will be of two worlds, and I was hoping we could adopt the Terran style of parenting in regard to raising our children."

A beaming smile lights her face as happiness flows through the connection between us.

"This pleases you?"

She gives me a fervent kiss. "When you say something like that it makes me want you even more."

I bask in the warmth of her love as it floods across the faint bond a moment before panic threatens to overwhelm me again as thoughts of the Mosaurans and Anguis fill my mind. I cannot bear the thought of anything happening to her. She is my life and my future.

Sensing my worry, her ocean-blue eyes search mine in confusion. "What's wrong?"

I still. I had not wanted to distress her unnecessarily.

She reaches up to gently cup her hand to my face. "Something is wrong. I can feel it. Is it because of what happened at the station today?"

Drawing in a deep and steadying breath, I struggle to push down the panic and fear I'm unintentionally sending her through our bond. "Yes. I do not know why the Mosaurans are so interested in you, but I trust neither them nor the Anguis. The Mosaurans we encountered are now demanding to speak with you."

"Why me?"

"I do not know. I only know that I do not want them anywhere near you."

"You think they're dangerous?"

"They are a warrior race, known to be aggressive and unpredictable."

She looks away a moment before returning her gaze to mine. "Why did your people bow to me? Why do they address me as if we're already bonded?"

"Ryven says that many have been anxiously awaiting your arrival. They have already accepted you as K'Sai of House D'enekai."

"They have?"

I nod.

"But they all stared at me like I was—"

"Beautiful," I finish her sentence. "Unlike anyone they have ever seen before." I run my fingers through the long, silken strands of her crimson hair. I lower my head to the curve of her neck and shoulder, breathing deeply of her delicious scent mixed with a hint of jasmine. I'm humbled that she has chosen me when she could have had anyone she desired.

"Why did you leave me here?"

I still as her displeasure flows across the bond, and choose my next words carefully, knowing that the wrong ones could ignite her fiery temper. "I fear the Emperor may try to harm you. I did not want to leave, but I am trying to make sure you are protected."

She pulls back just enough to give me a pointed look. "I'm not helpless."

She is right. My Si'an T'kara is strong and fierce. But my people are much stronger than her, and this is the source of my worry. I meet her eyes evenly so that she can see the truth of my words. "I know you are not helpless, but Terrans are much smaller than V'loryns and—"

Tilting her head back, she meets my eyes evenly. "I know you are trying to protect me, but I need to be involved instead of left behind. You left me here today, and I felt useless, Marek. That's not who I am. I'm not some helpless creature that needs to be sheltered. You're worried, and I understand that. So I've given this a lot of thought. On Terra, I trained with Taven in k'atana, and now I'd like to continue my training with one of your guards."

JESSICA GRAYSON

I jerk my head back in surprise. "They are much bigger than you and could injure you."

"And that's exactly why I have to know how to defend myself against one of your people. The Emperor is a threat, and I need to be ready if he tries to harm us."

I blink at her in shock. Does she doubt the ability of our guards? "All my guards are sworn to protect you and—"

She shakes her head softly. "I know they are. But I need to be able to do this in case something happens. If the Emperor were able to somehow get to us alone, I need to be prepared, Marek. Both for myself and for you."

My heart stutters. I cannot bear the thought of her in danger. "Elizabeth, we are leaving in the morning. This is madness, and I will not risk losing you."

"No." Her voice is firm and resolute. "We're not running away. If we run now, the Emperor wins, and your House loses everything. What's to stop him from hurting you if you abandon your House and your people? This is your home. And you were just talking about a nursery." She gestures to the adjoining room. "Someday all of this will belong to our children." Reaching up, she cups her hand to my face. Her luminous eyes stare deep into mine with a look of intense determination. "We *will not* run from him."

I open my mouth to protest, but I know that she is right. What would stop the Emperor from killing me *and* Elizabeth if I were to abandon my House? The only reason he dares not do so now is because House D'enekai has more support from the Lower Houses and the people than any of the other Great Houses. I realize now that we have always been in danger. The moment I chose Elizabeth as my mate, I put her life at risk.

Clenching my jaw, I close my eyes and press my forehead to hers as a long exhale escapes my nostrils. "We will speak with my guards tomorrow about your training."

CHAPTER 13

MAREK

Staring at my guards, I allow my gaze to travel over each one before I speak. Elizabeth stands at my side. Their eyes are all locked on her, and I know they are wondering why she is here.

"I have asked you here today to request a volunteer to train K'Sai Elizabeth in the ways of our combat so that she may be more prepared in the event of an attack on her person."

A look of shock flickers briefly across Ryven's face. "Do you doubt our ability to keep her safe?"

My guards all nod, and a general hum of discontented murmurs drifts throughout the room.

"I do not doubt your abilities."

All eyes snap up to meet mine, and I continue. "Kalvar and I have never asked anything more of you than what we ourselves would do as well. The K'Sai is of the same mind as we are. Just as V'loryn females used to train in combat before the destruction of V'lorys, the K'Sai wishes to do so as well."

Ryven steps forward and looks to Elizabeth. "K'Sai, you are the future of our House. You are Si'an T'kara to T'Hale Marek. We would not risk you or your health in such rigorous training. Forgive me"—he bows a moment before straightening—"but, at no fault of your own, your species is much smaller than ours. I speak for all the guard when I say that we have no wish to risk hurting you."

Elizabeth meets his eyes evenly. "Your acceptance and concern touch me deeply. But just as you would risk your life for T'Hale Marek, so would I. I want to be able to defend him if I need to. Teach me your ways so that I am prepared to defend myself and my mate if I must."

With a slight clench of his jaw Ryven studies her. I know him well enough to recognize that he is at war with himself. It goes against everything in him to put a female in harm. There are so few on our planet now that they are the most important people on V'lora. He darts a quick glance at me before returning his focus to Elizabeth.

He dips his chin in a subtle nod. "As you wish, K'Sai. I will assess your skill. Follow me."

As they walk to the training area, I know he thinks this will be over quickly. That he will find her skills severely lacking and put this all behind us. But I've seen her spar with Taven. He does not know how formidable she is in combat, but he is about to find out. She may be small, but she is fierce, and while I fear her injury, I know she is more skilled than he realizes.

I stand with the other guards just off to the side as Ryven leads Elizabeth to the center of the training mat.

The rest of the guards glance nervously between Elizabeth and myself. They believe I will put a stop to this at the last second. They do not know that I cannot do this. Not only would I risk incurring her wrath, but she has already made me promise not to interfere, and I will not break my vow. I curl my fingers reflexively into my palms as I struggle against the want to rush to her side and pull her behind me as she stands before him, readying to fight.

With one final glance at me, Ryven turns his attention back to her.

He spreads his feet, raising his arms in a defensive stance. "Defend yourself," he tells her.

They circle each other, each in a different fighting pose as their eyes remain locked.

Ryven strikes first, and Elizabeth spins away, easily missing his aim.

He strikes again, and she ducks just out of his reach before kicking out her leg, catching the back of his knee and causing him to stumble.

He barely manages to regain his balance in time, avoiding a fall. It is easy to read the surprised look not only on his face, but also on the rest of the guards. They did not think she would last this long, much less actually make contact with him in any meaningful way.

Ryven lunges at her, and she rolls to the side and behind him, quickly spinning around and kicking out again. She makes contact with his back and he falls forward, catching himself at the last moment.

Spinning quickly on his heels, he charges her again, and she twists, grabbing his arms and using his own forward momentum to push him away, and he stumbles onto the ground.

Picking himself back up, he turns to face her with a look of intense concentration. Feigning a step to the right, he changes position and goes left instead. Elizabeth barely corrects herself in time to avoid his strike, but her balance is affected enough that he grabs her arm to haul her to him.

Instead of trying to jerk away as he'd expected, she turns into his grasp, and pulls the knife from his belt and swings it toward him, stopping just at the edge of his throat.

His eyes widen in shock as he stares down at the blade a moment before releasing her arm.

Panting heavily, she opens her hand, allowing the blade to fall to the ground at their feet.

The eyes of every guard stare at her in shock.

"You *are* a warrior," Ryven whispers more to himself than to her.

"Who still has much to learn," she replies. "Don't hold back next time. I need to learn to fight you at your full ability so that if the time comes when I need to defend my Si'an T'karan, I will be able to do so," she adds, tilting her chin up slightly in a fierce warrior stance.

In this moment, she reminds me of a picture I've seen of one of V'lorys's ancient queens. Queen S'Mara was a warrior who fought for her people and led them to victory in the last Great War.

Ryven bows to her. "We will continue with your training tomorrow morning, K'Sai."

Elizabeth tilts her head down slightly in acknowledgment of his words, in her best impression of my people before turning to walk back to me.

As she draws closer, she flashes her brilliant smile.

She does not notice the effect this has on my guards. They are as mesmerized as I was the first time I saw her smile. I still am.

Ignoring their blatant stares, she stretches up on her toes, wraps her arms around the back of my neck, and presses her lips to mine. Pulling her close against me, I open my mouth and deepen our kiss.

Kalvar comes down the steps, clearing his throat as he approaches.

Elizabeth smiles against my lips before pulling away, a pink bloom spreading across her cheeks as we turn to face my uncle. This is not the first time he's witnessed us kissing, nor will it be the last. I am addicted to the soft press of her mouth to mine.

V'loryns do not kiss, and I notice the shocked and confused stares on the face of every guard. If any of them are ever blessed to find a Terran bondmate, they will wonder how our people have lived all these millennia without kissing.

With a slight quirk of his brow, Kalvar's gaze drifts over the guard before he looks to us. No doubt he noticed their shock at our blatant display of affection. He arrived on a transport just this morning. His travel was delayed by one day so he could brief his temporary replacement at the V'loryn Embassy before he left.

He steps forward, a hint of a smile on his otherwise stoic features as he greets us. "It is agreeable to see you both." His eyes shift to Elizabeth. "I trust you are settling in well?"

She smiles. "Yes. It's lovely here."

His expression softens. "I am pleased you find it so. This is as much your home now as it is ours."

Her happiness is easily read, through our connection, at his words. "Thank you," she replies.

He dips his chin in a subtle nod. "Perhaps when we return, we can all share a meal. But for now, we must ready for the interment ceremony."

Elizabeth and I head back to our rooms.

"I need to shower and change first," she tells me. But when I notice her heading toward the cleansing room in the adjoining apartment, I motion for her to follow me into the main one for this area.

Her jaw drops as soon as the doors open.

~

ELIZABETH

I thought the cleansing room I'd used this morning was the master, but I was definitely wrong. This space is palatial to say the least. I recognize the tile that I should press to make the sink and cabinet come out from the wall, but it is the large bathing pool in the center of the floor filled with clear light-green water that draws my attention. Big enough to easily fit at least four people, steam rises from the surface, and it looks so enticing I can hardly wait to get in. Turning to Marek, I gesture to the pool. "I thought water was scarce here compared to Terra."

He quirks his brow. "That's why we have developed excellent water recycling technologies."

I try but fail to suppress a grim look as I consider exactly where that water may have been recycled from. As if reading my thoughts, a small smile tugs at the corner of Marek's lips. "This water is not recycled. It is part of a natural spring, constantly refreshing. Our technology keeps it warm. There are a surprising number of springs in many of the desert caves as well. It's why the t'sars make their homes there."

"Oh," I reply, trying not to let my relief show too much. I shouldn't be so disturbed by the thought of recycled water anyway. I know that's what they have on the ships.

"The shower is this way." He points toward the opposite wall.

"Where?"

"Just here." He touches another tile, and a glowing green panel appears. With another touch, water sprays from the ceiling and walls, stopping abruptly at some unseen energy barrier.

I turn to Marek. "How do I get through that invisible barrier?"

"You step through," he explains, waving his hand to the spot. I marvel as he cups his hand, gathering water before pulling it back through to show me.

Unfastening the clasps of my tunic, I move to pull it from my body, but Marek places his hands on my arms to stop me. "Please wait until I've left, my Si'an T'kara."

I start to protest that we're engaged and it's ridiculous that we haven't seen each other naked yet, but when I see the hungry look in his eyes and the slight tic of his jaw as his gaze travels down my body, I know he's struggling against the urge to claim me. He's only saying this because he doubts his resolve in this moment.

A smile tugs at my lips as he gives me another heated gaze before turning and leaving the room. Perhaps it's wrong, but I love that I have this effect on him.

MAREK

When Elizabeth emerges from the cleansing room, she is nothing short of stunning. She had chosen several swaths of fabric to be sent here to V'lora ahead of us, along with her measurements, so that she would have a choice of V'loryn clothing to wear once we arrived. She knew it would be difficult to procure clothing otherwise due to her small size compared to V'loryn females.

Taven's sister, Tayla, made sure the clothing was made to Elizabeth's exact measurements.

She's dressed in an iridescent light blue and flowing dress-like tunic, with matching pants and boots. The silken fabric highlights both her long scarlet strands and her ocean-blue eyes. She is nothing short of breathtaking.

"What do you think?" She twirls around once.

I open my mouth to speak, but I cannot find the words. She is perfection in every meaning of the word. "You are more beautiful than the nightblooms of the k'nshara," I finally manage, and I'm rewarded with her brilliant smile. I clear my throat. "It is only missing one thing."

She frowns. "What is it?"

"This," I reply, handing her a small box carved from L'kir.

She opens it and gasps lightly when she finds the necklace inside.

Handed down over many generations, it is the v'rach sigil of House D'enekai. Green eterna stones mark the eyes, and the intricate v'rach is pure L'omhara that sparkles brilliantly beneath the lighting. Its value is priceless—worth more than the Estate and all the ships docked on the V'loryn orbital station. "Every K'Sai of House D'enekai has worn it over the past four thousand cycles."

Tear-filled eyes gaze up into mine as she takes in a shaking breath.

"It belonged to my mother. It was the last thing she gave me before I boarded the evacuation ship. She wanted me to give it to my T'kara."

"It's beautiful, Marek. Of course, I'll wear it." She stares in wonder at the pendant. "Will you help me put it on?"

I nod, and she hands me the necklace, lifting her hair from her shoulders. The sudden movement fills the air with her delicate fragrance mixed with a soft hint of jasmine. My gaze drifts to the pulsing artery along her neck, and my heart pounds as I fasten the small clasp to secure the necklace.

I've long desired to seal her to me in the S'acris. Tilting my head to the side, I lean forward just enough to skim the tip of my nose from her temple and down the elegant line of her neck.

She shivers and inhales sharply, and for a moment I wonder if I've scared her. But when I detect the sound of her heart quickening its pace, my nostrils flare at the scent of her arousal. A low growl rumbles deep in my chest as I wrap my arms around her waist and pull her back against me.

A soft puff of air escapes her lips in a breathless moan as I press a line of soft kisses from her jaw down to the curve of her neck and shoulder. She reaches back, running her delicate fingers through my hair before tilting her head up and gently guiding my mouth to hers.

I want her more than anything I've ever wanted before, but I force myself to pull away from the temptation to claim her in this moment. "We should go," I whisper.

She smiles against my lips. "Only if you promise to kiss me all night when we return," she teases.

A smile tugs at the corner of my mouth. That is a promise that will be easily kept.

CHAPTER 14

ELIZABETH

The Great Assembly Hall is nothing short of impressive. Tall, platinum, dome-capped towers of muted white stone like marble stand proudly in the heart of K'ylira. Almost as large and impressive as the Temple, it's a bit sleeker and more modern, reminding me more of the design of the V'loryn cruisers than ancient Terran buildings.

The crowd parts as Kalvar, Marek, and I ascend the steps and enter the main rotunda. Hundreds of people line either side, waiting to be allowed in to pay their respects. Their glowing green eyes watch us intently. The gentle press of Marek's hand on my lower back is reassuring as he moves in step beside me.

The seating inside reminds me a bit of the great Coliseum of Rome but indoors instead of out with white carved marble stone cordoned off into sections. Each is an area designated for members of the Great and Lower Houses. Marek guides me to a location only a few sections up from the floor level.

Vanek arrives, wearing the colors and sigil of his House A'msir—

one of the seven Great Houses of V'lora—just as we are dressed to represent House D'enekai. He dips his chin in a subtle nod and takes the seat beside me, instead of sitting in the area designated for his House. But I suppose he does this to openly show his support for D'enekai. Ryven and the rest of Marek's guard sit on either side and behind us, alert for any threat or danger as they form a barrier between us and the rest of the crowd.

Milena, K'Sai of the Great House L'eanan and ally to both D'enekai and A'msir, takes a seat in the section beside ours. With her light-brown hair braided and styled in an elegant design atop her head and dressed in the dark green colors of her House, she appears as regal as a queen of ancient Terran legend. Her emerald-green eyes meet mine briefly as she bows her head slightly in a subtle acknowledgment and greeting.

Once everyone is seated, the space becomes eerily silent. Footsteps echo loudly beneath the dome, drawing my attention to the far side of the structure where several more of Marek's guards carry in the stasis pod that contains Kaden and Brienna. The High Omari follows behind them, her head bowed slightly in reverence.

All eyes fall upon the pod, and several gasp when they notice Brienna's red hair, their gazes darting to me before turning their attention back to the Prince and Princess.

As soon as the stasis pod is in place, directly in the center of the room, Kalvar and Marek stand and walk silently side by side toward it. Kalvar moves to a silver bowl of L'sair crystals beside the casing. Lifting one of the muted orange crystals, he gently taps it to another beside it, activating the rest, illuminating the entire space with an otherworldly soft, warm glow.

He and Marek then turn to face their ancestor and his bondmate, each of them closing their eyes and bowing their heads. The High Omari hands them a small glowing stone. I recognize these. They are remembrance stones, the same as the one Marek left at my mother's grave. Holding it tightly to his chest a moment, Marek places it reverently atop the casing.

No one speaks, and the silence is deafening. V'loryns honor the dead in this way. Words are considered too inadequate to ever encompass the devastation of loss and grief.

We remain there in quiet observance as members of the other Great Houses go to pay their respects as well, each of them leaving a remembrance stone for the Prince and Princess. Vanek leans over to whisper. "You can go with me if you'd like," he offers.

I give him a subtle nod, and we walk together. The Omari hands us each a stone, and I lower my head, saying a silent prayer before placing it atop the casing. When I am finished, I turn to find Vanek waiting patiently for me. As we pass Marek and Kalvar, Marek's eyes meet mine, sadness reflecting behind them. I know that Brienna and Kaden's tragic story still haunts his dreams. He's told me before that it reminds him of when I died in his arms.

I asked him once to show me the memory. Reluctantly, he opened a connection between us to allow me a small glimpse of the pain he carries from that day. Experiencing his anguish and devastation even in this muted form were overwhelming. Now I understand why it is the source of his greatest fear.

"I know what it is to lose you," he had whispered. *"And it is something I never want to experience again."*

On our way back to our seats, something draws my attention off to the side to find deep-set glowing green eyes practically boring into mine. It's V'Meia. I recognize her from our meeting on Terra. When she told me she was Marek's betrothed.

Dressed in the muted gold color of House K'voch with the image of the poisonous k'mal embroidered across her chest, she sits proudly beside a man dressed in similar attire.

He stares at me with barely contained anger behind his gaze, and I realize it must be her father—the Emperor. Each of them wearing the same cold expressions, they watch me a moment more before turning their attention back to the center of the floor.

When we finally sit down, I notice members of the other Great and Lower Houses staring at me as well. Vanek's gaze sweeps the room before he leans down to whisper. "It is good that the people already embrace the K'Sai of House D'enekai."

A small smile curves my lips. "We're not bonded yet, but I appreciate the sentiment."

He arches a brow at me. "Your bonding is but a formality. Everyone already considers you to be K'Sai." His eyes drift over the crowd. "All have seen the footage of you sacrificing yourself to save Kalvar. If not for the si'an'inamora, Marek would have been unable to restore your life. You would be dead, and our people would still have honored you as a hero. But the fact that you not only live, but that you lived because of the fated bond and are here walking among them alongside your Si'an T'karan, Marek—the most respected of any T'Hale..." He trails off a moment before he turns to meet my gaze evenly. "You bring hope to our dying race, Elizabeth."

Confused, I whisper back. "Dying race?"

He tips his chin toward the mass of people. "Look around you. The males greatly outnumber the females of our species. The Goddess has gifted the sacred blessing of the si'an'inamora outside of our race not once"—his gaze darts briefly to Kaden and Brienna's stasis pod before returning to me—"but twice now with your species. Many believe it is a sign, not only that the Goddess has blessed the union of our people to yours, but that House D'enekai should be in power instead of House K'voch."

Shocked by his bold words I dart a quick glance around the room, hoping that no one can hear our conversation. "That's—" I start to whisper but he cuts me off.

"Treason." He nods, finishing my sentence. "I know, but it is truth."

As his eyes meet mine, everything comes into razor-sharp focus. The warning of the High Omari floats to the surface of my mind. "That's why the Emperor is so upset about our bonding. He thinks the people will see it as a sign. And that makes me a threat to him," I say more to myself than to Vanek as I put the pieces together.

"Yes. It is also why you are in such danger." He darts a quick glance in Marek's direction. "Both of you."

Ice fills my veins, but I force myself to push down my worry. I will not allow the Emperor or the people to see me afraid. As if my thoughts have summoned him, the Emperor approaches. Before today, I'd only seen images of him in the Terran newsfeeds when he signed the alliance with my home world. Up close, he is much more intimidating in person as he stares down at me with piercing, emerald-green eyes.

"Elizabeth Langdon of Terra," he says, and I note the bitter tinge in his voice.

"Emperor Zotal." I stand, forcing myself to hold his gaze as I tilt my chin up slightly. I will not show this man my fear.

He arches a condescending brow. "Ah. So, you know who I am. This is agreeable. I dislike the formality of initial greetings."

Vanek moves closer to stand protectively beside me.

"Vanek," the Emperor says with a subtle inclination of his head. "I've heard the search for Menov does not go well." His sinister gaze shifts to me. "Regrettably, the K'Sai remains in much danger whilst he is still at large."

His curled fists tremble at his sides as Vanek practically glares at the Emperor. He has hunted far and wide for Menov—the Emperor's nephew—ever since he determined that he was behind the Embassy attack on Terra and attempted assassination of Kalvar. Above all else, however, he believes Menov was acting on the Emperor's orders.

Inwardly, I shudder as I think on what might have happened if I hadn't been able to stop the terrorist that day.

Emperor Zotal tips his head slightly to the side. "It is a shame you've been unable to locate him after all this time."

"I do not believe Menov acted alone," Vanek says evenly. "And I suspect many believe this as well."

The Emperor narrows his eyes. "And just who do you suspect might have been working with him?"

My heart stops, and I hold my breath as I wait for Vanek to answer, wondering if he's actually going to come out and say it. Despite his stoic mask, his eyes betray his anger, and I pray he doesn't snap.

From seemingly out of nowhere, Marek appears on my other side.

"Ah, Marek," the Emperor turns to him. "I was meaning to speak with you. I wish to offer the protection of my guards for your betrothed."

Marek opens his mouth, but the Emperor quickly continues. "As your Emperor, I insist."

He's trying to back Marek into a corner, but it's not going to work. Tilting my chin up in defiance, I meet the Emperor's gaze evenly. His eyes widen slightly in surprise before he regains his composure. I dart a quick glance to Ryven, standing off to the side with the rest of the D'enekai guards. "I appreciate your concern, Emperor, but I have the utmost confidence in the guards of House D'enekai."

His nostrils flare slightly. "You are refusing my guard?"

"Yes," I state firmly.

Vanek's head snaps toward me. A look somewhere between disbelief and admiration flickers across his expression, but it's gone too quickly for me to be certain what it was.

Marek steps forward. "House D'enekai has the utmost confidence in our guards to protect us and the future of our House."

The Emperor's expression becomes almost haughty as his lips curl up ever so slightly in a tight smirk. "The future?" His gaze darts to me. "Yes, we are fortunate it turned out this way. It would have been a bit more...difficult if it had not."

Anger flashes behind Marek's eyes at the mention of the Emperor's desire to enslave Terra, but his expression remains impassive.

"We will meet before the Elders soon," the Emperor continues. The way he says it makes it sound more like a threat than a statement. "I look forward to our next meeting."

Without another word, he turns and leaves with his guard. Marek gives me a concerned look while Vanek's eyes show nothing but approval with just the barest hint of amusement. The slight twist of his lips into a subtle smile tells me I'm right before he even opens his mouth. "You may be small," he says, "but you are fierce."

I grin.

He continues. "Marek told me about the day you met. He said you were as fierce as a Mosauran warrior. At the time, I'll admit that I doubted his words, believing them clouded by attachment to his Si'an T'kara. But now"—he arches a brow—"it appears I have once again underestimated your people, Elizabeth Langdon of Terra."

CHAPTER 15

MAREK

When we finally return to the Estate, we are silent as the guards set Kaden and Brienna's stasis pod on one of the many polished stone slabs inside the crypt. Although they are the only ones here, this space is huge. As an exact recreation of the original D'enekai crypts, it had to be. The one on V'lorys was filled with the remains of my ancestors.

Kalvar's gaze drifts to the distant corner and remains there a moment before he returns his attention to the High Omari. His family —K'Lena and their two children—were interred in that spot on the original Estate. Beside it were my grandmother and grandfather—his brother.

After a moment, the High Omari places the House D'enekai banner atop the casing. The soft whisper of silken fabric sliding over the metal and glass echoes softly throughout the crypt.

I take one final look at Kaden and Brienna before it covers them. Locked together in their embrace, they appear as though they are merely asleep. Tears sting my eyes, but I blink them back. How devastating it must have been for Kaden to have saved his Si'an T'kara from the A'kai only to have her die from the heavy blood loss soon after. He didn't just lose his bondmate, he lost his future with the death of their child. I don't know that I would have been able to go on either. As my gaze drifts to Elizabeth, standing beside me, I know that I would have chosen to die with her as well.

Out of the corner of my eye, I notice Kalvar. He watches me with a pained expression, and I suspect it is because he already knows my choice and my decision. Because she is Terran and will die much sooner than I, my lifespan will be less than half what it should be. I've already spoken with him about this, but he refuses to accept it. In his desperation, he has already tasked a team of scientists to search for any way to extend the Terran lifespan.

He has lost so much, I suppose I would do the same if it were me in his stead. Gently, he places his hand on my shoulder. His expression is impassive, but it does little to mask the sadness behind his eyes as they meet mine. Many only know him as the stoic leader of our people. They do not realize the deep scars he carries inside.

Once everyone else has left, he walks over to the far corner where his family would be if this were V'lorys. Standing before the empty slab, he slowly lifts his arm to extend one hand out before him, his palm open and trembling slightly as it hovers directly over the spot where the stasis pod casing would be.

Elizabeth moves toward him. Sensing her approach, he curls his fingers into his palm and lowers his hand back down to his side.

I follow behind her, and when we reach Kalvar, we say nothing. Words are inadequate to express such a deep and terrible loss. Standing together, we bow our heads in reverent silence before he lifts his gaze to us.

"My son was here…on V'lorys that was." His eyes remain fixed on the smooth white stone. "When we boarded the transport, he begged me to trade places. He enjoyed looking out the window." With a slight clench of his jaw, he closes his eyes as if reliving the painful memory. "When we crashed, he was killed instantly. It would have been me if I —" Drawing in a deep breath, he shakes his head softly. "It should have been me and not him who died that day."

Elizabeth places a hand on the sleeve of his forearm.

He continues. "I understand what it is to lose those you cherish above all else. That is why I have tried so desperately to avoid civil war. I refuse to lose anyone else I care about. And if the Emperor gives any indication that he is a threat to our family after we present him with the irrefutable proof of the fated bond between you, I swear on the Goddess S'Lena that I will strike him down. I care not if it leads us down a path of chaos and destruction. I have lost everything before, and I will not lose it again. I swear it to the stars. My vow."

***

It has been a very long day. When we finally return to our chambers later in the evening, I know just how much I am in need of meditation. Not only am I still angered by the Emperor's threats, but the desire to claim Elizabeth is almost overwhelming. Among my people, the act of joining is normally only done during the mating cycle. This almost always results in the creation of new life—a direct defiance of death. Perhaps that is why my thoughts turn so strongly to this now.

Something dark and primal within me demands that I bind her to me—mind, body, and soul—so that all will know without a doubt that she is mine. My need to claim her has grown more intense over the past few weeks, and I know not if this is because my mating cycle approaches or if it is merely a response to her close proximity.

I shake my head softly as I turn away from her. I cannot claim her and seal us in the S'acris until the official sanction from the Emperor. To do so before then would be viewed as an affront—an open act of treason—since I have already publicly refused V'Meia.

Informing Elizabeth of my intent to meditate, she presses a quick kiss to my lips and goes to the cleansing room, smiling over her shoulder as she expresses her eagerness to soak in the large bath.

It would be so easy to follow her into the room—to join her in the bathing pool and kiss every inch of her bare skin as I've longed to do for so many months. With great effort, I push the errant thought from my mind as I turn in the opposite direction toward the meditation firepot.

∼

ELIZABETH

Peeling off the last of my clothes, I step down into the bath. Soothing warmth envelops me as I dip beneath the water to wet my hair. Allowing myself to enjoy the moment, I float peacefully on my back as my muscles slowly relax and unwind.

They've been aching terribly since my sparring session with Ryven this afternoon. I didn't want to tell Marek because I know how worried he'd be, but that session was pretty brutal. I do appreciate Ryven not holding back, however. He knows how important it is that I learn to defend myself against one of their people. The Emperor's words were certainly proof of that today.

I don't know how long Marek plans on meditating, but this is my version of meditation and I'm going to enjoy it for just a while longer. And to think—I worried that I'd have to take sonic showers the rest of my life if we decide to stay on V'lora. But this? I sigh softly in contentment. *This* I could get used to.

When I'm finished, I step out of the pool and dry off before wrapping myself in Marek's soft, plush robe. I love surrounding myself in his scent. That's why I often sleep in one of his shirts. I tuck my nose into the fabric and inhale deeply. It smells just like my beloved, a strong cinnamon earthy undertone that is both masculine and comforting.

As soon as I step into the bedroom, I shiver slightly as the cold night air drifts in through the open window. Marek gives me a concerned look. "I apologize. I was giving Errun his fish earlier."

My eyes search the balcony. "Is he still there?"

Closing the window, he shakes his head. "According to Ryven, he spends most of his time in their cave now." He quirks a brow. "And I believe he may be watching their egg."

Picturing a cute baby dragon, I smile. "You think they're going to have a baby v'rach?"

He nods. "V'rachs usually experience their first mating cycle shortly after bonding with their mate."

At the mention of the mating cycle, his expression darkens and he turns his gaze back out to the sea. I know what he's thinking. He's worried that his time will come soon.

Walking up behind him, I wrap my arms around his waist and rest my left cheek against his back. He covers my hands with his before turning in my arms to face me. "We'll be all right, Marek. Brienna survived the mating cycle, and I will too."

He clenches his jaw. "Not without great injury to herself."

Reaching up, I cup his cheek. "Neither of them knew what to expect. But you and I are prepared." Trailing my hand down his arm, I thread my fingers through his, tugging gently for him to follow me. "Let's go to bed, my love."

Not bothering to change into my nightgown, I lay down, and he slips under the covers beside me. Wrapping his arms around my waist, he pulls me back against him into the solid warmth of his body.

The movement pulls my robe back just enough that it opens to reveal my bare leg up to the top of my thigh. Marek's warm hand trails down my hip, and goose bumps form on the exposed flesh, not from the cold but from the almost electric touch of his skin to mine as the tips of his fingers skate lightly down to my knee and back again.

Reaching up, he pulls my hair to the side; his breath is warm as he whispers against the shell of my ear. "Eh'leh-na, my Elizabeth."

Small shivers of pleasure ripple through me as he gently caresses my neck, lightly pushing at the hem of my robe and sliding it down to expose the bare curve of my shoulder. He nuzzles my hair a moment before skimming the tip of his nose along my neck and pressing soft kisses to the curve at the base.

A soft moan escapes me with each touch of his soft lips over the sensitive flesh. Closing my eyes, I tip my head to give him better access to the curve of my neck and shoulder as I reach back and run my fingers through his hair, gently encouraging him to continue his ministrations. After a moment, however, he pulls away, carefully covering my shoulder with my robe as he settles in behind me.

Frustrated, I turn in his arms to lay on my back and reach up to cup his cheek as he leans over me, braced on one arm. "Don't stop, my love."

His eyes burn with desire as he shakes his head softly. "You know I must. I cannot risk losing control with you."

I trace my thumb across his full lower lip. "We're going to be bonded soon, Marek, and I've never even seen you fully undressed. I... I don't even know what you look like or if"—my cheeks heat in mild embarrassment—"we'll fit."

A light green bloom spreads across his face and the tips of his ears. "You've seen pictures of V'loryn anatomy. L'Tana showed you and—"

I press my finger to his lips, staring deep into his glowing green eyes. "Yes, but I've never seen *you*, my love. And—you've never seen me."

His brow furrows softly. "You wish to see me unclothed?"

"Yes," I whisper. "And...I want you to see me."

A mixture of desire and anticipation rushes through me as I take a deep breath and carefully untie my robe. With my eyes locked on Marek's, I pull the material back, sliding my arms free so that I lay completely bare beneath his gaze.

His mouth drifts open as he stares down at me in wonder. Words escape his lips that I've only ever heard in ancient V'loryn poetry. He speaks of beauty and worship as his eyes travel over my form. Cautiously, he reaches out to touch me but stops short as he lifts his eyes to mine. "May I touch you, my Elizabeth?"

I smile up at him. "I'm yours."

He studies me with a heated gaze. The tips of his fingers trace a line down my neck and between the valley of my breasts. He cups his hand gently over one of the soft globes, and a small shiver of anticipation runs through me. His thumb brushes lightly across the hard-beaded tip, and I inhale sharply as my nerves light up in delicious sensation beneath his touch.

"I want to see you, my love," I whisper as I push back through our connection, sending him a wave of love and desire as I dip my hands beneath the hem of his shirt and touch his bare skin.

Dazed, he nods and pulls it over his head, discarding it to the floor. He watches me with an intensity that steals my breath as I run my hands along the hard planes of his chest. His shoulders are broad, and his entire body sculpted of lean muscle, lacking even the slightest bit of softness in his flesh. He is breathtakingly perfect, and I bite my lower lip in nervous anticipation as I reach to undo the fastening of his pants.

Lightning fast, he grips my wrist to stop me, and I gasp in surprise. His gaze burns into mine, and his voice is rough like gravel as he barely manages to whisper. "This is dangerous, Elizabeth. We should stop."

His green eyes darken and begin to swirl with black, and his fangs extend into sharpened points as he struggles at the edge of his control. I reach up and cup the back of his neck, pulling his lips down to mine in a gentle kiss. "I just want to see you, my love. That's all. I'm not asking for anything else."

With a slight clench of his jaw, he nods and then pulls back. He draws in a shaking breath but remains perfectly still as I unfasten the clasp of his pants and slide them down past his hips. V'loryns do not wear undergarments, and so as his pants fall away, I look down at his l'ok and my mouth goes dry. When L'Tana said that V'loryn male anatomy is much larger than Terrans, I realize now that she was not exaggerating. All the images I've seen, however, do not even come close to his.

Ridges line the entire length of his fully erect l'ok. Softly biting my lower lip, my thighs squeeze together involuntarily as I imagine what that might feel like inside me. I gently trace my fingers along his length. A large bead of milky colored precum forms at the end. When I brush my thumb across the tip of his l'ok, he shudders and pulls back with a sharp gasp, panting heavily as his eyes meet mine.

I rub the fluid between my thumb and forefinger. Instead of feeling sticky like I'd imagined, it is liquid silk. Scent marking is very important between bonded pairs, and he watches me with a heated gaze as I trail my finger from the valley of my breasts and down to my stomach, marking me with his scent. He inhales sharply, and the low rumbling purr of his tr'llen sounds deep in his chest.

Feeling bolder, I try to wrap my fingers around his girth, but he's so large they cannot quite reach all the way around. He shudders and grasps my wrist again as he shakes his head.

I know we should stop, but I don't want to. I want to explore him and for him to explore me. Seeing the evidence of how much he desires me makes warmth pool deep in my core.

His nostrils flare as his gaze burns into mine. "I can scent your need," he rasps, and I can tell it is taking every ounce of his control to remain still.

I know this is difficult for him, and I told him I only wanted us to see each other. We have, and with a heavy sigh, I move to grasp the edges of my robe to wrap it around me again, but he catches my wrist, stopping me abruptly.

I open my mouth to speak but close it again. He pins me in place with his glowing green eyes as his hand trails down my abdomen to cup my mound. I gasp as he dips one finger between my already slick folds.

His tr'llen grows louder. With his gaze locked on mine, he whispers. "Show me how to touch you, my Elizabeth."

I'm about to reach down to guide him, but then his finger brushes against the small bundle of nerves at the cleft, and I gasp and arch up against his hand. He growls low in arousal as he concentrates on that spot, and I realize he doesn't need any instruction.

Pinning me with a hungry gaze, he continues to gently tease his fingers up and down my folds while using his thumb to brush over the sensitive pearl of flesh, driving me mad with desire. He lifts his hand and dips his fingers into his mouth. Closing his eyes, he groans low in his throat as if savoring the taste of me.

When he opens his eyes again, the normal glowing green color is gone, replaced with black as he stares down at me with a ravenous gaze.

JESSICA GRAYSON

~

MAREK

The taste of her sweet nectar lingers on my tongue, and I long for more. Everything about her is perfection, and I desire to kiss every inch of her beautiful form.

I dip my fingers again between her warm, slick folds. When I press my thumb to the small bundle of nerves at the top, she gasps, arching against my hand as a low moan escapes her. Opening a small connection between us, I shield her from my desire so I may concentrate on hers alone. Learning with each reaction to my touch what pleases her more, I concentrate on the areas that make her cry out with pleasure.

Terran females release a bonding hormone when they reach their climax. It binds them more firmly to their mate. I want to bring Elizabeth to release. If I cannot yet bind her to me in the ways of my people, I wish to bind her to me in the way of hers.

Her breath quickens and I capture her mouth with my own, swallowing her small cries of passion. Fervently, I stroke my tongue against hers in a claiming kiss and when I finally pull back, my name escapes her lips in a breathless whisper. Through the contact of our skin, I am able to sense the tight coil of need that builds deep in her core, and I know it won't take much to push her over the edge.

Dark and primal desire consumes me as she writhes beneath my touch. I press a line of soft kisses down the elegant curve of her neck to her chest. Closing my mouth over her left breast, I run my tongue over the stiff peak. She threads her delicate fingers roughly through my hair to pull me closer, and I growl low in arousal as she arches into my mouth. "Marek," she breathes my name between soft gasps of pleasure.

I turn my attention to her other breast and my name escapes her lips in a low moan.

Releasing her breast, I trace a line down her abdomen, tasting the sweet salt of her skin. When I reach her soft folds, the delicious scent of her arousal is intoxicating, and I long to taste her again. Lifting my head, I search her eyes. "May I put my mouth on you?"

She stares at me through a half-lidded gaze, her beautiful full breasts rising and falling with each panting breath as she barely manages to nod.

Without hesitation, I place my hands on her inner thighs and gently push them farther apart, opening her to my gaze. She is perfect and I want only to please her. Carefully, I guide her legs over my shoulders and then dip my tongue in her soft folds, drinking of her sweet nectar. I gently tease my tongue around the soft hooded flesh at the top, and her entire body lights up with pleasure.

Through the faint connection, it is easy to sense that she is close to finding her release. My l'ok throbs with painful need, but I push my desires aside to concentrate on hers. I want this to be about her; I want to prove that I am a worthy lover to my Si'an T'kara.

She says my name over and over between small gasps and moans as her hips move softly against my mouth. Banding one arm across her lower abdomen to keep her in place, I continue teasing my tongue through her soft folds as I slowly insert one finger into her core. She is so small I worry she will be unable to take my l'ok into her channel. But as I carefully insert another finger, I feel her body slowly stretching to accommodate the extra girth. The small muscles quiver and flex around me and I groan as I imagine my l'ok sheathed deep inside her warmth.

"So close," she breathes as my tongue continues to gently tease at the small bundle of nerves while my fingers move in and out of her warm, wet heat. Her entire body goes taut. The small muscles of her channel clench tightly around me as she cries out my name. As she reaches her climax, I drink greedily of her nectar, moving my tongue through her folds to prolong her orgasm until her body relaxes beneath me.

When I finally lift my head, I find her collapsed and panting heavily. The rise and fall of her chest draws my attention back to her breasts, and although I long to take them in my mouth again, I know she is tired and needs rest.

I pull myself up alongside her. She turns to press her lips to mine in a tender kiss before pulling back, panting heavily. "That was amazing," she breathes, her luminous eyes filled with wonder as they stare deep into mine.

Her hand drifts down to my waist, and she wraps her delicate fingers around my still hardened l'ok. She gives me a questioning look. "You didn't—"

I press my lips to hers in a claiming kiss before I pull back to stare deep into her eyes. "I wish for the first time I release to be when I'm inside you."

Wrapping my arms tightly around her, I pull her against me, nuzzling her hair as my tr'llen grows slightly louder in contentment.

Her warm hands trace delicate patterns along the muscles of my abdomen and chest as she nestles closer against me. Through the faint bond, I can feel her longing to touch me, to remain closely tucked against my warmth. Echoes of her climax still linger through our connection as the effects of the bonding hormone circulate through her body. I reach across and brush the dampened hair back from her face, running my fingers through the soft, scarlet strands as I stare at her in wonder, in awe that I am allowed to touch her in this way.

A soft smile curves her lips. "What are you thinking, my love?"

I stare into her luminous blue eyes. "That you are everything to me, my Elizabeth."

She nestles into my side, and I wrap my arms around her, breathing deeply of her intoxicating scent. She is mine, and I am hers.

CHAPTER 16

ELIZABETH

Staring in the mirror, I tie my hair back from my face. I don't bother with a shower because I know I'm about to have another brutal training session with Ryven.

Warm hands come to rest on my shoulders, and I softly bite my lower lip as Marek pulls me back against him. Wrapping his arms around me from behind, he leans down and gently skims the tip of his nose from my temple to my jaw and down to my neck as his purring tr'llen begins low in his chest.

Reaching back, I tilt my head up and run my fingers through the small hairs at the nape of his neck to gently pull his lips down to mine. I'm ready to cancel my morning training session and spend the rest of the day touching and kissing him, but after a moment, he gently pulls away. "Are you ready?"

I turn to give him a questioning look. "You're going to watch me train?"

To my surprise, he nods. Earlier, he said he cannot bear to watch me spar with Ryven. He said it drives him to the point of madness because of the biological imperative to protect one's mate.

When we reach the training area, we find Ryven already sparing with Vanek.

They spin and kick out at one another. Moving with a fluid and deadly grace, Ryven's movements are controlled and measured precision, while Vanek fights like a man possessed. Brutal and effective, he easily adapts to any changes in Ryven's form as they continue, and I wonder if he would be willing to teach me his technique.

As if sensing my thoughts, Marek's hand on my forearm brings my attention back to him. "I do not want you to spar with Vanek, and I… do not think he would want this either."

My head jerks back slightly. "Why?"

"I fear he may hurt you."

I open my mouth to protest, but he raises his hand in a gentle bid to allow him to speak. So, I patiently wait for him to continue.

"Something happened to him during our time in the Defense Force. It…changed him. Irrevocably."

My brow furrows softly. "What happened?"

"We boarded an Anguis vessel suspected of trafficking slaves. Vanek reached the cargo hold first while the rest of us subdued most of the crew on the bridge. He found one of the Anguis slavers violating an Aerilon female. He killed the Anguis, but it was too late; the damage had already been done." Lowering his gaze, he clenches his jaw, as if what he is about to say is too painful to speak of. After a moment, he continues. "When Anguis mate, they inject their partners with venom; it is a fatal paralytic to any except another Anguis."

I stare at him in disbelief. "There's no cure? No antivenom?"

He shakes his head.

"What happened?"

His expression is pained when he lifts his eyes to mine. "Trying to offer her comfort in her final moments, Vanek linked with her mind in the al'nara." He pauses. "When we found him…I'll never forget the haunted look on his face as he held her limp form in his arms."

Tears sting my eyes, and I struggle to blink them back. I know how strong the al'nara is. Even the briefest connection is intensely intimate. For Vanek to have linked with her…he experienced her life, her pain, and finally, her death. And I cannot imagine how terrible that must have been.

"He accompanied her body back to Aerilon—to her family." Marek's gaze drifts to his friend. "It changed him. He has never been the same since that moment. I have sparred with him many times since then and through the brief contact of his skin when we fight, I know that when he spars…in his mind, he returns to that terrible day. He does not see the opponent before him. He fights not to train, but to exorcise the demons that still plague his memories." He pauses. "He's refused to be betrothed to anyone, despite the fact that he is near the Age of Joining. He does not wish anyone to experience his painful memories through the al'nara and the S'acris."

As I turn to watch Vanek, still sparring with Ryven, I view him through an entirely different lens. When I first met him, I thought he was a man bored with his place in the grand scheme of things. Always with a ready glass of s'lir close by and a sort of relaxed almost flippant detachment in his manner. I realize now it is all just a carefully constructed façade—the alcohol an unhealthy coping mechanism to mask the extent of his pain. He's not a man bored with life; he's struggling to survive it.

As we continue toward them, Ryven's head snaps in our direction, and he waves his hand. The distraction causing him to narrowly miss a blow from Vanek.

"Stop!" he cries out, and Vanek stills, blinking several times as if coming back to himself. He turns his gaze to us as well and they both walk over.

I smile in greeting. "Good morning."

Instead of replying, Vanek and Ryven stare at me in shock a moment before quickly recovering. "Good morning," they reply in almost perfect unison.

Ryven inclines his head in a subtle bow. "Forgive me, I started without you. I did not expect to see you so early this morning."

I give him a confused look. "Why?"

His cheeks and the tips of his ears flush light green as he drops his gaze to the ground. Clearing his throat, he hesitates a moment before speaking in a voice so low I barely catch it. "My quarters are just next to yours."

My face heats in embarrassment. I didn't think I was that loud, but then again, V'loryns do have superior hearing. We're definitely going to have to figure out some sort of soundproofing for our rooms.

Ryven swallows thickly and then turns his attention to Marek. "I see you changed your mind?"

Marek nods.

"Changed your mind about what?" I ask.

He turns to face me. "Ryven insists that I train as well." He sighs heavily. "He is right. It has been too long since I last sparred with him. And—you need to learn the different holds and how to break them. He says I must be the one to train you in this way."

"Why?" I ask, wondering why I've never heard about these "holds" from Taven after hours of k'atana lessons with him.

"Because the holds are very…intimate."

"Oh," is all I manage to say. If the holds are *that* intimate, no wonder Taven never brought it up. I'm glad Marek will be teaching them to me. My mind drifts back to what happened between us last night and my body flushes with warmth. Perhaps these "lessons" can lead to something else when we're alone again tonight.

Ryven continues to spar with Vanek while Marek demonstrates the different holds and the techniques to break them. He locks one arm around my waist from behind, pinning my arms to my sides as he holds my back flush against his front and uses his other hand to hold my neck, cupping my jaw so that I'm immobilized.

"This is the Drogev hold—the most dangerous of any you may find yourself in." He leans down, his breath warm against my ear as he whispers. "Now, focus. Remember what I taught you. Try to break free."

Using all my strength, I struggle against the cage of his arms, and when he doesn't even budge, fear trickles down my spine. And now…I understand just how much of his strength he's held back from me. How much Ryven has held back from me.

My chest rises and falls rapidly as I try to push down my panic, thinking of how hopeless it would be if one of the Emperor's guards caught me in this way.

He inhales sharply, no doubt having scented my fear. His expression is pained as he looks down at me. Loosening his grip, he lowers his head in shame. "Now you know," he whispers, refusing to meet my gaze.

"Know what?"

"The source of my fear regarding my mating cycle."

His words shake me to my core. He's right. As strong as he is, if he loses control like he worries he might, I wouldn't be able to fight him off. Drawing in a deep breath, I tilt my chin up and cup my hands to either side of his face, forcing his gaze to my own. I stare deep into his glowing green eyes. "Brienna survived the mating cycle with Kaden. I trust you, Marek, and my love for you is stronger than my fear. I will not let anything keep us apart. I swear it to the stars. My vow."

After a moment, he reluctantly nods before dropping his forehead gently to mine. "We will practice more tomorrow," he says softly.

While Marek begins sparring with Vanek, I walk over to Ryven. "Don't go easy on me today," I tease.

He draws in a deep breath, a brief flicker of worry crossing his expression. I know this is difficult for him. But from what I've observed, he seems to be a pragmatist, and I know he understands the importance of what I'm asking of him.

Reluctantly, he nods. "Your people are smaller than ours, and your structures more fragile. You were correct when you accused me of being careful when we sparred." He pauses, his eyes meeting mine intently. "You are also correct that I will need to use my full strength and abilities to better prepare you for what may happen if you find yourself alone and fighting one of the Emperor's guards."

"You believe the Emperor would attack us," I say this as a statement, but it's really a question, one that I want him to deny.

"It is something I believe we should be prepared for, but I hope will never happen."

I meet his eyes evenly. "We have a saying on Terra: hope for the best but prepare for the worst."

He cocks his head to the side. "Your people are wise."

When we spar this time, he does not go easy on me. Countering every one of my movements, I'm surprised by his speed and maneuverability, and it isn't long before I begin to tire.

He pauses a moment and quirks his brow. "Enough?" he asks.

I shake my head. "I need to push myself."

Ryven hesitates a moment, but seeing the determination in my expression, he finally nods. "As you wish."

When we're finally done, I'm winded and breathing through pursed lips before I practically inhale my entire bottle of water. Sitting beside me, he lowers his head until his eyes meet mine in a questioning look.

"I know. Pretty pathetic compared to a V'loryn, right?" I blow out a quick puff of air, wincing slightly at the pain in my sides from, what I'm almost certain are bruised ribs.

He cocks his head to the side. "Quite the opposite, actually. You use your small size to your advantage. You force a change in my center of balance with your quick movements, and to be honest, I am impressed at your skill in combat."

I straighten. "You are?"

He inclines his head. "Are all Terran females trained as warriors?"

"I can't speak for everyone, but I know a lot of women train in the martial arts."

He gives me a cautious look. "It is...dangerous on your world?"

I shrug. "It can be, I suppose, but...apparently, it can be here too. I mean, you protect Marek and Kalvar, right?"

"And you, K'Sai. I would defend you with my life if necessary."

I smile. "I meant no offense, Ryven. And, please, call me Elizabeth."

"Only when we are alone...Elizabeth," he says, although the way he says it suggests he is a bit uncomfortable. "In public, I will address you as K'Sai, as I address Marek as T'Hale."

"Agreed," I reply.

I'm glad to have this moment alone to speak with him because there's something that I've been needing to tell him, and I knew I couldn't say it in front of my overprotective V'loryn fiancé. "You trained with Marek, right?"

He nods.

"He regards you like a blood brother, Ryven."

"As I do him."

"Then, we are agreed that his safety takes priority over mine."

Ryven's eyes widen in shock.

I meet his gaze evenly. "When we meet with the Emperor, Marek's safety comes first, Ryven. Promise me this."

"You will not be meeting with the Emperor, Elizabeth."

His answer shocks me. "What?"

"Marek does not want you there. He is afraid the Emperor may try something. He has entrusted me to guard you and to make sure you return safely to Terra if something should happen to him. I have sworn a blood oath to protect you."

I clench my jaw. "Then you will be present when Marek goes before the Emperor, because *I* will be there too. I *will not* allow my Si'an T'karan to go before the Emperor alone. He will need both of us. Do you understand?"

Ryven's mouth drifts open slightly before he quickly snaps it shut and inclines his head in agreement, as if thinking better of arguing with me. It seems Marek already warned him of my supposed "fiery" temper.

More determined than ever, I stand. "Let's continue our training."

When we're finished, I'm a sweaty mess. Marek swears I smell enticing when I'm like this, but I certainly don't feel sexy at the moment as I take a seat and watch him begin sparring with Ryven.

They fight with a sort of fluid grace that belies the strength and brutality of their motions as they move through the various forms. I know now why Marek doesn't like to watch me spar. I'm on the edge of my seat with worry. They move with a speed that doesn't seem possible, and I bite my lower lip, waiting anxiously for them to finish.

"Greetings," Vanek's voice calls out. He gives me a V'loryn barely there smile as he sits down beside me.

I smile. "You fight well. Your technique is impressive."

His brow creases into a small frown. "I...cannot train you, if that is what you were hoping, but I will tell you the secret to beating your opponent."

"What is it?"

"When you fight, you must imagine that your enemy is trying to take away the one thing you hold most precious in this life. That if you lose, you lose that which you absolutely cannot live without." He pauses. "When you fight, you fight not for yourself, but for the life of another—the one you hold most dear. And in understanding this, you become the more dangerous opponent. For you, there can only be victory or death. Because, knowing what you could lose, you will hold nothing back when you fight...no matter the cost to yourself."

His words settle deep in my chest as I turn my gaze to Marek. And I know Vanek's words are true. I would do anything to keep Marek safe.

We sit in contemplative silence for a few moments before I finally turn back to him. "Marek said L'Tana might return to V'lora even sooner than everyone else so she can help set up the Med Center at the Terran Embassy here."

He arches a teasing brow. "And she will be speaking to the V'loryn Healers, that will be joining the staff, preparing them to handle emotional Terrans."

I laugh.

A hint of a smile tugs at his lips. "In truth, I look forward to my sister's return." He leans back with an almost thoughtful expression. "I've heard that many children become extremely jealous when their parents have a second child, but it was never this way for me. Growing up, she was my constant companion and playmate...from almost the very moment she first learned to walk."

I smile, imagining L'Tana as a small child, toddling after her older brother.

"Yes." He nods. "It has been too long since she has been home."

"I'm sure your father must have missed her too."

His expression falls. "I suppose he has...in his own way."

"What do you mean?"

"After my mother died, it destroyed him. I believe the only reason he survived L'talla is because she made him promise, on her deathbed, to do whatever it took to survive for me and my sister."

"Marek said it's almost impossible for someone to survive the effects of L'talla. He said Kalvar's mind was too damaged from the loss of his bondmate and children that he couldn't form the familial mental bond—the T'ama—with either Marek or his mother."

He nods. "Any who survive L'talla are broken in some way or another."

Now it all makes sense. I understand why Vanek, although only Second T'Hale of House A'msir, is the one who sits in on all the High Council meetings to represent his House. He does this because his father cannot.

Vanek turns to me. "I've heard that this is not the case for your people. That you are able to adapt to the loss of a bondmate whether by death or…abandonment." His gaze darts briefly to Marek before returning to me. "But for V'loryns, it is not this way."

I understand the message behind his statement. He is worried I'll grow tired of Marek and leave him for another. I move to reassure him, meeting his eyes evenly so he can see the truth of my words. "The only thing that will ever separate me from Marek is death. I swear it to the stars. My vow," I say, speaking a solemn promise that I know he will understand.

He quirks his brow, a hint of a smile playing on his lips as he stares down at me. "Marek is like a brother to me, and I do not wish to lose him. So, I suggest that you endeavor to live a long and healthy life then."

I smile in return. "That's the plan, Vanek."

∼

MAREK

Once we're done sparring, Ryven and I walk over to Elizabeth and Vanek. A smile crests her lips and I find myself irrationally jealous that she is speaking to Vanek as she does this. I'm both surprised and concerned by my reaction. Vanek is much like a brother to me, but I recognize this for what it is: my mating cycle will come soon. It could be as long as a couple of months or as little as a few days before it overwhelms me, but I can already feel the beginning of its pull.

When we reach them, I wrap a possessive arm around Elizabeth as I struggle to suppress the urge to growl at my best friend.

Elizabeth gives me one of her brilliant smiles, and my heart stutters, making my earlier jealousy of Vanek disappear instantly. That she is able to affect me like this, with the simplest look or touch, is nothing short of fascinating.

She looks to Ryven. "Marek said you were both in the Defense Force, but how did you two become friends?"

Ryven cocks his head to the side, a subtle smirk on his lips. "You did not tell her?"

I give him a warning look and subtly shake my head. While Ryven is one of my closest friends, the way we met was not one of my finer moments and definitely not one that would impress my future bondmate.

Elizabeth's face lights up in a grin. "Now, you *have* to tell me."

With a questioning quirk of his brow he looks to me, and I reluctantly nod. Sitting beside Elizabeth, I stare across at my friend and try to decide which embarrassing story I will share about *him* after he's done telling her mine.

"As you know, we were both in the Defense Force," he begins. "Both of us fresh out of training, we were assigned to the same squadron. Our team was tasked with boarding an Anguis vessel suspected of transporting drogai."

Her brow furrows softly in confusion, so he explains. "Drogai is a highly addictive stimulant substance. It usually comes in a white, powdery form. It is very profitable for smugglers because it is illegal in almost every quadrant and difficult to obtain."

She leans slightly forward in her chair, staring at him in rapt fascination.

He continues. "The moment we boarded the transport, the Anguis captain knew he had been caught. The entire ship smelled so strongly of drogai, there was no mistaking that he was transporting large quantities of it."

"Then what happened?" she asks.

"His crew scattered. Where they thought they were going, I have no idea. The rest of our squadron went after them, but Marek and I"—he looks to me—"we chased the captain as he attempted to reach one of the escape pods."

He pauses for dramatic effect as Elizabeth waits with bated breath for him to continue.

He leans forward, his lips quirked up slightly in a V'loryn smile. "The captain had a pack with his illegal contraband slung over his back as he tried to escape."

"How did you catch him?"

"He was almost to the escape pod, when Marek pulled out his blaster to stun him and took aim." He darts a quick glance to me, his eyes sparkling with barely restrained amusement. "I yelled for Marek to stop, but it was too late."

Elizabeth grins with excitement. "What happened?"

"The blast hit him square in the back. His pack exploded in a puff of white powder, coating everything in the small hallway, including the two of us."

Her jaw drops.

Shaking his head, Ryven quirks his brow as a small smile twists his lips. "We were high for two days."

My Si'an T'kara doubles over with laughter—the light and cheery sound almost musical as it fills the cabin around us.

"Our commander remanded us to shared quarters. He basically quarantined us from the rest of our squad for the next two days while it worked its way out of our system." Ryven turns his gaze to me. "We have been friends ever since."

~

ELIZABETH

I leave Marek with Vanek so that Ryven can familiarize me with the controls for the transport. I want to be as comfortable flying it as I was with the old Z30 my grandfather had—the one he taught me to fly when I was in college. After all, Marek and I will be going back and forth between here and the Terran Embassy once it's completed while we work on the V'loryn LRCSA project.

As he points out various command sequences on the control panel, Ryven turns to me, arching a brow. "Your command of our language is excellent, and your piloting skills are exceptional."

Practically beaming with pride, I smile brightly at him.

His eyes widen, and my expression falters.

As if sensing my confusion, he looks down a moment before softly shaking his head. "Forgive me. Your smile." He clears his throat. "I have never seen anything quite like it before." He pauses. "Is it truth that all of your people are this expressive of their emotions?"

I shrug. "A majority of them are. I can hardly wait for you to meet my best friend, Anton."

He sits back in his chair. "Ah, yes. Marek has told me much about him. He said you have been friends since childhood."

"Yes. He lived next door to me when we were growing up."

Ryven turns to me. "I look forward to meeting him. Does he fly as well?"

"No."

With a subtle quirk of his brow his lips curve up slightly at the edges in a subtle V'loryn smile. "Then perhaps by the time he arrives, you will be able to teach him."

∼

MAREK

When Elizabeth leaves with Ryven to learn how to pilot one of the transports, Vanek gives me a concerned look. "Your eyes swirled black for a moment. Are you unwell?"

Ashamed that he noticed my unwarranted response to his nearness to my Si'an T'kara, I shake my head. "I fear my mating cycle will come soon."

Instead of giving me the pitying look I'd expected, his lips twist up in a slight smirk and he claps a hand on my shoulder. "I am flattered your instincts would think I am a rival for her attentions. I've always been the more handsome of the two of us after all. Surely, she has noticed this."

I narrow my eyes. And although I know he is only teasing a low growl rumbles deep in my chest. As soon as I realize it, I stop, and my eyes widen slightly in shock.

His expression sobers, concern evident in his gaze. "Unfortunately, I fear you are right, my friend. Your cycle must be approaching."

With a slight clench of my jaw, I look down at my hands as I admit the fear deep in my heart. "I am afraid for her, Vanek. I do not know what to do."

He says nothing. When I lift my gaze, he gives me a solemn nod. "I understand, Marek. But Kaden's bondmate survived it, and so will yours."

At that moment, the transport flies low overhead. Elizabeth's red hair is visible in the pilot's seat and as they swing back for another pass, my heart stops when the wings dip left, right, and then left again.

Fear steals my breath. Is the transport having problems? I tap my communicator to contact Ryven. His face appears instantly in the viewscreen. Words leave my mouth in a panicked rush. "What's wrong? Are the engines malfunctioning?"

Elizabeth's sparkling laughter fills the background, and he quirks a brow as he stares at me through the display. "She was demonstrating the Terran pilot signal they use to indicate to others that they are… friendly—allies instead of enemies."

Elizabeth's face comes into view as she leans next to him. "My grandfather taught me that maneuver, so I was showing it to Ryven."

My shoulders sag forward in relief. Ryven must notice this because he gives me a solemn nod. "All is well, T'Hale. We will make another few passes over the Estate and then we will return."

When the viewscreen cuts off Vanek claps a hand on my shoulder again, drawing my attention back to him. "It is not good to worry as much as you do. There are some things you must leave in the hands of the Goddess."

I know he's right, but it is difficult to suppress my fears where my Si'an T'kara is concerned. Taking a deep breath, I change the subject. "I did not expect to see you here this morning, but it was a welcome surprise."

He nods. "I actually came here to bring you some news."

Something about his tone suggests that whatever he has to say is not good, and I brace myself. "What is it?"

"L'Tana has refused a match proposed by the Elders."

I cock my head to the side. "I did not know that they sought to match her to anyone. Who was it?"

"K'Sai L'Mira's son, Niren. He is the heir of House S'tiran."

My eyes widen slightly.

Vanek continues. "I've heard he is an honorable male, but L'Tana, it seems, has spent too much time on Terra." With a slight quirk of his brow, a small smile tugs at his lips. "She believes her bondmate should be *her* choice and not someone chosen for her by the Elders."

"She is right," I reply. "It should be her choice."

"I agree, my friend. It is a tradition that I believe our people would be better served without." He gives me a slightly hesitant look before he continues. "But her refusal to bond with Niren has created an entirely different and more concerning problem."

"What is it?"

"Although we've tried to reassure them otherwise, S'tiran views the refusal as a slight to their House. I've heard rumors that L'Mira has approached the Elders to match her son to V'Meia now instead."

This is indeed disturbing news and could be devastating if it comes to pass. "If she aligns herself with the Emperor's House, it would tip the balance on the Council in his favor."

"Precisely," Vanek agrees. "And although it is only mere rumor at this point, I felt that I should tell you in case we need to prepare."

"Prepare for what?"

His glowing green eyes meet mine evenly. "Civil war."

From his grim expression, it seems he already believes this is a forgone conclusion. He gives me a pointed look. "I know you do not want war, but it is inevitable, and I cannot understand why you and Kalvar refuse to see it."

Frustration burns through me. "Think of how many lives could be lost. And for what? The Emperor may be power hungry, but surely even *he* recognizes that war would be devastating to our people."

Vanek gives me an incredulous look. "He is mad, Marek, and he must be deposed. Why will you not recognize this?"

My friend has more reason than most to despise the Emperor, but his hatred could be reckless if left unchecked. "If war is to come, it *will not* be started by my House," I warn him.

With a slight clench of his jaw, he turns away, his gaze scanning the ocean below. "You've asked me before why I do not want to lead."

It is truth, but I say nothing, waiting for him to continue.

He sighs heavily and then turns back to face me. "It is because I have known you all my life."

His statement confuses me. "What are you talking about?"

"Where I am quick to judge, you wait. I am fast to anger, and you are calm." He pauses and then gives me a pointed look. "I know I am all these things that a V'loryn should not be. But in *this*...I know that I am right when I tell you that we must take down the Emperor before he comes at us. Because I know for certain that he will, Marek." His gaze darts to Elizabeth. "And I fear that the price of that terrible day will be more than you are able to bear."

His words strike fear in my heart. Deep in my soul, I know they are truth. Movement catches the corner of my eye, and I turn to see Ryven and Elizabeth approaching. "I need you to prep the transport and ready our cruiser," I tell him. "The K'Sai must return to Terra at once."

Elizabeth gives me a shocked look. "What are you talking about? I'm not going anywhere."

"Elizabeth, you should—"

She puts her hand up to silence me. "What happened? Why are you saying this? I thought we already settled this, Marek."

With a heavy sigh, I proceed to inform her of everything Vanek just told me.

When I'm finished, she crosses her arms over her chest and purses her lips. "Don't you have the numbers?"

Confused, I quirk my brow. "What…numbers?"

Her gaze darts briefly to Vanek and then back to me. "Even if House S'tiran aligned with the Emperor, your two Houses, along with Milena's—House L'eanan—have more of the Lower Houses pledged to you than any of the other Great Houses combined. The Emperor knows this. I doubt he'd risk a war that he knows, more than likely, he'd lose."

Ryven steps forward. "This is truth. I do not believe he would risk a war. No." He shakes his head. "The Emperor's sigil is the k'mal. Poisonous, deadly, treacherous. The k'mal is a creature that hides in the shadows before striking. He would never come at House D'enekai directly. He would find other ways to weaken it."

Vanek turns to Elizabeth. "He is merely trying to protect you. *You* are Marek's greatest weakness. The Emperor would come for you, to use you as leverage against House D'enekai."

Indignation burns in her eyes as she meets his gaze evenly. "I am *not* Marek's greatest weakness. Although we are not yet fully bonded, together we are stronger than either of us alone. I am his, and he is mine. If what you believe is true—that the Goddess bestowed her blessing on us for a reason—how would it make sense to separate us?" She pauses. "If the Emperor decides to come for either of us, regardless of if he does so in the shadows or in the open, it wouldn't make a difference where we were. Terra or V'lora. It wouldn't matter to him." She gives me a determined look. "I refuse to hide somewhere in fear. We're not going to argue about this anymore. My place is here. I'm not going anywhere."

CHAPTER 17

ELIZABETH

When Vanek finally leaves at the end of the day, we return to our chambers. I press a quick kiss to Marek's lips as we step into the bedroom. His face is impassive, but his eyes speak for him. I know he's worried, but I refuse to change my mind. And although he is afraid for my safety, deep down he knows that I'm right. Am I scared? Yes, I am. But I also know that all we have is right now. The future isn't set. And I don't want to waste my time upset about something I can do nothing about.

Staring deep into his eyes, I reach up and gently brush my fingers across his brow, creased with concern. "Do you remember what I said when you asked if it bothered me that the Terran lifespan is so short?"

He doesn't speak, but he doesn't have to. His intense sadness flows across our faint bond.

I continue. "I told you that no one is promised tomorrow. All we have is right now." I press my lips to his. "I love you, Marek. I choose you above everything else. In a few days, we'll go before the Council and the Elders to approve our bonding." Cupping my hand to the back of his neck, I run my fingers lightly through his hair as a slow smile curves my lips. "I'm going to bathe and then…" I trace my finger lightly down the front of his chest, "maybe we can spend the rest of the evening holding each other."

His cheeks and the tips of his ears turn a light shade of green as desire flares brightly through our connection.

I quickly bathe in the pool, eager to spend the rest of the evening in Marek's arms.

When I enter the room, in only my robe, he stares at me with a hungry gaze. The slight tic of the muscles along his jaw as his nostrils flare tell me that he is struggling to maintain his control.

I walk toward him, allowing the tie of my robe to hang limp at my waist. The top hangs a bit loose, exposing the valley between my breasts. His eyes rake over my form a moment before I stretch up on my toes to wrap my arms around his neck and brush my lips against his.

His tongue finds mine and deepens our kiss.

When he finally pulls back, I'm dazed and breathless as I stare up at him. "Dress quickly," he says. "I have a surprise for you."

I blink up at him in shock. This is definitely not what I was expecting. "A surprise?"

He flashes his V'loryn smile. "Yes."

As soon as I return from dressing, I find Marek standing on the balcony with a pack over his shoulders. I start to ask him what it's for but stop abruptly as a thunderous roar breaks the silence.

My jaw drops as I look up to see Errun circling overhead. The wind whips through my hair as his wings billow out, slowly lowering himself to land on the balcony beside us.

He cocks his head to the side, staring between myself and Marek. Although I don't know very much about v'rachs, the intelligence is obvious behind his large green eyes. He studies me a moment, his cat-like irises expanding slightly before Marek distracts him with a dried bit of fish, patting his snout in an affectionate gesture.

Errun's enormous tail curls behind Marek as he gently nuzzles his hand again, apparently begging for more fish. A loud rumbling vibration fills the air.

Marek turns to me. "V'rachs purr. Much like the felines of Terra."

I don't know any cat that sounds that loud or ominous, but I suppose it's a halfway decent comparison.

While he runs his hand gently back and forth over Errun's snout, Marek pulls another bit of dried fish from his pocket and hands it to me as the v'rach closes his eyes, relishing the affection he's receiving.

I lift the fish to him, and his nostrils flare. He turns his massive head toward me, interest sparkling in his gaze. Gently, he nuzzles my arm as he scents my hand.

Very cautiously, his lips curl around the fish, and I appreciate that he takes great care to keep his teeth far from my skin as he plucks the treat from my hand. When he's finished, he gently bumps my arm, and I reach up to pet his snout as I watched Marek do earlier.

Marek lightly scratches under Errun's jaw, eliciting another rumbling purr from the v'rach. A smile tugs at the corner of his mouth. "Errun likes you."

I smile. "How do you know?"

His eyes dart to his hand on Errun's scales and back to me. "I can sense it."

My head jerks back slightly in surprise. "You can communicate with him through touch?"

Marek tips his head to the side in a thoughtful look. "In a way, yes. But it is more a communication through the projection of images instead of emotions or thought."

I stare at Errun in wonder.

He nudges Marek's arm before lowering himself farther to the ground.

Marek takes my hand. "Are you ready?"

His question catches me off guard. "Ready for what?"

He arches a teasing brow. "To ride a v'rach, of course."

Errun's head turns toward me, and I could swear there's a glimmer of amusement in his eyes at the stunned look on my face.

Marek helps me up onto Errun's back before settling behind me. His scales are soft and smooth like silk beneath my fingers. When he stands, I inhale sharply, afraid of losing my balance. Marek wraps one

JESSICA GRAYSON

arm solidly around my waist, pulling me back against his chest as he uses his other hand to hold onto one of Errun's neck spikes to steady us. "We are safe," he says softly. "I promise."

I tip my head back, twisting slightly to press a quick kiss to his lips. I trust him. Completely. And I relax in his embrace.

Errun's muscles tense a moment before his enormous leathery wings extend, expanding like great sails as he lifts into the air. As we rise above the ground, I stare in awe at the landscape below as I watch the castle grow smaller beneath us.

Without warning, Errun turns abruptly and headlong into the wind. Catching the current, we sail out over the ocean. The light of the twin moons scatters shimmering reflections across the rolling waves.

With a bellowing roar, he cries out near the cliff wall, and I startle when it's answered in kind. I turn toward the sound. It's his mate. Ryven says they named her A'ravae—Huntress. It is fitting. Her black scales are a near perfect camouflage in the darkness around us.

In perfect synchronization, they weave around one another as if in greeting. Her glowing green eyes meet mine a moment before they turn as one, dipping their wings into the wind and making a long, slow arc to head back over the land and out toward the vast expanse of the desert plains in the far distance.

An ocean of sand undulates and flows beneath us like water as wisps of dust and mica sweep across the dunes. Towering rock formations spiral toward the darkened sky, standing proudly in the desert sea like skeletal islands amid the vast expanse of barren land.

The landscape is both harsh and beautiful all at once, and as the wind whips around my body, I've never felt so alive. Marek's solid presence behind me is a soothing comfort as we glide over the rock and desert below.

Pulling his wings closer to his side, Errun begins to descend, gliding low over the plains. He slows just a bit and then begins to circle, readying to land upon the large rock formation below us. When he finally does, I barely feel the impact of his body touching down upon the stone—as if he were light as a feather instead of a massive v'rach.

Errun lowers himself to the ground even more, and Marek helps me to slide off his back. His mate hovers above, patiently waiting for him to rejoin her.

Marek runs his hand lightly across the v'rach's jaw in an affectionate pat before Errun turns and lifts off. I stare at him in wonder as he soars up into the sky, joining A'ravae in an intricate dance of give and take as they circle one another before flying off into the night.

"They go now to hunt," Marek whispers.

"What do they hunt?"

"T'sars," he says softly, and I still.

Sensing my fear, he cups my cheek. "Do not worry. This is where Errun always leaves me. He stays nearby. No t'sar will come within several acrums of this area while he patrols the skies."

Pale moonlight reflects off the smooth stone casting enough contrast against the desert sand that I am able to make out the large shape of the formation around us.

Marek pulls a blanket from his pack and spreads it out across the surface. He sits and motions for me to do the same. Once I'm seated, he lays down, gently pulling me with him so that we are side by side. His fingers thread through mine as we stare up at the star-filled sky.

The cool breeze blows across the desert, sending a slight chill through my body. Marek pulls out another blanket, this one thick and soft, and drapes it over us. I move closer to him, snuggling into his warmth as he wraps an arm beneath my neck, and I rest my head on his shoulder. "Where is Terra?"

He points to a cluster of stars in the southern sky. "Just there," he whispers. Pressing a gentle kiss to my temple, he tugs me closer. "I've come here for many cycles. Even as a child, I was always drawn to that particular grouping of stars." He turns to face me, his eyes staring deep into mine. "Perhaps something inside me always knew you were there. Waiting for me to find you."

A smile curves my lips at the thought. "That's beautiful, my love." How many nights did I stare up at the stars too? Wondering if there was any other life out there? His heart beats a steady rhythm beneath my open palm as I rest my hand over his chest. I love being here with him, just the two of us. "How did you first find this place?" I whisper.

A small smile tugs at the corner of his mouth. "When Errun grew too large to sleep inside the Estate, he took to sleeping on the balcony just outside my window. I would spend many hours out there to keep him company. Sometimes I'd even fall asleep against him." He pauses. "Kalvar would often find us together like that, with Errun's tail wrapped around me.

"We fed him all the fish he could possibly eat, but Kalvar insisted that he must learn to hunt as well. Or else he'd never have a chance at finding a mate. You see, to Errun, Kalvar and I are part of his pack. We are his family."

"So, you taught him to hunt?"

He shakes his head. "No. But v'rachs tend to hunt in packs. He brought me with him, but left me on this rock, returning for me a few hours later." His lips quirk up slightly. "It became our routine. The night sky has always fascinated me, and I enjoy coming out here with him. And—he can sense it when we communicate."

As he speaks, I trace lazy circles across his chest with my fingers. Marek begins his purring tr'llen. I look up to find him staring at me with a heated gaze, and I shiver against him.

He turns to face me, pulling me close against his warmth. Leaning forward, he gently skims the tip of his nose from my temple down to my jaw. An involuntary gasp escapes my lips as he cups my breast, brushing his thumb across the sensitive peak. He trails a line of soft kisses down my neck.

Running my fingers through his hair, I pull him closer, wanting so much more than teasing kisses. "Marek," I breathe as his hands slip beneath my shirt and his fingers trace across my bare skin.

He lifts his head, staring at me with a hungry gaze. "May I touch you?"

Already breathless with anticipation, I barely manage to nod yes.

Carefully, he unfastens the clasps of my tunic and pants. His warm hands dip beneath my waistband as he slides the fabric down my hips, pulling it free from my legs. Within seconds I'm naked beneath him, and he stares down at me in wonder. "You are perfect, my Elizabeth."

Running my hand across his now bare chest, I bite my lower lip as I trace the muscles of his form. Like masculine perfection brought to life, he watches me as I reach up to undo the clasp of his pants, and when I wrap my fingers around his hardened length, he inhales sharply. I swipe my thumb across the tip of his l'ok, gathering the precum that beads at the end.

Holding his gaze, I bring my thumb to my mouth and take a tentative lick. I'm surprised at how amazing he tastes—a strange but pleasant mixture of spice and cinnamon. Not salty or bitter like I've heard Terran men are. His mouth drifts open as he watches me intently, and when I reach down to gather another beaded drop, he hisses through gritted teeth, his entire body shuddering at my touch.

Remembering how much he enjoyed it the other night as I marked myself with him, I rub his scent across my bare abdomen.

A low growl of arousal rises in his throat, and I turn my head slightly, extending my neck and offering myself to him. His eyes swirl in a mixture of green and obsidian pools as his fangs slowly extend.

"Seal me to you, my love," I whisper softly. "I don't want to wait any longer to be yours. Take me here beneath the stars."

He breathes in shaking breaths as he stares down at me intensely. After a moment, he hangs his head, closing his eyes as his body trembles slightly above me. "I want you more than anything, Elizabeth. But I cannot seal us yet. I won't risk you, my Si'an T'kara. You mean too much to me. If something were to happen out here while we are alone, I would be unable to find help soon enough."

He's worried once he tastes my blood to seal me to him in the S'acris that he'll be unable to stop. While I understand his concern, disappointment washes through me. I trust him. Completely. And I know his fear is unfounded. Marek would never hurt me.

I reach up to lightly touch his lips. "Then let me love you as you loved me last night," I whisper.

His brow furrows slightly in confusion. I move down his body and wrap my fingers around his l'ok. The breath explodes from his lungs as soon as I swipe my tongue across the tip, tasting him again.

Before I can do anything more, he grips my arms and pulls me back up the length of his body, holding me close to his chest as he breathes in shaking breaths, trembling as he struggles to maintain his control.

"Please, Elizabeth," he rasps. "I am not as strong as you think I am."

I'm about to protest, but before I can speak, he growls and then flips me onto my back. I don't even have time to look down before he dips his fingers into my soaked folds. I cry out, but he quickly seals his mouth over mine, swallowing the sound as his tongue curls around mine. I arch against his hand as his thumb brushes over the small bundle of nerves at the top.

Overwhelmed with myriad sensation, desire pulses strongly through the faint bond between us. I move my hands over his body, wanting desperately to touch him everywhere. I gasp when he pushes one finger just inside my entrance. His touch is electric and fire all at once, and I allow myself to be consumed by it.

He growls low in arousal as he stares down at me with a possessive gaze, deep and intense and so completely V'loryn before capturing my mouth in a passionate kiss.

"Marek," I barely manage to breathe through my pleasure, but the rest of the words get lost as he dips a second finger into my core. My inner walls stretch to accommodate him.

I sob his name as my release rapidly approaches, digging my nails into his back. I want him to feel as amazing as I do, so I reach down to touch his hardened l'ok. He growls low in warning and removes his hand from my center.

I gasp, panting heavily at the sudden loss and open my mouth to speak but quickly shut it again as he moves down my body and runs his tongue through my folds.

Intense pleasure ripples through me. Arching my back, I cry out his name. My hips involuntarily move against him and he clamps one arm over my lower abdomen, anchoring me in place. A tight coil of need builds in my core as his tongue continues to tease at my sensitive flesh.

Overwhelmed by sensation, I run my fingers through his hair. And when he growls, I feel the vibration straight through me, sending me over the edge and into a beautiful wave of oblivion as I climax harder than I ever have before as I cry out his name.

Marek continues to taste me, prolonging my release until only small aftershocks remain and wash through me.

I'm dazed and breathless as he moves back up my body. And when he seals his mouth over mine, he gives me a claiming kiss. He takes my hand in his and I feel him searching my mind. For what, I'm not sure. Intense possessiveness fills me, and I know it is his. A low moan escapes my throat as ecstasy spirals through me…almost as intense as when I found my release only a moment ago.

When I finally come down from my pleasure, he runs his fingers through my dampened hair and stares down at me with an intensely possessive gaze. "The flush of your skin is so beautiful after you have found your release, my Si'an T'kara."

I forget how well he can see in the dark, and I smile at him before pressing my lips again to his. "How did you learn how to do this, Marek?"

"I studied many books on Terran mating rituals. But the most informative were *Forbidden Longings* and the *Kama Sutra*."

My mouth drifts open in shock. "You read *Forbidden Longings* and the *Kama Sutra*?"

He nods. "After I discovered what you were reading when we were in San Francisco, I knew I needed to study those books in order to learn more about the Terran mating ritual. In my study of your species, I read that it is important for Terran females to achieve release. I knew you had concerns about our…sexual compatibility, and I wanted to make sure that I pleased you."

He pauses. "While my people form mental bonds with their mates, yours form physical ones. Only when Terran females reach their climax, then their bodies release the bonding hormone oxytocin, strengthening the connection they have to their mates."

"You read all that?"

He stares intensely into my eyes before he leans down and skims his nose alongside mine and then presses a tender kiss to my lips. Fierce possessiveness floods the connection between us as he whispers, "I can feel the bonding hormone coursing through your system, binding you more strongly to me even now."

I smile against his soft lips. "I already am bound to you, my love." Running my fingers through his hair, I find his tongue and deepen our kiss. I knead the muscles along the length of his spine and wrap my leg over his hip, moaning softly into his mouth as I arch against him.

His nostrils flare slightly as he pulls back just enough to stare across at me. "You desire my touch again so soon?"

The idea that he researched this so thoroughly just to bring me pleasure is a potent aphrodisiac. I cup his cheek. "Yes, my handsome V'loryn scientist," I whisper as I pull him back down to my lips.

~

MAREK

Terran females seem to possess the same level of sexual energy as V'loryn males. We've been taught it is important to suppress this urge because our females only tolerate a mating once every six months to one year. To know that Elizabeth still desires more even after she's found her release is a pleasure I had not even imagined. Perhaps I will not have to suppress my mating urges with her. To be honest, I could have pleasured her all night, but she was tired after she reached her third completion.

I've read Terran males require a refractory period between matings, but my people do not have this problem. I've also read that Terrans can be very vocal during matings, and *this*, I've discovered, is truth. Elizabeth cried out so many times and so loudly, Errun circled overhead at least twice to make sure we were not in distress.

As I hold her in my arms, I gaze at her in wonder. She responds so beautifully to my touch. I love the sounds of pleasure she makes and the way she writhes beneath me when my mouth is on her body.

She opens her eyes and gives me a sleepy smile. "What time is it?" she whispers.

I turn my gaze up to the sky. "Errun should be back for us soon. Until then...rest, my Elizabeth. I have you."

She releases a small sigh of contentment and snuggles into my chest. She closes her eyes, drifting off to sleep, and I'm touched again by her complete and utter trust in me. That this beautiful and perfect female would allow me to hold her like this, to bring her to a place so different from her home, to love me even knowing what I am... Words cannot express the depth of my feelings for her.

Errun's shadow circles overhead. Fully extending his massive wings, he gently drifts down beside us. I pull Elizabeth close against me to protect her from the swirling dust and wind as he lands. He cocks his head to the side, regarding me curiously.

His mate flies low overhead, probably anxious to return to their cave. I suspect, by now, they probably have a nest with at least one, maybe two eggs awaiting them. Pressing a gentle kiss to Elizabeth's forehead, I whisper her name to wake her.

She opens her eyes, and a beautiful but tired smile curves her lips. I help her up onto Errun's back, and as soon as I'm settled behind her, she falls asleep against me. As if conscious of this, Errun takes great care in his flight and subsequent landing on the balcony, touching down so gently I pause a moment, uncertain if we're actually on the ground or not.

Holding Elizabeth tight to my chest, I slide off his back. "Goodnight, my friend," I whisper.

He waits to take off until after I'm inside our room with the glass door shut behind me. Laying her gently down into the bed, I crawl in next to her and curl myself protectively around her, allowing myself to drift off to sleep as well.

We have an early day tomorrow. She desires to explore the city, and I am eager to show her around.

CHAPTER 18

ELIZABETH

When we step off the transport platform and into the City Center, I have a hard time trying to decide what to look at first. Everything is so picturesque. Rows of quaint little shops line the streets. There are hints of Terran European old-world architecture in all of these buildings, but they are also modern in such a way that it is easy to identify them as distinctly V'loryn. Sleek lines blend seamlessly with intricate touches of ornate L'kir moldings and the platinum-colored L'omhara finishes. Just like on the orbital station, everything here is immaculately clean. The stone walkways are well-maintained but, like everything else, appear as if they have been here for far longer than the past couple of decades.

Looping my arm through Marek's, several people openly stare at us as we walk past. Some seem curious, others...I cannot be sure, but they look almost disgusted. I suppose this is what Marek and his people must experience when they're on Terra. Now that the tables are turned, I have an entirely different understanding and appreciation for the prejudices they face on my home world.

The V'loryn sun burns brightly overhead, but I'm not uncomfortable in the least. The crisp saline breeze from the coast is cool and refreshing against my skin as we make our way through the crowds. I look up at Marek. "K'ylira is just as it was on V'lorys?" I ask again just to be sure. I still have a hard time wrapping my mind around the fact that everything has been recreated in exact detail from their original home world.

Marek's brow creases into a frown. "There is one thing that is different."

"What is it?"

Ryven and the two guards trail behind us as he leads me down another walkway. When we reach what I recognize must be the heart of the city, the first thing I notice is the beautifully manicured grounds that surround us. Carved L'kir benches are scattered throughout the large park-like area and a three-tiered fountain sits in the center of the plaza, flowing with clear sea green water cascading from each level.

On V'lorys, this must have been the focal point of the plaza, but the tall, obsidian obelisk beside it is easily the primary focus now. Striking but somber, this piece stands out among everything around it.

It is inscribed with silver V'loryn glyphs. I study it closely to translate the words and whisper them aloud. "Grief is the deafening silence that echoes in the darkness." Realizing now what this is, a lump forms in my throat, and tears gather in the corner of my eyes as I stare at the engraving. This is a memorial to V'lorys that was.

Marek's sadness bleeds through the connection between us. "It is to remember those who died in the destruction of our home world."

Gently squeezing his hand, I reach my other palm forward to rest it on the marble-like stone as I often do at my mother's grave. Almost as soon as my skin touches the cold, smooth surface, a holographic display appears before me. Scanning the words, it takes me a moment to realize it is a list of names—the people who died. At the top of the list, I notice two names in particular: K'Sai L'Nara and T'Hale Toven of House D'enekai—Marek's parents.

A V'loryn woman with long dark hair, stares at me through tear-filled eyes as she places a necklace around my neck. "You will give this to your T'kara someday," she whispers. The image fades and is replaced by another. I watch from the viewscreen as my planet is destroyed. Overwhelming sadness fills me, and I feel as if I'm drowning in it.

But this planet is not mine. It is his.

Almost as quickly as they'd appeared, the images fade. My gaze drifts to Marek. Those were *his* memories.

He gives me a pained look. "I am sorry," he whispers, gently dropping his forehead to mine.

This has been happening more often lately. Flashes of memory, images, emotions... Although we have yet to form the permanent bond, the faint one that exists between us is growing stronger. Part of me wonders if it would eventually just form on its own without any other intervention. Marek worries about this, despite my attempts to reassure him that I'm fine.

"There is nothing to be sorry for, my love. You don't have to carry this sadness alone anymore. I'm here." I cup my hand to his face. "My soul grieves with yours."

As we continue past the structure, I glance back and notice each of the guards, including Ryven, placing their open palm reverently on the stone as they pass. This, I realize, is the only marker they have to remember their dead. Everything else is gone.

Although we walk side by side with our fingers entwined, I feel nothing flowing across the tenuous connection. He must have his shields up, trying to protect me again from his sadness. Gently, I squeeze his hand to remind him that I am here for him. He returns the gesture, and a small bridge opens between us. Marek and I understand each other in a way that only those who have experienced great loss can be understood.

After a while, he stops abruptly and turns to face me. His eyes reflecting with something akin to joy instead of the sadness I saw at the memorial. "I wish to show you something."

"What is it?"

He quirks a teasing brow. "It is a surprise."

I smile and follow him down the bustling sidewalk without question, curious to know what it is. It seems that my V'loryn fiancé is full of surprises lately. The nursery, the necklace, the last two nights of amazing…

All thoughts leave my mind as we turn the corner. My eyes go wide at the beautiful park-like forest before me. Large trees with massive trunks that twist at odd angles, as if competing with each other for a small patch of sun, create a beautiful canopy overhead. Heavily laden with heart-shaped leaves in varying shades of reds and orange, it reminds me of the autumn season on Terra. Thick carpets of deep-green grass spread out beneath them, dotted by several shrubs and flowering plants in a vast array of colors. Flowers of red, orange, purple, yellow, and green.

It's even more impressive than the gardens on the Estate. This is like finding an oasis in a vast stretch of desert. Not that everything is sand and dust elsewhere in the city. It's just that the amount of vegetation gathered in this one spot is so much that everything else seems to pale in comparison. "Is *this* what V'lorys used to look like?"

"Yes." That one word so full of joy and yet such longing as it leaves his lips.

We walk side by side. A small stream winds along our path. Something moves in the bushes and I gently tug on Marek's arm to stop him so I can get a better look. It's a small creature the size of a mouse with light gray fur. It looks something like a cross between a rabbit and a squirrel with a long puffy tail. "Is that a ritak?"

"Yes."

I smile. "They're so adorable."

It tips its head to the side to regard me warily. At least ten more smaller ones come out from the bush and circle around the first one.

I'm about to ask if those are her babies, but Marek answers my unspoken question. "Ritaks can have up to a dozen offspring each litter and they often have several litters per cycle."

I knew they reproduced rather quickly but I had no idea it was that extreme. I purse my lips as L'Tana's comment floats to the front of my mind when she said Terrans mate and breed like ritaks.

Having sensed my annoyance, Marek turns to me. "What is wrong?"

I huff. "Do you remember what L'Tana said about Terrans and ritaks?"

His amusement bubbles through the link between us a moment later and his lips quirk up in his V'loryn smile. "You *do* want a rather large family."

I roll my eyes in mock frustration. "Four kids is not extreme, Marek." I place a hand on my hip. "How many do *you* want? Just one?"

"No." He cups my face, staring down at me with a look of intense love and devotion. "I want as many as you will give me."

Happiness blooms in my chest and a slow smile curves my lips as he sends me an image of an infant with pointed ears, dark hair, a light dusting of freckles across the bridge of his nose, and glowing blue eyes. The same child I have imagined many times since he first told me it would be possible for us to have children.

We continue along the pathway, until we reach a waterfall. Crystal clear sea green water cascades over an alabaster rock formation into a large pool below. Flat white stones span the entire length from one side to the other. Marek guides us toward them.

At first, they don't look too difficult to cross, but upon further inspection, I realize they're better suited to legs a bit longer than mine. I'll have to hop from stone to stone if I want to get across. Eyeing the first one, I take a deep breath to steady my nerves. My balance is good, so I shouldn't have any problems.

Before I can attempt it, however, Marek surprises me by sweeping me up into his arms. I let out a surprised laugh. "You don't have to carry me, you know."

He arches a teasing brow. "You would deny me the pleasure of carrying you?"

Softly biting my lower lip, I smile. There's just something so sexy about the way he quirks his brow. Movement catches my attention over his shoulder, and I realize we've drawn an audience. While Ryven and the two other guards watch us closely, I notice their eyes are trained on the people around us as well.

Trying to ignore the not-so-discreet stares of the now gathering small crowd, I turn my gaze toward the opposite end of the pond. I twine my arms around Marek's neck as he easily carries me across each stone until we reach the other side.

I take his hand in mine after he gently sets me back on my feet. His gaze darts briefly to the people observing us. "Do not concern yourself with their stares. Many of them are merely curious. I fell in love with a Terran. My people will either accept you or they will not, but I will never ask you to change. You are mine, and I am yours. And I love you just as you are, my Elizabeth."

My heart practically melts. How could I not love this man? "Eh'leh-na, Marek."

His lips quirk up in his V'loryn smile. "Now, let us find a few new foods for you to try."

I don't know what I was expecting, but when we reach the open-air food market I'm surprised by how many merchants are here. Carts and displays overflow with strange and colorful items as far as the eye can see. The soft scent of spice and cooked food drifts through the air, and it smells so enticing I want to try everything. Marek points out the various fruits and vegetables he thinks I might enjoy, as well as the ones he believes I will not.

"Why not this one?" I ask, pointing to a purple fruit that looks something like a cross between a prickly pear and a watermelon.

"Levina is very bitter," he explains. The vendor agrees, but still hands me a small slice to sample after I insist. I take a small bite and instantly wrinkle my nose as the sour taste explodes across my tongue.

Amusement dances behind Marek's eyes as he quirks his brow at me in his "I told you so" look. As we continue on, the scent of s'lara spice drifts on the wind. I love V'loryn tea blends because of this distinct flavor. Excited, I turn to him. "Where is that coming from?"

He guides me to a small spice shop just across the way. When we enter, I stop and inhale deeply, enjoying the strong scent of rich V'loryn spices. Barrels overflowing with dried leaves, flowers, and fruits fill the small but cozy space. I'm so excited I don't know which to sample first. A V'loryn man calls out from behind the counter. Bent over something before him, only his back is visible as he speaks in a gruff voice. "Help yourself, I will be with you in a moment."

"Thank you," Marek replies.

The man goes still and then straightens. Turning, his gaze goes wide, and he rushes to the front. "T'Hale." He bows low before Marek. "I did not expect you to—" He stops abruptly as his eyes land on me.

"Greetings," I tell him in V'loryn. "It smells wonderful in here."

Despite his impassive expression, the shock is easily read in his eyes. "You…like V'loryn teas and spice?"

I grin. "I love it."

He dips his chin in a subtle nod and then turns to one of the barrels, scooping several herbs into a small pouch. "Here," he hands the bag to me. "Kali berries are in season, and this batch of s'lara has a hint of their sweetness that I believe you will enjoy."

I smile brightly. "Thank you. How much do we owe you for this?"

His gaze darts briefly to Marek and then back to me before he bows deeply. "There is no charge, K'Sai. It is a gift."

According to what I've learned of Marek's people, it's an insult to refuse a gift, so instead of insisting we'll pay, I thank him. We wander around the store a bit more and I ask him about various spices. He mixes another pouch full of herbs and gives them to me. "Try this mixture," he offers. "It is a bit more robust, but it's balanced by the crisp bittersweet taste of citrona leaves."

Before he can gift this to me as well, Marek gives him payment. He accepts, and when we finally turn to leave, he bows low again as we exit.

When we get far enough away that I don't think he'll hear us, I turn to Marek. "Do people normally bow to you this much?" It feels like it has been happening all day, and because I'm not used to it, it catches me by surprise almost every time.

"Not as much as they have been since we arrived. I believe they are trying to show their support of my choice of bondmate."

Fast movement catches my eye, and I turn just in time as a small

V'loryn child stops in front of us. Glowing green eyes stare up at me in fascination.

A smile curves my lips as I drop to one knee before him so that his gaze is level with mine. "Well, hello, little one," I say in V'loryn. "What is your name?"

His jaw drops and his brows shoot up toward his dark brown hairline. "You speak our language?"

I grin. "Yes."

"My mother says that you are the one that was promised in the Ancient Tomes," he whispers in amazement. "Is it truth?"

High Omari L'Naya's words fill my mind and I turn to Marek. I'd forgotten until now to ask him more about this. Now, I'm even more curious.

The boy's mother calls out. "Torvan, leave the T'Hale and K'Sai in peace."

The little boy runs back to his mother, who bows as they move past us.

I look back to Marek. Worry flickers briefly behind his eyes as they meet mine. "It is getting late. We should probably return to the Estate."

His expression tells me there's more he wants to say, but not here. As we make our way back to the transport, I notice a large group of aliens gathered nearby. Some species I recognize from the V'loryn orbital station, but many I've never seen before.

Feathers, scales, horns, claws, wings. I know there are so many different races my people have yet to encounter, but to see all the various ones before me now makes me realize there is so much more out here in space than I could have ever imagined.

They stand huddled together just outside a clothing shop. It's only now that I notice how their coverings all appear tattered. A V'loryn man and woman motion for them to go inside, I assume to procure new clothing. But this is very strange.

I thought Marek said most trade was done on the station—that most off-worlders were not allowed down on the surface. I turn to him. "Who are all those people?"

He gently squeezes my hand, and through our bond I feel a strange mixture of both worry and empathy as his gaze follows mine. "They are recently freed slaves. It is a crime punishable by death to traffic slaves anywhere within our borders. So when my people discover any slave ships operating in V'loryn space, the masters are executed immediately and the slaves brought here until we are able to help them return home." He pauses. "Judging by their appearance, they must have only recently been freed and now my people are procuring new clothing for them before they are taken to their temporary accommodations for processing."

Stunned and horrified by his words, I cover my mouth in shock. My heart bleeds for these people and what they must have gone through.

One of them turns. Her eyes go wide as they lock on mine and she calls out in V'loryn, "Are you Terran?"

Surprised by her question, I nod. "Yes."

She breaks from the line and moves toward me. Despite her worn and tattered clothing, she is beautiful—like a fairy princess straight from one of my childhood books. Taller than me, although not as tall as Marek, she has long, flowing silver-white hair. Her skin is pale violet, and her eyes are a striking reflective golden color. This must be an Aerilon. Two large sparkly wings flutter at her sides, and I notice they appear grossly deformed. I inhale sharply when I realize that they're broken.

Her gaze follows mine to one of her broken wings before she looks back at me. Tears gather in the corner of her eyes, but she blinks them back. "One of my masters," she explains. "My name is An'ari. Were you rescued as well?"

"No. My name is Elizabeth. I came here with my betrothed." I gesture to Marek. "How do you know what I am?"

Her head jerks back slightly in surprise as she looks at Marek, blinking several times as if she cannot believe what I've said.

"He is your betrothed?" She cocks her head slightly to the side, her sharp gaze scanning Marek from head to toe. "I did not think V'loryns took mates outside of their race."

"We are the first," he tells her.

She nods and turns her attention back to me, her gaze traveling over my face. "I have seen your people before. You look much like the V'loryns, but your ears and your eyes, they are different."

"Where have you seen my people?"

"The slave stations. Your kind are very rare and worth thousands of credits for the slavers. The Mosaurans and the A'kai…they are searching for Terrans, paying handsomely to purchase them."

Marek visibly stiffens beside me, his panic seeping through our faint bond. "Why do they want Terrans?"

She shakes her head. "I do not know. I only know that they seek those of your race." Her eyes brighten with tears. "The first Terran female I saw was several months ago. An A'kai bought her and one of my people from an Anguis." She shakes her head as her bottom lip trembles. "She was so brave. She tried to shield my kinsman from the A'kai and he—" her voice catches. "He didn't even wait…"

Ryven steps forward and although his face remains impassive, I can tell from the tense set of his shoulders that he is on edge. "Wait for what? What happened to her?"

"R'ugol," she whispers in a voice so faint it takes me a moment to realize she's even spoken.

Alarm floods the connection between us, and I look up to see unmistakable panic and fear behind Marek and Ryven's eyes, despite their carefully guarded expressions.

Confused, I ask Marek. "What is R'ugol?"

He swallows thickly. "Mind rape."

Fear twists deep in my gut, and I struggle to swallow against the bile rising in my throat as the meaning of his words sink in. The A'kai are touch telepaths like the V'loryns. It is believed they share a common ancestor, because despite their green skin and silver hair, their features are remarkably similar. They are blood drinkers, just like the V'loryns had been during the time of Kaden.

Her golden reflective eyes search mine as she takes my hand, a low, mournful trilling hum rising in her throat before she speaks. "The same Terran female was then stolen from the A'kai by a Mosauran warrior in the heat of his mating cycle."

Marek's eyes go wide. "What?" he asks, and it is easy to hear the alarm in his normally even tone. "Mosaurans do not mate outside their species. Are you certain?"

She nods. "The A'kai offered a huge reward to anyone that could find her. It was all the masters spoke of for several weeks."

Marek steps toward her. "Please"—he inclines his head—"will you speak to one of our officials? Tell them what you know? What you have seen?"

She nods. "I will do so, but it must be done now. I am eager to return to my people. I have been gone for at least three cycles, and I miss my family terribly. I have passage on an Aerilon freighter. It leaves in a few hours."

Marek nods and begins typing on his communicator to contact Kalvar.

I turn back to An'ari. "What did she look like? This Terran woman that you saw?"

"Dark brown hair with skin close to the shade of your mate." She looks to Marek. "I didn't see much else. She was close enough that I knew she was different from the V'loryns, but far enough away that I could not make out any more details." She hesitates a moment before taking my hand in her own. Closing her eyes, she lowers her head. Warmth spreads out from the contact of her skin against mine, encompassing my palm.

Marek tenses beside me, but I give him a look to tell him I'm okay.

After a moment, she releases her grip and turns a soft gaze to me. "I have taken your measure. You are a kind and good person. There is talk amongst the slaves of your people—the ones who look like V'loryns but are not. I fear there are many of them who are being traded."

Her words fill my veins with ice, and when I look to Marek it's easy to read the panic etched in his features.

When Kalvar arrives, An'ari recounts everything she witnessed to him. After she's finished, we escort her to the transport hub. Marek, Kalvar, and the rest of the guards give her a slight dip of their chin in polite parting, but I move forward and wrap my arms around her, giving her a hug. My heart clenches in my chest when she returns it, embracing me tightly.

When she finally pulls back, dark tears stream down her face. "Thank you for your kindness. I will say a prayer to the Creator that you find your people safe."

When we board the transport to return to the Estate, Ryven is the first to speak. "I do not understand. How are there Terrans beyond your star system? Your first deep-space ships have only just been built."

Long, icy tendrils of fear unfurl from deep within, coiling tight in my chest as the terrible truth dawns on me. "The missing transports," I barely manage as an image of my Aunt Liana fills my mind. "The ones traveling between Terra and Mars. There have been several that have gone missing over the past fifty years. The most recent ones within the past three cycles."

Kalvar turns to me. "I must speak with your government immediately. Your people will begin arriving to staff the Terran Embassy soon. They must be made aware of this threat."

CHAPTER 19

ELIZABETH

When we return to the Estate, Kalvar wastes no time contacting the Terran Prime Minister.

I contact Anton, telling him everything the Aerilon said, including my theory about the missing transports.

He stares at me intently. "All this time…maybe your Aunt Liana is still alive."

As I suspected, his thoughts went exactly where mine did. I give him a pained smile. "I just hope…" Emotions lodge in my throat and the words won't come. Marek rubs my shoulders in a soothing gesture, the tips of his fingers resting lightly against the skin just above my collar as he projects a wave of warmth and comfort across the link.

"I know," Anton's voice quavers slightly. He loved my Aunt Liana too. Like me, he's held onto hope all these years, that she might still be alive.

I meet his eyes evenly. "I don't think it's safe for you to come to V'lora, Anton."

He crosses his arms over his chest, pursing his lips. "You really expect me to just stay here? To miss my best friend's wedding?"

A small smile tugs at the corner of my lips.

"We'll be fine, Elizabeth. Besides, two V'loryn cruisers are going to accompany our ship to V'lora."

Taven steps forward from behind him. "V'loryn cruisers are heavily armed. We should not encounter any problems."

Marek nods in agreement. "He is right."

Anton's eyes light up as he moves closer to the screen. "Oh my gosh," he says in that tone that tells me what he's about to say is breaking news. "I almost forgot to tell you what happened."

"What is it?"

"The Elders contacted L'Tana and told her she was going to be matched to some guy she barely even knows. Can you believe it?"

I've already heard this from Marek, but I know how much Anton loves to tell a story, so I stay quiet and let him finish.

"And *get* this," he says animatedly. "She turned him down, because she thinks V'loryns should be able to choose their mates just like Terrans do. And you know what? I think they're right." He gestures to Taven. "And Taven thinks so too. Don't you?"

Taven nods in agreement. Anton claps a hand on his shoulder and grins. "So now, we just need to find you a nice Terran girl."

Taven quirks his brow. "I do not need your help finding a bondmate."

"Of course, you do," Anton scoffs. That's why you're lucky you have me as your friend. I'm going to help you."

Inhaling and exhaling deeply through his nostrils, Taven levels an irritated gaze at my best friend. "I do not want your help. You embarrassed me at that karaoke bar," he adds. "That is not an experience I am eager to repeat."

A surprised laugh escapes me. "You took *Taven* to a karaoke bar?"

Marek's hands still on my shoulders.

Anton shrugs. "It's a good place to meet people, you know?" He looks over at Taven, rolling his eyes. "How was I supposed to know he'd clam up when I put him up on the stage. I mean…it's not *that hard* to follow along with a song."

Taven purses his lips. "V'loryns do not…karaoke."

Anton gives him an exasperated look. "All you had to do was read the words on the screen, Taven. How hard is that?"

Unable to help myself, I start laughing again as I imagine Taven trying to karaoke. Anton opens his mouth to speak, but the screen distorts and the display cuts off.

With a heavy sigh, I turn to Marek.

"When the V'loryn LRCSA is complete, this problem should not happen anymore," he offers.

He's right. I suppose we're lucky that we can even communicate with Terra at all. And since we've already worked out most of the problems with the Terran LRCSA, we should be able to get the V'loryn one up and running in half the time.

~

It isn't quite bedtime yet, but so much has happened it feels like it's been a long day. Marek brings me a cup of s'lara tea as I sit on the balcony, staring out at the ocean. So strange how easily I can forget I'm on an alien world as I watch the rolling waves. In the darkness, the sea looks just like the ones on Terra and the primary moon, though larger, is not very different from ours.

In two days, we will stand before the Council and the Elders with the High Omari to sanction our bonding. With everything that happened today, I forgot to ask Marek my burning question. As he sits in the chair beside me, I turn to face him. "What are the ancient tomes that the V'loryn child and the High Omari mentioned?"

Marek is silent a moment, a look of deep contemplation on his face as worry pulses through our connection.

"Well?"

He meets my gaze evenly. "They were speaking of the Ancient Tomes of the Saraketh."

"What are the Saraketh?"

"They were a race of seers, rumored to be able to travel through time—to view many possible futures."

"What happened to them?"

"No one knows. They disappeared thousands of cycles ago. All that remains of their race are the ancient tomes—their recorded prophecies."

"Where are the tomes now?" I ask, curious to read more about this race of mysterious beings.

He shakes his head. "Gone. The Garkols once had a Great Library in their capital city. They were considered the keepers of knowledge during the time of my ancestors. Their library housed hundreds of thousands of works from species all across the known universe that dated back to the ancient times." He pauses. "But it was destroyed during the last Great War, many cycles ago."

"Along with the Tomes of the Saraketh?"

Taking a sip of his tea, he nods and then sets his cup down beside him. "Only a few of the writings survived. It was rumored that the Garkols saved the tomes, and that they still study their riddles, trying to unravel the secrets contained in the prophecies."

"What does this have to do with me though?"

"There is a prophecy of the Great Uniters." His glowing green eyes meet mine evenly. "They will be off-worlders that bond outside of their race. Their bonding is fated by the Great Creator of all things. Some of them are destined to rule; they will usher in an era of peace."

"Do you believe the prophecies in the tomes?"

He lowers his gaze. "I am conflicted."

I stare at him in disbelief. "But this prophecy is considered a myth, right? I mean, for all we know, the tomes weren't even real."

"It matters not. The Emperor is a believer. He has studied what remains of the prophecies in great detail. Kalvar says it is his greatest obsession."

Exasperated, I huff. "But they're just myths, Marek."

"I used to believe this as well." He meets my eyes evenly. "But so were the vampires and dragons of Terra."

CHAPTER 20

ELIZABETH

When I wake in the morning, it's to Marek's warm arms wrapped solidly around me as he nuzzles my hair, skimming his nose along my jaw and down my neck before he presses a series of soft kisses to the curve of my shoulder.

I turn in his arms and before I can speak, he captures my mouth in a searing kiss. His tongue is warm and insistent as it strokes against mine. His hands skate lightly over my skin, beneath my robe.

I smile against his lips. "Well, this is a wonderful way to wake up."

He stares at me with a half-lidded gaze as I reach across to trace the tip of his left ear with my fingers. I figured his ears were sensitive, but it's confirmed as his tr'llen begins low in his chest.

His hands are warm as they trace along my outer thigh before cupping the back of my knee and pulling my leg up over his hip. The hard length of his l'ok presses insistently against the warmth of my center, through the thin fabric of his knit pants that separate us.

He shifts to pull me closer, and I moan as the movement hits me in just the right spot, lighting up every nerve in my body and melting my core. His nostrils flare as he scents my arousal, and with a low growl he moves down my body, closing his mouth over my breast. With a quick swipe of his tongue over the already stiff peak, I arch up off the bed beneath him, wanting more.

"Marek, please," I breathe between soft pants and gasps as he turns his attention to the other breast.

He lifts his head, staring at me with a heated gaze. "Tell me what you desire, my Elizabeth."

"You. Just you," I breathe, threading my fingers through his and pushing my longing toward him.

∼

MAREK

I inhale sharply when she makes the connection. Desire pulses strongly across the link; it takes everything within me to maintain my control. I love the way she responds so beautifully to my touch and how she cries out my name as she finds her release. But most of all, I love to experience the effects of the bonding hormone coursing through her system, binding her to me in the Terran way.

I know not if it is the approach of my mating cycle that demands that I bind her to me or if it is just a natural impulse because of our faint bond, but I can barely keep my hands off her when we are alone. And when we are surrounded by others, my possessive instincts flare and it is even more difficult, but somehow, I manage.

As she writhes beneath me, I fight the impulse to seal her to me, right here and now. "Marek." She moans lightly in my ear. Her warm tongue traces over the sharp peak and a low groan escapes me.

I kiss a heated trail down the curve of her neck, my tongue tasting the sweet salt of her skin as my fangs extend in anticipation of binding her to me in the S'acris. Grazing my teeth over the pulsing artery along her neck, I feel my control slipping away.

"Yes, Marek," she whispers. "Make me yours."

Fierce possessiveness rushes through me, but I force myself to pull away just before I pierce her skin.

She reaches up to cup her hand to my face. My obsidian eyes and sharp fangs reflect in her luminous eyes as she stares up at me, filling me with guilt. I avert my gaze, not wanting to see the monster I am—the one that nearly lost all control.

Love, brighter than a thousand stars flows across the bond between us, drawing my gaze back to her in wonder for I know she has projected this.

"I love you," she whispers. "Both your darkness and your light. You are mine, and I am yours. I'm not afraid of you, and I'm not afraid of forming the S'acris."

Cupping her hand to the back of my neck, she pulls my lips back down to hers and then smiles up at me. "Will you go over the defense holds again with me this morning?"

My thoughts return to the grim stories of enslaved Terrans that the Aerilon female spoke of yesterday. I must prepare my Elizabeth to defend herself against a violation of her mind. "There is something else I must train you for."

Her brow furrows softly. "What is it?"

"I must teach you how to resist the R'ugol."

She stills. "Why?"

With a slight clench of my jaw, I meet her gaze evenly. "Although it is a crime punishable by death among my people to use the R'ugol on someone's mind, V'loryns are just as capable of doing this as the A'kai." She inhales sharply, her fear seeping across the bond. "You must be taught how to resist in case the Emperor or one of the A'kai ever try to—" Emotions lodge in my throat, rendering me incapable of speech as the nightmare of Elizabeth locked in the deadly embrace of an A'kai floats to the front of my mind.

She presses her forehead to mine, gently tracing her fingers across my cheek. "It's all right, my love. I'll be fine."

Unable to speak, I nod. It is difficult to train her to defend herself against my race. I want to protect her, not attack her. Hold her, not overpower her. I hate that my own people are as much a threat to her as the A'kai, and I vow that if any dare try to harm her, I will end them without hesitation. I swear it to the stars. My vow.

ELIZABETH

My muscles ache in protest as I practice sparing and holds with Marek. With my back flush against his front, he bands one arm around my waist, pinning my arms to my side, while his other hand immobilizes me as he cups my chin firmly, keeping me in place. I struggle, but I cannot break free of this hold.

"You must not panic if you find yourself in the Drogev position. Remember to use your smaller size to your advantage," he whispers against my ear. "It changes my center of balance enough that what should be mere muscle memory when I utilize this hold, takes concentration—breaking my focus and leaving me vulnerable to counterattack."

Gritting my teeth, I twist from his grasp and spin to face him. Sweeping my foot out, I catch the back of his ankle and he loses his balance.

Marek recovers quickly, and we each form a defensive stance as we begin to circle each other. A large shadow passes overhead, blocking out the light from the sun. Despite my intent to focus on my opponent—like Marek and Ryven have instructed—I look up, fully expecting to see Errun.

My heart stops as a deafening roar splits the air. A massive silver-gray dragon circles overhead. With iridescent scales that shimmer beneath the V'loryn sun, this is not Errun nor his mate.

Ryven's voice cries out. "Protect the K'Sai!"

The world shifts into slow motion as Marek throws himself over my body, shielding me from the swirling wind and debris as it flaps its great wings above us.

Just as suddenly as it started, it stops as the v'rach lands, shaking the ground beneath us. My eyes go wide as it transforms into a man.

Silver reflective eyes lock on mine. Ice fills my veins as I recognize the Mosauran from the orbital station. "Release the Terran!" His words are harsh and guttural as he speaks in his native tongue.

Marek growls low in his throat as he pulls me behind him, anger rolling off his body in heated waves as he glares at the man. "No." His voice is quiet but deadly.

"Give her to me."

"She. Is. Mine," Marek grits out through his teeth as his nails extend into sharp and deadly claws. "You *will not* come near her."

Ryven and his men surround us. "Leave this place or you will die, Mosauran."

Without warning, the Mosauran transforms back into an enormous dragon. His tail lashes out, knocking Marek and the rest of the guards out of the way. The world shifts into slow motion as massive claws wrap around me.

Marek jumps up, rushing toward me only to be knocked back by a violent gust as the Mosauran flaps his enormous wings, lifting into the air in a rush of wind. A terrified cry erupts from my throat as Marek's body slams against the far wall with a sickening thud.

"Marek!"

His head jerks up, and his eyes meet mine full of unbridled fear. I cry out his name once more as I'm ripped away into the sky.

The vise-like grip of his massive clawed hand squeezes the air from my lungs, abruptly cutting off my scream as we ascend above the castle. I twist and thrash against his hold, but he tightens his grasp so much I can barely move. I claw and bite at his scaled hand, but his hide is too thick to do any damage.

Desperation and anger steel me. I *will not* go quietly. I'd rather fall to my death than end up a slave.

A thunderous cry fills the air, and I turn toward the sound. Errun flaps his wings furiously as he races toward us. He barrels into my captor's side, clamping his jaws around his neck.

He's much larger than the Mosauran in dragon form, and my captor roars in pain, releasing me from his grip.

Wind whips around my body as I tumble through the air in a terrifying freefall. Unbridled fear steals the air from my lungs as the ground rushes toward me.

A clawed hand grips me, abruptly halting my descent. I look up to see Errun above me. Relief floods my veins, but it's short-lived when the Mosauran sinks his teeth into Errun's neck.

Errun releases a bellowing roar, spinning and tumbling as he shakes violently in an attempt to free himself, but he doesn't let me go.

I cling tightly to him. If he lets go, I don't want to fall. Not anymore. I'd rather go down with him than be taken again. A large, raven-black form soars past us as A'ravae comes to defend her mate.

Realizing he's outmatched, the Mosauran's eyes meet mine a moment before he roars in anger and races away.

Black blood runs down Errun's neck to his chest and down his leg, dripping around the clawed hand that holds me. His wings falter as he struggles to fly with his injury. A'ravae circles. Pain visible behind her eyes as she stares at her failing mate. She releases a series of sorrow-filled cries.

Raw pain and emotion wash through me. Tears stream down my face and I choke back a sob as Errun struggles to fly to the Estate. Despite his pain, he holds me gently as he hovers above the balcony.

Marek and Ryven rush toward us as Errun begins to falter, extending his wings as he struggles to land. As soon as we touch down, he releases his hold and with a low rumble in his chest, rolls to the side and away from me. I scramble toward him, running my hands over his injury. His cat-like glowing green irises contract and expand as he lifts his head a moment before collapsing again.

The balcony shakes beneath us as A'ravae lands on his other side, a low mournful sound in her throat as she nuzzles her mate and extends her wing over his body as if to protect him.

Strong arms wrap around me from behind and pull me away. I cry out. "No! He needs help!"

"Where are you hurt?" Marek's panicked voice calls out above me.

"I'm not hurt. Take care of Errun. He saved me. You need to help him."

"You're bleeding, Elizabeth!"

I struggle against his hold. "I'm fine! You have to help Errun!"

Marek turns me in his arms to face him, panic evident in his glowing green eyes. "Ryven and one of the Healers will help him.

Let the other Healer treat you. You are hurt, my Si'an T'kara. Please."

Everything is chaos and yelling all around me as Ryven orders the guards. Marek scoops me in his arms, rushing me inside.

I look down at the black and red blood smeared across the torn fabric of my tunic. Extending his claws, Marek slices the material away from my body to reveal several large scratch marks across my abdomen and back. Only now that I see them, do they begin to burn in agony.

One of the Healers scans me from head to toe while Marek watches with barely contained panic etched in his features. "There is heavy bruising, but nothing is broken. The wounds are superficial and should respond well to a dermal regenerator," he reports.

The Healer runs the medical device over me a few times and the wounds begin to heal at a rapid rate as new tissue and skin knit together.

Marek dismisses the Healer when he's done. I'm still in mild shock from what happened, so I don't protest when he lifts me into his arms. He carries me to the cleansing room. I open my mouth to speak but emotions lodge in my throat and the words won't come.

He doesn't bother to undress either of us before he walks into the bathing pool, gently lowering us both until only are heads are above the warm and soothing water. The sea-green liquid swirls with red and black. Marek's gentle hands remove the shredded remains of my tunic and pants to wash away the blood stains on my skin.

He cups the back of my neck and presses his forehead to mine. With shaking breath, he closes his eyes. "I thought I'd lost you again." His voice quavers slightly, and it's only now that I'm aware of his all-consuming fear bleeding through our connection.

The look on his face is nothing short of devastated and I wrap my arms tight around his neck, running my fingers through the hairs at the nape as I whisper. "You didn't. I'm here."

"Elizabeth, I almost lost you today. We should never have come here. I don't care about all of this." He waves his hand, gesturing to our chambers and, by extension, the Estate and his title. "All I care about is you. You are more important than any of this, and I will not risk your life for it. We should return to Terra. It is safer for you there."

I reach forward and cup my hands to either side of his face. "If everything you've told me about the Emperor is true, you cannot just leave. You, Kalvar, Vanek, and Milena are all that stand against him—protecting both your world and mine. If you left you would forfeit everything, including the ability to vote against him on the Council. If he enslaved my world, there would be nowhere for us then, my love. And if the Mosaurans and the A'kai are hunting Terrans, we cannot survive on our own." Softly, I shake my head as his glowing green eyes stare deep into mine. "This is not just about you and me anymore. It's about all of us. Your people *and* mine."

He says nothing, but I feel the heavy weight of his resignation through the bond. He knows I'm right.

The initial shock is gone, and despite my attempt to calm myself, my body trembles slightly with the echoes of remembered fear. As I rest against Marek, words will not come for either of us and it feels like forever before he finally moves back just enough to pull the remainder of my torn and wet clothing from my form.

He removes his clothing as well before carrying me out of the water, wrapping me tightly in a large plush robe. Pulling back the comforter, he lays me gently down in the bed. He moves to his dresser and changes into soft knit pants before laying down beside me. Curling himself protectively around me, his warm hand brushes the hair back from my face as he whispers in my ear. "Rest now, my Elizabeth. Your body will finish healing while you sleep."

As I lay wrapped up in his arms, exhaustion steals through me. My eyelids flutter closed, and I struggle to blink them open but it's no use. Marek whispers words of love and devotion in hushed and soothing tones as I drift away into sleep.

∼

MAREK

I could have lost her. The image of her being carried away is burned into my memory, filling me with fear. She is supposed to be safe here on the Estate. If I cannot keep her safe here, she is not safe anywhere on V'lora. She closes her eyes and as soon as I realize she's asleep, I gently rise from the bed and quietly step out onto the balcony to check on Errun.

He lies on his side with his mate curled around him. She lifts her head to stare directly at me but lowers it again when she realizes I am not a threat. I place my hand on his neck just below his injury, and he opens his eyes to look at me. "Thank you, my friend. I can never repay you for saving my mate."

Through the touch connection, an image of A'ravae flashes through my mind, telling me he understands. He blinks several times and after a moment, closes his eyes again. I look to his mate. "Go check on your offspring. He is safe here with us."

She raises her head and studies me a moment as if gauging the truth of my words before she stands and extends her wings. Lifting off the balcony, she dives over the side of the cliff and disappears.

"They understand more than we realize," Ryven says as he stands from his chair.

I had not realized he was here. I turn to face him. "Yes, they do."

His eyes shift to the door. "Go to the K'Sai. I will stay with Errun. We're well acquainted, he and I."

I raise a questioning brow.

A small smirk twists his lips. "Who do you think fed him fish while you were away all that time on Terra?" He pauses, dropping his eyes a moment to the ground before lifting his gaze back to mine. "I thought it was foolish…dangerous to allow a v'rach to make its home so close to the Estate, even if you did raise him. But now"—he looks to Errun—"we would not have gotten her back without him…without them both."

"How are our defenses?"

"The shield is up, but it is useless against a Mosauran."

I clench my jaw. Force shields are only meant to keep out technology and blades, not organic matter.

He continues. "I've doubled the guard. Everyone is instructed to search the sky and the ground, but I doubt he will try to return now that he knows we have these two." He looks to Errun, studying him a moment before continuing. "I've never seen a Mosauran shift before. I'd heard of it, but to actually see it is another thing entirely. I also issued a planetary alert. Hopefully, he will be discovered before he is able to leave the planet."

"Why do you think he wants her?"

He shakes his head. "I do not know, but I also do not want to find out."

"Agreed."

A'ravae circles above us, drifting down again beside her mate. I meet Ryven's eyes with a knowing look. "I suspect there will be more v'rachs on the Estate soon, and I am pleased it will be so. Now more than ever."

He nods. "I'll order extra fish to keep them both fed until he recovers. And when the little ones come, we will feed them as well so they will learn that we are friends."

With a subtle dip of my chin in parting, I walk back into our rooms and activate the privacy screen. The glass frosts over immediately, and I quietly lay down in the bed beside Elizabeth, wrapping my arms around her sleeping form.

~

When she wakes, she turns a sleepy gaze to me. "Why do you think the Mosauran wanted me?"

I trace my fingers lightly across her cheek, shuddering inwardly as the memory of her being ripped away into the sky replays in my mind. "I do not know. I thought they detested slavery as much as we do…and yet, he tried to take you away."

"You think he wanted to make me a slave?"

As I pull her close against me, her heart beats rapidly against my chest as she tries to contain her worry. "I do not know."

"How was he able to turn into a v'rach? Are his people able to change into any form at will?"

"No. They are only able to change into their draken forms—similar to v'rachs but smaller. Scientists speculate the Mosaurans are somehow related to v'rachs. V'rachs *did* originate on the Mosauran home world, but my ancestors captured hundreds of them to be used as machines for war during the time of the Ancient Ones."

She shifts in my arms, squeezing her eyes shut as she winces slightly in pain.

Panic races through me. "Are you—"

Pressing her lips quickly to mine, she smiles softly. "I'm fine. Just a little sore." She pauses. "When do we meet with the Emperor?"

After everything that's happened, I refuse to risk her any further. "*I* will meet with him. *You* will stay here."

She frowns. "You're not going without me."

Shaking my head, I brace myself for her wrath. "After what happened today, I don't want you leaving the Estate until it is time for us to return to Terra."

Her head jerks back in surprise before her expression soon becomes angered. "The Emperor is a dangerous man. I'm not going to let you face him alone."

From the look on her face and the emotion that seeps through our connection, I know there is no changing her mind about this. I will take Ryven and several of our elite guards and pray to the Goddess that the Emperor sees reason when we go before him for the sanctioning of our bond.

CHAPTER 21

MAREK

While Elizabeth readies herself for our meeting with the Emperor, I seek out Ryven. I find him in the courtyard giving instructions to the guards that will be traveling with us. When his eyes meet mine, he gives me a knowing look. "Have you convinced the K'Sai to remain here?" he asks, hopefully.

Drawing in a deep breath, I shake my head. "She refuses."

He looks down a moment before lifting his gaze back to mine. Crossing his arm over his chest, he gives me a solemn nod. "I will guard her with my life."

I place my hand on his shoulder. "Thank you, my friend."

As she walks down the staircase, the entire house staff and guards stare up at her. Dressed in the colors of House D'enekai, she looks both fierce and regal all at once as befits the K'Sai of a Great House. Wearing a long white dress tunic with silver V'loryn glyph embroidered on the hem, and light gray leggings with gray boots, it is the silver threaded v'rach sigil across her chest that draws my attention. The v'rach necklace hangs just above it, and it is as if she was always meant to be here. To be K'Sai of our House. To be mine.

When she reaches the bottom of the stairs, she takes advantage of the height added to her stature by the last step and wraps her arms around my neck, pressing her lips to mine. Vaguely aware of the many curious stares that watch us, I care not. Their K'Sai is Terran, and our children will be of both worlds. We are forging a new future that will be a blending of our two cultures.

Pulling back from the kiss, she steps down and loops her arm around mine as we make our way to the courtyard and the transport.

Just before we step onto the ramp, Ryven turns to me, his eyes darting briefly to Elizabeth and back again. "Are you certain about this?"

I dip my chin in a subtle nod.

As we sit side by side on the transport, Elizabeth takes my hand, entwining our fingers. Even with my mental transference shields up, her anxiety is still palpable through the faint bond, but she tries to mask it with an impassive expression. As we head out across the ocean, a bellowing roar sounds out nearby. Turning to look out the viewscreen, we see Errun and A'ravae flying in tandem beside us a moment before breaking off to circle back to their cave.

Elizabeth smiles widely, squeezing my hand in her excitement. "He's better."

Ryven rolls his eyes in mock frustration. "You wouldn't know it this morning though. You should have seen the pitiful look he gave me, begging for extra dried fish."

Elizabeth laughs.

A hint of a smile curves Ryven's mouth as he stares across at her.

The mood is light for a bit as Ryven tells her more stories about our time on the Defense Force together, including the time Vanek was clawed by a Lycaon during a ship's search. He made us stay up all night with him during the next twin full moons because he worried the stories about shifting after a scratch or a bite from a Lycaon were truth.

The lighthearted feeling is short-lived however as we near the Emperor's home.

Ryven leans forward in his seat, his gaze darts briefly to mine before he looks to Elizabeth. Pulling a knife from his belt, he holds it out to her. "I want you to keep this on you at all times."

I expect her to protest, and it would appear he did as well, because his brows rise briefly toward his hairline as if surprised as she tucks it just inside her boot without question and then meets his eyes evenly. "Thank you."

"We are approaching the K'voch Estate," Tolav says from the pilot's seat.

Elizabeth's jaw drops as she stares out the viewscreen at the massive floating structure.

Though the Emperor's Estate is vast, his palace is on a floating island above the main grounds. Powered by L'sair crystals, I suppose it could remain in the air indefinitely if he wished, and perhaps that is his intent. He is paranoid and has always been thus as far as I know. He insists that almost all Council meetings be held here. It is rare to ever find him outside of his home. That he came to Kaden and Brienna's ceremony was not only shocking but one of only a few times he's left his Estate this cycle.

∼

ELIZABETH

The Emperor lives on a floating island—a technological marvel suspended above the vast, green ocean that borders his lands. Although mechanically made, it's so green and lushly overgrown with plant-life, it looks almost natural, reminding me of the park in the city center. We are not yet over the water and as my gaze drops down to the ground below, I'm shocked to see so much foliage. If Kalvar's greatest indulgence is the courtyard at the Estate, the Emperor's eclipses it one hundredfold.

I turn to Marek. "How is it that your people struggle to terraform your planet and yet, the Emperor lives as though it's already done?"

A hint of irritation crosses his expression as he stares at the Emperor's property. "This excess is but one example of how unwisely he wields his power. Much of our planet's resources are dedicated to the upkeep of his lands."

I open my mouth to speak but stop abruptly as we fly out over the ocean, approaching the island. I'm surprised by the sheer size of it; I can't imagine how much L'sair is needed to keep it suspended above the sea. While Marek's Estate looks more like a castle, the Emperor's reminds me of the grandiose palaces of ancient Terra. Built more for aesthetics than for defense, it is larger than any palace I've ever seen.

Light shimmers around it—reflecting the sun in an iridescent glow reminiscent of a soap bubble, but on a much larger scale. It covers the entire floating structure; it must be his defense shield.

The grounds—covered in green and red foliage stretch out for several acrums, extending as far as the eye can see. It is as if it's a separate ecosystem apart from everything else on this planet. Nothing like the barren landscape that covers more than half of V'lora.

"He has recreated V'lorys that was on his lands and his Estate," Marek explains, answering my unspoken thoughts.

As we touch down on the surface, I look to Ryven, hoping he understands the subtle reminder of the promise he made to protect Marek first if anything should go wrong.

After a moment, he lowers his gaze, inclining his head just enough to indicate that he understands what I'm silently trying to convey with my eyes.

Marek helps me down from the transport, and we're greeted by two of the Emperor's guards. Both large and imposing men, they wear plated armor of muted gold with the sigil of their house emblazoned across the front—the poisonous and deadly k'mal, similar to a black cobra, coiled and ready to strike.

The first one meets my eyes, and a look of shock flickers briefly across his expression before he returns it once again to a stoic mask. "This way," he says, motioning toward the palace behind him.

The smooth walls of the castle glisten with a pearlescent black sheen with row upon row of large, open windows, reinforcing my belief that it appears this place was built for aesthetics instead of protection. As if in response to my observation, my eyes are drawn again to the subtle glimmer of the force shield as it closes over us, covering the entire Estate and the dozens of laser cannons along the outer wall. It seems he does have plenty of fortification after all.

The guard leads us through a large outer gate and into a courtyard. If I thought Kalvar's multitude of plants on the D'enekai Estate was an indulgence, this one is outrageous. Several fountains filled with precious water are interspersed throughout the grounds and several small streams wind throughout courtyard.

Massive doors shimmer and open, revealing a rather impressive and opulently decorated entryway. Almost everything in here is made from some sort of precious metal. It gleams brightly beneath the harsh lighting within, rivaling the midday V'loryn sun. Its purpose is probably meant to impress, but everything screams of excess gaudiness. It looks nothing like the subtle, yet natural beauty of the L'kir moldings that define the castle of House D'enekai.

Walking farther in, the doors reappear and seal behind us with a resounding echo that reverberates throughout the large structure, following us down a seemingly never-ending hallway.

When we finally reach the end, another set of doors opens into what looks like a throne room. The Emperor is seated in the largest chair, while V'Meia is seated beside him in the smaller one. A woman sits on the other side of him, and I realize this must be the Empress—his bondmate and V'Meia's mother.

From what I've learned of the Great Houses, Empress V'Mika is of House G'alta, as is her sister, who is bonded to the Emperor's younger brother. Her eyes rake over me with an intense gaze, colder than even Milena's was the first time she met me.

Holding Marek's hand, I force my attention to remain locked on the Emperor as we stand before him. Members of the High Council, including Kalvar, file into the room, taking their seats along either side of Emperor Zotal and his family.

I notice Vanek, Kalvar, and Milena all sit to one side, representing the Great Houses of A'msir, D'enekai, and L'eanan, while three others sit on the opposite side of the Emperor. Dovak of House G'alta, L'anrul of M'theal, and L'Mira of S'tiran. It is easy to see how the

JESSICA GRAYSON

Council is split. One side supporting Marek and Kalvar, and the other supporting the Emperor.

A group of at least a dozen V'loryns, each dressed in long, flowing green robes enter the room, taking the row of seats just off to the side. They must be the Elders. Although, seeing as how Marek's people do not outwardly age, aside from the darkening of their green eyes, none of these people appear elderly at all. The High Omari sits beside them.

∼

MAREK

Emperor Zotal scans the room, his gaze sweeping across the Council and Elders before he turns to address Elizabeth and me. "Your bonding has been approved."

I'm so shocked by his statement it takes me a moment to respond. As I look to Vanek, Kalvar, and Milena, I notice they are equally as surprised as I am. V'Meia's face remains stoic beside her father, but something just behind her eyes fills my veins with ice when her gaze meets mine.

I force myself to bow to the Emperor as is expected of any T'Hale. "Thank you. We will perform the ceremony as soon as we return to K'ylira."

"May the Goddess bless you," Emperor Zotal replies, but something about his tone sounds almost mocking, as if it's taking everything within him to remain impassive.

Taking Elizabeth's hand in mine, I turn back to the door to leave, but the Emperor's words stop me abruptly and I spin back to face him.

He darts a quick glance to the Elders. "I heard about the Mosauran attack on your...betrothed. I have issued a planetary alert and warning concerning this. We have reason to believe he has not left the planet. We are continuing to search for him."

Something feels off but I force my expression to remain neutral as I incline my head in acknowledgment. "Thank you for your concern.

That is why we have brought many guards with us today," I reply. Although, that's not the only reason why, but I'm sure he already knows that I do not trust him.

"Of course. Safe journey, T'Hale Marek."

With that, I turn back to the door. Elizabeth and I walk as quickly toward the exit as we can. Panic floods my system so intense it feels as if I'm drowning in it, and I struggle to remain calm. Something is wrong. Stopping abruptly just as we enter the courtyard, I turn to Elizabeth and give her a curious look. "Are these feelings coming from you?"

Her eyes are full of worry as they meet mine. "Something isn't right, Marek. Did you see the way they looked at us? We need to leave. Now."

I nod and turn to find Ryven and Kalvar entering the courtyard. "Let us leave. Quickly," I tell them.

"Agreed," Ryven replies, and we head toward the shuttle. As we make our way across the Estate, the same sense of panic claws at my throat that I felt when we were on the station and the Mosaurans and Anguis approached us. My every instinct is telling me to lift Elizabeth into my arms and race toward the transport, but we are being watched closely by the Emperor's guards. If I did this now, it would only signal to them my distrust of the Emperor, and I do not want to anger him anymore than he already is. My people do not need a civil war because I'm unable to control my fear.

We reach the courtyard, and I can see our transports just beyond the walls. V'Meia cries out, stopping me in my tracks. "Marek, wait!"

I turn to face her.

Her cold gaze rakes over Elizabeth, and I clench my jaw, biting back my anger. The last thing I want is a war between our Houses. "What do you want?" I ask in as even a tone as I can manage.

She steps toward me, her eyes fixed on my Si'an T'kara with an almost predatory gaze. "I would speak with you alone."

I open my mouth to protest, but she continues. "I promise to be brief." A hint of irritation crosses her features. "If you want peace between our Houses, I suggest you hear what I have to say."

Running a frustrated hand through my hair, I look to Elizabeth. I do not want to leave her. Not even for a moment. Especially not here on the Emperor's Estate.

Elizabeth threads her fingers through mine, sending a wave of love and reassurance to me through the faint connection. "I'll be fine, my love." She looks to Vanek and Ryven. "We'll be right here, waiting for you."

After a moment, I nod and turn to follow V'Meia. I make sure to never lose sight of Elizabeth as we move off just enough to speak privately.

I look to her expectantly. "How do you suggest we maintain the peace between us?"

Her ice-cold gaze locks on mine. "Isn't it obvious? I want to form the bond with you to unite our Houses. I'm offering you one final chance to see reason and change your mind before it is too late."

I shake my head. "Your father already sanctioned my bonding with Elizabeth. You and I do not have to be bonded to have peace, V'Meia."

"We do if you want to avoid a war."

"House D'enekai has been loyal to House K'voch for over a thousand cycles. Why should it be any different now?"

Her eyes shift back to Elizabeth with a hint of disgust in her expression. "Because of your Terran," she says in a low and threatening hiss, "many of the people believe *she* is the one spoken of in the Ancient Tomes of the Saraketh. Already, threats of dissent and rebellion are being whispered throughout V'lora. And *she*"—she points to my Si'an T'kara—"is the cause."

"My House does not seek to rule, V'Meia." I meet her eyes evenly. "You know this is truth."

She studies me with a dark gaze, reminding me once again of the deadly k'mal. "It matters not. It is a personal slight against me, and I will not tolerate it. I am the Princess of V'lora and heir to the crown. As long as you show the people that *she* is your choice instead of me, they will continue to believe in the superstitious riddles of an ancient book. It will undermine my House and my claim to the throne."

"I will not do what you ask," I state firmly. "I am hers, and she is mine. I will take no other as my bondmate."

Her nostrils flare, and her voice is low and threatening as she speaks. "You will remember this moment, Marek, as the biggest regret of your existence."

I don't bother to reply. Instead, I turn and walk back to my Elizabeth. Our guards quickly ready the two weapons transports that will escort us back to the Estate as we board the personal transport with Ryven and Kalvar. Vanek's face appears in the viewscreen as he hails us from his ship. "The transports of House A'msir will escort you back to the Estate."

I nod. "Thank you, my friend."

The screen goes dark, and Tolav's hands fly across the control panel, activating the startup sequence. We lift off, and I'm anxious to put as much space between us and the Emperor's island as possible. As we set out over the ocean, I reach across to take Elizabeth's hand in mine, thankful that we are finally on our way.

Kalvar looks to Tolav. "Alert the Estate that we will activate the shield as soon as we arrive."

Tolav's shoulders visibly stiffen as he goes still, hesitating with his hand over the comm panel. Curling his fingers into his palm, he retracts his arm and spins to face us, a blaster in his other hand. Before I can react, a blast of light erupts from the barrel, and Elizabeth crumples in her seat beside me.

I roar and lunge for his chair, but he shoots again. Pain explodes across my chest, and my world goes black.

CHAPTER 22

ELIZABETH

A throbbing pain in my skull calls me back into awareness. Every muscle in my body seems to scream in protest as I begin to move. My eyes snap open to near darkness, and I turn onto my side to find Marek beside me. His eyes are closed. Worried, I cup his cheek. "Marek? Marek?"

He doesn't even move.

My chest tightens as I run my hands over his still form, praying that he's not dead. "Marek?"

He moans low in his throat. Relief rushes through me, and I lean forward, brushing my lips against his. I'm so thankful he's alive. I run my hand down his arm and take his hand in mine.

His shields are down and, although he's not fully awake, he is aware of me beside him. I brush my fingers lightly across his face, tracing the line of worry that creases his brow. "I'm here, my love. I'm here."

As I scan the area around us paralyzing fear snakes through me when I realize we're in a cell. A whisper of sound across the cold metal floor makes me still. The hairs rise on the back of my neck, and my skin prickles with the sudden awareness that we are not alone here.

Breathing through pursed lips, I hug Marek close, wanting to protect him as I turn to face whatever approaches from the shadows.

Two pairs of menacing eyes stare across the cell. My breath catches as I recognize the silver reflective gaze. Cold fills me. I know these eyes; they are neither V'loryn nor Terran. Jumping to my feet, I form a defensive stance between the two Mosaurans and Marek.

Just behind them, I notice Kalvar and Ryven in the next cell over, their expressions full of unmistakable panic.

The Mosaurans stalk toward me.

A loud bang from behind startles them both as Ryven throws the full weight of his body against the cell bars, growling and desperate to reach us. "Do not dare approach them, Mosauran!" he yells. "For it will be your end. I swear it to the stars. My vow."

They say nothing, and I glare at them. "You *will not* touch him," I grit through my teeth in the harsh guttural tones of Mosauran. "He. Is. Mine."

They halt, and their eyes go wide. "You speak our language?"

Despite my fear, I tilt my chin up defiantly, pushing down my panic to face my enemy. I will die before I let them touch Marek. "Stay back," I growl, "or I will kill you where you stand."

The one with the silver eyes steps forward, his massive body towering over mine. With smooth scales stretched tight over a heavily muscled form it is easy to see he is a warrior. His sharp gaze scans me from head to toe. "We are prisoners here as well. We mean you no harm. For one so small, you are very brave."

Despite his words, I stand my ground, curling my hands into fists at my side. "Stay back," I command in a threatening voice.

He moves closer. "I do not—"

Lightning fast, I react. Jumping up, I spin and kick out with my left foot. His head whips back as I make contact with his face. He roars in anger as he stumbles to the side, slamming against the wall.

The other one rushes me.

I duck and grasp his forearm, twisting my body beneath his.

Pulling the hidden knife from my boot with the other hand, I come up behind him, knocking him off balance. He crashes to the ground, and I scramble over his back. Grasping his hair firmly in one hand, I pull back his head and place my blade to his throat with the other and growl low in his ear. "Don't. Even. Breathe."

"Wait!" the other one cries out. "Do not kill him! Please! We came here to save you!"

Panting heavily, I make sure to keep my grip tight as I lift my head to meet worry-filled silver eyes staring across at me.

"Don't believe him!" Ryven cries out. "He is the one that tried to take you. Mosaurans are violent and unpredictable. Do not trust his words."

Corded muscles tense and flex beneath me as the one I'm holding growls low in response. "V'loryns are the duplicitous ones," he hisses.

The other one moves closer. "If you follow the path revealed only by moonlight, along the wandering stream…where time stands still in the deep and dark forest, where would that take you?"

My brow furrows deeply and I blink several times in shock as I recognize the well-known phrase of a classic Terran fairy tale—a common bedtime story told to children by their parents. *Did he really just quote a phrase from The Elf Prince?*

He cocks his head to the side. "Do you not understand my question?"

Still stunned, it takes me a moment to respond. "It…it would take you to the Land of Silver Dreams. The Kingdom of the Elf Prince," I whisper in shock. "Where did you learn that phrase?"

"I am Prince Rowan of House Mosaura and he"—he gestures to the man beneath my knife—"is Tharin. My brother's Ashaya is Terran. We rescued her from an A'kai slaver." He pauses. "She said if we ever came across another Terran they would understand this phrase and know that we mean them no harm."

"What is 'Ashaya'?"

"Fated bondmate."

I can't hide my shock at his words. A Terran bonded to a dragon warrior? I open my mouth to speak, but he continues.

"She is now a Princess of Mosaura, and my mother the Empress sent us ahead to search for her home world."

"Your mother is the Empress?" Kalvar says from his cell, a hint of disbelief tinging his voice. "You lie. If all this were truth, your brother would be Outcast. Mosaurans do not take bondmates outside of their race."

Rowan shoots an agitated glance at Kalvar. "I do not speak lies," he grits through his teeth.

Still regarding him warily, I meet his eyes evenly. "Why are you here? And—why did you try to take me?"

His expression darkens. "My brother's bondmate searches for her home. Your people so closely resemble the V'loryns we hoped it was more than coincidence…that perhaps they evolved on a planet near their system. But when we saw you on the orbital station, we thought you were being held against your will."

I balk. "Why would you think that?"

"The V'loryns are much like the A'kai—capable of mind manipulation. It is well-known that V'loryns are desperate for females, and it seems yours are breeding compatible with many species, according to our Healers." His eyes drift to Marek. "We saw you on the station and when *he* would not allow us to speak with you, we assumed the worst. When I found you on the Estate fighting him, I thought you were their prisoner, and I was trying to help you escape."

"How did you end up here?"

He growls low in his throat, his hands curling into fists at his side. "After our failed attempt to free you, we sought an audience with the Emperor, but were received by the Princess instead. We demanded the release of any Terran slaves, threatening war with our Empire if they did not comply."

My brow furrows softly in confusion.

"She explained that your people were allies. We told her if she was lying, V'lora would become an enemy of our Empire. And that any who trafficked Terran slaves would meet the same fate as Talel—brother of the First Prime of A'kaina. He died at the hands of my brother's Terran bondmate when he tried to capture her again. After that, the Princess became enraged and ordered our imprisonment." He pauses. "We are searching for your world to warn them."

"Warn them of what?" Ryven bites out.

Tharin growls. "The A'kai hunt the Terrans. They are searching for their planet to enslave them."

My heart stops. "Why should I trust you?"

"Do *not* trust them." Kalvar's voice is low and deadly.

Rowan's eyes meet mine evenly. "Because we were with you the entire time you both lay unconscious in this cell. If we had meant you harm, we would have done so then."

His words make sense, but I still have questions. "What do the A'kai want with Terrans?"

"They are blood drinkers. Your Terran blood is valuable to them. They claim it has restorative properties unlike anything they've had before. If they find your world, they will enslave and slaughter your people by the millions." He looks to Marek and growls low in his throat. "The V'loryns are touch telepaths—able to manipulate minds through the R'ugol. Their ancestors were blood drinkers as well, like the A'kai." He narrows his eyes at my beloved. "I must ask again: Do they keep you against your will?"

I tilt my chin up as I meet his gaze evenly so he will see the truth of my words. "Marek is mine, and I am his."

His mouth falls open in shock. "You are his mate?"

I nod.

"But…V'loryns do not take mates outside of their species."

Tharin grumbles. "The same was true of our own species only a few months ago, but you and your brother changed that."

I study him warily. "Why haven't you shifted into your other form? You could easily escape."

"The Emperor's guards put a device here." He points to the back of his neck. "If we attempt to shift, it will kill us. The tools to disable it are back on our ship."

"You have a ship in orbit over V'lora?"

He nods. "Cloaked and waiting for our signal. I'm certain they've already sent word to the Mosauran Empire that we've gone missing.

Several Mosauran cruisers are probably already en route to V'lora as we speak."

"He lies," Kalvar growls. "It would take weeks to get a signal back to their Empire."

Rowan narrows his eyes. "Not with the use of the Passage."

Marek mentioned the Passage before. Said it was something used during the time of Kaden to travel quickly between systems. But he told me that Kaden had destroyed it to maintain the peace.

As if echoing my thoughts, Kalvar continues. "The Passage was destroyed thousands of cycles ago."

Rowan turns to face him. "We only recently found a way to restore it."

Holding his gaze, I struggle with indecision. Hope finally wins out and I decide we have to trust him. We can't escape without their help. As I pull back, Ryven's voice whips through the darkness. "Don't release him, K'Sai!"

I stop short, but keep my eyes trained on Rowan. "He is right, Ryven. He could have hurt us while we were unconscious and...if we don't work together, we will not get out of here alive."

I stand, and Tharin quickly rolls away, springing to his feet beside Rowan. He glares at me.

Rowan sighs heavily and looks to him. Rolling his eyes, he shakes his head in mock frustration. "Do not be upset that she bested you. You should have been prepared. You know how fierce Terran females are." He turns his attention back to me. "Tharin is young. You have wounded his pride."

I start to answer, but Marek's low growl draws my attention.

Off to my side, I can just barely make him out in the darkness as he slowly stands to full height, his chest rising and falling as he seethes with barely contained anger. His glowing green eyes turn black as he bares his fangs. His voice is low and deadly as he speaks. "You dare to threaten my mate?"

"No," Rowan replies, putting his hands up before him in a placating gesture. "*She* attacked us."

Marek tips his head to me. His eyes swirl from black to green, and

I recognize the confusion that flashes briefly behind them. I shrug. "I did, my love. I was afraid they were going to hurt you."

He wraps a protective arm around me, pulling me behind him as he growls again at the Mosaurans—the terrifying sound causing the hair to rise on the back of my neck. "She is mine. If you dare try to harm her, I will end you both."

Rowan straightens and then bows slightly. "You have my vow as a warrior of Mosaura, we will not harm either of you. I swear it to the Creator."

Marek narrows his eyes, studying him a moment before slightly relaxing the tense set of his shoulders, but he continues to stand between me and them.

I move to Marek's side and take his hand. "We have to find a way out of here."

The Mosauran tips his head back, studying the cell. "What do you propose?"

I scan our surroundings. "This hold looks like it was built for cargo, not for keeping people imprisoned," I say, more to myself than to anyone in particular. My gaze comes to rest on a vent high up on the side wall. "Can you lift me to that grate?" I point toward it. "If I can make it to another room, perhaps I can get this cage open from the outside."

Marek shakes his head. "It is too dangerous. We do not know how many others are on this ship. I doubt Tolav is the only one here."

Rowan steps forward. "He is right. V'loryns are faster and stronger than you. If you are caught, you will likely be killed."

Inhaling and exhaling deeply, I clench my jaw and look him straight in the eye. "If we do nothing, we could still die. Do you understand?"

His brows go up in surprise a moment before he nods.

Ryven calls out from across the room. "No, K'Sai, there has to be another way."

"You trained me, Ryven. I can do this. I've got this."

Rowan tips his head to the side and gives me a curious look. "What?"

"My brother's Ashaya uses that same phrase."

Marek studies the panel again and shakes his head softly. "It is too dangerous."

"I have to try, my love."

"She is right," Rowan's deep voice rumbles. He steps toward us. "We will have to lift you so that—"

The low, menacing growl from Marek stops him short. "Do *not* touch her. *I* will lift her."

I turn and stretch up onto my toes. Twining my arms around his neck, I brush my lips against his in a soft kiss. When I pull back, he drops his forehead to mine. Worry pulses through our connection. "I can do this, my love. I will save us."

He holds me tighter to him. "You said this to me once before. The day that you—" He doesn't finish his sentence, but he doesn't have to. Overwhelming sadness and pain fill me, and I know it's coming from him. He's speaking of the day I died in his arms.

"I want our future," I whisper. *"This* is the only way."

With a slight clench of his jaw, he reluctantly nods.

I turn to face Rowan. "I've heard much about Mosauran warriors. There are many words in your language about honor. Swear on your honor as warriors of Mosaura that you will not betray us."

He thumps his closed fist to his chest. "On my honor as a warrior, we will not harm you or your mate." A smile tugs at the corner of his lips. "You are as fierce as my brother's Terran mate."

Marek doesn't seem fully convinced. His eyes bore into Rowan's as a low and threatening growl rumbles deep in his chest.

I place a hand on his forearm, drawing his attention back to me. He pulls me protectively against him, so tight his embrace is almost crushing. Through the bond, I can feel his panic and desperation to keep me safe. "Please be careful, my Elizabeth."

I reach up and cup his cheek. "I will, my love. I promise."

Marek lifts me up to the panel. Prying the vent from the duct, I swallow nervously when I see how small the opening and crawlspace are. Panic fills me as my claustrophobia rears its ugly head. There's barely enough room for me to squeeze inside.

"What's wrong?" Rowan says below me. "I can scent your fear. What do you see up there?"

Marek growls at him again.

My throat is so dry it takes me a moment to reply. "It's...small."

"Will you fit?"

Unable to speak, I nod. I can do this. I *will* do this. I *have* to do this. If I don't, we could all die.

Marek pushes me a bit higher, and I cautiously pull myself into the vent. Shimmying just enough that I can slide the rest of the way in with minimal noise, I hear the soft click as the panel is returned to its position on the wall behind me.

Paralyzing fear wraps tight around my spine, threatening to render me immobile, but I force myself to push past it and focus. I have to get through to the next room. I can do this. I've got this.

My back hits the ceiling of the crawlspace, and I close my eyes as dark memories wash over me. *I'm back in the transport as it fills with water. Bear's bark echoes loudly throughout the enclosed space as he frantically tries to wake up my mom. I pound on the glass as water rushes in. Oh God, we're going to drown!*

A deep voice snaps me back into awareness, and I open my eyes to see light filtering into the crawlspace. Dragging myself toward it, I look down to see two of the Emperor's guards. "We must set the transport to self-destruct. We need it to look like the Mosaurans crashed the vessel after they kidnapped the others."

"We should not do this," the other one says. "It is wrong."

"Be quiet and do as you're told."

They leave the room, and I count out a full thirty seconds before carefully pushing the grate open. The hinge creaks lightly and my heart stops. A bead of sweat trickles down my forehead and drips onto the cold metal beside me. The sound of its splash is almost deafening in the near silence as I wait with bated breath to see if I've been discovered. When I don't hear or see any movement below me, I cautiously exit the crawlspace, hanging for a moment on the lip of the metal before allowing myself to drop to the ground below. The dull thud along the floor as I fall is much louder than I'd anticipated, and I cringe as I wait for someone to burst through the doors.

I pause for a moment, and when nothing happens, I scour the room for some kind of weapon. I still have my knife, but I'd like to have something else for backup as well. A large metal latch on a nearby crate that's about the length of my arm and as thick as two of my fingers looks like it will work. I pull it free and press the door control to exit.

Quietly, I hug the walls as I carefully make my way to the cargo bay. As soon as I reach it, I press my hand to the control to enter. My heart pounds, and I freeze when I notice one of the Emperor's guards inside.

He spins to face me with a surprised look on his face. Taking advantage of his confusion, I rush toward him. He pulls out his blaster, and I spin and kick out with my left leg, knocking it from his grip.

The blaster flies from his hand, slamming against the metal bars and bouncing just outside Ryven and Kalvar's cell. Grunting in desperation, Ryven struggles to reach it through the bars as I narrowly miss the next blow from my opponent.

When he charges me, I twist to the side and swing the latch, hitting him square across the face. He turns and rips it from my grasp, throwing it off to the side. Growling, he moves toward me. He feigns right and I duck. Too late I realize it was a ploy. He lunges and rams his fist into my side, forcing the air from my lungs and throwing me against the bars. Pain explodes across my back, and I slide down to the floor in a boneless heap. A hand grips me through the bars. "Elizabeth, get up. You have to get up." Ryven's voice is in my ears and I turn my head, blinking several times as I struggle to focus.

The guard stalks toward me, and I manage to roll onto my side, trying to get up, but he kicks me in the ribs. The air escapes my lungs in a sudden rush as I slam again against the metal cage. "You foolish Terran," he snarls. "How dare you try to ruin the Emperor's plans."

The guard looms over me, glowing green eyes staring down with a look of sick fascination. "I wonder just how pliable your mind is? Perhaps I should see for myself."

Fear ignites my mind and body back into awareness and I scramble away from him as he approaches. My eyes dart to the blaster just off to his side.

Gritting my teeth, I draw in a deep breath and lunge for the weapon. The guard grabs my ankle and jerks me back. Instead of trying to pull away, I allow him to take me. He drags me up even with his face. In one quick motion, I pull the knife from his belt and shove it up under his jaw, cutting deep into his throat.

Thick, warm, obsidian blood gushes from the mortal wound, spilling over my hands and down my arms as he stares at me in shock. Even as he dies, he refuses to release his grip. Dropping to his knees, he pulls me down with him, glaring at me as the light slowly fades from his eyes. His body goes limp and his hands fall away.

Drawing in a deep and steeling breath, I use the last of my strength to force myself to my feet. Bracing my arm across my aching ribs, I stumble to the access panel. I press the release and the cell doors open as I slump to the floor in exhaustion.

Warm arms wrap around me as Marek cradles me to his chest, holding me tightly against him. "Thank the Goddess you're all right," he breathes the words against my skin.

"I'm fine. We have to get control of the transport. They're going to set it to self-destruct...blame the Mosaurans for our death."

Ryven calls out. "Quickly! We have to go."

Only now do I notice the three more of the D'enekai guards emerging from the other cells. Glowing green eyes stare at me with a mixture of awe and wonder as Marek holds me tight in his arms.

I cup my hand to his cheek, drawing his attention. "I can walk."

"Even so. It is faster if I carry you."

Normally, my pride would make me argue, but instead I nod as we file out into the hallway.

Rowan comes up beside us, staring down at me intently. He dips his head in a subtle nod. "You are just like my brother's Ashaya. You are small but fierce. A true warrior."

Ryven takes the lead. They open the door and we slip down the hallway in single file, making our way to the bridge. Marek's people are not only fast, they are silent as they move through the ship with a stealthy ease that belies their imposing figures. We encounter two guards along the way, and Ryven makes short work of them, breaking their necks. The sickening crunch makes my stomach twist, but I force myself to swallow against the bile rising in my throat. I have to keep it together.

Reaching the entrance to the bridge, Ryven puts out his hand in a silent countdown before slamming it against the access panel. As soon as the doors whoosh open, the bridge erupts into chaos. Marek pulls me behind him as the world shifts into slow motion.

Out of nowhere, a guard rushes up behind me, and I spin to face him while Marek fights two in front. Just like during training, I push beyond my pain, focusing on being aware of every movement of my opponents. Ducking and spinning away, giving them no time to react as I use their momentum against them.

Strong hands grip my arm, pulling me away from Marek. I twist in my attacker's hold and hook the back of his knee, making him stumble to the side. I take advantage of his imbalance and sink my blade deep into his chest with a sickening squelch. He looks down at his wound and back to me in shock before collapsing to the floor in a pool of blood.

Marek pulls me back behind him as another guard rushes forward. He moves with a fluid and deadly grace as he fights, and it isn't long before the guard is lying dead at his feet.

Ryven kills the last guard, and Marek turns to me. His eyes go wide as he rakes over my form. Covered in blood, I must look terrible. "Are you hurt?" he asks, pulling me against him as he searches for any injury.

Panting heavily, I look down at my body, my clothing stained black with the blood of my enemies. I don't see very much red, so I assume I must be okay. "I'm fine."

A strange mixture of worry and relief flood the link between us at my words.

My gaze drifts to Tolav, struggling to breathe as he lies in a pool of his own blood on the floor. His face pale and drawn, he lifts a pitiful gaze to Kalvar. "They set the ship to self-destruct. You don't have much time."

Kalvar's eyes flash with anger. "Why did you do it? Why did you betray us?"

He lowers his head in shame. "They had my brother. They told me they'd spare him if I helped them. But they lied to me. My brother is dead. As am I."

"Who was it?" Marek roars. "The Emperor or V'Meia?"

"Both," he whispers, his skin growing more and more pale from the loss of his lifeblood.

"Can you stop the self-destruct?" I ask.

"No, and the communications are disabled. You must alter course. The Emperor was going to retrieve his men at a predetermined location. He'll find you if you eject the escape pods along this programmed route."

I look to Marek. "We need to alter course and rig the transport to blow prematurely so the Emperor doesn't figure out that we escaped. He'll think everyone died aboard instead." I move closer to the panel, studying the controls. "I can do this. Get everyone to the pods."

Ryven's gaze darts to the two Mosaurans. "What about them? We cannot trust them not to betray us. They are Mosauran."

Rowan and Tharin growl low in their throats, extending their claws as they face Ryven.

I step between Ryven and them. "They helped us. We will not leave them to die."

With a slight clench of his jaw, Ryven reluctantly relaxes his stance, bowing slightly to me. "As you wish, K'Sai."

Marek moves next to me. "I will help you with the ship."

I want him to go to the pods...to escape and be safe. But we don't have time to argue. Even if I begged him to save himself, I already know he would never leave my side.

Kalvar places his hand on Marek's shoulder, worry flashing behind his eyes. "I do not want to leave you."

"I will be fine, Uncle. But you must go with Ryven."

"You are the future of our House," Kalvar argues, his gaze sweeps to mine. "Both of you."

My heart clenches at his words. Marek is the only family he has left, and I understand his fear. "This"—I gesture to the computer—"is what we are good at. We can work much faster than anyone else here. Please, trust us. We are wasting time, and you need to go."

After a moment, he reluctantly agrees, his eyes drifting once more to Marek before he and the rest of them leave.

Together, we work quickly to reprogram the transport's flight path. As soon as we're finished, Marek lifts me into his arms and races down the hallway, moving with inhuman speed toward the escape pods.

Everyone else is already gone when we finally reach them. We slam into our seats, fastening our harnesses securely before pressing the release. The pod ejects violently from the transport, spinning away before suddenly righting itself as the thrusters fire up.

As we stare out the viewscreen, the ship erupts in a brilliant ball of light. The explosive shockwave slams against the outer hull, throwing us back against our seats. Alarms begin blaring as red lights fill the cabin. Marek's face is a mask of panic as he looks over at me. His worry pulsing across our bond.

"Brace, brace, brace," the computer repeats as the ground races toward us. We're going to crash and there's nothing we can do about it.

I hold tight to Marek's hand as he stares across at me.

"Eh'leh-na," he whispers.

"I love you."

A thunderous boom splits the air as we slam into the ground, and the world goes black.

CHAPTER 23

ELIZABETH

Red lights blink rapidly around the edges of my vision as I struggle to open my eyes. Alarm bursts through me as the scent of smoke fills my nostrils. A deafening clang echoes throughout the structure as the floor trembles beneath me as if keeping time with the resounding noise.

I lift my gaze to find Marek braced against one of the panels, kicking at the hatch. He grits his teeth as he pounds against the door, trying to force it open.

The metal grates and groans under the assault. A sliver of light seeps in through the small opening, bathing the interior in a glowing soft orange color and illuminating the thick layer of smoke inside the cabin.

Panic claws at my throat as the smoke grows thicker, burning my lungs with each inhalation. Gasping for air, I cough and sputter as I struggle to catch my breath.

Marek's glowing green eyes dart quickly to mine as he continues to pound on the door. "Almost." He throws his weight against the hatch. "There," he grits through his teeth as he slams against it once more.

The metal groans loudly as the door comes loose from the structure and falls away from the opening.

Marek gathers me in his arms and carries me to safety. Setting me gently on the ground, he turns and then races back to the pod. Fear twists deep in my gut as he rushes inside. ·

I scramble to my feet and hurry back to the opening. Barely able to breathe through the heavy fumes, I call out to him. "Marek!"

He appears a moment later with a large pack slung over one shoulder. Although the pod is almost completely buried in the sand, dark smoke billows from the open hatch, spiraling up to the sky and announcing our presence like a beacon. His eyes meet mine. "We cannot stay here."

Out of habit, I glance down at my wrist, shaking my head in frustration when I remember that our communicators were taken from us while we were unconscious.

Shading my brows with one hand, I squint my eyes against the brightness of V'lora's sun. I scan the stark and barren landscape, searching for any sign of the other pods, but see nothing.

Dry wind whips around my form. Wisps of dust and mica float like silken waves across the red sand, whispering through the maze of canyons and rock formations that jut up from the earth like towers. Composed of alabaster stone streaked with black and gray veins, they are like skeletal islands, dotting the bleak terrain. I lift my gaze to his. "Where do you think we are?"

Marek's expression is unreadable, but his eyes betray his worry. "According to the pod's readings before we crashed, we are still deep in the Emperor's territory."

Fear spikes through me as my thoughts turn to Kalvar, Vanek, and the rest of our companions. "What about everyone else? Do you think they made it out of here?"

"I hope so." With a slight clench of his jaw, he turns to me, his gaze full of concern. "The Emperor's lands border that of House S'tiran and

House G'alta. G'alta's border is much closer"—he points off to the right—"but I know for certain they are allies of the Emperor." He looks back to the left. "If we travel to S'tiran's lands, I am uncertain of their allegiance. We could be escaping one danger only to be walking into another."

"Then we should head for the border with S'tiran. At least there's a chance they might help us."

Instead of agreeing, he gives me a hesitant look.

"What's wrong?"

"It is many days' journey in either direction." His glowing green eyes study my body in concern. "Your people cannot go as long as mine without water, my Si'an T'kara. The heat of the sun may be more than your Terran physiology can handle. The sooner we reach one of the cities, the better."

I gently squeeze his hand. "We can't risk going somewhere that we know isn't safe. Even *if* it is closer."

His resigned expression tells me he knows that I'm right. To be honest, I'm worried, but I won't let him see it. The deserts on Terra are one of the most unforgiving places on my home world and, from everything I've learned of V'lora so far, I know its great desert plains are even more dangerous. T'sars and all manner of large predators roam this terrain. Even the v'rachs hunt the skies in the darkness. But we don't have a choice.

He lifts his gaze to the sky. "I do not know how long we have before the Emperor realizes something went wrong. Before he begins sending out ships to search for us." His eyes meet mine. "We have to leave. Now."

I take his hand and we start in the direction of House S'tiran's territory.

The dry wind moves across the sand, carrying a heavy blanket of dust that flows over the dunes and around the rocks like water. A soft hint of spice permeates the air, reminding me that despite how familiar this desert may seem to the ones of Terra, I am on an alien world.

The fine crimson grains are soft, and my feet sink deep with each step. My muscles burn with effort as the sun beats down relentlessly upon us. The air carries not even a hint of moisture as it whistles through the canyons.

I've read stories of people who were lost in the desert and remind myself that despite how desperate our situation is right now, it is not impossible to survive in a place like this. If the large predators of V'lora can make their homes here and thrive, so can we. It's all in the knowing of where to find water, shelter, and food.

Ryven did me a great service when he insisted on making me learn the secrets of V'lora's deserts. I watched several modules detailing how to survive in this harsh environment.

Although much of the terrain consists of the vast and great desert plains, we are fortunate that the area we crashed in has several rock formations and canyons spread throughout. There is water to be found in many of the caves, and roots that may be dug up and harvested for food if we grow desperate.

My grandfather loved to camp and taught us all about survival. He warned that most people who become stranded in the wilderness merely die of lost hope. They give up and, in doing so, their minds shut down completely. It is the ones who keep their wits about them that survive—the ones who never allow the possibility of failure to seep in and take hold of their thoughts.

We walk for what feels like an eternity. As the sun dips low on the horizon, Marek gently squeezes my hand to draw my attention and points up ahead. "We will shelter just beneath the top shelf of that stone formation."

With the promise of rest in sight, my body gets a second wind and I pick up my pace, taking advantage of my surprising burst of energy.

Unfortunately, it's much farther than it seems. I'm so exhausted I feel like I'm going to collapse. Night descends quickly, casting sinister shadows across the sand. It isn't long before I can barely see anything, relying on the pull of Marek's hand to guide my steps.

This is the worst time to have been stranded here. The larger of the twin moons is almost completely eclipsed, and the smaller one gives off only the barest of light. Marek stops abruptly and then turns to face me. His glowing eyes are the only thing I can make out in the dark. "We will have to climb."

"Climb?" I tilt my head back as if I can see where and how far up he's talking about, but it's useless. I'm essentially blind right now.

"Yes."

"I can't see where—"

"You will have to hold onto me."

Fear spikes through me but I push it back down, reminding myself that Marek can see very clearly with his superior night vision. He wouldn't suggest this if it weren't necessary; I trust him to keep us safe.

Carefully, he crouches low and guides me onto his back. He stands, and I realize we're missing something. "What about the emergency pack?"

"I will come back for it after I get you to the top."

Despite my trepidation, I nod. "Okay."

"Hold on tight," he whispers and then begins to climb.

With my legs wrapped tightly around his waist, it's hard not to hold just as firmly with my arms around his neck, but I don't want to choke him. The muscles of his form flex beneath me as we make our way up the rock. I thought it would be a strenuous journey for him, but there is little hesitation in his movements as he climbs.

When he finally reaches the top, he grips my forearm and gently pulls me around to face him. I barely move a muscle even after my feet touch down on hard stone. I'm worried I'll somehow lose my footing and tumble over an edge I cannot see. A few stray pebbles scrape beneath my shoe and I kick them away to make my footing more secure.

They roll and then clack against the stone. Their clicking noise as they tumble down the side seems to go on forever before it finally stops when they reach the ground. Sweat trickles down my spine and I swallow thickly.

The dry desert wind pulls at my form. It is much stronger now that we're up here. I close my eyes, breathing through pursed lips as a wave of panic threatens to consume me.

Marek must notice my trepidation because he pulls me tight to his chest. Brushing the hair back from my face, he tucks it behind my ear as he whispers soothingly. "I must go back for the emergency pack, but I will return quickly. You are safe up here from any predators. My vow."

Despite my determination to push down my fear, my voice quaver slightly as I ask, "What about v'rachs?"

"Reach up," he says softly.

With one arm wrapped around him, I cautiously extend the other above my head. The tips of my fingers brush against smooth, cool stone and a smile tilts my lips. "We're underneath a ledge?"

"Yes." He takes my hand and guides me a few more steps. Our footsteps echo softly, telling me we're in some sort of cavern. When we stop, he reaches our joined hands out before us until my fingers touch cold stone again. "Place your back to this wall, and you will be safe here while I climb down."

Panic twists in my gut. I don't want him to leave me here. And despite how easily he seemed to climb this rock, I'm terrified he could fall. But we don't have a choice. We need the emergency pack. Carefully I sit back against the smooth stone, reluctant to let go of him.

He raises my hand and places a kiss to my open palm. "I won't be long, my Elizabeth."

Unable to speak through my fear, I nod.

His footsteps begin to retreat, followed by a soft scraping noise against the stone and another cascading tumble of small rocks. I imagine him going over the edge to climb down. Without my vision, my sense of hearing seems to increase tenfold. I hold my breath, listening intently to every scrape or skid along the rock wall.

Even though I know he's strong, my pulse pounds in my ears as I wait for him, worried that he might lose his grip and fall to his death. Inhaling deeply, I blow out a frustrated puff of air. I hate feeling so helpless. Despite my attempt to remain calm, goosebumps prickle my flesh and the hair rises on the back of my neck when a low howl sounds in the distance followed by a chorus of several more. Those must be t'sars.

Marek's told me they hunt in packs. Although I've yet to see one up close, the images Taven and Marek showed me were more than enough to give me nightmares. Easily three times the size of a Terran panther, they have long sabretooth fangs, glowing green cat eyes, and dark scales that can change color to match their environment.

Pulling my knees to my chest, I wrap my arms around my ankles and breathe as shallow as possible, listening for any sign of Marek. The smaller of the twin moons seems almost anemic compared to Terra's one, casting barely enough light to even make out its shape in the sky.

A soft scuffle of rocks and dirt draw my attention. I recognize Marek's steps as he moves to my side. His warm hands cup my face before he presses a soft kiss to my lips and pulls me into his chest, wrapping his strong arms around me. His body is so warm against mine, I instinctively nestle against him. "The scent of your fear is strong, my Elizabeth. But I promise you, we are safe up here from any predators."

What he doesn't say, and what we both know, is that even if we're safe from the t'sars and the v'rachs, there is always a chance that the Emperor's guards could still find us here. As if in answer to my dark thoughts, Marek whispers, "The winds are strong. The sand has already covered our tracks from the pod."

I sag against him in relief. Just that simple act and my fatigue hits me like a giant wave. Barely able to keep my eyes open, I trace my hand up his arm and neck to gently cup his face. "Is there space to lay down?" I ask, because I haven't moved from this exact spot since he left me here. I was too nervous to explore in the dark and risk falling over the edge.

When he doesn't answer right away, I start to worry all over again. Wondering how high up we are and how narrow the ledge. Sensing my panic, he brushes the soft pad of his thumb across my cheek. "There is room. But first you must eat and drink something."

He rifles through the emergency pack and a moment later, places a bottle of water in one hand and a nutrient bar in the other. Eagerly, I drink from the container. The cool water quenches my parched throat. As soon as I realize I don't hear him doing the same, I hold out both items. "What about you, my love?"

His warm hands cover mine, gently pushing the water and food back to me. "I do not need them yet. I can go a few more days before I will have need of sustenance."

I've studied V'loryn anatomy. He's right, and I'm too tired to argue.

When I'm finished, he gently guides me to lay down beside him with the stone wall against my back so that he acts as a barrier between me and the edge of the ledge we are on. He pulls an emergency blanket from the pack and drapes it over my body, carefully tucking it around my form before settling in next to me.

I press myself into his solid warmth as he holds me close, no space between our bodies. Despite knowing the danger we're in, I can barely stay awake. "I love you, Marek."

"Eh'leh-na, my Elizabeth," he whispers. "Rest now while you can. I've got you."

Safe in his arms, I close my eyes and allow myself to succumb to my fatigue.

CHAPTER 24

MAREK

My Elizabeth falls asleep almost instantly in my arms. I hold her close to my body, glad that she feels secure enough to rest as she needs. We are safe here as long as the Emperor's guards do not find us.

We walked far today, but we have much farther to travel tomorrow. It will be at least several days to reach the edge of S'tiran's territory. From the rather small amount she drank, it is easy to guess that she is trying to ration our water. But it will run out long before we reach the city. Many of the caves have small natural springs. Although I dread entering one of the caverns for fear of finding a t'sar's den, I will eventually have to in order to replenish our supply.

A low growl drifts up from the ground and my body instinctively tenses. The t'sars know we are up here. Even now, they circle the towering rock, searching for any way to reach us. Closing my eyes, I focus on the padding of their footsteps as they scrape against the stone in an attempt to climb up. Flaring my nostrils, I scent the wind and determine there are at least five of them below us.

Although I know they cannot possibly climb something this steep, irrationally, I still fear for Elizabeth's safety. Violent images of claws and teeth raking across her petal-soft skin fill my mind. An involuntary shudder moves through me and I pull her closer into my chest. I wish I'd never brought her to V'lora. I knew the Emperor was a dangerous man.

My thoughts drift to Kalvar and everyone else. I can only hope they made it to safety.

～

As the morning light dawns along the far horizon, Elizabeth has not yet awoken. I am reluctant to wake her now that she is in such a deep sleep, but I must. The temperature dropped so low, she shivered most of the night despite the emergency blanket and the warmth from my body. Carefully, brushing the hair back from her face, I softly whisper her name. "Elizabeth?"

Her eyelids flutter and open, and she smiles warmly at me before she jerks up. The fog of her sleep lifted as she stares wide-eyed at our surroundings. "We're so high up," she says, her voice barely a whisper.

"It was the only way to be certain nothing could reach us, my Si'an T'kara."

Speechless as she gazes down to the ground below, she nods shakily in response.

I take the pack down first, not wanting to leave her alone at the bottom for fear of any lingering predators. When I climb back up to retrieve her and it's time to descend, her grip is much tighter around my neck than it was when we initially climbed but not tight enough to impair my breathing.

As we make our way down the rock wall, her anxiety taps at my mind through our faint connection like an insistent drum. My nostrils flare as the acrid scent of her fear floods my senses. I try my best to send her a wave of reassurance, but it is difficult. Fierce protectiveness fills me, and my claws and fangs extend as my body responds instinctively, wanting to protect her against any and all distress.

When we reach the bottom, she stares wide-eyed at the many footprints of the t'sars that were here last night. "There were so many of them," she whispers in shock more to herself than to me.

"We should be safe during the day," I reply, trying to assuage some of her worry. "They are nocturnal hunters."

She looks once more to the newly disturbed sand before turning her attention back to me. "Let's go."

Throwing the emergency pack over my shoulders, I take her hand in mine and we begin to walk.

Side by side, we make our way across the crimson sands in silence. I focus my senses on the environment around us, straining to listen for any sounds from a transport or predators. As my gaze sweeps across the desert, I pray the Emperor believes we are dead so that he does not search for us.

As the sun moves slowly overhead, beating down with its relentless heat I watch as she keeps a steady pace without complaint. Her fatigue seeps through the bond and I know she is at the limits of her exhaustion, but she refuses to stop for more than a few seconds at a time. Trying to ration our supplies, she stubbornly refuses to take any more than a few drinks of water and tiny bites of a nutrient bar.

My heart clenches at the determined look etched in her features. She is strong, my Si'an T'kara, but I know this environment tests her Terran physiology. Despite anticipating the answer to my question, I cannot help but ask just the same. I gesture to the closest rock formation and the shade it casts beside it. "Do you need to rest?"

∼

ELIZABETH

Marek asks me if I want to rest a moment. I want to. Desperately. But I know if we stop now, it will be that much harder to continue. "We should keep going."

He stops, halting my steps in the process. His eyes search mine in concern as he touches the back of his hand gently across my forehead and then against my cheek. He clenches his jaw. "We must. You are too warm; your skin is already turning red—burning from the sun."

His words conjure the memory of when I found out he believed a sunburn meant that Terran skin would peel away from the body, exposing the raw muscles and tissues beneath. A delirious laugh bubbles up from my throat, and he stares at me curiously.

When I notice the hint of worry that flashes behind his eyes, I shake my head softly. "I'm fine, Marek."

He gives me a firm look. "No, you are not. I refuse to go any farther until you at least drink some more water and eat a few bites of your nutrient bar."

Too exhausted to argue, I'm only half listening to his attempts to convince me to rest when something strange catches my attention over his shoulder. I squint my eyes, trying to determine what it is. Off in the distance, a dark wall stretches across the sky, blocking the sun. "What is that?"

His gaze follows mine and his eyes widen in unmistakable panic. "A sandstorm! It's moving fast! We must find shelter!"

He sweeps me up into his arms. Tucking me close to his chest, he races across the sand with the inhuman speed possessed of his people.

The wind whips around us, howling through the canyons. The sky darkens as the massive storm front draws closer. Coarse grains of sand scrape at my exposed skin, stinging my eyes.

"Cover your face!" Marek cries out.

I squeeze my eyes shut and press my head against his chest.

My pulse pounds in my ears, but it's quickly drowned out by the deafening roar of the storm as it approaches. Wind and sand claw at us both as I hold tightly to Marek. His intense panic floods across the bond, adding fuel to my own fear as he races to find shelter.

When we stop, it's so abrupt I feel as though I'll pitch forward from his arms. But he holds tightly to me, and as I look up from his chest, the world spins as he sinks to his knees and then onto his back, collapsing to the floor in a crumpled heap.

Panic grips me in an iron vise as I look down to see his eyes closed and his chest rising and falling rapidly as he struggles to catch his breath. "Marek!"

Unable to speak, he reaches his hand up weakly to take mine, projecting a wave of reassurance to me through the link. His exhaustion, an overwhelming force in the background that seems to echo my own.

It's dark in here and the air is still. This must be some sort of cave. The wind howls outside the entrance, forming an impenetrable dark wall of thick, swirling dust that blocks out the sun. Only the barest of light fills the space, but it's not coming from outside. Hundreds of L'sair crystals embedded in the rock emit a soft yellow-orange glow, illuminating the interior to reveal red sandstone walls that open up into a large, empty chamber.

A shimmering reflection along the back wall draws my attention, and I'm so exhausted I almost cry when I notice the small, clear pool bubbling up from the ground. A light mist of steam hovers just above the liquid surface. "Marek, there's water back here." I stand and start toward it, but he reaches up and grips my forearm, stopping me abruptly.

"Wait." His voice is an urgent whisper, a strange edge of caution in his tone. His nostrils flare. "There are t'sars here." In one fluid motion, he's on his feet and pulling me behind him. With his body crouched in a defensive position, he peers into the darkness at the back of the cave.

His body tenses, and my heart stops. The hairs rise on the back of my neck as a low growl rumbles through the cavern. Large glowing green eyes seem to float up ahead, staring at me intently. Cold fills me as the creature moves into the light.

Large fangs the length of my forearm drip with saliva as the t'sar bares its teeth in a feral snarl. With smooth, hairless black scales stretched taut over a menacing muscular form, it stalks toward us on silent paws. I've seen images of t'sars but they're even more terrifying up close, at least three times larger than the size of any panther or tiger I've ever seen on Terra.

Sweat trickles down my spine as two more move in behind the

first one, flanking it on either side as they move toward us with their heads lowered as if ready to charge at any moment.

Panicked, I palm the knife from my boot, slowly drawing it from its sheath. It may not be much against these creatures, but it's better than nothing.

My eyes track the closest one, and I draw in a shaking breath, trying to steel myself as its dark gaze holds mine intently.

It growls low in its throat, carefully approaching like a predator closing in on its prey while the other two move silently behind it. As they watch us, I can almost see the gears turning in their minds, studying us as if to determine how easily we can be defeated.

I ball my shaking hands into fists as I position myself in a defensive stance. The lead t'sar's eyes shift to me, and I know he thinks we will be easy prey.

Marek's eyes are black as he bares his fangs. A deep growl rumbles in his chest as his claws extend into sharpened points. In this moment, he looks every bit as terrifying and deadly as the predators before us.

I turn my attention back to the t'sars. No. Marek and I will not die today. I am certain of it.

Taking a small step to the side, Marek's voice is low as he extends his arms behind him, urging me to move back. "Elizabeth, stay behind me."

"We live together, or we die together," I reply in as even a voice as I can manage. "There are three of them. You cannot face this alone."

The lead t'sar lowers its head, its lips pulled back in a feral snarl, readying to charge. I spread my feet a bit farther apart, bracing myself for attack.

In an explosion of movement, the t'sars lunge forward as one, and the world shifts into slow motion as Marek takes the brunt of the attack, drawing away the first two.

The third one rushes me, and I spin to the side, slashing out with my knife and kicking out with my leg. My blade tears through flesh, and my foot connects with its body; it yelps out in surprise. I turn to face it again, readying myself for another charge. Blood trails down its chest as it gnashes its teeth and then rushes me again.

I feign to the left. but too late; it anticipates my movement and corrects its course. It swipes at me, catching my side. A pained cry rips from my throat as sharp claws rake across my abdomen, slamming me against the rock. Pain explodes through my body and I crumple to the ground.

A deafening roar splits the air; wind whips through the cave as a blur rushes past me, barreling into the t'sar.

So fast it doesn't have time to react, it's thrown back against the far wall.

I'm frozen in place as my mind struggles to register the scene before me. Marek's arms are wrapped around the t'sar in an iron embrace. It thrashes wildly in his hold, and I watch in horror as he opens his mouth and sinks his fangs deep into the thick cord of its neck.

Its loud cries die down to mere whimpers as it slowly begins to still, sinking to the floor while Marek holds it in place and drains it of its lifeblood. The glow fades from its eyes and its head lolls to the side just as Marek releases his grip, ripping his fangs from its throat.

When Marek lifts his gaze to mine, dark, feral obsidian orbs stare across at me, his fangs bared and dripping with blood.

The caustic burn of adrenaline still courses through my veins, and I don't know if that's why I'm shaking or if it's the shock of what I just witnessed. Off to the side, the bodies of the other two t'sars lie lifeless in the sand.

Instantly, Marek's eyes return to their normal glowing green and his expression is pained as he rushes toward me. Scooping me into his arms, he carries me to the water and gently lowers me to the ground.

His clothes are torn and stained dark with blood. Deep claw marks span almost the entire length of his arms and chest. I reach up to cup his cheek, wincing slightly as pain shoots through my body with the movement. "You're hurt, my love."

He shakes his head softly. Worry pulses through the bond between us as he stares down at my wounds. "The blood I consumed," he says softly. "My people are able to heal when we…" His voice trails off, but

I already know what he was going to say. Blood has restorative properties for V'loryns.

Looking down at my torso, I gasp. Five deep jagged lines, left by the t'sar's claws, span across my abdomen. Crimson blood pools at the site, and Marek removes what's left of his tunic to quickly wrap it around me.

I suck in a sharp breath, gritting my teeth in agony as he tightens it.

He stares down at me in panic. Placing his large hand over my abdomen, he lowers his head and closes his eyes.

"No!"

His head jerks up and he gives me a questioning look.

"You cannot use your energy to heal me, my love. You need your strength."

"But, Elizabeth, I cannot stand to see you like this. Not when I could heal you."

I place my finger to his lips to silence him. "We didn't see any signs of the other pods. We don't know if anyone else lived or if any help is coming. You need your strength. If I can't make the entire journey, you're the only one who can walk us out of here, Marek."

His hand trembles as his fingers flex weakly over my abdomen. Through the faint bond, I can feel him struggling to force himself to pull away. He shakes his head, tears gathering at the corners of his eyes. "You cannot expect me to let you suffer like this. I—I cannot do it. I love you too much, my Si'an T'kara."

I reach up to gently take his hand. "You cannot weaken yourself to heal me, Marek. You need your strength," I whisper. "You know I'm right, my love."

∼

MAREK

I know she is right, but I cannot stand to see her in pain. With a trembling hand, she reaches for me, threading her fingers through mine. It opens a small connection between us. Her love for me floods across the link, filling my body with warmth as she whispers softly in my mind. *"I will be all right, my love."*

Gently probing the bond between us, I know she is trying to hide the extent of her pain. Her ocean-blue eyes stare deep into mine, missing their usual spark. Resting my forehead gently against hers, I clench my jaw, angry at myself for not reacting sooner—for not intercepting the t'sar before it attacked her.

As if reading my mind, she shakes her head softly. "Don't blame yourself."

I blink several times in shock. Is the bond that strong between us now that she can sense even my closely shielded emotions? "Can you sense my thoughts?"

"I don't have to read your mind to know that you feel guilty when you shouldn't. It's not your fault, Marek."

My heart clenches at her words. She believes this, but I know otherwise. If I'd been faster, the t'sar would never have been able to harm her. I failed to keep her safe when she needed me.

She gently tugs at my arm for me to lie down with her. "We need to rest while we can."

Carefully, I lay down beside her, and she nestles against me. Wrapping myself protectively around her as she closes her eyes, I make sure to remain alert. We were fortunate to only have stumbled upon three t'sars. They usually live in much larger packs.

The storm still rages outside, but that does not mean we are safe. Staring at the mouth of the cave, I watch and listen for any sign of approaching predators. T'sars are the largest creatures in the desert, but they are not the only things that hunt among the dunes.

CHAPTER 25

MAREK

The morning light filters in through the mouth of the cave. The storm finally stopped at least three hours ago. It raged all through the night, and I worried for how long it might last. Some have been known to linger for days. We are fortunate it is already over.

Elizabeth is still asleep in my arms, and although I am loath to do so, I know I must wake her. Leaning forward, I gently nuzzle the back of her head.

She stirs softly, and when she turns in my arms to face me, she inhales sharply, banding her arm across her waist. Breathing through pursed lips, she struggles to sit up as she grits her teeth in pain.

Carefully, I help her the rest of the way, watching her in concern.

"I'm okay. Just a bit sore. But I'll be fine."

Everything inside me wants to argue that she's not. My fingers flex and extend at my sides with want to place my hands to her injury, to use the Balance to heal her. But I know that I cannot. To do so would render me unconscious for at least several hours, perhaps even an entire day, while my body recovers from the transfer of energy. I cannot afford to be vulnerable for that long. Not while the Emperor may be searching for us, and not with the ever-constant danger of lurking predators.

Slipping the pack over my shoulders, I reach out and take Elizabeth's hand in mine, gently helping her to her feet.

When we step outside, I squint as my vision adjusts to the bright assault of the harsh V'loryn sun. To my great relief there are no tracks indicating any nearby predators. But there is also hardly any wind, so our footprints will be easily visible in the sand if any transports are searching for us.

As tempting as it is to remain in the cave, we must take the risk of being discovered as we trek through the desert. My Si'an T'kara needs a Healer for her injuries.

∼

Time seems to move so slowly as we make our way across the sand. Through the bond, I can feel Elizabeth's determination as she struggles against her pain and fatigue. I offer several times to carry her, but she refuses.

When the sun begins its slow descent upon the horizon, I scan for any nearby place to shelter. Amid a sea of towering rocks, I choose the one that looks most difficult to climb, knowing that if it is hard for me, it would be even harder for any predators to reach us.

Elizabeth holds tightly to my back as I scale the cliff wall; her muscles tremble against my form as we make the climb. When we reach the top, I quickly locate a spot beneath a rock ledge to shelter beneath. I lead her away from the edge as we settle with our backs against a solid stone wall.

As the last rays of the sun sink beneath the crimson sand in the distance, the two moons rise above the desert, casting sinister shadows of creatures that begin to stir below, searching for prey. Most of them recognize my scent and know I am the superior predator, but there are some, like the t'sars, that would challenge me if they approached. So far, we have not come across any more of their kind since she was attacked, and for that I am immeasurably grateful.

As if sensing my thoughts, she looks up at me. "Thank goodness we haven't seen any more t'sars."

I nod but do not tell her that they are not the only things we need to fear in the desert. A pack of e'lans trail us. They have been for the past few days now. They are mostly scavengers, but I worry they will become hungry, desperate enough to attack. But so far, they keep to the shadows, waiting for us to weaken and become easy prey.

Terran night vision is poor compared to my people, and I am glad she cannot see the things that move across the dunes just below our shelter. She needs food and water, so I move to our pack to retrieve them.

"Marek?" She reaches her hand out to me, her eyes staring unseeing into the darkness.

"I am here," I whisper and move back to her side. Slipping my arms around her waist, I pull her into my lap as we settle against the back wall. Through our bond, I can sense the fear she tries to hide from me. It must be terrifying to be unable to see in the dark, and my heart clenches at how vulnerable she appears in this moment.

Taking her hand, I place the water container in her grasp. "You must drink, my Elizabeth."

She nods, and I frown when she takes only a few sips.

"You need more than that."

It is telling just how exhausted she must be, because rather than argue with me, as she normally would, she sighs and then takes another drink.

After she's finished, she leans into my chest. Her breath catches as she shifts slightly, and I bite back my frustration that I cannot heal her. Brushing the hair back from her face, I place a soft kiss to her temple. "I must tend to your injuries, my Si'an T'kara."

Reluctantly, she nods and then moves off my lap. Carefully unwinding the cloth from her torso, I clench my jaw as my gaze travels over the red, inflamed skin along the jagged edges of her wounds.

I tear a piece of cloth from my ever-shrinking undershirt and dampen it with water to cleanse the deep crimson marks on her flesh. In this moment, I curse my people's ability to heal ourselves so efficiently. It is because of this that our emergency packs do not contain healing gels like the ones I've seen in Doc's medical kit.

"It doesn't hurt so bad anymore," she says. But as I run the damp cloth across her skin, it doesn't escape me the way her hands ball up into fists at her side as she grits her teeth silently in pain.

Despite our best efforts to protect her from the sun's burning rays, her delicate skin is now redder than I've ever seen it before. It is peeling in many places and her normally soft, pink lips are dry, cracked, and bleeding. Dipping a piece of cloth into the water, I gently run it across her mouth to soothe the damaged flesh and my heart clenches as a small sigh of relief escapes her. It is her wounds that concern me most, however. She has assured me that her people are slow to heal, but I worry that they do not heal faster.

She takes my hand and gives me a weak smile. "It's already starting to feel better."

She is trying to be brave for me and it is breaking my heart.

After I rewrap her wounds, I lay down beside her and she snuggles against me, resting her hand trustingly over my chest. Shuddering inwardly, I think of the shock on her face when I killed the t'sar. Although she has seen me kill before, I worried she would be afraid of me when I reached for her. But she has not shown any fear since then.

CHAPTER 26

MAREK

We have been walking the desert for five days. The harsh rays of the sun beat down upon us as we move across the dunes. She holds my arm for support, still refusing to allow me to carry her. She wants me to save my strength, even though I have more than enough compared to her.

My Si'an T'kara is strong. Although her body may be weaker than mine, her strength of will is far greater than many of my people. I've seen males injured during training cry out in agony, insisting they could not move or go on, and their wounds were not even half as bad as hers. And yet, she does not complain, blinking back tears each night when I cleanse her wounds.

I point up ahead. "We can shelter at that next formation."

She grips my arm as her steps begin to falter. Abruptly, she stops, tugging at my hand as she does.

I spin to face her. Something…an emotion I cannot quite place slowly filters through our connection despite her desperate attempt to hold it back. Concerned, I cup her chin, tipping her face up to mine.

Ocean-blue eyes stare up at me and I still. It is despair that I sense from her.

Gone is the light that so brilliantly defines her luminous gaze, replaced by a tired and worn expression that I've never seen on her before. Panic steals my breath as I place my hands on either side of her face, studying her in concern. "Elizabeth, are you—?"

The words die in my throat as her knees give out. Catching her before she falls, I scoop her into my arms. With one hand behind her back and the other under her knees, I lift her smaller form, cradling her to my chest.

Her eyes snap open, and she looks up at me with a pained expression. "I'm sorry. Put me down. I can—"

Her pain and exhaustion bleed through our bond as I hold her tight against me. "No. I will carry you."

She opens her mouth as if to resist but closes it again and gives me a small nod. As I walk, she tucks herself close to my chest, resting her head under my chin.

That she allows me to do this without protest tells me she feels much worse than she has let on. I do not need to probe the connection between us to know that she is trying to protect me with false reassurances that she is well. If it were just me out here, I would not worry so much about survival. I can go several more days without food or water before my body will begin to feel the effects. She cannot, and it is not her fault. Her species is different from mine. If we do not find help soon, I worry she will die.

As the sun begins to set, a faint glimmer of light catches my eye in the distance. Hope fills me. Increasing my pace, I squint my eyes against the harsh glare of the last rays of the sun and study the glowing horizon a moment more before deciding that it is indeed a sign of civilization.

I lean down and gently nuzzle the top of her head. "Elizabeth, look."

Her eyes blink open and she stares up at me in confusion a moment before turning her head. "Are those—"

A smile tugs at my lips. "Yes."

"How far away do you think it is?"

"If we do not stop tonight, we should reach it before dawn."

Her brow creases into a slight frown. "But you need to rest. You can't carry me all day *and* all night."

"I can and I will," I state firmly.

"But—"

"No," I snap. "You need a Healer, and I will not stop until we reach one. I swear it to the stars. My vow."

CHAPTER 27

MAREK

My muscles burn in protest as I continue on through the night, but I refuse to stop. I scent a pack of e'lans behind us, but they are far enough away that they are not a concern. For now.

Elizabeth has grown quiet, drifting in and out of consciousness over the last few hours. She needs a Healer. Desperately.

My thoughts drift again to Kalvar and Ryven. I wonder where they are. If Kalvar and I had the familial bond between us, I'd know for certain if he were alive. For a moment, irrational panic grips me at the thought of him and Ryven dead, but then I realize they are both V'loryn and, like myself, much better suited to surviving the desert. Despite not having the familial bond between us, the emotional connection that Kalvar and I do share tells me that he is alive and I will see him again.

I do not know what we will face when we reach the city. House S'tiran has never had clear loyalties. They are known for choosing whichever side they believe will benefit them most. Once we're discovered, K'Sai L'Mira may order us arrested and turn us over to the

Emperor immediately. But I have no choice. We cannot stay hidden in the desert. Elizabeth's health is failing, and she needs a Healer. I can only hope that when we arrive, we will be received as friends instead of enemies.

~

When we reach the outskirts of the city, I'm on the verge of collapse. As I glance down at my Si'an T'kara, fear ripples through me. Although she is breathing, her quiet stillness worries me.

I dart a quick glance at my clothing and am glad it is still night. Until I know for certain of House S'tiran's loyalties, we must remain hidden. I will not risk Elizabeth's safety by delivering her into the hands of my enemies. It matters not that she is not V'loryn. If S'tiran is allied with the Emperor, they are just as likely to kill her as they are to take her prisoner.

Removing what's left of my undershirt, I cover Elizabeth as much as I can, making sure to hide her Terran features and red hair. Holding her tightly to my chest, I quietly slip into a narrow alleyway behind a row of houses.

The cobbled roads of the city are in a terrible state of disrepair. The loose stones make it difficult to move with any kind of stealth. I'd heard that S'tiran's cities were run down, but I never expected this level of neglect. The houses and shops appear as worn as the streets. Many of them with broken windows and poorly patched roofs. It appears that rumors of their Great House caring very little for their people must be truth.

A small beam of light cuts through the darkness, and Elizabeth's eyes slowly blink open and closed as she looks up at me, placing a hand against my chest. "Are we safe?" she whispers.

Through the soft touch of her skin upon my own, not only can I feel her lifeforce beginning to fade, but from the transfer of heat from her body I recognize the fever burning through her from the infected wounds. I have to find somewhere to hide so I may heal her. She cannot continue like this. "Not yet, my Elizabeth. I will—"

The words die in my throat as a female steps directly into our path. Unaware, at first, of our presence she bends down to pick up a box but stops abruptly to spin toward us.

Her sharp intake of breath fills me with panic. Her eyes dart to Elizabeth and then back to me, having made the connection. "T'Hale Marek?"

Ice floods my veins. She knows exactly who we are. Curling my arms even tighter around Elizabeth, I gather her closer to me as I hold the female's gaze, uncertain if I should run or remain still, hoping that she is an ally and not my enemy.

A male's voice calls out behind me, and every muscle tenses; I'm ready to race away if I must.

She motions to the open door beside her. "Here," she whispers. "You may shelter in my home. Hurry."

Everything inside me is telling me to run. But the fact that Elizabeth doesn't even respond makes the decision for me. I have no option but to trust this female. My Si'an T'kara needs healing.

Moving to the side to allow us entrance, she quickly shuts and seals the door behind us. A tiny gasp draws my attention to a small V'loryn child no more than five cycles old. His glowing green eyes stare transfixed on Elizabeth, his mouth gaping open. "What is she?"

"My mate." The words escape my lips before I even realize I've said them aloud.

He gives me a curious look. "But why does she look so different?"

"Tyvek," his mother's voice calls sharply behind me, and he goes ramrod straight as his head snaps toward her.

"Yes, Mother?"

"Seal the front door and darken the windows."

He cocks his head to the side. "But—"

She cuts him off abruptly. "Just do as I say."

Her sharp gaze darts briefly to mine before she steps forward and motions for me to follow her.

"You will help us?" I ask cautiously as I trail behind her.

She leads us to a small room with a bed. From the various toys strewn throughout and the child-size table and chairs, I can only assume this must be Tyvek's room. "Yes," she replies. "I am M'Rena. You may rest here." She gestures to the bed.

Carefully, I lay Elizabeth down, fighting the panic rising when she barely stirs as I settle her atop the blanket. As I begin to pull away, her small hand grips my forearm tightly. Her eyes snap open, and my heart clenches when I notice their luminous spark is still missing. Her skin is dry and reddened; her lips are cracked and peeling. "Don't go," she whispers softly.

I kneel beside her, pressing my forehead gently to hers. "I won't leave you, my Si'an T'kara. My vow."

Still holding onto Elizabeth, I glance back over my shoulder. "Water. Please. She needs water."

"Of—of course," M'Rena stumbles over her words.

The slight scuffle of retreating footsteps follows a moment later.

As my gaze scans the room, I'm struck by how sparse and bare it is. Everything here seems so run down...dilapidated. Strange. This should not be so. As I think back on the state of the streets when we entered the city, I realize every location we passed was the same. All of it in various states of decay, as if nothing has been properly maintained. I've heard rumor that House S'tiran hoards food, credits, and water meant for their people, but I did not believe it was truth until now.

The female returns a moment later with her son in tow. "Here." She moves beside me and offers me a glass of water. The way she stares at it as I take it from her hand tells me it is a rare and precious commodity, confirming my suspicions about House S'tiran.

"Thank you."

Turning my focus back to Elizabeth, I carefully help her to sit up. "Here is water, my Si'an T'kara. You must drink."

She nods weakly as I press the cup to her lips. Taking only small sips at first, she soon begins taking larger gulps. After finishing one glass, the female quickly pours her another, and she drinks that one too.

When she twists on her side to sit up even more, a sharp hiss of pain escapes her lips as she bands her arm across her torso.

Carefully peeling back the makeshift wrap, I clench my jaw when I see the angry red marks that mar her delicate skin.

M'Rena inhales sharply behind me. "She needs a Healer."

Turning to face her, I meet her eyes evenly. "House S'tiran. Tell me. Are they aligned with the Emperor?"

My gaze never leaves hers as I wait for her answer. If S'tiran is on our side, we are saved. If they are not…

"Yes."

My heart sinks.

"K'Sai L'Mira has pledged the support of House S'tiran and all its forces to the Emperor."

Fierce protectiveness rushes through me and I move to place myself between M'Rena and Elizabeth. My gaze shifts to the door and I inwardly brace myself, waiting to hear the impending sound of heavy-booted steps at any moment. I should never have brought my Si'an T'kara here.

She continues. "Everyone believes you are dead. Including T'Hale Kalvar."

My head snaps toward hers. "Kalvar is alive?"

"Yes. He and T'Hale Vanek of House A'msir have joined with K'Sai Milena of House L'eanan and declared war on the Emperor and any who ally themselves to him."

"I must get word to them. Please, I need to—"

She shakes her head. "There are no communications allowed to leave this city, aside from government and military channels."

Standing to my full height, I meet her eyes evenly. "Will you turn us in?"

A strange look of shock flickers briefly across her features. "Never. You are the heir of House D'enekai. The one who should be on the throne." Her eyes shift to Elizabeth. "And *she* is the one foretold in the ancient tomes, is she not?" Conviction burns in her gaze as she turns her attention back to me. "One of the Great Uniters that signals the end of the Emperor's reign."

I give her the only answer I can. "The High Omari believes that she is."

"And you?" She gives me a wary look. "What do you believe?"

With a slight clench of my jaw I give her my truth. "She is my Si'an T'kara. Of that, I am certain. But I have never wanted war, and I have no desire to rule. I only wish to live a life of peace with my bondmate."

My words seem to please her as she dips her chin in a slight nod. "The greatest rulers in our people's history have been those who had no thirst for power and yet bore the burden of rule in pursuit of peace." She bows slightly. "You are safe here."

I narrow my eyes as I study her, still suspicious of her intent. "I must heal her."

She gives me an earnest look. "I vow that I am not your enemy, T'Hale Marek."

A light touch on my back draws my attention behind me to Elizabeth. I spin to face her, kneeling before her as I brush the hair back from her face and then cup her cheek. "What is it, my Si'an T'kara?"

"She could have exposed us when we were outside, Marek. But she didn't."

Reluctantly, I nod. She is right. M'Rena could have turned us in then. She recognized me the moment she first saw us.

Elizabeth takes my hand in hers, opening a small connection between us. Her mind whispers to mine. *"We will trust but we must stay alert and cautious."* Her blue eyes hold mine a moment before she turns to M'Rena. "Where is your cleansing room?"

"Just down the hallway," M'Rena says. "Last door on the left."

Carefully, I lift Elizabeth off the bed.

～

Standing under the cleansing unit, I hold Elizabeth in my arms. My skin tingles slightly as the ion cleanser pulses around us. I only wish there was actual water for the shower, but from what I've gathered about our surroundings, such a use of water would be a luxury in this place.

Elizabeth looks up at me. "There are several exits," she whispers, her eyes shifting to the door. "Just in case we need them."

My lips quirk up slightly at the edges as I gaze down at her. My Si'an T'kara is wise. Even injured and exhausted beyond measure, her mind is still sharp. "I took note as we made our way here," I inform her.

"I am well enough to stand," she offers, and I tighten my hold on her form.

"Not until—" The words die in my throat as she places a finger to my lips to silence me.

She gives me a pained look. "I know that you want to use the Balance to heal me, my love. But we cannot risk it." She cups her hand to my cheek. "You are exhausted, Marek. You haven't slept longer than a few hours in the past several days."

She is right, but that does not matter. I shake my head. "We cannot allow your wounds to grow worse. You already have fever."

We change into the clean clothing left by M'Rena and then make our way back to the small room. I gently lay Elizabeth down on the bed. M'Rena and Tyvek enter a moment later with more water and a small tray of food. She places the food on a table beside us, bowing slightly as she does. "I apologize, T'Hale. This is the best I could find." She gestures to the pitiful protein supplements.

"It is more than enough," I assure her as I take one and hand it to Elizabeth, encouraging her to eat.

My heart stops, and I still as booted steps sound down the hallway. Stepping protectively in front of Elizabeth, I spin to face the door. A low growl of warning escapes my throat, and my claws and fangs extend into sharpened points as a male moves into the entryway. My eyes rake over his form as I ready to strike. He is dressed in the guard's uniform of House S'tiran, and from his strong build I know my exhaustion will make it difficult to defeat him.

M'Rena has betrayed us.

The male's eyes widen as they meet mine in shock.

"Father!" Tyvek shouts.

I retract my claws and fangs as Tyvek rushes to greet the male.

M'Rena moves beside him, gesturing to me and Elizabeth. "Kovan," she says evenly, "this is—"

"T'Hale Marek," he finishes her sentence. His eyes are still fixed on mine in a look of disbelief as the words escape his mouth in barely a whisper, "Everyone believes you are dead."

Instead of answering him, I narrow my eyes. "You are a member of House S'tiran's guard."

He nods and then cranes his neck just enough to look at Elizabeth behind me. His jaw drops as he stares at her a moment before quickly snapping it shut. "I—I vow to the goddess that I will not harm you. Either of you."

I give him a wary look. "You will help us then?"

"Yes," he replies earnestly. "In any way that I can."

I study him a moment, trying to determine if he speaks truth. Although I can see no hint of deception in his eyes, I am hesitant to trust him. He is, after all, a member of House S'tiran's guard. The markings on his shoulder tell me he is not among the higher ranks. "You are a member of the House Guard. Why do you offer to help us?"

He steps forward, his gaze darting briefly to Elizabeth and then back to me. "You are the heir of House D'enekai—the only living son of the Great K'Sai L'Nara and T'Hale Toven who sacrificed their lives to save their people. Even if this were not so, everyone on V'lora saw the vidcam footage of you using the Balance to restore the life of your Si'an T'kara. At that moment, there was no doubt that you have been blessed by the Goddess herself and she"—he points to Elizabeth—"is one of the Great Uniters foretold in the Ancient Tomes of the Saraketh." He pauses. "There are many who are angered that your choice was the catalyst that has led us to war, and not all who would meet you would render you aid. But I am honored that the Goddess chose my family to help you. And we will do whatever we can to see you safely returned to your House."

After so many days of walking in the desert and very little sleep, fatigue threatens to overwhelm me, and I turn my attention back to Elizabeth. If I am to heal her, I must do so now. Before I collapse.

I look to Kovan and M'Rena. "I need to heal my Si'an T'kara. But the Balance takes a toll on my body when I do so."

Kovan steps forward. "You have my vow that I will protect you with my life."

I'm barely able to keep my eyes open, and I realize that I have no choice but to trust their word that they will not turn us in. Elizabeth's wounds are worse. The infection has already settled in the tissue surrounding her injury. A quick glance around the room reminds me that there is nothing I may draw energy from to heal her. I must hope that my lifeforce is enough.

Exhausted, I drop to my knees before my Si'an T'kara and carefully peel back her bandage. The deep, jagged red lines that mar her flesh stand out in sharp contrast to the purple and discolored bruising on her skin from where she slammed against the rock wall. Kovan's voice sounds out behind me. "What did this?"

I look back at him. "A t'sar."

He blinks several times in shock as his eyes rake over Elizabeth in disbelief. "We have heard their bones are like glass. How did she survive?"

Elizabeth clears her throat as she stares up at him with pursed lips. "We are not as fragile a species as your people believe."

Her V'loryn is perfect, without even the slightest hint of an outsider's accent, and I watch as a stunned expression crosses his face. A hint of a smile tugs at my lips as her agitation pulses weakly through the bond. My Si'an T'kara may be physically injured, but her fiery spirit is still intact.

His cheeks flush light green in embarrassment. "Forgive me," he tells her. "I have never met your kind before, and I realize now that much of what I've heard is probably rumor. If you require anything, please let us know."

Drawing in a deep breath, I struggle against a wave of overwhelming fatigue. I give him a subtle nod and then turn back to Elizabeth. Placing my palm over her abdomen, she gives me a pained smile and then places her hands over mine.

Too tired to care if Kovan and M'Rena are still here in the room, I bow my head and begin.

Through the touch of my palm over her bare skin, the connection flares brightly between us. Swirling currents of energy flow from the tips of my fingers and join with the beating pulse of hers.

Squeezing my eyes shut, I focus on the ebb and flow of the lifeforce that moves through her body. Fire builds and then burns along every nerve ending as my mind connects with hers. Her wounds are a raw and unshielded force that stabs at my consciousness. Absorbing her pain, I make it my own as I strengthen her with the lifeforce that flows within me.

I sense the moment she feels me growing weaker; she begins to pull away, not wanting to take what I offer her freely. Enveloping her mind in warm layers of soothing comfort, I whisper, *"Allow me to heal you, my Si'an T'kara. Please, do not pull away."*

Creating a shared construct to tether her consciousness to, I walk toward her on the beach. Waves lap gently on the shores of our combined thoughts as I wrap my arms around her, pulling her close.

Her luminous ocean-blue eyes, even bluer than the ocean beside us, stare up into mine as she reaches up to cup my cheek. *"I can feel how much you are taking from yourself to give to me, my love. You must stop."*

"You are mine, and I am yours." I whisper as I gently press my lips to hers. *"I would give you everything I am just to make you whole."*

CHAPTER 28

ELIZABETH

His words wash over me like a gentle caress as his glowing green eyes stare down at me full of reverent devotion. In them, I see the truth. He *would* give everything to me and more, no matter the cost to himself. *"Marek, I—"*

A sharp cry pierces the air around us. The construct shatters, and I'm ripped from the connection.

Rough hands pull at my arm, and my eyes snap open to find a stranger staring down at me. "What is wrong with him? Why will he not wake?"

I jerk up from the couch, spinning so that Marek's unconscious form is behind me. "Who are you?"

From the pattern of his clothing, I recognize this man as one of House S'tiran's guards, just like Kovan. Fear snakes down my spine, but I force myself into a defensive stance as I hold his gaze.

His eyes widen slightly as they meet mine in a look of undisguised shock before he retrains his expression into an impassive mask once more. "I am Aemar, and this"—he looks over his shoulder to another guard standing sentry—"is Garen. By order of the K'Sai of House S'tiran, we are to bring you to her immediately."

Despite my panic, I notice something odd about the way he says these words. Very loud and perfectly enunciated as if he's speaking them in a manner so as to be overheard outside of this room.

"No." I level a dark glare at him. "We will not go with you."

He darts another glance over his shoulder to Garen, and something passes between them as they both give a subtle nod before Aemar turns back to me. He leans forward slightly and then speaks in a low voice. "We have no choice. K'Sai L'Mira requested that you be brought to her dead or alive. And...Garen, Kovan, and I would prefer that you both live."

His words shock me.

He continues. "There are others with us, just outside the house, who would wish otherwise."

Desperate, I look down at Marek, placing my hand over his and then lift my gaze to Aemar. "Please, help us escape then."

Something akin to guilt flashes behind his eyes. "I would, but then we would all die, including Kovan's family," he explains. "The best I can do is make sure that many see you are both still alive before we take you to the K'Sai. We will do all we can to help you escape, but it cannot be done now."

I turn a sharp gaze to Kovan standing off to the side but direct my question to Aemar. "How did you find us?"

Kovan steps forward. "Our neighbor. He must have seen you. He reported his suspicions that you were here." He looks to Aemar. "We train together, so he made certain his regiment responded to investigate my home."

Fear wars with uncertainty as I stare deep into his eyes, studying his expression to search for any hint of a lie even as part of me realizes that I don't have any choice but to trust them.

As if reading my intent, he pulls a small blaster from his belt and holds it out to me.

Worried this may be a trap, I cautiously take it from him.

"Keep it hidden and use it only if there is no other option."

My gaze never leaves his as I tuck the blaster into the waistband of my pants, beneath my tunic.

"Forgive me, but I must bind your hands."

Swallowing against the knot of worry in my throat, I turn back to Marek, placing my hands on either side of his face as I rest my forehead against his. It breaks my heart how defenseless he is…and all because of me. "Eh'leh-na, my love," I whisper against his lips.

When I turn back to Aemar, I find him watching me with an indiscernible expression. I lift my hands to him, and he binds them loosely. This is either an elaborate trap of some kind, or he's telling the truth and really does intend to help us. Only time will tell, and I steel myself as I wait for the verdict to play out.

Aemar nods to Garen and Kovan, and they both move to Marek, carefully lifting his limp form from the bed. Carrying him, they lead me out the front door.

When we step outside, I'm shocked by the large crowd that has gathered here. Curious stares greet me as an audible gasp comes from somewhere among the people.

"It is truth," a voice says in a hushed whisper.

"T'Hale Marek and his betrothed are alive," another says.

One of the outside guards moves toward me, his gaze cold as he looks to Kovan and Aemar. "You were instructed to cover their faces," he whispers in a voice so low, I'm almost certain no one else can hear him. "Now, everyone has seen them."

Kovan meets his eyes evenly. "Forgive me. It was difficult to restrain the Terran. As you are aware, they are very fragile, and it was challenging to bind her hands without causing her injury."

"What does it matter?" the guard snaps. "The K'Sai said she wanted them dead or alive." A low growl rumbles in his chest as he looks at Kovan, eyeing him suspiciously. "How is it they were in your home and you were unaware?"

Kovan glares at him, pretending offense at the question. "I tried to call several times to inform the authorities once I discovered them. But, as you know, communications are not functioning properly ever since we cut off contact with those outside S'tiran's holdings."

A small puff of air escapes the guard in a huff as he turns his attention to me. "If it wasn't for you," he says accusingly, "our people would not be at war right now."

Indignation burns through me. "House D'enekai did nothing to provoke the Emperor. The si'an'inamora is a blessing from the Goddess herself that the Emperor refuses to accept," I state loudly, using the power of their beliefs as a weapon.

It works.

A voice cries out from the crowd. "Release them!"

It's followed by another. "They have been blessed by the Goddess. You must let them go!"

Soon a chorus of voices is echoing similar sentiments as the guard roughly motions us into the transport.

I move closer to Marek's unconscious form and carefully brush the hair back from his brow. Several other guards file into the transport and it doesn't escape me that Kovan, Garen, and Aemar sit between us and the rest of them as if forming a protective barrier.

The viewscreen is so dark, I can't see anything outside. We arrive at our destination and I'm shocked when we exit the transport into a nearly pitch-black room. I blink several times, trying to adjust my vision to the dim lighting. I reach over and take Marek's hand in mine as he's carried out by the guards. Even though he's still unconscious, I'm hoping he'll be able to sense me somehow.

We move rather quickly. I don't think these guards know my people have such terrible night vision compared to theirs, and I'm not about to give myself away. So, I walk as confidently as I can beside my beloved.

Several pairs of glowing green eyes watch us as we pass—like disembodied spirits floating in the darkness—as the guards lead us down a long hallway. Aside from the sound of our footsteps, this place is eerily quiet. There's just enough light that I can barely make out the shapes in front of me aside from the back of another guard as he leads us presumably to the K'Sai.

Kovan and Aemar walk beside me, carrying Marek on some sort of hovering stretcher device. I hold even tighter to him, making certain

JESSICA GRAYSON

we are not separated. Despite my worry, I train my expression into a stoic mask, like a V'loryn. I don't know what awaits us when we reach K'Sai L'Mira, but I refuse to show her my fear.

The guards in front stop abruptly. A soft hiss of air fills the silence as something shifts just in front of us. I realize only a second later that it's a door opening, because when we step through, the sound of our footsteps changes and we're plunged into total darkness. The echo is even louder now, so it must be a huge, cavernous space we've just entered. A pair of glowing eyes stare up ahead in the darkness, and I inhale sharply as they race toward me with inhuman speed.

They stop just in front of my face. My pulse pounds in my ears. "Leave us," a voice rasps, the breath so close it fans across my forehead.

The hairs rise on the back of my neck as the glowing eyes stare down at me and then disappear in a blink. A light whisper of sensation skates across my cheek. Despite my fear, I tilt my chin up defiantly.

A lock of my hair lifts away from my face and I turn in that direction, as if I could see who is there. But everything is pitch black and I can already guess at who it is.

The deep sound of a man's voice practically purrs in my ear. "You are different than I imagined."

I'm wrong. This isn't the K'Sai.

Drawing in a deep breath, I steel myself. "Let us go," I state firmly. "Return us to House D'enekai."

"Yes," the voice answers. "I have heard you are brave."

"Who are you?"

"Niren, heir of House S'tiran. My mother, the K'Sai, is indisposed at the moment."

Niren? His name sounds familiar, and I realize why. He is the man that the Elders wanted to betroth L'Tana to, but she refused him. A sharp sting rakes across my cheek and I gasp, instinctively jerking away from the unexpected pain. I reach up to touch the site, and my fingers smear over something wet and warm as the scent of iron touches my nostrils.

"It is truth. Your skin is paper thin." He pauses. "How does he keep from harming you, I wonder?" A soft tsk sounds beside me, and I move closer to Marek placing myself between him and Niren. "I suppose I will never get to ask him this question."

My veins fill with ice, and I glare into the darkness. "Your people have seen us. They know we're alive. It's only a matter of time before this information reaches Kalvar. If you harm us, how long do you think he will let you live once D'enekai, A'msir, and L'eanan have won the war?"

Silence greets my question, but I know I have his attention.

I continue, "I am certain it will be the end of your line and your House once Kalvar finds out that you played a hand in his nephew's death."

Glowing green eyes snap open in front of me. After being in complete darkness for so long, even that minimal amount of light affords me the terrifying sight of his angular face; his fangs extended as he growls low in his throat, looking every bit as terrifying as the ancient vampire myths of old. "Guards!" he calls out in a booming voice and then turns his attention back to me. "You and your Si'an T'karan," he says the last words in a mocking lilt, "will be taken somewhere to rest while I decide what to do with you."

The soft whooshing sound of the doors opening is followed quickly by booted steps and several pairs of glowing eyes as they walk toward us.

A small thread of light filtering in from the open doors allows me to just barely make out Kovan's features. "This way," he says.

As we make our way down a long hallway, I'm able to see the shapes of only a few of the other guards around us, but I listen carefully, trying to determine how many others are nearby. I want to say something to Kovan, but I don't know who else is here and I cannot expose his vow to help us.

After walking in the near darkness for what feels like forever, we stop abruptly. A soft glow zips before us in the outline of a door that suddenly disappears into the wall. Light pours in as soon as it opens. I blink my eyes several times as my vision adjusts.

JESSICA GRAYSON

We step into a small room. Sparsely furnished, it contains only one bed and a chair. The soft light of the morning dawn filters in through the single window across from us. Kovan and Aemar bring Marek inside and gently place him on the bed near the wall.

I open my mouth to speak but stop abruptly as Kovan interrupts. "We will return with food and water shortly."

Without hesitation, he and Aemar disappear back out into the hall, sealing us in. I move to the doorway and run my hands over the panel, but it won't open, and I suspect we've been locked in here under the orders of Niren.

Palming my blaster beneath my tunic to reassure myself that it's still there, I walk over to Marek and sit on the edge of the bed. As tired as I am, I will not fall asleep. I must keep watch until he awakens.

~

MAREK

As my mind slowly comes back into awareness, I reach out to Elizabeth through our connection. Uncertainty along with a strong undercurrent of fear flow through our faint bond. My eyes snap open and I jerk up from the bed to find Elizabeth sitting beside me.

She spins toward me and then throws her arms around my neck. "Marek, thank god you're awake.

I scan the room behind her, and nothing is even remotely familiar. "Where are we?"

She pulls back slightly, and my gaze is immediately drawn to her cheek. I reach out to trace my fingers across a small red line with dried blood that stains her otherwise smooth skin. She places her hand over mine. "Niren," is all she says in way of explanation. "We're prisoners in House S'tiran."

Anger rushes through me as Elizabeth explains how we got here and her conversation with K'Sai L'Mira's son. I curl my hands in to fists at my side. I will end him for touching her.

The doors whoosh open, and Kovan appears. His eyes widen

when they meet mine before he retrains his expression into a stoic mask. "Thank the goddess you are awake," he says. His gaze darts to Elizabeth and then back to me. "You know what has happened?"

I nod and then meet his gaze evenly. "You must help us get out of here."

"I have a plan."

~

Kovan's plan is sound, but I worry for him if the K'Sai and Niren find out that he aided our escape. "You should come with us. I do not know what L'Mira may do if she finds out you helped us."

He shakes his head softly. "It is a risk I must take. I cannot leave M'Rena and Tyvek. My punishment, if I were to go missing, would extend to my family. But if I remain and they suspect me of anything, it is only *I* who would suffer any consequences."

Reluctantly, I nod. He is right; he cannot risk his family to House S'tiran's wrath.

Elizabeth squeezes my hand, her concern for Kovan and his family bleeding across the tenuous connection between us as she looks to Aemar and Garen. "What about your families?"

Garen's expression softens as he looks to her. "Thank you for your concern, but we are unbonded and...we have no family."

Aemar hands Elizabeth and me each a guard's cloak to shield our appearance and a pair of boots. They turn their back as she changes into my tunic to mask her scent as much as possible.

When Elizabeth pulls the cloak over her shoulders and then stands, it is obvious to see the clothing is much too large for her Terran form. And as she steps into the boots, her gait is awkward despite the material we've stuffed into the toes to help with her balance. But there is nothing we can do for it now. As if sensing my worry she places her hand over my own. "It's all right, Marek. Kovan says we don't have far to go. I'll be fine."

Aemar stares at her uncertainly, but after a moment, resignation flashes across his face as he realizes what I already have. There is no other choice. We'll either make it, or we won't.

Kovan turns toward the door, but I place a hand on his shoulder, stopping him. He looks back at me with a puzzled look. "Thank you for all your help. May the Goddess bless your path."

He inclines his head in solemn acknowledgment of my words and then leaves.

Aemar steps forward. "We must go. Now."

When we step out into the hallway, we're plunged back into darkness as soon as the door seals behind us, cutting off the minimal light from the window in the room.

Elizabeth's eyes blink several times as if trying to adjust. Her expression betrays nothing. When I take her hand in my own, despite the fear that I sense, her steeled determination is the stronger of her emotions as it flows across the link.

We debated several times whether to bring a light for my Si'an T'kara but decided it would draw too much attention if we ran into anyone else. According to Kovan, this is how L'Mira always keeps her House. Only the natural lighting from the sun ever brightens the exterior rooms.

I wonder if it is because her House may be heavily in debt as we've long suspected. L'sair crystals may be plentiful on V'lora, but they are not inexpensive. Perhaps S'tiran sells or hoards what they mine instead of using any for the upkeep of their House and lands. Thinking back on the decaying state of the city surrounding her home, this theory makes sense.

As we make our way down several different hallways, we are mindful of our stride as Elizabeth struggles to keep up in her ill-fitted footwear. Bootsteps echo up ahead, but we maintain our pace. There is nowhere to hide, so we must continue and hope that our presence is ignored as we pass whomever is coming our way.

I guide Elizabeth behind me, placing her hand on the back of my cloak so she can follow easily and hopefully remain unnoticed. My pulse pounds in my ears as the constant tempo of steps up ahead grows louder as it approaches.

Rounding the corner, I lower my head, trying to cover my appearance as much as possible with my hood. Anger fills me when I recognize Niren with one of his guards. It takes everything inside me not to attack him.

Niren's nostrils flare as he passes us. He stops and cries out. "Halt!"

We watch in silence as he approaches Garen. "Do you scent that?"

Rage wars with my anxiety, but I force myself to remain still as the first hint of the acrid scent of Elizabeth's fear begins to overcome the masked scent of my clothing covering her.

Niren's guard steps forward. "Even out here, the Terran's scent is strong."

Garen looks to him. "We've just come from her room. Perhaps it clings to our clothing."

Niren's nostrils flare again and his gaze shifts to me, his eyes widening as recognition sweeps across his face. "T'Hale Marek." His voice is low as if he cannot believe what he's seeing. He taps his communicator, yelling into the display. "Guards! The T'Hale has escaped and—"

I rush forward, slamming him against the wall, while Aemar and Garen blast the guard beside him. Wrapping my hand around his throat, unbridled rage consumes me as I bare my fangs and growl low in my throat. "You dared to touch she who is mine."

His eyes bulge with fear as I tighten my grip. He opens his mouth, struggling to gasp for air, but it is futile. He harmed my Elizabeth and now, I will end him for it. Just as I will kill the Emperor and V'Meia for their treachery.

A blast of light flares and shoots through the darkness, barely missing my left arm. Another quickly hits the wall beside me, forcing me to drop Niren.

"Stop them!" a voice cries out down the hallway.

Taking advantage of our distraction, Niren charges me. Aemar blasts him, and he crumples to the floor. "We've been discovered. We must hurry!"

I gather Elizabeth in my arms and we race down the hallway.

The resounding echo of dozens of booted steps seems to come

from everywhere as we make our way to the transport bay. Fear spikes through me as another beam of light races past us, barely missing its goal.

My muscles burn in protest as we hurry to the nearest transport.

The outer door slides open. A blast hits the outer hull next to my head, temporarily blinding me with its brightness as we rush inside. I blindly manage to stumble forward and slam my palm against the panel, sealing the hatch behind me.

I blink several times, adjusting my vision as I quickly follow Garen and Aemar to the bridge.

They slam into their seats. Their hands move quickly across the control panels to start up the ship as I place Elizabeth in one of the other chairs, tightening her harness before doing the same for myself. With a sudden jump, we lift off.

Loud sirens and flashing red lights fill the hangar. The outer doors of the transport bay begin to slide closed as we fly toward them. The open gap is narrowing fast as we approach.

Garen cries out, "We're not going to make it!"

"Yes, we are," Aemar grits through his teeth.

He punches the accelerator and jerks the transport sideways. The sharp screech of metal scrapes along the outer hall as we barely manage to squeeze through the narrow opening. Garen rights the vessel and then slams his fist on the controls, bringing up the communications display. A red light blinks rapidly across the screen, indicating no signal. He growls in frustration and then glances back at me. "Will your guards shoot us down once we cross into your territory?"

Panic spirals through me. "Yes. If we cannot alert them who we are, they will fire on us."

A deafening boom splits the air, and the ship rocks violently to the side.

"There are two transports behind us," Garen yells, his eyes glued to the display. "They knocked out our weapons!"

Elizabeth turns to me. "I have an idea."

"What is it?"

The transport shudders turbulently as another explosion hits the outer hull.

Garen darts a glance at her over his shoulder. "Whatever it is, we need it fast. We're approaching the border to your territory."

Elizabeth unclasps her harness and moves to his side. "There's no time to explain. I'll need the controls."

I rush to her, bracing one arm around her back and one hand on the control panel to steady us in case of another hit. Without hesitation, he moves from his chair, giving her his seat. She squeezes my hand. "Strap in, Marek. I've got this."

Although I'm reluctant to leave her side, I do as she says, securing my harness.

Despite his even tone, worry flickers across Aemar's expression. "Ten seconds to the border."

A silent countdown begins in my mind. Fear snakes down my spine as myriad scenarios play out in my head of how this will end. None of them in our favor. House D'enekai's defense of our border is tight and efficient. They'll blow us out of the sky the moment we pass into the territory.

Elizabeth's hand is poised over the control panel. I don't know what she intends, but I hate that I'm not by her side.

As we reach the final two seconds, I grip the handrails of my chair so tightly, my fingers press indentations in the metal as I brace myself for the inevitable.

A moment before we cross the threshold, Elizabeth's hands fly deftly across the controls and the ship tilts slightly, dipping the wing left, right, and then left again in a subtle rocking sensation.

My heart hammers in my chest as bright light illuminates the viewscreen. I recognize the weapons fire from the border cannons, and I look to my Si'an T'kara. The last image I want in my mind, before we pass from this world to the next, is her face.

Aemar gasps as the blasts zip past our vessel. A reverberating boom followed quickly by another thunders behind us, and the transports in chase drop from the viewscreen.

With a cry of joy, Elizabeth raises her arms in triumph.

A moment later, Ryven's face appears in the display. His eyes widening slightly as they look from her to me. He blinks several times in shock. "I—I'd hoped it was you. But I couldn't be certain. We thought you were dead. I almost—"

"I understand," I reply quickly, cutting him off. "Alert Kalvar and Vanek of our arrival."

Elizabeth smiles back at me and then looks to Ryven. "We're coming home."

CHAPTER 29

MAREK

We touch down in the courtyard mere moments later, and as she stands from her chair, I rush to embrace my Elizabeth, holding her tightly. "You saved us, my Si'an T'kara."

Garen looks to me, confusion etched in his features. "I do not understand. Why did they not shoot us down?"

Elizabeth smiles. "That maneuver I did…dipping the wings side to side. Terran pilots used to do this to indicate to others they were 'friendly.' My grandfather and my aunt taught it to me, and I showed it to the captain of Marek's guard."

Aemar's lips quirk up slightly as he dips his chin in a subtle nod. "Thank the goddess for Terran pilots, then."

A rush of pride fills me as I look to my betrothed. She is the most brilliant female I've ever known, and her intelligence and bravery are the reason we are alive. She stands beside me, her hand in mine as we wait for the outer doors to open.

Kalvar stands at the bottom of the ramp. His glowing emerald-green eyes stare up at us, bright with tears. I watch as he struggles to blink them back. The deep circles under his eyes tell me he has not slept properly in many days. No doubt because he believed we were dead. Everyone did. Ryven stands behind him with a stoic expression, but his eyes betray his joy at our return.

When we reach him, my uncle opens his mouth as if to speak but says nothing. With a slight clench of his jaw, he places one hand on my shoulder, squeezing it as if to reassure him that we are real. A puff of air escapes his nostrils as he shakes his head. He doesn't say anything, but he doesn't have to. His eyes speak for him. I can only imagine the depth of his despair when he thought we were dead.

Without warning, Ryven tenses, anger burning in his gaze as he looks behind us.

The rest of the guards raise their weapons toward the transport. I spin to see Aemar and Garen at the top of the ramp, both of them dressed in their House S'tiran uniforms—the House of our enemy.

"Stand down," I command. "These men risked their lives to help us escape."

Ryven narrows his eyes at them. "Even so, they are guards of House S'tiran. They betrayed their vow to their own House. I suggest they be placed under close watch."

I step toward him. "They *ignored* their vows to do what was right and just, instead of blindly following orders. Is that not a good reason to betray the loyalty they gave to their House?" I place a hand on his shoulder. "I have always valued your counsel in the past, but in this I am asking you to trust me. They are not the enemy, my friend."

His gaze holds mine a moment before he reluctantly nods and then looks to one of his guards. "Find them a place to rest. They are guests of House D'enekai and will be treated as such."

ELIZABETH

I turn to Kalvar. "Has everyone been found?"

"Yes."

As my gaze drifts over all the D'enekai guards and the Estate grounds around us, I release a heavy sigh of relief. Marek winds his arm around my side, and I sag against him in exhaustion. It's good to be home again.

Kalvar gives us a pitying look. "Both of you have been through much. You should rest."

"What of the Emperor and V'Meia?" Marek asks darkly. "Do they still live?"

Ryven steps forward. "They are in seclusion on their Estate, hiding behind their force shield. The Great Houses of G'alta and M'theal have asked for a temporary truce." A slight smirk tilts his lips. "And I suspect S'tiran will request one shortly as well."

Marek growls low in his throat, but I place a hand on his forearm to draw his attention. "You need to rest, my love."

"She is right," Kalvar adds. "All is well for now. Our enemies cannot touch us here. We can discuss our plans after you have both rested."

Marek reluctantly agrees, and we make our way up the stairs to our rooms. Too tired for an actual bath, we forgo the tempting hot water for a simple ion shower. I change into a robe and Marek into his soft knit pants. We curl up in the bed together as he pulls the comforter over us. Wrapping his arm around my waist from behind, he pulls me close to his chest, tucking my body into his.

The tightness in my shoulders slowly begins to relax as my fatigue moves through me. It's hard to believe we're safe. It feels like an eternity since we've been in this room and this bed. Part of me worries it's a fever dream...that we are still walking in the desert, searching for an end to the endless waves of crimson sand and towering stone.

Sensing my fear through the bond, Marek tips his head slightly to me. His breath is warm against my ear as he whispers, "Eh'leh-na, my Elizabeth. We are safe. My vow."

A deep sigh of relief escapes me as I snuggle deeper into his embrace and close my eyes, allowing myself to fall away into a peaceful sleep.

∼

The soft scent of spice—cinnamon and earth—surrounds me. I inhale deeply, and my mind drifts back into awareness. I yawn as I stretch out in the bed. Marek's arm tightens around my waist as he gently nuzzles my temple. I turn to face him.

He reaches forward to run his fingers through my hair and then brushes his lips against mine in a tender kiss.

I smile. "How long have I been asleep?"

He frowns, lowering his gaze with a look that tells me he's doing some sort of calculation in his head. After a moment, his eyes snap back up to mine. "Twelve point four hours."

I jerk up in the bed. "What?"

Marek gently pulls me back down into his arms. "All is well, my Elizabeth. Now that you are awake, we will meet with the Council to discuss our next steps."

I stare at him in confusion. "Now that *I'm* awake?"

He regards me curiously. "It matters not that we are not officially bonded yet. You are K'Sai of House D'enekai; your voice will be heard along with everyone else who represents their Houses."

A smile curves my lips, and I lean forward to kiss him, but a loud knock on the door startles me.

"Hello?" Anton's voice calls out from the hallway.

I grin and Marek purses his lips. "He's been demanding to see you."

My head jerks back slightly in shock. "You haven't let him?"

He blinks several times, as if surprised by my question. "Of course, I have. But I wanted to be alone with you this morning while I finally slept as well."

Only now do I notice the dark circles under Marek's eyes, and I reach forward to cup his cheek as I stare at him in concern. "How long has it been since you had enough sleep?"

He covers my hand with his. Turning his face into my touch, he presses a soft kiss to my palm. "Truthfully? Not since the pod crash."

I hug him tightly, and he relaxes in my embrace, lowering his head to rest at the curve of my neck and shoulder as a long exhale escapes him. "Doc and L'Tana said you would be fine," he whispers. "But I was worried because you slept for so long. And because the Emperor and V'Meia are still alive, I've been unable to rest because I worried that I needed to be ready in the event that they mounted an attack." He pulls back just enough to stare deep into my eyes. "Eh'leh-na, my Si'an T'kara. I will make certain the Emperor and V'Meia can never threaten us again. I swear it to the stars. My vow."

I open my mouth to ask what he means, but he stands from the bed and moves to the door.

I stand as well to greet my best friend.

As soon as it opens, Anton rushes in. "Thank God you're awake!" he cries out.

He wraps his arms tightly around my neck. His eyes are bright with tears. "When we heard about your transport. They said you were dead." He shakes his head softly. "Lucas was so..." His voice trails off, and my thoughts turn to my cousin. He must have been beside himself with worry. Anton continues. "He dropped everything at the cafe to get here, to come search for you. He didn't believe it, and neither did I."

Emotions lodge in my throat, and I hug him tighter a moment before pulling back to stare up at him. "You know I wouldn't just leave you like that." I give him a small teasing smile. "Someone has to keep you in line you know."

Despite his sadness, a slow grin curves his mouth. He turns to Marek and stares at him a moment before embracing him in a warm hug as well. "I'm so glad you're both okay," he whispers.

Awkwardly, Marek returns the gesture. "Thank you, my friend."

Anton steps back just a bit and sniffs as he blinks back tears. "Come on. Lucas is anxious to see you two."

I change out of my robe and then walk with Marek and Anton down to the main entry room. As soon as we descend the stairs, sparkling blue eyes meet mine. A wide smile splits his face and Lucas runs toward me, sweeping me up into one of his giant bear hugs and spinning me around.

Marek's guards watch with wide eyed expressions, obviously not used to such visible displays of affection.

When he sets me back down, he gives me his signature crooked grin and I notice he's grown a short beard to match his red hair. I wonder if it's just the result of worry and neglect while I was missing or if it's a new look. "I didn't believe it for a second," he says. "You're stronger than anyone I know. I knew you weren't dead."

I'm surprised to see Tayla and Taven standing behind him, and I smile brightly at them.

"We are glad you are well," Taven says, a small version of his V'loryn smile on his face.

Tayla hugs me warmly. "I am glad you are unharmed," she whispers. "My brother and I were so worried."

I pull back just enough to give her a warm smile. "Thank you."

I look over my shoulder to find Lucas staring at her with a softened expression. And I recognize that look on his face. He's fallen. Hard. When she steps back and her eyes meet his, a light-green bloom spreads across her cheeks and the tips of her ears. An answering red blush creeps across the bridge of Lucas's nose, accentuating his freckles.

It's only now that I realize Marek hasn't mentioned the Mosaurans, and I turn to face him. "Where are Rowan and Tharin?"

"They returned to their ship. Rowan was anxious to see his mate again. He promised they would be back soon, however. They claim to be able to use the Passage for faster travel. I am curious to know if it is truth."

Off to the side, I notice L'Tana, Vanek and Doc. L'Tana's lips quirk up slightly as her eyes meet mine. "It is good to see you awake."

Doc smiles brightly. "Yeah, we're so glad you're both all right."

Out of nowhere Maya rushes forward and throws her arms around me. "Thank God you're okay. We were all so worried."

Ruvaen moves to her side. "When we learned what happened,

everyone feared you were dead. But Maya," his eyes dart briefly to her, "and Anton believed that it was not so. They refused to give up hope, and insisted that we leave immediately to help search for you both."

It's wonderful to be surrounded by all our friends and family. I only wish things were more settled now that they're here. The Emperor is still a problem and the truce between the Great Houses may not last long if we do not form a plan.

CHAPTER 30

ELIZABETH

When we reach the Great Assembly Hall, Marek leads me to our seating area. The one reserved for House D'enekai. Kalvar sits on the other side of me, his face stoic as we watch the rest of the Council file in.

Across from us, members of the other Great Houses take their seats. The large section reserved for the Emperor sits empty between the Houses that typically align with the Emperor and the ones aligned with ours. It would appear to be an even split, but as the Lower Houses come in, it is easy to see that House D'enekai easily has far more support than the other Great Houses.

The Lower Houses were not present the last time we were here. As my gaze sweeps the room, I cannot believe the Emperor was foolish enough to start a war there is no way he will ever win.

Dovak G'alta, L'anrul M'theal, and L'Mira S'tiran stare across at us with stoic expressions, but I can see the contempt reflected from behind their eyes. Niren is not seated among them and I wonder at his absence. Garen told us he stunned him with the blaster instead of killing him. Perhaps L'Mira has hidden him because she's worried for her son's life after what he did to Marek and me.

My gaze darts to my beloved to find him glaring across at her. From the anger pulsing through the bond, I know she is right to fear him.

Ryven and several of the guards sit behind us, and after everything that has happened, I am glad they are here. I look back at Ryven and smile warmly. He dips his chin in a subtle nod before turning his sharp gaze back to the crowd around us, scanning for any threats.

Marek takes my hand, drawing my attention back to him as he threads his fingers through mine. Opening a small connection between us, he sends me a wave of love and reassurance as Kalvar stands.

His voice is loud and authoritative as it echoes through the assembly. "We are here today to address the crimes of House K'voch."

Dovak G'alta shoots up from his seat. "There has been no crime committed by his House that I am aware of. Tread carefully, Kalvar. Such accusations can be construed as treason."

Kalvar's gaze darkens. "We have proof of his treachery. Of his attempt to murder myself and the heir to my House."

L'anrul M'theal quirks her brow in condescension. "Of what do you speak?"

Movement out of the corner of my eye draws my attention to the floor. Vanek steps out from under one of the many columns supporting the colossal structure, and I'm surprised when I notice Tolav and one of the Emperor's guards beside him. I thought Tolav was dead.

Anger flashes behind Vanek's eyes as he looks up at L'anrul. "Here is your proof." He grits through his teeth as he roughly pushes Tolav and the guard to the center of the room.

L'anrul, Dovak, and L'Mira all turn a nervous gaze to the guard, and I know now from their expressions that none of them are innocent. All of them were aware of the Emperor's plan.

Rage floods the link between us as Marek glares at them with a

JESSICA GRAYSON

murderous gaze, a low growl rumbling deep in his chest. "They will all pay," he whispers under his breath.

One of the Elders steps forward in his long, flowing green robes. "I am Elder Vendak. I will hear your statement. State your name and position."

Tolav does so with a repentant glance to Marek and Kalvar. "I am Tolav, and I have served House D'enekai for one hundred and seventy-nine cycles."

My eyes widen in shock. I didn't realize he'd been with them for so long.

He continues. "The Emperor had my brother. He threatened to kill him if I refused to betray House D'enekai." He turns to face Marek and Kalvar, dropping to his knees. "Please, T'Hale Kalvar, T'Hale Marek, and K'Sai Elizabeth. Please forgive me. I had no choice."

Dovak gives him an outraged look. "You dare to accuse the Emperor of such a thing."

Tolav's head snaps toward him. "Yes, because it is truth."

L'anrul narrows her eyes. "I will hear no one speak against our Emperor!" She motions to her guards as she stands. "I refuse to stay here and entertain such ridiculous slander! My House will—"

Elder Vendak interrupts in a thunderous voice. "You will all remain here."

She shoots him a venomous gaze as she and her guards take their seats.

"And what of you?" Vendak motions to the guard next to Tolav. "We would hear your testimony as well."

The guard steps forward, the golden insignia across his uniform marking him as one of the Emperor's elite. He scans the Council, the upper tilt of his chin lending him a pompous air. This man is not repentant of his actions in any way. He finally returns his attention to the Elder. "My name is First Elite Dukar. I have served my Emperor for forty-two cycles. How can you"—he narrows his eyes—"accuse our leader of treason when his word is rule?" He turns a cold gaze to Kalvar, Marek, and me. "House D'enekai has long been a problem for House K'voch. The Emperor would have accepted you into his House in a bonding to his daughter. But you chose that"—his eyes rake over me with a look of disgust—"creature instead."

Marek shoots up from his seat, his eyes obsidian and his fangs fully extended, growling low in his chest as he glares at Dukar.

Vendak however, appears unfazed. He cocks his head slightly to the side as he regards him. "So, you admit to playing a part in the attempts on House D'enekai's lives on behalf of the Emperor." He says this as a statement, but I can tell it's actually meant as a question.

"As I said." The guard meets Marek's eyes evenly. "I do what my Emperor asks of me as a loyal subject of the crown."

A general rumble comes from the Elders and it is easy to read their shock at his admission.

Elder Vendak turns a sharp gaze to Dovak, L'anrul, and L'Mira, all of whom watch the guard with stoic expressions, giving away nothing to suggest they had anything to do with the attempt on our lives. Without taking his eyes off them, he addresses the guard. "Are there any others who may be implicated in this plot besides House K'voch?"

At this, Dovak narrows his eyes at Dukar, and I don't miss the way L'anrul and L'Mira seem to shift nervously in their seats. Ryven appears to notice this as well because I hear him whisper to Daenor, "If any of their guard makes a move, above all else, protect the K'Sai and the T'Hales."

Heavy silence settles over the room. The atmosphere is tense as Dukar hesitates in his answer. Marek's arm wraps around my waist as he pulls me against his side as if bracing to shield me.

After a moment, Dukar turns to Elder Vendak. "No."

With a dismissive wave of his hand, Vendak gestures to Dukar. "Take him away."

Two guards from House A'msir move forward, roughly grabbing his arms and escorting him out of the chamber. To where, I don't know.

Tolav's eyes widen as he gives Kalvar a pleading look. "Please, T'Hale. Forgive me my transgressions against your House. I had no choice. I—"

Kalvar stands, cutting him off abruptly. Leveling a dark gaze, his voice is low and accusing as he addresses Tolav. "But you *did* have a choice. You should have come to us when the Emperor first threatened your family. We would have helped you get your brother back. Instead, you allowed *my* family to be taken from me the same way yours was taken from you. And that"—his fisted hands shake at his sides as he bares his fangs—"is unforgiveable." With a quick jerk of his chin, he looks to Daenor. "Remove him from my sight. He is no longer welcome in our House."

Daenor and another guard escort Tolav from the room.

Dovak addresses the crowd. "This meeting must be postponed. The Emperor is not even here to defend himself against these false accusations!"

The Assembly erupts in a chaos of voices. I've never seen so much anger and emotion among Marek's people.

Marek's voice thunders over everyone else as he stands, pulling me up with him as he calls for silence.

All eyes turn to him as his piercing gaze sweeps over the room. "House K'voch tried to end the line of my House, and I will not allow this treachery to go unpunished. House D'enekai no longer recognizes the authority and title of House K'voch to rule V'lora. The Emperor will answer for his crimes. I swear it to the stars. My vow." He turns to face L'Mira. "Where is Niren of House S'tiran?" he growls. "Where is your son that dared harm my mate and threatened to kill us both?"

K'Sai L'Mira's eyes flash with panic, but her face remains neutral. "Gone. He disappeared shortly after you..." she pauses as if searching for the right word before finally settling on, "left. Perhaps it was in shame for what he had done." She tilts up her chin. "If I had been there to receive you, your...visit to my home would have gone much differently than it did," she adds cryptically.

Marek levels a dark gaze at her. "When I find your son, he will pay for harming my mate. I swear it to the stars. My vow."

L'Mira visibly pales at his words.

Everyone stares at us, Marek's hand in mine as we stand united before the Assembly.

He continues. "I call upon all the Great and Lower Houses allied with House D'enekai to end the reign of House K'voch. Who stands with us?"

Vanek steps forward. "House A'msir is with you."

"So is L'eanan," Milena adds.

"We stand with House D'enekai," a K'Sai of one of the Lower Houses says.

One by one, over two-thirds of the Lower Houses pledge their support while the Great Houses of G'alta, M'theal, and S'tiran watch in angry silence.

After each House has spoken, Dovak stands. "The High Council appears to be evenly divided. Therefore, a consensus cannot be reached."

Marek glares at him. "You misunderstand my intention here." His voice is a low and deadly growl. "I did not call for a vote. I called for support to end the reign of a murderous tyrant. He tried to end the line of House D'enekai without provocation, and I will not live in the shadow of his threat any longer."

Dovak's eyes widen slightly as he looks around the Assembly, finding little support for the Emperor here. "*You* provoked him"—he points an accusing finger at Marek—"when you chose a Terran breeder over his daughter, the Princess."

Milena stands. "The High Omari validated the fated bond. T'Hale Marek and Elizabeth Langdon have been blessed by the Goddess herself with the si'an'inamora. Who are you to question her will?" She gestures to the Emperor's empty seating area. "For the crimes of House K'voch, the Emperor has forfeited his right to rule. House L'eanan will no longer recognize his title or authority."

"House A'msir seconds that motion," Vanek calls out.

Dovak's eyes are cold as he looks between Marek, Vanek and Milena. "The truce between our Great Houses remains, but I refuse to take part in deposing the Emperor." Spinning on his heels, he turns to leave, exiting the Great Assembly with his guards trailing behind him.

House S'tiran and M'theal both make mirroring statements, vowing that they are no longer at war with us and leave soon after, without saying another word.

Vanek walks up to us, his eyes burning with anger as he watches the last of House S'tiran exit the Assembly Hall. "If they cross us, we will depose them as well," he says under his breath.

"Let's hope it does not come to that," Marek replies. "Our people do not need a civil war."

Kalvar sighs heavily. "Is that not what this already is?"

Marek shakes his head. "We will give the Emperor a choice. Surrender and accept his punishment according to our laws, or fight and be destroyed. His forces are no match for ours, and I doubt he believes he would stand any chance of winning if it came down to a real war."

CHAPTER 31

MAREK

It's only been two days since the Council meeting. Elder Vendak sent a courier to the Estate, requesting reassurance that we have no intention of restarting the civil war that had been declared while we were lost in the desert. Elizabeth sits beside me while Vanek sits directly across from us, thrumming his fingers anxiously on the chair handrails. Milena's face is a stoic mask as she listens to Kalvar read aloud the last of the Emperor's message.

When he's finished, he lifts a heavy emerald gaze to me. "The Emperor refuses to step down."

My hands curl into fists at my side as I draw in a deep breath. This is not what I wanted. I turn to my Si'an T'kara to find her eyes already upon me. It was never my intent to place her in danger, and yet that's what has happened almost from the very first moment she stepped foot onto my home world.

As if sensing my dark thoughts, she takes my hand. Through the tenuous link she sends me a wave of reassurance, letting me know she is not afraid. I am glad she feels this way because I suspect I carry enough worry for us both.

Vanek's fingers stop abruptly. He stills and looks between us. "Then, there is no choice. We must depose the Emperor by force."

Milena dips her chin in agreement. "He is right."

Reluctantly, I look back to Ryven, standing just behind us, near the door. He and the captains of House L'eanan and A'msir step forward, bowing slightly before meeting our eyes. Ryven taps his communicator, and a 3D projection of the Emperor's Estate floats on a screen before us. "I've studied the Emperor's defenses and believe I may have a plan."

∼

After we finalize our strategy to move on the Emperor, Milena remains talking with Kalvar, while Vanek, Elizabeth, and I step out onto the balcony.

Elizabeth's communicator chirps with a message from Anton, and she moves back inside to speak with him, leaving Vanek and I alone.

As soon as she's gone, he turns to me, arching a questioning brow. "You are certain it is wise to take her with us when we storm the Emperor's Estate?"

With my hand on the railing, I turn my attention to the sea. Although it is green, it reminds me of the oceans of Terra and the first time I looked into her luminous blue eyes. Inhaling and exhaling deeply, I watch the waves roll in, crashing against the sharp rocks below. "In truth, I wish she were anywhere but here, my friend. I would force her to return to Terra if I thought she would actually listen. But she will not." A small puff of air escapes me as a smile tugs at my lips when I think of how fierce she is when someone tries to convince her to do that which she does not want. "So, if she is to remain here, the safest place for her to be is at my side and among my guards. The Emperor would never suspect that I would bring her with me. And as K'Sai of our House, it is her right to see to its defense just as much as it is mine or Kalvar's." I lift my gaze to Vanek. "If I should fall in battle—"

He cuts me off and meets my eyes evenly. "If you fall, I will protect her for as long as I draw breath. I swear it to the stars. My vow."

CHAPTER 32

MAREK

Ocean-blue eyes stare intensely into mine a moment before we turn our attention back to the viewscreen and to the Emperor's Estate. Worry floods across the faint bond, and I do not know if it is mine or hers. Perhaps it is a mixture of both. I do not doubt that we will win this battle today, but I would be more at ease if my Si'an T'kara had stayed home in the safety of our Estate.

The floor trembles beneath our feet as the ship's weapons power up. Vanek's face appears in the display. "We will begin our attack on their defense shield generator on your mark."

My eyes drift out the viewscreen to the many ships from L'eanan, A'msir, and D'enekai as well as dozens from the Lower Houses that support ours, surrounding the Emperor's island Estate. That the other Great Houses are not here today speaks volumes. Their refusal to help us end the Emperor's tyrannical reign will not be forgotten.

Ryven turns his gaze to mine, waiting for the signal to begin firing. I dip my head in a subtle nod, and he turns back to the screen. "Now!" he cries out.

Each ship aims their weapons on the generator. The light from the lasers all concentrated on one spot are so bright it is almost blinding. The force shield's glow begins to waver, flickering off and on beneath the assault a moment before the generator explodes in a brilliant display of color.

The shield collapses around the Estate and, as one, our armada of ships begin to close in.

Vanek's ship moves in first, touching down on the surface only a moment before ours. I glance over my shoulder at Kalvar and Elizabeth once more. Worry visible in her expression, she mouths, "I love you," as I stand readying to exit the ship with Ryven.

She tried to talk me out of storming the Estate with my guards, but how can I lead them if I ask them to do something that I do not? My time on the Defense Force prepared me for this. I am no stranger to command or battle.

The transport doors slide open, and I charge down the platform with Ryven and the rest of our guards. Vanek and his men are the first ones into the courtyard. As we race toward the palace, he glances back to us with a puzzled expression. It is strange that we meet no resistance from the Emperor's men. Worry gnaws at the back of my mind at the thought that we are moving into an elaborate trap. And yet, we have no choice but to press forward.

Storming the palace entrance, Vanek, Ryven, and I share another confused look.

Ryven speaks first. "Where are the guards?"

Vanek looks toward the hallway that leads to the throne room. "Perhaps they are all concentrated in one place. We should be prepared. This could be a trap."

His words almost perfectly echo my own thoughts, and I nod in agreement as we continue on.

When we reach the throne room, my heart pounds as Vanek forces the doors open. Charging inside, we stop almost in unison as we take in the mostly empty chamber around us. No one is here but the Emperor, the Empress, and V'Meia, seated on their respective thrones. A flicker of fear steals across the Emperor's otherwise stoic expression as he glares down at us. In V'Meia's eyes, I see only burning anger as her gaze falls on mine.

"Seize them!" Vanek orders his men.

Ryven and a few of my guards move forward as well, roughly pulling the Emperor from his seat and binding his hands behind his back.

As two of Vanek's guards do the same to V'Meia, one of them turns back with a questioning look as he stands before the Empress—her mother. Although she is bondmate to the Emperor, we have no proof that she was involved with their plans and therefore have no grounds to imprison her.

I look to the guard. "Take her to one of the ships and see to it that she is transported back to House G'alta—the House of her birth."

Her eyes widen in shock when they meet mine.

I continue. "Unless we find evidence of her conspiring with her bondmate and daughter, we have no valid reason to hold her."

He bows slightly before turning his attention back to the still-stunned Empress.

V'Meia's cold gaze locks on mine. "If you murder us, the other Houses will wage war," she seethes.

Barely able to contain my anger, I grit through my teeth. "My House is not dishonorable like yours. We do not seek to assassinate those who stand in our way. You will be tried according to our laws. And if you are found guilty, you will be punished as befits your crimes against my House."

In truth, I want them both dead now. But Kalvar is right. We cannot trade one tyrannical regime for another. Once they are found guilty, they will be executed anyway.

She sneers. "And that's why you will lose, Marek. Because Empires are not built by those with honor. They are forged in fire and blood by those who are willing to do anything to seize power and hold onto it." Her eyes rake over me with a look of disgust. "You. Are. Weak. We have more support than you think. We will not be imprisoned for long."

Growling, I turn to the guard. "Take her away."

"Wait! You cannot imprison the Princess!"

I spin to find one of House K'voch's Healers rushing toward us. A concealed panel along the wall slides closed behind him and alarm burst through me as I scan the room, wondering what other hidden passages may be here.

As if reading my mind, Vanek's eyes meet mine briefly before he commands his guards. "Search everywhere! Make certain no one else is hiding within these walls."

Ryven and another guard intercept the Healer, binding his hands behind him. He drops to his knees and looks up at me with a pleading look. "Please, T'Hale. She is with child. Surely you would not imprison her."

My head snaps to V'Meia. "Is this truth?"

She says nothing. I look to her parents and they glare at me in return but remain silent as well.

All eyes turn to us with varying looks of shock and surprise. I motion to the Healer. "Unbind him and give him a scanning device."

Ryven shakes his head. "But, T'Hale, he—"

"Do it," I snap.

Reluctantly, Ryven unbinds the Healer as one of the guards gives him a scanner.

Narrowing his eyes at me, his nostrils flare as he runs the wand low over V'Meia's abdomen. With a flick of his wrist, he projects a 3D image of a fetus on a floating display in the center of the room.

My gaze shifts between V'Meia and her father. "If we had bonded, I would not have lived long after our ceremony, would I?"

Her nostrils flare in anger, and that is all the answer I need to confirm my suspicions. She would have been unable to hide the truth of her condition if we'd formed the S'acris. So she would have made certain that we never did. I would have been murdered on our joining night. The Emperor and Empress, however, are staring at their daughter with a shocked gaze.

Vanek, no doubt having reached the same conclusions I have, glares at her. "Who is your mate?"

The scanner beeps twice, and the Healer's jaw drops as he stares at the information on his display.

"What is it?" Vanek asks.

The Healer's eyes are wide as he looks to us. "The child is half A'kai," he states, and the look on his face is one of shock and disbelief—an expression that is mirrored on the face of everyone in the room, except for V'Meia.

V'Meia's lips pull back in a feral snarl as she turns a dark gaze to me. "I carry the child of Talel—brother of the First Prime of A'kaina. Now that he is dead, this child is the only living relative of the First Prime. The A'kai honor blood above all else, and I promise you, he will come for me once he finds out we are being held prisoner."

Anger sweeps through me. "You would bring death and destruction to our world by aligning yourself with the A'kai?" I look to the Emperor. "I knew you desired power, but I never thought you would go to such lengths. The A'kai will bring nothing but death to our people."

He shakes his head emphatically. "I only sought to take control of your House. Even *I*"—he stares wide-eyed at V'Meia—"know better than to deal with the A'kai."

V'Meia narrows her eyes. "My alliance with the A'kai will save us, Father. You will see."

He blinks several times in shock. "No, it will not. You—you do not understand what you've done."

He is right. She does not. But the rest of us know. I look to Ryven, and he answers my unspoken question. "Kalvar has had all signals blocked from leaving the planet's surface ever since he was recovered from the desert."

Relief washes through me. At least two weeks have passed since then. If V'Meia had been able to send word asking for help from the First Prime of A'kaina, their ships would have already been in orbit several days ago. That she would endanger our planet and our people so recklessly is something I'd never imagined. My gaze shifts to Ryven. "Take her away."

As they lead her down the hallway, she calls out. "The A'kai will come for me, Marek. I promise you. They will come. And when they do, none of you will be safe."

Cold fills me as my thoughts turn to Elizabeth's nightmares—her visions of dark ships descending from the skies. I fear she is right. Her dreams are a warning.

CHAPTER 33

MAREK

When I inform Kalvar of V'Meia's child, his eyes widen slightly before he quickly retrains his face into an impassive expression.

"Do you think the A'kai will come for her?"

He meets my gaze evenly. "Let us hope not. If they do, it would be better if we just give her to them, rather than risk a war."

My hands curl into fists at my side. "The Mosaurans said the A'kai are searching for Terrans. If V'Meia is freed, she will tell them about Terra, and their people will be enslaved."

"Then perhaps despite the reservations of our scientists, we will have to share more of our technology with the Terrans so they can defend themselves if necessary." He pauses and then leans forward to tap his communicator. "Now, we must contact Dovak."

As soon as Dovak's face appears in the viewscreen, he glares at Kalvar. "Why have you contacted me?"

"I wanted to inform you to expect your sister, the former Empress." Kalvar puts slight emphasis on the word "former," and Dovak pales. "She is on her way to you now."

Dovak's mouth drifts open before he quickly snaps it shut. "Does this mean that the war has already begun?"

His face is impassive as he asks this question, but it is easy to read the fear in his eyes. He knows if we declared war upon his House there would be little he or the others that support him could do to stop us from overthrowing his power.

Kalvar shakes his head. "No. The Emperor and the Princess are to be imprisoned. We will convene the High Council in three days. V'lora has many enemies that would take advantage of a moment they perceive to be weakness. We cannot afford to be divided right now."

Despite his attempt to appear unfazed, Dovak frowns in confusion. I'm certain this is not what he was expecting when Kalvar first informed him of the return of the former Empress to his House and the imprisonment of the Emperor and V'Meia.

Although this new development will undoubtedly cause some unrest among the Great and Lower Houses, I rest easier knowing the Emperor and V'Meia are no longer a threat. For now.

When I leave his office to return to Elizabeth, my communicator chirps loudly. Glancing down, I tap the display, and Vanek's face appears in the viewscreen. "We have located the rest of the Emperor's missing guards."

My first instinct is to order their imprisonment, but when I remember that they abandoned their House during its hour of need, it is easy to see that they are not loyal to the Emperor. The question now is: would they be loyal to us? I look to Vanek. "What should we do with them?"

"We should divide them among our Great Houses: D'enekai, L'eanan, and A'msir," he states. "You and I served with some of these males during our time on the Defense Force. I doubt most of them realized the treachery of their Emperor. We cannot judge them all equally just because they served his House."

My thoughts drift to Kovan, Garen, and Aemar of House S'tiran. Without them, Elizabeth and I might never have escaped. Vanek is right. "We will have the captains assess each of them to determine if their service may be pledged to our Houses."

"Agreed," he replies. "I will inform House L'eanan."

He leans forward to shut off the viewscreen, but I stop him abruptly with a question. "Did you locate Kovan and his family?"

Vanek nods. "They have already been retrieved and settled in K'ylira. Kovan is to report to Ryven in the morning to begin his training as one of your guards, along with Aemar and Garen."

"Good," I reply. "Thank you for taking care of this, my friend."

He dips his chin in acknowledgment and then shuts off the display.

～

Tightening my arms around Elizabeth, I think on V'Meia's treachery and how it almost cost my Si'an T'kara her life.

Pulling back from my dark thoughts, I listen carefully to the soft and even sound of her breathing as she sleeps beside me. After I informed her of V'Meia, she experienced her recurring nightmare of the black ships again last night.

She insists it is a warning. A sign that something terrible is coming. I am now inclined to believe this.

My thoughts turn to the A'kai and the warnings from the Aerilon female and the Mosaurans. Ice fills me as I think on my own nightmares—my vision of Elizabeth in the deadly embrace of an A'kai as he drinks of her lifeblood. Aside from V'Meia, it has been at least a thousand cycles since we've had any sort of contact with the A'kai.

I've researched all I can about Terran precognition and have found documentation to support the idea that this does exist among a very small number of her population. I dare not inform Kalvar or L'Tana, though, for fear that word would get out and others would wish to study her. Perhaps our scientists might even suggest one of the Healers join with her mind to analyze what she is experiencing.

But I know Elizabeth does not want this. Neither do I. I dislike the idea of anyone else in her head almost as much and perhaps even more so than she does.

As if sensing my thoughts, her eyelids flutter and open and she smiles sleepily at me. She is precious, cherished, beloved…the other half of my soul. As I stare into her luminous eyes, I long to make her mine according to the ways of my people—to seal her to me in the sacred blood ritual of the S'acris.

I reach forward to tuck a stray tendril of hair behind her ear, running my fingers through the long, silken strands before cupping her jaw and running my thumb lightly across her soft, full lips. "Eh'leh-na, my Elizabeth," I whisper softly.

Her mouth curves into a stunning smile. "I have an idea," she bites her lower lip in the way that drives me mad.

I quirk my brow, curious to know what it is. "What is it, my Si'an T'kara?"

"Everyone is already here. And we have no reason to wait any longer." She brushes her lips against mine, smiling against them. "Let's have our bonding ceremony tomorrow."

Happiness fills me and my tr'llen begins deep in my chest. I capture her mouth and stroke my tongue against hers in a claiming kiss.

When I pull back to stare across at her, doubt fills me once again.

She runs her finger lightly across my cheek, then traces my jaw. "What are you thinking, my love?"

"I—" I stop, not sure that I should share this with her, but she wants no secrets between us. "I am afraid."

She shakes her head. "Why?"

My gaze drifts down to the curve of her neck and shoulder, resting briefly on the pulsing artery just beneath the delicate skin before lifting my eyes to hers once more. "You saw what I did to the t'sar. You listened to Kaden's logs. You heard what happened when he formed the bond with Brienna. How could I not be?"

She leans forward to brush her soft lips against mine in a gentle kiss. "I trust you," she whispers. "I know you won't hurt me."

Her words simultaneously fill me with joy as well as guilt. Illogically, I wish I were Terran. I desire more than anything to bind her to me in the sacred blood ritual of my people. Even knowing the risks, I am too selfish to ever give her up. "Then, we will do as you wish. We must speak with Kalvar about the arrangements."

I start to rise from the bed, but her warm hand on my forearm stops me and I turn back to face her with a slight quirk of my brow.

"We can't forget Anton," she grins. "He'll be so upset if we make plans without including him."

I sigh heavily in mock frustration as the edges of my lips quirk up in a teasing smile. "Of course. *How* could we forget Anton?"

CHAPTER 34

MAREK

The Terran tradition of the male being kept from his mate the night before the bonding ceremony is absolute torture and, in my opinion, completely unnecessary. Is this done because Terran males lack self-control?

I barely slept last night. I long to see Elizabeth, to hold her in my arms. But, according to Anton, their people believe it is bad luck for the betrothed to see each other before the ceremony. Although, I would argue that it is ridiculous to honor a ritual that seems to be nothing more than mere superstition.

But it is her choice to honor this tradition, and I respect her decision. So, I have tasked Ryven and the rest of our guard to make certain that we are kept from accidentally seeing each other prior to the ceremony.

"She is well?" I ask Ryven anxiously as he enters the room.

He quirks his brow. "Yes."

"And the High Omari is ready for our arrival?"

Restrained amusement dances behind his eyes as he regards me, crossing his arms in front of his chest. "Yes."

"Kalvar is already with her?"

Vanek walks in. "Yes, yes, and yes," he says in mock frustration, a hint of a teasing smile threatening to quirk his lips. "It is time. We must leave now so you will be in position before they arrive…or before you lose your sanity," he mumbles under his breath.

I narrow my eyes at him, and he claps a hand on my shoulder. "You know I merely jest." He shakes his head. "I believe I am almost as eager as you are that this day is finally here."

"I agree." It feels as though I've been waiting for this day for forever.

The three of us make our way to the garden, overlooking the sea. The last of the sun's rays spread out across the water in a sparkling display of shimmering light that dances across the rolling waves. Almost the entirety of the Embassy staff has gathered here, including the Terran Ambassador. All of them either know us personally or are here to witness this historical moment between our two peoples. Either way, we turned no one away from the Embassy that wished to be here today.

As people began to file in earlier, Ryven voiced how fortunate we are that only the bare minimum of staff are currently in the Terran Embassy now. The rest will not arrive for another few weeks. Even so, as I glance at the crowd gathered here, I know this is by far the largest bonding ceremony I've ever attended. There are at least thirty people here, not including my guards.

Most bonding ceremonies include only the closest family and friends. It is not unusual for fewer than ten people to be in attendance, even if it is a bonding between the Great Houses.

Our guests squint against the setting sun as it begins its descent into the ocean just beyond the Estate. They are seated in several rows of carved L'kir benches that have been grouped to form an aisle between them. This is for the bride and the person "giving her away" to walk between.

As Anton explained, it is usually the Terran female's father who "gives the bride away," but as Elizabeth has not seen hers since she was seven cycles old, she asked Kalvar to stand in for her. Although his expression remained ever stoic, it was easy to see the emotion that flashed behind his eyes at her request; he was honored that she would choose him for something so important.

A series of gasps from our many Terran guests gives me a moment of panic, but as I turn to look over my shoulder, following the path of their wide-eyed stares, a smile threatens to quirk my lips.

Their gazes are locked on Errun and A'ravae riding the wind currents along the cliffs just over the ocean. They gasp again, almost in unison as Errun releases a bellowing roar and A'ravae answers with one of her own. It occurs to me how strange it must be to see something before your very eyes that you'd always believed was only myth.

I turn my attention back to face the Estate, anxiously awaiting my Si'an T'kara. I stand in the wide circle of glowing L'sair crystals, their soft light beginning to grow brighter as the sun dips lower into the sea.

V'loryn bonding ceremonies are held just before twilight—a time that represents an end to all the days past. When the sun rises on the following day, the newly bonded couple are already awake to greet it. A symbol of a new beginning—having already formed the S'acris the night before—they are now irrevocably changed and ready to begin their lives anew as one.

Our bonding is a blend of both Terran and V'loryn tradition. Kalvar will escort Elizabeth to my side, and Anton will stand beside her as "male of honor," while Vanek stands beside me as "best male." I am not entirely sure of the exact distinction between these two titles, but that is of little concern.

Although I am anxious to be formally bonded to my Si'an T'kara, lingering fear gnaws at the back of my mind that she may be hurt during our mating. So I've asked L'Tana to remain on the Estate overnight just in case. Her eyes had widened slightly in shock at this request before she quickly retrained her expression into an impassive mask. As one of my oldest friends, but also as a concerned Healer, she agreed without issue.

Elizabeth has reminded me several times that Brienna and Kaden only had problems during their first mating because she was unaware of our ways—unprepared to form the S'acris. Her logic is sound, but it does not completely erase my fears.

Our bond is so strong, I sense her approaching even before she arrives. Her emotions—a strange mixture of both happiness and anxiety—thrum through the connection between us. When she comes into view, I inhale sharply. She is more beautiful than I could ever have imagined...and I have imagined this moment many times since I first fell in love with her.

Her silver bonding robes are made of the finest silkara. It flows softly around her as she walks down the aisle with Kalvar, the material shimmering as it catches the last light of the setting sun. Her long red hair is tied back in a series of intricate braids with a few stray tendrils that hang loosely to frame her face. She is at once beautiful and ethereal and, for a moment, I worry that this is all a dream. Too perfect to be real. My fingers curl reflexively into my palms with want to touch her.

I watch in rapt fascination as she steps into the circle, staring up at me with a dazzling smile that rivals the brightness of the V'loryn sun.

Gently, I place a wreath of white heather atop her head, then I kneel slightly as she places a similar one atop mine as well.

As the High Omari recites the ancient words of the bonding ceremony, Elizabeth's luminous blue eyes stare deep into mine, full of love and affection. I cannot believe this day is actually here. I've waited so long to claim her.

The High Omari speaks of Empress K'Lura and her Si'an T'karan. How their bonding ended the hundred cycle war between their Great Houses. She heralds our bonding as the dawning of a great change for our people—blessed by the Goddess herself. We are a new beginning and the first of many to come.

In Elizabeth's gaze I can already see our future, and I am happy and whole in a way I never imagined I could be.

The High Omari gives us her final blessing, and I raise my open hand out to my Si'an T'kara, trembling slightly as desire and anticipation course through me. She lifts hers and aligns our palms. She threads her fingers through mine, and a long exhalation escapes my parted lips as my mind pours into hers like liquid pouring into a glass as we form the al'nara.

Happiness brighter than a thousand stars floods the link between us. "You are mine, and I am yours," I speak the sacred bonding words aloud.

Elizabeth smiles brightly as she replies softly in return. "I am yours, and you are mine." In the ocean of our combined thoughts, she whispers in my mind. *"I will love you for the rest of my life. You and no other, my love."*

My heart is full as I wrap her up in my arms and capture her mouth in a claiming kiss. I believe I understand the purpose of this tradition that signals the ending of the Terran bonding ceremony. It is both a seal and a promise. Elizabeth is mine, and as my tongue curls around hers I deepen our kiss, leaving her breathless when we finally pull away and turn to face our family and friends. The Terrans cheer and clap while the V'loryns observe in curious silence.

Elizabeth's happiness bleeds through our bond as she smiles brightly to our guests. With her arm linked through mine, we walk through the courtyard toward the central area that has been cleared for our reception. The last rays of the sun are now no more than a thin line of light just above the lip of the ocean. Dozens of L'sair crystals scattered throughout the gardens create an almost ethereal glow all around us—as if we were floating through a dream.

Her gaze drifts over the various decorations. Pots full of flowering heather, both lavender and white, interspersed with various L'sair crystals in shades of muted yellow and white outline the area that Anton has turned into an outdoor dance floor. She turns to me, a stunning smile on her lips. "It's so beautiful, Marek."

I wish I could take credit for giving her all of this, but it is Anton who has done this for her.

As if my very thoughts have summoned him, he appears. "What do you think?" he asks, his boyish grin lighting his face as he motions to the decorations.

"It is perfect," I tell him, and his brows go up slightly in shock as he turns his gaze to me.

His smile grows even wider. "High praise from a V'loryn," he teases.

A smile tugs at the corner of my lips. "It is truth."

"He's right, Anton. It's magical." She pauses and turns to me, stretching up on her toes to press a soft kiss to my lips. "It's everything I could have ever imagined, and more."

Maya steps forward, her arm looped through Ruvaen's. "We helped decorate too, you know," she teases.

Elizabeth hugs Anton and Maya warmly. "Thank you," she whispers. "Everything looks amazing."

"Okay," Anton waggles his brows. "Now it's time for some dancing." He gives me a conspiratorial wink. "Bride and groom get the first dance."

After I vowed to learn how to dance for Elizabeth, I naturally went to Anton for advice on where to begin. He began giving me secret lessons a few months ago. It was very difficult having to lie to Elizabeth and tell her that I would be working late with Lorne, when in fact, I was learning how to dance with her best friend. I disliked keeping this secret from her. But Anton reassured me that it is a good secret if its intent is to surprise and please one's bondmate later.

Taven, Ruvaen, and Lorne saw us in the Embassy gym, and once my fellow V'loryns discovered how important dancing is to the Terran courtship and bonding ritual, they inquired about lessons as well. Our private lessons quickly became group ones, and as I glance around at our guests, a small smile curves my mouth at the number of curious V'loryn faces that watch us. I suspect many will want to learn this new skill after today.

With her hand in mine, I guide my beautiful bondmate out onto the dance floor. She stops and gives me a hesitant look. "I know your people don't dance, Marek. We don't have to—"

I don't let her finish her sentence. Stepping back, I pull her toward me, spinning her into my arms before dipping her back just enough to press a quick kiss to her lips.

Her eyes light up with delight and surprise. "I thought you said your people didn't dance."

I quirk my brow. "That may be, but I've learned a few things since then."

She gives me a beaming smile.

My eyes dart to Anton briefly before returning to her. "And I had an excellent instructor."

She tips her head back with a small laugh—the sound light and musical, touching something deep in my soul as I stare across at her, completely enchanted. My love for her is immeasurable.

Off to the side, Anton gives me another wink and the song he helped me choose for our first dance begins to play over the speakers. Her face lights with a brilliant smile as the first strings of the violin begin to play.

Her jaw drops, and she covers her mouth in stunned surprise. "How did you know?" She grins. "This is my favorite song."

I tip my head to Anton, and she mouths, "Thank you," to him as I pull her farther onto the floor and wrap my arms around her as we begin. The words are perfect—telling her exactly how long I will love her.

Forever.

One song turns into the next, and Elizabeth's joy floods the bond between us as we dance. Several Terran couples join us on the floor, but only a select few V'loryns make the attempt. Many of them awkward, except for the ones who've had instruction from Anton... including Ruvaen, who is surprisingly graceful in his movements as he dances with Maya.

I'm surprised to see Doc and L'Tana out on the floor. How he convinced her to dance I'm uncertain, but they appear to be enjoying themselves.

Lucas and Tayla spin past us, and I am surprised at how easily she catches on to this Terran tradition without any instruction before today. A beaming smile lights her face as she stares up at Lucas, Taven watching from off to the side with a softened expression on his face. I believe the Terrans may be one of the best things to ever happen to his sister. She now has a people that make her feel not only welcome, but also accepted for who she is.

At Anton's insistence, even Kalvar takes the floor. His movements and rhythm lack the polish of someone who has had lessons, but Elizabeth smiles all the same as they dance. Vanek and Ryven make their way to me as my eyes track my Si'an T'kara, marveling at how blessed I truly am.

Vanek places his hand on my shoulder. "I am pleased for you, my friend."

"As am I," Ryven adds. "The Goddess has chosen well for you." He pauses. "Your bonding has given all of us hope."

I agree. "This is a new beginning for our people. Perhaps the Goddess will bless others with a Terran mate."

Vanek lowers his gaze to the floor, a deep frown creasing his brow. I know what pains him. If not for his upcoming mating cycle, he has said he would prefer to never take a bondmate. The familiar haunted look he has carried since our time on the Defense Force flits briefly across his expression before he lifts his gaze to mine. I only hope that he finds someone who truly understands him the way Elizabeth understands me.

As the evening draws to an end, our guests begin to file out, returning to their homes and the Embassy. The High Omari motions for us to follow her, and I take Elizabeth's hand in mine.

Through the touch of her skin, I know she is as nervous as I am about what happens next. The High Omari leads us back into our chambers and motions for Elizabeth to stay in the main bedroom while I am ushered into the one that would be hers if she were V'loryn and we did not share a bed.

Another Omari enters the room, instructing me to change into my ceremonial Joining robes. She leaves while I dress, and when she calls me back into the main bedroom, I notice Elizabeth standing behind her. The sheer reflective silver robe does nothing to hide her naked form just as it hides nothing of my own. A pink bloom spreads across her cheeks as her gaze finds mine, and my body fills with warmth.

The High Omari instructs us to face one another while she recites the fertility blessing. When she is finished, she quietly exits the room.

Now that Elizabeth is standing before me, I am almost afraid to touch her. I tremble with want and desire, and I struggle to maintain my control.

She reaches out to take my hand, threading her fingers through mine. I lower my shields to open a small connection between us, sending her a wave of love and warmth across the bond. Something lingers just at the edge of her thoughts, and as I explore this small recess in her mind, I pull back immediately when I see what it is. She is afraid, and I move to step back from her, but she holds firmly to my hand, stopping me.

"Not of you, my love," she whispers. "I'm just nervous. I've heard that the first time can be a bit painful."

Reaching across, I brush the hair back from her face and gently run the soft pad of my thumb over her cheek. "We do not have to mate until you are ready, my Si'an T'kara. We can wait."

"No. I want this, Marek." She stretches up on her toes, wrapping her arms around me. "I want you," she says, pressing her soft lips to mine.

After a moment, she steps back. With her eyes locked on mine, she carefully unclasps the fastening of her robe. It slides from her shoulders and pools around her feet. My eyes travel over her bare form and I am afraid to move, afraid to breathe because my desire for her is so great.

She gives me a soft smile and begins unfastening the clasps of my robe. When it is loose, she pushes it back from my shoulders, allowing it to fall to the floor. My l'ok is erect and painfully hard with want to sheathe myself deep inside her warmth.

She takes my hand and places it on her left breast before her eyes drift down to my l'ok. Softly biting her lower lip, she gently touches my length. A shiver of pleasure runs through me, but I force myself to remain still as the tips of her fingers trace lightly over my already sensitive skin.

A glistening bead of fluid gathers on the end, and she brushes her finger across the tip. My breath catches in my throat as she rubs it across her abdomen, marking herself with my scent. Her eyes search mine as she whispers softly. "Make love to me, Marek. Make me yours."

I gather her in my arms and move to the bed, gently lowering her into the soft nest of blankets. When I lay down beside her, she turns to face me, cupping her hand to the back of my neck and pulling my lips to hers.

She traces her tongue along the seam of my lips, asking for entrance, and when I open my mouth, I deepen our kiss as my tongue finds hers. I wrap my arms tightly around her, pulling her body against mine until there is no space between us. My l'ok is hard against her stomach, and as she moves her leg over my hip to pull me closer, the scent of her arousal is overwhelming, and my fangs extend with want to claim her.

But I want to give her pleasure first, so I force them to retract. I roll us both so that she is beneath me. She opens her thighs to cradle my hips as I settle between them. Nothing separates me from her entrance, and desire courses through my body so intensely that I struggle to maintain my control as I kiss a heated trail down her elegant neck to the valley of her breasts.

Turning my attention to her left breast, I close my mouth over the soft peak. I caress the tip with my tongue and as it tightens into a hard bead, she presses against me, running her fingers through my hair to pull me closer.

I love the soft moan that escapes her lips as I cup my hand over her mound and gently part her already slick folds. Something dark and primal stirs within me as I press soft kisses down the length of her body, and the thought suddenly strikes me that she is completely mine. Mine to touch. Mine forever. And as my thumb presses against the sensitive pearl of flesh at the apex, she gasps and arches up against my hand. Fierce possessiveness rushes through me.

Moving down between her thighs, I carefully guide her legs over my shoulders, opening her to my gaze. She looks down at me with heavy-lidded eyes, and her mouth drifts open as I gently drag my tongue between her slick folds.

She moans loudly when I reach the small bundle of nerves at the top, teasing my tongue around the softly hooded flesh in the way I've learned makes her cry out in pleasure. She writhes beneath me, and I band an arm across her hips to hold her still while I continue to taste the sweet nectar of her channel.

Lowering my shield, I can feel the tight coil of need that builds slowly in her core. I concentrate my touch to the areas she loves best, and she cries out my name in blinding ecstasy as she finds her release, flooding my tongue with her sweet taste.

My l'ok is painfully hard against the bedding, and I long to sink deep inside her warm, wet heat. I move back up her body until my face is even with hers. Propping my weight on one elbow to avoid crushing her beneath me, I reach my other hand to gently cup her face as I search her eyes for permission. I want to make sure she wants this as much as I want her.

As the connection opens between us, her want and desire crash against mine like waves upon rock. She desires this as much as I do. Opening her thighs even wider, I settle between them. The tip of my l'ok bumps softly against her entrance. Reaching up to cup my face, her luminous blue eyes stare deep into mine as she wraps her legs around me in encouragement.

~

ELIZABETH

His intense V'loryn gaze pins me in place as he moves his body to cover mine. Wrapping my arms around his back, I shift slightly to open myself as his hips come to rest in the cradle between my thighs. The tip of his l'ok pushes lightly against my entrance, and the sensation is almost more than I can bear as I close my eyes and moan softly in anticipation of him entering me.

Gazing down at me with half-lidded eyes, he lowers his lips to mine, and I love the weight of his body over me. His eyes search mine for silent permission, and I speak the words softly. "I want you, my love."

JESSICA GRAYSON

As he slowly enters my channel, he clenches his jaw, and I can tell it's taking everything in him to move slowly, not wanting to hurt me. I angle my hips to push up against him and gasp as the crown of his l'ok breaches my entrance. He stops and goes completely still, and I know he's worried that he has hurt me.

"I'm all right." I whisper. "It's just really sensitive...but in a good way."

Unable to speak, he nods. Reaching my barrier, he grits his teeth, and I urge him to keep going, gasping at the small ripple of pain and pleasure as he sheathes himself deep inside me, the burn of my body stretching to take him completely. The tip of his l'ok presses at the entrance to my womb, and I've never felt so full.

"So tight," he rasps. "Are you all right, my Elizabeth?" Worry flashes behind his eyes as he waits for my answer.

Cupping the back of his neck, I pull his lips back down to mine and whisper against them, "Yes, my love."

His tongue finds mine, deepening our kiss as I marvel at the exquisite feeling of fullness inside me.

When he pulls back from our kiss, his glowing green eyes turn into obsidian orbs. His fangs slowly extend into sharpened points as he stares down at me with a look of intense possession. With my gaze locked on his, I tip my head back, offering my neck to him. "Seal us in the S'acris, my love. Make me yours."

Lowering his head, his lips find mine again in a searing kiss, stealing the breath from my lungs. He runs his fingers through my hair, gripping the long strands in his strong hand as he gently pulls my head to one side to kiss a heated trail down my neck. I run my hands up and down the muscles along his back, wanting to touch him everywhere. I love the weight of his body over mine, and as his tongue lightly traces over the artery of my neck, the soft graze of his teeth follows after, sending ripples of pleasure through me.

The small muscles of my channel clench involuntarily around his hard length, and without warning, he surges against me, sinking his teeth deep into my neck.

My mouth opens in a silent cry as I arch against him. Intense pleasure mixed with just a hint of pain, the gentle pull as he drinks of my blood is a heady mix. Warmth spreads out from the site, filling my body as he injects me with the hormone that will mark me as his and join our minds in the permanent bond.

∽

MAREK

Sinking my teeth deep into her flesh, the sweet taste of her blood explodes across my tongue. Rich and unlike anything I have ever known, I close my eyes and relish the flavor of the warm, viscous nectar that flows from her artery.

The tight clasp of her channel around my l'ok as I pin her in place and seal her to me gives rise to something dark and primal, clawing its way to the surface of my mind. As I drink deeply of her intoxicating blood, savage instinct strips bare the last of my control, and it crumbles before my dark desire.

I wrap my arms tighter around her form, and a deep growl of arousal fills my chest as pleasure floods my entire body. Overwhelming need rushes through me like fire, threatening to leave nothing but ash in its wake. I lose the war with the monster within, claiming my mate and binding her to me in the sacred and savage ways of my ancestors.

"I love you, Marek," her soft voice whispers in my mind, pulling me back from the dark abyss.

Carefully pulling my fangs from her neck, I trace my tongue over the two puncture wounds to seal them as I dive deep into her mind and lose myself as we become one in the ocean of our combined thoughts.

∽

ELIZABETH

The heavy press of his mind as he joins with mine is powerful. Pulled beneath a wave of overwhelming sensation, I spiral through thoughts and dreams that are mine and yet they are not.

"*They are ours,*" his mind whispers to mine.

Swept away in a tide of swirling thought and emotion, his consciousness sinks deep into mine and mine into his until we are one and I don't know where he ends and I begin. *Love*—the emotion rushing through me like a powerful wave, enveloping me completely as time slows down, drawn out between the combined beating of our hearts.

Our minds laid bare to each other, fierce possessiveness ripples through me. The intensity of his love is both alien and all-consuming. There are no words for what passes between us as I embrace the dark and primal emotion of his claim upon my body and mind. His consciousness sinks further into mine until I'm aware of every sensation coursing through his body and my own.

With his l'ok sheathed deep inside my body, I can feel all the effort it is taking him to remain still.

"*I want you. All of you,*" I whisper in his mind. "*You don't have to hold back.*"

He stares down at me, his gaze dark and possessive. His hips shift slightly, and I gasp as pleasure ripples through my body as he begins to move inside me. He shifts again, moving his arms to slip them beneath my back so his hands cup my shoulders as he drops down against me, holding me in place as he rocks back and forth, taking my body in long, even strokes. I hold tightly to him. The delicious friction of his ridged l'ok deep within my channel is so intense, I close my eyes as warmth pools deep in my core.

Lost in the sensation of this oneness between us, I arch my back to meet each of his thrusts, wrapping my legs around him as he sinks even deeper. His warm hand cups my face, and I open my eyes as he stares down at me intensely. "I want to watch you as you reach your release."

Unable to speak, I nod and keep my eyes locked with his. A low moan escapes me as my heart beats wildly, my every nerve ending alive with only the sensation of him. In complete surrender, I open myself even more to take him into my body as he moves deep within me, pinning me to the mattress in a delicious motion of back and forth.

Intense need spirals through me, and I dig my nails into his back, gasping with each glorious ripple of sensation along my inner walls as his ridged l'ok moves in and out. I feel him beginning to expand, my body burning slightly as it stretches to accommodate him, a mixture of pleasure and pain so powerful, my inner walls spasm and clench tightly around his length. A strong pulsing begins deep within. He roars above me, and I cry out as overwhelming sensation rushes through me as he fills me with his delicious warmth.

I don't have time to catch my breath as another wave rolls through me. A pinch of pain followed by overwhelming pleasure ripples through my core as the tip of his l'ok seals over the entrance to my womb. I gasp in surprise, holding him tighter to me and I cry out his name, as he surges deep within me, his l'ok pulsing as he fills me again with his warmth.

Barely able to catch my breath, I start to ask, "How many times do you—?" But the question dies in my throat as I feel another wave begin to crest...his l'ok vibrating deep within me, somehow even stronger. His base begins to expand within, stretching me almost to the point of pain but not quite.

"What's happening?" I gasp, barely able to speak as his hips surge forth and he buries himself impossibly deeper.

His glowing green eyes burn with desire as he stares down at me, panting heavily. "Knotting," he rasps.

The Healers told me about this, but I had no idea it would feel so amazing as the base of his l'ok expands to completely fill my channel, holding him in place inside me. My body hums in awareness of him, and nothing exists outside of this moment as his gaze remains locked on mine. He breathes words of love and devotion in the ancient tongue as he continues to move deep inside me, filling me with his seed. My thighs tremble slightly as he pins me with each thrust and another wave of warmth floods my body. It's so overwhelming; my mouth falls open, and a low moan escapes my lips as I hold to him tightly.

"Marek. It's so intense," I barely manage as another strong orgasm churns deep within me, carrying me on another blissful wave as he stares deep into my eyes.

He answers me in the ancient tongue. "You. Are. Mine," he growls. Wrapping his strong hand around my hip, he surges again, and I swear I see stars as his l'ok pulses even stronger within me causing another powerful orgasm to wash through me as my body eagerly takes in his seed. I cry out his name as he roars his pleasure above me.

Completely sated, I float in that place between sleep and awake as he stills. Gently, he rolls us onto our sides as he remains knotted inside me.

Brushing the dampened hair back from my face, he kisses me with a renewed passion and urgency that takes my breath away. My legs tremble slightly, and the dull ache between them becomes a sharp pain that steals my breath when he eventually pulls out. Fluid runs down my inner thighs as the combined sweet scent of our mixed fluids fills the air around us.

Nuzzling against me, his nostrils flare, and he pulls back quickly to look under the sheet between my legs. "You are bleeding," he says, a look of intense pain and horror on his face.

Reaching my hand up to gently cup the side of his face, I stare deep into his eyes. "We talked about this," I say softly. "It's normal for Terran females to bleed the first time they make love."

He captures my mouth in a searing kiss. "You are mine," he whispers against my lips, "and I am yours." He rolls us again and the tip of his l'ok is already at my entrance.

I put my hand to his chest and give him a questioning look. "Already?"

He stills, cocking his head slightly to the side. "Do you need to rest?"

Desire floods the bond between us, and I inhale sharply before pulling his lips back down to mine in answer to his question. I'm already addicted to his touch and I want him again.

He takes me slower this time, and when he knots inside me there's more pleasure than pain as he fills my open womb with his seed, causing another intense orgasm to wash over and through me.

After we've made love for the fifth time, I put my hand to his chest. Thoroughly sated and floating on a wave of pure bliss, I reach up to cup his cheek. "Marek, I'm exhausted…I don't think I can again. I need to rest."

He rolls us to the side once more, pulling my body flush against his. "Rest, my Si'an T'kara," he whispers, and I'm so tired I don't know if he's spoken these words aloud or if they're in my mind. But as I fall asleep wrapped in his arms, I dream of the blue oceans of Terra and know it is him remembering the first time he looked into my eyes.

CHAPTER 35

ELIZABETH

When I wake the next morning, the dull ache between my thighs fills me with warmth at the remembrance of his body joined with mine, reminding me that I've been thoroughly claimed by my V'loryn bondmate.

He skims his nose softly along my cheek, down my jaw, and to my neck, stopping at the spot where he gave me his mark. His tr'llen grows loud in his chest, and I run my fingers through the hairs at the nape of his neck.

He pulls back to regard me, his eyes drifting down to the mark as he gives me his V'loryn smile. "Can you feel my presence in the back of your mind, my Si'an T'kara?"

I look down a moment, concentrating, but suddenly realize I don't have to. The gentle hum of his consciousness fills me with a comforting warmth unlike anything I've ever experienced before. Relief washes through me, and I smile up at him.

He cocks his head slightly to the side as he senses my relief. "You were afraid the bonding would change you." He says this as a statement, but I know it is a question. "You worried that you would no longer be you—your own separate entity." He pauses, his brow furrowing softly. "And yet...you still chose to bond with me despite this fear."

I reach up to trace my fingers lightly across his lips, marveling in the perfection of his mouth. "I love you, Marek. And I decided that being bonded to you was worth the risk."

He flashes his subtle V'loryn smile before pressing his lips to mine in a gentle kiss.

I shift in his arms to pull him closer to me and wince slightly.

His eyes flash with worry. "You are hurt?"

Shaking my head softly, I run my fingers through his hair. "Just a little sore. That's all."

He stands from the bed, and I marvel at the perfection of his form. The thick corded muscles of his body flex as he reaches down to scoop me up into his arms and carry me into the cleansing room.

When he walks us into the warm pool of water, my aching muscles begin to relax in the soothing warmth.

I cannot help but touch him, running my hands along his broad shoulders before tracing my fingers across the muscles of his abdomen and chest as he watches me intently. "I can't believe you are mine," I whisper, more to myself than to him.

He gives me a heated look. "I'm yours, my Si'an T'kara."

Pressing his forehead gently to mine he whispers. "Are you ready to greet the dawn?"

This, I remember, is an important part of the V'loryn bonding ritual. The newly bonded couple watch the sun rise the morning after their first Joining—to symbolize this new beginning of their lives together as one.

He carries me out of the water and sets me on my feet a moment before wrapping me in a plush, thick robe. Wrapping another around himself as well, he takes my hand and we walk out onto the balcony. We sit on the far corner and he pulls me back against him, wrapping his arms around me from behind as I relax back into the solid warmth of his chest. As we watch, the first yellow-orange rays of the sun rise up over the red desert sand, shimmering off in the distance.

"Red like the red sands of V'lora." The words float through my mind, and I know they are his...from the first time he saw me.

As the sun moves higher up in the sky, his warm hand cups my chin, turning my head gently back to face him. He brushes his lips over mine, and I turn in his arms to face him.

The loud chirp of his communicator startles us both. With a heavy sigh, he rests his forehead against mine. "Can we start our honeymoon early?" I give him a teasing smile.

We had planned on returning to Terra for our honeymoon, shortly after our bonding ceremony here. But that was before everything that happened with the Emperor. Now, it looks like we probably won't get a honeymoon or a vacation anytime soon.

His communicator chirps again, and he presses a kiss to my forehead. "I'm sorry, my Elizabeth. I wish we could just—"

Pressing my finger to his lips to silence him, I give him a small smile. "It's all right, my love."

He nods, and we both walk back inside to see who it is. "It's Vanek," he calls out, staring down at the display.

Vanek's voice fills the room. "I hated to disturb you, but the Mosaurans are here. They are requesting to speak with the K'Sai."

CHAPTER 36

MAREK

All my guard are assembled and lining the entry room as Elizabeth and I descend the stairs. Kalvar follows close behind us. The Mosaurans, although surrounded, stand proud and unafraid as they await my Si'an T'kara.

Prince Rowan's silver reflective eyes stare intently at her, and something akin to admiration flashes behind them as she approaches.

He steps forward. "We owe you our lives, Elizabeth Langdon of Terra. When others would have left us to die"—his gaze flits briefly to Ryven beside me—"you saved us. You are as brave and fierce as a Mosauran warrior. As a Prince of the Mosauran Empire, I have come here today to offer you the protection of the Royal House of Mosaura."

He and Tharin drop to one knee before her, and her mouth drifts open in shock. An expression that seems to be mirrored on the faces of all those around us.

Pulling a blade from his belt, he holds it out, presenting it to her. The Mosauran blade glints beneath the light. Sharp and deadly, this steel is renowned for its strength—able to cut through almost

JESSICA GRAYSON

anything. My attention moves to the curved obsidian handle. The royal symbol of the House of Mosaura is engraved in L'omhara. This is indeed a generous gift.

Elizabeth carefully takes it from him, studying the blade intently.

Rowan lifts his gaze to her. "If you are ever in need of aid, present this blade to any Mosauran warrior and they will know you are under the protection of the Royal House of the Empire. They will fight and will even die to defend you if necessary."

My eyes go wide, and I look to Kalvar and Ryven. They appear to be equally just as stunned as I am.

She darts a quick glance at me and then turns back to Prince Rowan. "What about my bondmate?"

He stands. His sharp gaze scans me from head to toe. "Our people have a long history of mistrust amongst each other."

Elizabeth meets his eyes evenly. "Then let us end that today."

He cocks his head to the side. "What would you suggest?"

"An alliance with Terra—with my people and my family. And by extension"—she looks back at Kalvar—"one with V'lora."

He remains silent, his piercing silver eyes holding mine a moment before he returns his gaze to Elizabeth. "This is not a decision I can make on my own. I will have to speak with my mother, the Empress." He pauses. "My original intent upon coming here was to find your people and warn them. We have made several attempts to contact your Ambassador here on V'lora, but our requests to meet have gone unanswered. We need to warn them about the A'kai. If they find your home world, they will surely enslave your people."

"Why do they want Terra so badly?"

"They believe the blood of your species is...special." His gaze sweeps again to mine in an almost accusatory look. He knows how we form the S'acris with our mates, and from the way his eyes dart to the fresh mark on her neck, he knows I've already had Elizabeth's blood. He continues. "The A'kai are ruthless in their conquest of other worlds. Especially when those worlds have something they desire."

His words strike fear in my heart.

"Our Princess was the slave of an A'kai. When my brother and I rescued her, he had already tasted of her lifeblood. It restored his health after my brother gave him a mortal wound." He pauses. "Now, their race search for your people and your world."

Fear floods the link between us as Elizabeth grips my hand tightly. "If he had her blood, and saw into her mind, wouldn't they already know where Terra is?"

He shakes his head. "In addition to our Princess, we have rescued several other Terran females. A few were also slaves of the A'kai, and despite their use of the R'ugol—"

I inhale sharply, and many of my guards do the same, unable to contain our horror at these words.

He continues. "They have been unable to find Terra's location because your people do not even know how to find it themselves. Your species is only now beginning to venture beyond your own star system."

I wrap a protective arm around Elizabeth, and panic rises in my throat, but I force it back down. "What led *you* here?"

"The Princess searched the ancient star maps in the Great Library. She identified a system close to V'lora that she believes may belong to Terra. Tharin and I were already coming here to renegotiate a trade agreement between the Empire and V'lora for L'sair crystals. We planned to investigate the system after we left." He pauses. "We have just returned from there and it is exactly as she described. Eight planets orbiting a yellow dwarf star." He narrows his eyes. "We detected several of your vessels in that system."

Elizabeth gives him a wary look. Despite their words, she is wise to be cautious, especially now that he's told her they've found the location of her world. "You never told me the name of your Terran Princess."

"Her name is Liana Garza, and she is the bondmate and Ashaya of my brother, Soran."

Elizabeth inhales sharply, her eyes brightening with tears as she stares at him in shock. An expression that I am almost certain is mirrored on my face as well.

Rowan cocks his head to the side to regard her. "I—I do not understand." He looks to me in confusion. "I promise you that she is happy and well. They are expecting a child and—"

A broken sob escapes Elizabeth as she covers her mouth with her hand, shaking her head in disbelief. "Liana Garza is my Aunt." Her voice quavers slightly. "She is sister to my mother."

His brow furrows as he stares at her in disbelief. "You are her family?"

"Yes," she barely manages. "She disappeared sixteen years ago. We thought she was dead."

He smiles. "She is alive and well. She will be overjoyed to know we have found you. When she found out how long she'd been in stasis sleep, she feared that all her family were gone."

The tears she struggled so hard to hold back flow freely now at his words, and my heart clenches. Elizabeth and Lucas are all that is left of their family. "Her parents and my sister are all dead."

I wrap my arm tightly around her as if doing so can somehow shield her from the pain of all that she's lost.

He stares at her in shock as she continues. "My grandparents died during the last great pandemic, and my mother died in a transport accident a few years ago."

Rowan's face pales at her words. "I—I cannot tell her this. I wouldn't know what to say. We sent word already that we'd found her people, but I have yet to hear back. She is traveling with my brother. But I'm almost certain she will insist on coming when she hears we have found the location of her world."

Brushing the tears from her face, Elizabeth meets his eyes evenly. "I will tell her when she comes." She pauses. "And I will speak with my government about meeting with your people."

CHAPTER 37

MAREK

As Kalvar, Ryven, Elizabeth, and I travel to the Embassy, I am on edge at the thought of Elizabeth's people discussing the possibility of an alliance with the Mosaurans. Despite what they've said, I have a hard time reconciling the deep-seated mistrust that I hold for their people.

She takes my hand. "What's wrong?"

With a heavy sigh, my gaze darts to Kalvar before I speak. "All my life I've been taught that the Mosaurans are violent and unpredictable, with a thirst for war as great as that of our ancestors. I've always believed them to be conquerors—a people too aggressive and volatile to be trusted." I clench my jaw in frustration. "They took you from me. You could have been harmed and I—" I draw in a deep breath, attempting to calm the storm within. "Everything inside me wants to tear them apart for daring to lay a hand on you. And I dislike the idea of their Empire dealing with Terra."

She gives me an exasperated look. "They thought they were saving me, Marek."

Kalvar interjects. "That is what they claim, but their people are desperate for females. If what he says is truth about your aunt carrying his brother's child, I wonder at their true intentions for wanting to make contact with Terra."

She meets his gaze evenly. "Many V'loryns still view my people as nothing more than potential breeders. But *I* know that not all of them believe this."

He lowers his head in shame. "You are right. We hid our true agenda, and the madness of the Emperor from your people. I am sorry we kept the truth from you for so long."

"You misunderstand." She shakes her head softly. "I'm not saying this to make you feel guilty. I'm saying this because you cannot judge an entire race by the actions of only a few."

While what Elizabeth says is truth, I cannot help but still be wary of the Mosaurans.

∽

ELIZABETH

As soon as we arrive at the Terran Embassy, we are ushered inside. This is my first time coming here, and I'm surprised by how large it is. It was still unfinished when Marek and I were lost in the desert. All polished metal and stone, it looks nothing like the V'loryn architecture that surrounds it, and I'm suddenly a little bit homesick for Terra.

Ambassador Garcia comes out to greet us. If not for my v'oltir game with the Prime Minister requesting this meeting, it probably wouldn't have happened this quickly. When I'd first contacted him, he was more than a little reluctant to meet with the Mosaurans, despite my reassurance that they are here on friendly terms.

Although he must be at least in his late fifties or early sixties, the only thing that speaks to his age is his full head of silver-gray hair. His dark-brown eyes study me a moment before he gives me a polite smile. "I'm glad you are here. I was hoping"—his eyes sweep over Marek, Kalvar, and Ryven—"to speak to you in private."

From the tense set of Marek's and Kalvar's shoulders, I can tell this doesn't sit well with them.

"Marek is my husband now, and Kalvar is the Ambassador to Terra. Whatever you need to speak with me about, should be safe in front of them as well," I offer.

Standing a bit taller, he straightens his shoulders and shakes his head. "As I said," he states a bit firmly, "I would like to speak with *you*." His gaze shifts to Marek and Kalvar. "Only for a moment, of course."

Now Ryven's shoulders tense as well. How this man got picked to be the Terran Ambassador is beyond me. Does he not understand the political structure here on V'lora? I can only assume that he received such an important post because he's related to someone powerful back on Terra.

Marek looks to me. "We will remain here," he says.

I give him a quick kiss and then turn to follow the ambassador to his office. Our footsteps echo loudly throughout the empty halls. Only a skeleton staff has arrived, the rest will not be here for two more weeks.

I'm surprised when I step through the door. Instead of the usual pretentious furnishings that most Terran government officials seem to decorate their offices with, there are various collages of family pictures all over the walls and even on his desk. He must be a man deeply dedicated to his family, and I wonder if any of them have come with him to V'lora.

My eyes drift to a portrait of him and a woman I assume must be his wife. As if in answer to my unspoken question, he says, "My wife, Ofelia, will be here in two weeks along with the rest of the Embassy staff." A wistful smile crests his lips. "She's going to miss her garden, but I promised her she could help make the Embassy gardens as strikingly beautiful here as they are on the V'loryn Embassy on Terra." He nods to himself. "She's a botanist, so I believe she is up to the challenge."

He motions for me to take a seat and then sits down directly across from me instead of behind his desk. "What's this about?" I ask, wanting to get straight to the point.

He gives me a meaningful look. "As I'm sure you're aware, the Prime Minister arranged this meeting."

I hold his gaze but say nothing, I won't reveal my secret communication method to Prime Minister Martinez. Certainly not to this man.

He continues. "You're the first Terran to become intimately involved with a V'loryn. The first to actually *marry* one of them." He leans forward in his chair. "I have a few questions that I'd like to ask you."

Something about his tone puts me on edge. This sounds more like it's about to become an inquisition. "What is it?"

"How much do you remember about the night the V'loryn Embassy was infiltrated by the Terra United terrorist?"

I go still. Why is he asking me this? I've never been a good liar, but I've had a lot of practice training my face into an impassive mask like the V'loryns. So, I make sure to do just that before I answer. "Like all the other Terrans, I was unconscious."

His eyes narrow slightly as he leans back in his chair with a contemplative look. "You see, there are quite a few people in the Terran government who are questioning what happened that night."

"Why would the V'loryns lie?" I pose the most obvious question. The one that should make enough sense to him that he'll drop whatever line of questioning this is.

"That's what has been bothering me about this whole thing. I don't know why they would lie about what happened. But the truth is, the story they told us and the vidcam feed we received just isn't adding up."

I say nothing, waiting for him to continue.

He shakes his head. "Did you know that Terra United is so paranoid about aliens, that they make sure all their weapons are coded to only work for Terrans?" He studies me a moment, as if trying to gauge my reaction before continuing. "It's a rather ingenious little device they have, and it takes less than a minute to install. Now here's the funny thing," he continues. "The zbraun that the terrorist would have used to murder Kalvar was just such a weapon. And yet"—he tips his head to the side in a subtle shrug—"according to the vidcam footage and the information we received from the V'loryns, a V'loryn guard was able to use it to…neutralize him."

Leaning forward a bit in his chair, he narrows his eyes. "Strange, don't you think?"

"Why are you asking *me* about this?"

He doesn't answer, but instead continues. "And the fire that caught and burned beyond the Embassy. It was almost a perfect circle. It radiated outward from almost the exact position of the dead terrorist. And according to our investigators, the damage left in its path was unlike the damage from any fire they've ever seen."

He pauses a moment, waiting for me to say something, but I don't. I'm not going to play this game of cat and mouse or whatever this is.

Realizing I'm not going to offer him anything, he sighs heavily, steepling his hands in front of him as he sits back in his chair with a contemplative look. "Perhaps it's because of their refusal to share all of their technologies with us. You know how the government and the military are. They can't stand for someone—even an ally—to have the upper hand. It is creating mistrust between our two peoples. I, personally"—he puts his hand to his chest—"like the V'loryns. I'm glad we have the alliance with them. And if I didn't trust them, you can be assured that I would never allow my wife to come to this planet with me. But I need you to help me put something to rest that has begun circulating in the higher levels of our government."

"What is it?"

"The Terran Prime Minister was one of the people unconscious on the ground for who knows how long…and the V'loryns *are* touch telepaths."

My eyes widen slightly as I realize what he's implying. Anger sweeps through me, and I snap. "You're right. They are telepathic, but did you know that to touch someone's mind without their permission is the equivalent of rape in their culture? It's abhorrent to them, and the penalty for such a crime is death."

Now *his* eyes go wide.

"Although we are married, *Marek* won't even touch my mind without my consent. *That's* how sacred such an act is to them." Heat flushes my cheeks as I glare at him. "Let me ask you something that you can pass along to your superiors," I tell him. "V'loryn technology…their ships, their weapons…I've seen it up close. They're so far advanced beyond anything we have. Why would they need to read a government official's mind? If they wanted to, they could have easily conquered our world and our people a long time ago."

He looks down as if processing my statement. But even as the words leave my mouth, the horrible truth lingers in the back of my mind. Some of the V'loryns—including the Great Houses—still wanted to conquer Terra even after the formation of the alliance. Part of me feels guilty that it's never even occurred to me to warn my people or my government. But I also know that doing so would only widen the gap of mistrust that still exists between us, adding fuel to the movement of Terra United.

When Ambassador Garcia lifts his gaze, I can already see it in his eyes. My question has cleared the doubt from his mind. I can only hope it will do the same for his superiors. This is not the time we should be turning on our allies—the V'loryns. Especially not with the knowledge that other races are looking for our home world with the intent to enslave us.

So, I decide to remind him of this, knowing that everything spoken here will be passed along to the rest of our government. "You've read the report the Aerilon gave? The threat of the A'kai?"

He nods.

"Then you understand what's at stake here."

He gives me a grave look before nodding again. "Yes, the Prime Minister informed me in great detail of what you'd told her beyond the official reports."

"The V'loryns are not our enemies, and they are not conquerors. But the A'kai?" I meet his eyes evenly. "*They* are." I pause, allowing the weight of my words to settle in the space between us. "The Mosaurans came here to warn us. And this is a chance to gain another ally against what is coming. If the A'kai are as ruthless as I've heard they are, I think we should listen to what the Mosaurans have to say, don't you?"

He leans forward, his gaze heavy on mine as he speaks. "Where is the Emperor?"

I still.

He leans forward in his seat. "I thought it was strange that he wasn't there to greet me as planned when I first arrived. Instead, I met with Ambassador Kalvar."

Uncertain how much I should tell him, I say nothing, but I realize that even my silence speaks volumes.

He gives me a knowing look. "I've heard rumors from several sources, but I'm not sure which ones to believe. My goal"—he puts his hand to his chest for emphasis—"is to make sure our alliance remains intact. So, if there is anything that I need to know that could jeopardize that, I hope you'll keep me informed."

I meet his eyes evenly. "Our goals are the same then. The council is meeting soon, and I'm certain Kalvar will inform you of any changes that might affect the alliance."

CHAPTER 38

ELIZABETH

As we gather in the Great Assembly Hall, almost every eye is on Marek and me. Word of our bonding ceremony has spread to every V'loryn on the planet by now, and they all stare with open fascination.

Kalvar sits on one side and Marek on the other as Ryven and the rest of the guard sit behind us. The Emperor's seating area remains vacant. Members of House G'alta, M'theal, and S'tiran watch me closely, but with contempt instead of curiosity. No doubt they blame me for the rash actions of their Emperor.

Kalvar addresses them. "We are here to discuss the status of our alliance with the Terrans."

Dovak stands. "If that is the case, would it not be wise to hold this meeting without a Terran present?" His eyes dart to me.

Marek levels a dark gaze at Dovak. "I have taken Elizabeth Langdon as my bondmate. She is as much a V'loryn citizen now as any of us. As K'Sai of House D'enekai, it is her right to attend this Council meeting."

Dovak narrows his eyes as he slowly returns to his seat in silence, his anger visibly simmering beneath the surface of his stoic façade.

Kalvar continues. "Our House votes for the continued alliance of V'lora with the people of Terra."

"House A'msir votes the same," Vanek adds.

"As does L'eanan," Milena addresses the Assembly.

Dovak grits through his teeth. "I refuse to cast a vote. We have no Emperor, no one to lead us."

The Houses of G'alta, M'theal, and S'tiran all murmur an agreement.

Milena stands. "Then, let us vote for a new ruling House of V'lora."

The Assembly falls silent at her words, many staring at her in shock.

She turns to Kalvar. "I vote for House D'enekai."

Vanek stands. "House D'enekai should lead us. As they did during the time of Prince Kaden."

Dovak points to his sister—the former Empress. "House K'voch still has an Empress. And I vote for House K'voch to continue its leadership of our people."

L'anrul of House M'theal gives her agreement as well.

Now, it is down to L'Mira S'tiran. When she finally stands, the room falls silent. She looks across to Kalvar. "I vote for House D'enekai."

No doubt she has done this hoping to gain a pardon for the actions of her son, Niren.

The members of G'alta and M'theal go into an uproar, loudly voicing their protests.

Dovak steps forward. "I refuse to recognize the rule of any save House K'voch. If you won't accept the Empress, why not the Princess V'Meia?"

Kalvar's eyes flash with anger. "Because the Princess would deliver her people into the claws of the A'kai."

The entire room falls silent.

L'anrul interjects. "What is the meaning of this? What lies are you spreading now, Kalvar?"

"They are not lies," Vanek says. "The Princess is carrying the child of Talel—brother of the First Prime of A'kaina. She promised them our people and our planet would fall under their rule." With a dark look, he scans the room. "If you do not believe us, ask the Emperor's personal Healer." He points to the Healer beside him.

All eyes fall on him as he stands next to Vanek. "It is truth. The Princess carries a V'loryn/A'kai child in her womb. And"—he lowers his head in shame—"I was there when she informed T'Hales Marek and Vanek of her treachery."

All the color drains from L'anrul's face. Threat of an A'kai invasion seems to have swept everything else aside.

Milena steps forward, motioning for silence. After a moment, everyone looks to her. "The Council has voted. If any disagree"—she glares at Dovak and L'anrul—"know this. You will be starting a war that you *will not* win. Thousands will be lost to senseless bloodshed. We are so few compared to our numbers before the destruction of V'lorys, we cannot afford to lose any. We must unite despite our differences. Especially if the A'kai come to our planet intent upon conquest."

Dovak and L'anrul glare back at her but remain silent, as do the rest of their Houses. They know she speaks truth. The A'kai are an evil and dangerous enemy; we cannot afford to fight among one another while threat of a possible invasion looms.

Marek stands. "If our House is to rule, then I choose Kalvar to lead us, as he has always done so wisely in the past."

At his suggestion, I can see many of the members of the opposing Houses' expressions soften a bit. Kalvar is respected by many, despite the disagreements between the Houses. He is a good choice to lead V'lora.

In yet another vote, all but House G'alta decide in his favor. When the vote is finished, Vanek stands and then bows low before him. "Long live Emperor Kalvar of House D'enekai."

When we leave the Assembly Hall, half the guards leave with Kalvar as he goes to speak with the Terran Ambassador—to tell him the news of his new title and to begin a discussion of a potential alliance with the Mosaurans. I worry that my government, already distrustful of the V'loryns, will be reticent to entertain the idea of an alliance with the Mosauran Empire. I only hope that I am wrong.

As Marek sits beside me on the transport back home, he is oddly quiet. I gently probe the bond between us but do not understand what I'm sensing. Ryven says nothing, but it's not unusual for V'loryns to sit in comfortable silence amongst each other. It's just that this usually doesn't happen when I'm around. When we reach the Estate, we return to our chambers.

Although it bothers me that he is so quiet, I wait to speak until we are alone. As soon as we reach our apartments, I look at him expectantly, waiting for him to say something, knowing he can sense my growing frustration with his silence through the bond.

Instead, he walks to the balcony, staring out at the ocean, his brow furrowed deeply in thought.

"What's wrong?"

Although his expression is impassive, I can read the sadness behind his eyes. "I'm sorry, my Elizabeth."

Now I'm confused. "For what?"

"For everything."

I take his hands in mine. "What are you talking about?"

He gives me a pained look. "Your people are in danger because of mine," he says, and I know he is speaking of V'Meia.

Kalvar has them locked away under heavy guard as they await trial. But the only punishment that would ensure our safety is their deaths. And yet, that can never be an option. V'Meia is pregnant, and the child cannot be held responsible for the sins of the mother. Just as the Emperor's bondmate cannot be forced to suffer L'talla for his.

He continues. "This is not the life you expected when you chose me as your bondmate." Inhaling and exhaling deeply, he looks down at our joined hands.

"You're right."

His eyes snap up to meet mine.

Reaching up, I trace the sharp line of his brow as I study his features. "I never expected to fall in love with an alien." I smile, and he quirks his brow. "To get married and live on a planet outside my star system. To find out that my aunt, who I feared was dead all these years, is the bondmate of a dragon warrior and carrying his child."

I cup his cheek, and he leans into my touch.

"But my grandfather taught me that life doesn't always turn out how we expect it to."

Marek pulls me against him, gently cupping my chin to tip my head up to his. He runs the soft pad of his thumb across my cheek and then traces it down to my jaw.

Stretching up on my toes, I wrap my arms around the back of his neck and brush my lips to his. "I choose you, Marek. I choose *us*. You are mine, and I am yours, my love."

He flashes his V'loryn smile as happiness floods the bond between us.

Taking his hand again, I lead him to our bed. He whispers my name in awe-filled reverence as I join my mind and body with his. He makes love to me in the way of his people: all-consuming and intense.

The path that fate chooses for us is often different from the one we imagined. As I lay wrapped in Marek's arms, I reach up and gently trace the slight ridge of his brow, and the sharp pointed tip of his left ear, attempting to memorize this moment—to keep this perfect memory stored in my mind so that later, when I'm old, I can recall it with sparkling clarity.

I don't know what the future holds, I only know I'm excited to meet it. As Marek's glowing green eyes stare deep into mine, he whispers words in the ancient tongue. He takes my hand and places it over his heart, and I understand through the al'nara; he does this so I know that it belongs only to me.

There is no word for this—the sheer intensity of the love that exists between us. But the question forms in our combined thoughts just the same. A tethered connection binding us together, the ancient

V'loryn words fill my mind, and I do not know if they are mine or they are his. He smiles and presses his lips to my own, filling my mind with the poetry of his ancestors. *"I love you with a love that accepts all of your flaws and your unspoken truths and still recognizes that my soul is meant to be with yours."*

ABOUT JESSICA GRAYSON

Thank you so much for reading this. I hope you loved this story as much as I loved writing it. If you enjoyed this book, please leave a review on Amazon and/or Goodreads. Reviews are so very important. They are the lifeblood of Indie Authors.

Good news! I have more fairy tale retellings up for preorder below. I also have a completed Dragon Shifter Duology as well.

For information about upcoming releases Like me on Facebook at Jessica Grayson
http://facebook.com/JessicaGraysonBooks.

OR

sign up for upcoming release alerts at my website:
Jessicagraysonauthor.com

Aerilon Fae Series (Fae Alien Romance)
Trace The Sky

V'lory Series (Vampire Alien Romance)
Lost in the Deep End
The Thing We Choose
Beneath a Different Sky
Under a Silver Moon

V'loryn Fated Ones (Vampire Alien Romance)

Where the Light Begins (Vanek's Story)

Want more Dragon Shifters? I have a completed Duology.
Mosauran Series (Dragon Shifter Alien Romance)
The Edge of it All
Shape of the Wind

Fairy Tale Retellings (Once Upon a Fairy Tale Romance Series)
Taken by the Dragon: A Beauty and the Beast Retelling
Captivated by the Fae: A Cinderella Retelling
Rescued By The Merman: A Little Mermaid Retelling
Bound To The Elf Prince: A Snow White Retelling

Made in the USA
Columbia, SC
05 July 2025